D0925263

A Black Tie Affair
and Other Mystery Stories

Also by Elizabeth Elwood

Mystery Stories

To Catch an Actress and Other Mystery Stories

Plays

Casting for Murder
Renovations

Watch for The Next Beary Anthology

The Beacon and Other Mystery Stories

A wife is haunted by the beacon on the far shore that pinpoints the location of the house where her husband's mistress was stabbed to death. When her husband's body washes ashore near their waterfront home, suspicion immediately falls on her for both of the murders. Enjoy this intriguing story and other mysteries in the next Beary anthology.

Web site: **www.elihuentertainment.com**

A Black Tie Affair
and Other Mystery Stories

Elizabeth Elwood
Author of *To Catch an Actress and Other Mystery Stories*

To Leigh,
Congratulations!
Elizabeth Elwood

iUniverse, Inc.
New York Lincoln Shanghai

A Black Tie Affair and Other Mystery Stories

Copyright © 2008 by Elizabeth Elwood

All rights reserved. No part of this book may be used or reproduced by any means, graphic, electronic, or mechanical, including photocopying, recording, taping or by any information storage retrieval system without the written permission of the publisher except in the case of brief quotations embodied in critical articles and reviews.

iUniverse books may be ordered through booksellers or by contacting:

iUniverse
2021 Pine Lake Road, Suite 100
Lincoln, NE 68512
www.iuniverse.com
1-800-Authors (1-800-288-4677)

Because of the dynamic nature of the Internet, any Web addresses or links contained in this book may have changed since publication and may no longer be valid.

This is a work of fiction. All of the characters, names, incidents, organizations, and dialogue in these stories are either the products of the author's imagination or are used fictitiously.

ISBN: 978-0-595-42850-2 (pbk)
ISBN: 978-0-595-71233-5 (cloth)
ISBN: 978-0-595-87189-6 (ebk)

Printed in the United States of America

For Hugh

Contents

Acknowledgements

I would like to extend my thanks to my husband, Hugh Elwood, for researching material on a variety of topics and for providing guidance and information from his wealth of knowledge of outdoor recreational activities. A big 'thank you' also to Lorraine Meltzer for her invaluable assistance in proofing and editing my manuscript, and to Doris Von Zuben and Edna Lotocky for their willingness to read, discuss and provide feedback on the plots. Thanks too to my daughter, Caroline Mundell, for the ice-skating background for "The Mephisto Waltz Jump" and to my daughter, Katherine Elwood, who directed me on items regarding fashion, shopping and make-up. I also appreciated the input from several helpful police officers from both the VPD and the RCMP who provided information on protocol and told me about some of the pitfalls that present-day criminals face in today's modern world of technology. I have taken some latitude with the ranks of those forces, since readers of traditional 'cozy' mysteries are used to inspectors and sergeants being out on the street in the course of their investigations, so I greatly appreciated the cheerful attitude of the constables who acknowledged that some creative licence was perfectly acceptable.

I would also like to acknowledge the production team and cast of my play, *Renovations*, who helped make the play such a success that I was inspired to recreate the plot into the story, "Sisters in Crime", for this anthology. Finally, I should add a note regarding the settings and characters. The stories in this volume are set in the Greater Vancouver area, on the Sunshine Coast of British Columbia, and in the city of New York. Therefore many of the scenes and controversies described may seem familiar to residents of those areas; but the various political groups, theatrical associations and characters in these stories exist only in the imagination of the author and bear no relation to organizations or people in real life. However, although the people are imaginary characters, the dogs in the story, "A Political Tail", really did exist and were much loved pets in real life.

The Fall of Tosca

Ballantine Castle was built in 1892 by a social-climbing coal baron who had made a sufficiently large fortune from the natural resources of British Columbia that he could afford to emulate the extravagant lifestyle of the British aristocracy. He built his dream home on a five-hundred-acre estate overlooking the Fraser valley, and since his intention was to give the appearance of a family tree that went back several hundred years, he instructed his architect to create a design that suggested an ancient building that had weathered centuries of use and renovation. Thus, the castle was constructed with a Norman fortress at the centre, Tudor wings on either side, and a flagstone courtyard between the three sides of the edifice. The coal baron's fortune was immense, and his castle was huge to fit his bank balance, but sadly for the multi-millionaire, the stress of accumulating such wealth took its toll, and he died within months of the building's completion, leaving his wife and seven children to enjoy the landmark he had left behind.

A hundred years later, Ballantine Castle still cast its long shadow across the hillside, although the estate it stood on was now diminished to a mere hundred acres and the building was sorely in need of repair. It had changed owners many times since the family had been forced to sell during the Depression, and had served as a school, an orphanage, a military hospital, a monastery and an artists' retreat, but rescue came in 1994 in the form of another multi-millionaire, this time a music lover who had made his fortune in computers, and was now able to indulge his dream of creating a combination of Glyndebourne and Verona in his native province of British Columbia.

Within three years, the necessary repairs and renovations were complete, the gardens had been restored, and the Ballantine Festival Association was formed. A high-profile conductor—who was also fortuitously married to Giordana Bianci, one of the greatest dramatic spintos of the era—was lured from a prestigious European opera company and hired as artistic director. His presence, along with a generous budget, ensured that some of the finest voices of the day were heard throughout the three-month summer festival that combined recitals and chamber opera in the ornate ballroom and grand operatic spectacles in the castle court-

1

yard. The first season had been a sensation, largely due to the presence of the voluptuous Giordana herself, who was at the height of her career and renowned for her beauty and extravagant lifestyle as much as her lush soprano voice. The pathos of her Tosca seemed heightened by the eerie but perfect acoustics, subtly aided by technology since it was an open-air performance, and the looming Norman battlements which, if not architecturally correct for the Castel d'Angelo, were atmospherically compatible. The following year, she returned to sing Lady Macbeth—a role even more suited to the surroundings—and since the production was taped and broadcast by CBC, the festival gained even more widespread coverage.

By the millennium, everything that the multi-millionaire had envisioned became a glorious reality and the name of Ballantine's Castle became a familiar term amidst the international musical cognoscenti. The festival drew crowds of opera lovers, and the estate brought hordes of sightseers who toured the buildings, walked through the gardens, and photographed the waterfall that thundered down the cliff at the strategically placed viewpoint five miles down the road from the entrance gates. Seven years into the new century, to celebrate the tenth anniversary of the festival, a new production of *Tosca* was commissioned. Giordana was no longer quite at the peak of her talents—three years previously, she had been forced to cancel performances due to vocal problems, which were initially due to illness, and later the result of neglect as she had been involved in a tumultuous affair with Ballantine's head technician—but after a sixteen-month sabbatical and careful work with her coach, she was ready to re-launch her career and the world was eager to hear her again. The multi-millionaire, convinced that his festival was once more about to generate a world-wide sensation, poured money into the production; however, he would have been shattered if he had realized the kind of headlines that were in store. Giordana Bianci's Tosca had drawn bravos on every major opera stage throughout the world, but her fall from the castle tower was to become over time the ultimate and memorable performance that ensured that her name remained a legend long after many of her contemporaries were assigned to the annals of operatic history.

◆   ◆   ◆

Philippa Beary turned the windshield wipers onto high and slowed to take the corner. The road arced back so sharply around the escarpment that it felt as if she were heading straight into a void. Since turning off the highway, the drive that provided a breathtaking scenic spectacle for the hordes of summer visitors to the

Ballantine Festival had become a nightmare of slippery curves and poor visibility, with both mist and rain blanketing the cliff-top on this cold January morning, and a constant reminder of the precipitous drop into the valley every time she negotiated a bend in the road. As she came out of the curve, a massive outcropping loomed ahead, and she reduced speed yet again, cursing the fact that the festival director's flight to London had necessitated that her audition be set for nine o'clock in the morning.

The call from Gustav Werner had come the previous day, a timely lift to her spirits, since, other than her regular work with the opera chorus, there were no engagements in sight. To add to her melancholy frame of mind, her friend, Adam, had left for Hamburg, having been given a two-year contract with a company in Germany; so she was feeling forlorn and the opportunity to sing for a famous conductor was a welcome and exciting development. She was actually amazed that Werner had remembered her from their first brief meeting, but clearly he had. With impeccable Teutonic courtesy, he had given her careful directions, instructing her to call him when she turned off the highway so that he could make sure she took the correct road as the castle sign had been damaged in the winter storms and had been taken in for repairs.

Philippa had met Werner in September when he conducted *Norma* for the Vancouver Opera. Her expectations had been great, so she was disappointed to find that the maestro was a rather pedestrian orchestral leader, with a vague circular beat and total indifference to all but the principal players on the stage; but given his status in the world of opera, she had felt the need to make a good impression. Therefore, she had been delighted when she had been provided with the opportunity to attend a post-show reception with her father, Councillor Bertram Beary, who was at the function as an invited guest. Philippa had hung back shyly, waiting to find a propitious moment to talk with the influential man, but her father, who was never daunted by celebrity status, dragged his daughter forward and made the necessary introductions. Before long, Gustav Werner had been treated to the full Beary family history, including the detective son, the retired high-school-principal wife, and the three intelligent, and in Philippa's case opera-singing, daughters. Philippa squirmed with embarrassment as Werner graciously listened, assured her that he might well have something for her in the future, then, as soon as he could escape, sashayed neatly into the entourage surrounding the mezzo-soprano who had shone that night in the role of Adalgisa. At the time, Philippa had been furious with her father, but Beary had been unabashed, dismissing Werner as a cocky upstart who had ridden to fame on his wife's talent. Now, with the prospect of an audition for the Ballantine Festival in her immediate future, she blessed her father's shameless networking, although she would have been happier if the call for an interview had come with more clement weather.

The mist lifted momentarily, and Philippa caught a nerve-wracking glimpse of the rocks below. The sound of the rain seemed louder, even though the drops pattering on the windshield were diminishing, and she realized that she must be approaching the waterfall. Relieved because she was nearing her destination and would soon be past the most treacherous section of road, she checked her watch. It was only eight-forty. She would be on time.

Now that her apprehensions for her physical safety had abated, her anxiety about the coming interview returned. Werner had mentioned Mozart, specifically the role of Papagena, which Philippa had performed in the opera workshop. It was a small but charming role, and the prestige of performing the part at the Ballantine Festival would be a tremendous boost to her career. She had never been to the castle, but had read about Howard Grohman, the multi-millionaire who had created the festival, and she avidly followed reviews of the productions and listened to broadcasts of the operas. She wondered if Werner's wife would be present. Philippa half-hoped she would as she would love to meet the famous Giordana, but she was also aware that the presence of the prima donna could very easily exacerbate her nerves and throw her off.

Another corner loomed ahead, and Philippa braked and carefully steered around the bend, only to find that the road curved back in the other direction, snaking concavely against the rock-face, then disappearing into a tunnel that had been dynamited out of the granite. The noise of the falls became thunderous as the car entered the tunnel, and as it emerged at the far end, Philippa saw that the rain had stopped. Although patches of mist still hung below the cliff, her view was clear. At first she saw nothing but the torrential cascade pounding down the mountainside, but then she noticed another vehicle parked in the viewpoint. It was a gleaming red Jaguar. A woman was standing close by. She hovered at the edge of the precipice, a shadowy profile at first, but as Philippa drove closer, the sun burst through the clouds and the rays illuminated the figure so that the woman was instantly transformed into colour, lit as brilliantly as if she were standing in a spotlight. With a jolt, as if she had conjured the soprano by thinking about her, Philippa recognized the trademark leopard-skin coat, the silk Armani headscarf, tied Italian-style behind the neck, the pouting carmine lips and the Versace sun-glasses, always worn no matter what the weather. It was Giordana Bianci.

My God, thought Philippa, with a sinking lurch to her stomach, *she's going to jump.*

She pulled into the lookout and turned off the engine. The prima donna seemed not to notice the other car. She rocked back and forth, her arms clutched tightly around herself, the black gloves gripping the sleeves of her fur coat, and she continued to stare into the abyss.

As Philippa got out of the car, the cold air hit her cheeks and she shivered. She crossed the viewpoint, feeling the mist from the falls settling around her, and trod carefully as she approached the edge, conscious that the ground was slippery. The air smelled fresh and clean, but the damp was producing a bone-biting cold, and she could feel tension rising in her throat, an aria-deadening grip generated by adverse temperatures and apprehension. She hoped she would be able to persuade the woman to leave quickly.

"Miss Bianci?" she said quietly. "It is you, isn't it?"

There was no reply. It was as if Philippa had not spoken.

"Miss Bianci, I've always wanted to meet you. I'm one of your greatest admirers."

Nothing. Philippa tried a different strategy.

"I'm Philippa Beary," she said briskly. "I'm coming to sing for your husband today."

Finally the woman turned. The dark glasses stared blankly at Philippa. When Bianci spoke, her voice was deep and her Italian accent strong, but the despair in her tone was palpable.

"Don't sing, *cara*—it will break your heart—*he* will break your heart. Go away. Go back where you came from."

Philippa was at a loss, but she knew she could not leave the woman alone.

"Please, Miss Bianci," she ventured again, "let's leave this spot. It's cold and damp. Come back to the castle with me. If you don't feel well, I can drive you. I'm sure someone can fetch your car later."

Bianci turned back towards the cliff edge.

"No." Her voice quavered as if she were trying to stifle a sob. "I have no reason to go back."

"Miss Bianci—"

"I am not Bianci! I am Tosca. For love and art I have lived, but without them there is nothing. Everything … everyone has let me down … my voice, Gustav, Justin. I do not want to go on. Go. Leave me alone."

"I'm not going to leave you," Philippa said firmly, putting her arm around the diva and drawing her back from the edge. With her other hand, she reached into her pocket and extracted her cell phone.

"Now," she said, "I'm going to call your husband—"

"No!" The voice took on a note of fury. "Let me be. Do not interfere. Leave me alone."

Giordana pulled out of Philippa's grasp and ran to the Jaguar. She jumped in, started the engine and careened out of the viewpoint. Without looking back, she sped up the road and the car vanished around the corner.

This is unreal, thought Philippa desperately. *It's not really happening.* Dreading what lay ahead, for the coveted audition had taken on the guise of a bizarre and malevolent dream, Philippa got into her own vehicle and pulled back onto the road. The Jaguar was already out of sight.

She covered the last few miles as quickly as she could, given the unfamiliarity of the terrain, but the drive was easier now for the road had broadened out and was passing through level forested ground. Within ten minutes, the open gates of the Ballantine Estate appeared. She drove through and found herself on a narrow road that ran between two long stands of alder trees.

The rain had stopped, but water dripped from the alders and the asphalt gleamed wetly in the light that filtered through the branches. It seemed as if the woodland would go on forever, but suddenly the car shot out of the trees and the vista of the Ballantine Estate opened up before her. On either side of the road were lawns dotted with rhododendron bushes and edged with pine trees, distorted and stunted, their branches black and sinister in the winter light. The castle, so familiar from photographs and television broadcasts, looked strangely different and somehow unreal in its natural setting. A hundred yards from the portico, a huge Douglas fir with a massive trunk that had split into two catapult-like arms stood in solitary splendour, its thick branches spreading like a fountain and trailing back to the earth. Behind the fir, dwarfing it in spite of its size, the castle tower soared above the top branches.

The Jaguar was parked in front of the castle and its driver stood beside it. She was gesticulating wildly at a tall, thin man who wore a leather coat with a black fur collar—Saint Laurent, Philippa guessed, assessing the coat before she looked at the man—the monetary equivalent of three years tuition for singing lessons. The man looked round and Philippa recognized the angular features right away. It was Gustav Werner. He appeared to be trying to calm his wife, but with no success, for after a moment, the prima donna delivered one last imprecation, then pushed him aside and raced into the building.

Philippa got out of her car, flinching as the chill wind bit into her face. Werner moved forward to meet her. He looked flustered and harried, but he took her hand and greeted her courteously.

"I'm sorry, Miss Beary," he said. "My wife is upset. I will have to go to her."

Philippa nodded.

"Yes, of course. I understand. I saw her at the lookout near the waterfall. She was distraught."

Werner looked at Philippa sharply.

"How do you know? What did she say to you?"

Philippa suddenly felt uncomfortable. She had not anticipated an inquisition. Torn between truth and diplomacy she chose her words carefully.

"She talked about her voice letting her down and …" Her voice tailed off, but Werner continued to stare expectantly, so bravely she went on. "She talked about people letting her down too."

She paused and bit her lip.

"Miss Beary, you don't have to spare my feelings. Tell me what Giordana said. Did she say *I* had let her down?"

Philippa sighed.

"Yes," she admitted finally, "and she mentioned someone called Justin."

Werner frowned.

"Justin Williams. He's our resident technician. Giordana was … fond of him. Too fond, perhaps." He looked anxiously at Philippa. "Did she say anything about their relationship?"

"No, there was nothing else, but she was in an awful state. I was honestly afraid she might do something desperate. I think you ought to have someone with her."

Werner paled.

"Yes, of course. I will go right away. Perhaps you can wait inside and my sister will get you some refreshment. She is in the office on the ground floor. I will take you to her."

He took Philippa's arm, but as they turned towards the house, the door flew open and a statuesque blonde appeared on the front steps. Philippa shivered. The newcomer looked intimidating—an avenging Brünhilde in a modern-day business suit. With apprehension, she noted the cold blue eyes and thin, unsmiling mouth.

The woman spoke in English, but there was a hint of a German accent. In spite of her daunting appearance, she sounded concerned.

"Gustav, is Giordana all right? I heard you quarrelling. She sounded hysterical."

"She's completely distracted. I must go to her and calm her down. She ran inside. Did you see where she went?"

"I heard the elevator, so she must have gone up to your apartment."

"I will go up. Hilde, would you please look after our guest." Werner turned to Philippa. "Miss Beary, this is my sister, Hilde Brandt. She is the festival administrator."

Philippa followed her hosts up the steps and into the entrance hall. Once through the main portal, the Norman fortress was transformed into a mock-Tudor banquet hall, with brown beams, stained-glass windows and a minstrels' gallery overlooking the tessellated floor. A massive oil painting of Giordana Bianci as Tosca hung directly opposite the entrance. It was a dramatic portrait, predominantly black and gold, with the prima donna's ebony hair and gown ornamented with gold braid and jewellery that matched the ornate gilt frame; yet within the grandiose setting, the dark, brooding eyes looked strangely vulnerable.

The room was vast and the temperature inside did not feel any warmer than outside, though Philippa realized that her frozen state was the result of her stop at the waterfall and that she was probably chilled right through. In spite of her discomfort, her eye took in anomalies introduced by each of the millionaire owners: a nineteenth-century fireplace with stonework depicting native Indian customs, a Victorian-era dumb-waiter, a modern-day elevator, and to the right of the entrance, a glass-paned door through which was visible a computerized, state-of-the-art office, presumably where the formidable Hilde spent her days. As if reading her mind, Werner's sister opened the office door and gestured to Philippa to come through. Werner went straight to the elevator. As Philippa entered the office, she felt a welcome blast of heat, and she gratefully slipped off her damp coat and handed it to Hilde. She was about to sink into a chair when she heard a strangled cry from the hall.

"Hilde! She has gone to the tower!"

Hilda Brandt threw Philippa's coat on a chair and ran out into the hall. Philippa followed her. Werner was standing by the elevator and pointing at the panel beside the door. The very top button on the panel was lit up. Werner pressed the control to bring the lift back to the main floor, but as they waited impatiently for it to descend, they heard a blood-chilling scream echo in the distance. Then, as abruptly as the sound began, it was cut off.

◆   ◆   ◆

"We'll take more statements and check her rooms, of course, and we'll look around the building," declared Constable Hillerman, "but I think it's a pretty clear case of suicide."

Hillerman had not been entirely convinced after hearing Werner's sad tale of a prima donna whose voice was deteriorating and whose broken love affair with Ballantine's resident technician had left her shattered and insecure, especially as the employee in question had been close at hand in the on-site recording studio when the soprano fell to her death; but once the constable had listened to Philippa's account of her meeting with Bianci earlier in the day, his mind was made up. He considered Philippa, with her connections to the law and the lawmakers, the perfect witness, and had complete confidence in the truth and accuracy of her statement.

But Philippa was not happy. She had been asked to remain in case there were further questions, so as her audition was clearly to be postponed, she asked Hilde if she could borrow a dry coat so she could walk in the grounds. As she proceeded along the path that led around the shallow lake on the west side of the castle, she was haunted by the image of Bianci's body, a sodden rag doll lying in the flag-stone courtyard, the leopard-skin coat flared out beneath her, the sunglasses broken a few feet away. *If only I could have found the right words to help her*, she thought sorrowfully. *Why couldn't I get through to her?*

She rounded the end of the lake and started to walk back on the far side, shivering as she passed the stunted pines. Before long, the trail curved away from the water and she found herself in a wild garden with a network of paths, ornamental ponds and a strange variety of trees, some allowed to twist and turn towards the light, and some shaped neatly by a topiary artist. She passed a yew that had been sculpted into a series of pompoms and an eerie ash-grey eucalyptus, which, according to the wooden tag at its base, was called a snow gum. The path veered again and turned into a narrow dirt trail that ran between a brick-lined pond and a high rock wall. Halfway along the wall, a wrought-iron gate was set into the stonework, and through it, Philippa could see the bare stumps of the rose garden. Suddenly, amid the scent of damp leaves, Philippa became aware of the smell of smoke. It was coming from a gazebo at the centre of the pond. A man was leaning against the railing. He was smoking a cigarette and staring stonily into the water.

Philippa paused, hesitating to disturb him, but the man sensed her presence and looked up. He waved to her.

"You must be the singer," he called. "Come out here. I want to hear what she said to you. There's a bridge further along the path."

Philippa continued until she reached the bridge that linked path and gazebo. She crossed over and joined the man. He was young, not much older than herself, and attractive in a quiet way, but his eyes were sad. Philippa suddenly realized who he was.

"You're Justin Williams, aren't you? You're ..."

Her voice tailed off, but the man smiled ruefully and nodded.

"The techie she had the scandalous affair with—yes. It's all right. Everyone knows about it. Giordana's affairs were common knowledge. Every couple of years she'd have a passionate fling with someone like me—then let them down kindly and go back to her husband. I knew I'd go the same way ultimately, but it didn't change my feelings."

"You really cared for her?"

Williams nodded.

"I was crazy about her. She was outrageous and fascinating and extravagant. She bought diamonds as if they were bottles of wine, and she flaunted her leopard-skin coats in the faces of the eco-fanatics. She was vain and self-centred, and I'd have done anything for her. It's not true, you know, what they're saying about her being depressed over the end of our affair. She was the one that called a halt—not me. If she was so desperate that she killed herself, then it'll be that cold bastard of a husband who drove her to it."

"If her husband was so unkind, why did she stay with him?"

"They were a team. He was part of her career. He wasn't the greatest conductor in the world, but he was her vocal coach, and a superb one at that, not only because he concentrated exclusively on her, but because he understood her voice—she relied on him."

"Did you sense that she was unhappy?"

Williams frowned.

"No, that's the ridiculous part. She'd been down for a while about her vocal problems, but Giordana was a survivor. She'd beaten cancer two years ago, and she was determined to regain her strength and technique. She was working her way back, but she used to joke that when her voice finally packed in, she would fall back on her certified pension."

Philippa looked mystified.

"Grohman," he explained. "He adored her. This whole festival was set up originally as a showcase for her. Werner was only hired as the director because he was married to Giordana. It was Grohman's way of ensuring he'd establish a long term relationship with his idol."

"Then why do you think she jumped?"

"I can't explain it. Maybe, for all her bravado, she really couldn't face the prospect of a fading career. Werner may have known how to get the best out of her voice, but he didn't leave her any illusions. He was brutally frank under that smarmy exterior."

Philippa stared at the lily pads on the surface of the pond and tried to blank out the thought of Bianci hurtling through the air from the top of the tower.

"You were in the castle when she fell?" she said finally.

The man nodded.

"Yes. I was the only one there."

"But surely they need a big staff to run such a large building?"

"Yes, when it's occupied. But it was going to be empty for three months. There were a lot of people here over Christmas—a big house party—Grohman loves that sort of thing—but everyone left after New Year's Day and the house was to be closed for the rest of the winter. The staff left yesterday, and Giordana was going to leave today with her husband and his sister. I was staying on for a couple of days until the caretaker arrived. I was doing some editing for a recording, and it was a good opportunity to work in peace. That's why I was in the sound studio this morning."

"Then you must have seen her on the tower. Surely the booth overlooks the courtyard?"

"The booth does, yes—that's where I control the lights and sound for the opera productions—the piped in music for social events comes from there too—but the recording studio is on the second floor. There aren't any windows there. I didn't see a thing."

"I suppose it's a sound-proof room—you wouldn't have heard her either."

"Actually, I did hear the elevator going up. I'd been under a headset since eight o'clock, and I always stopped after an hour to have a short break. I was just going back into the studio when I heard the sound of the lift."

"But you didn't hear her scream?"

"No." Williams sighed. "She loved the tower, you know. She'd go up there in all weathers. She said it was her way of being on top of the world. I like to think that the view from there was the last thing she saw."

Philippa nodded, but Williams had already turned away and she sensed he wanted to be alone. She left the gazebo and returned to the path. It soon led her to the Italian garden, which was always featured in the brochures as a riot of red tulips and golden daffodils, but now lay as barren and bleak as the stones in the wall that surrounded it. At the end of the walled garden, she came to an odd-looking copper beech with three Cyclops-like eyes in the centre trunk where the branches had been lopped off. As she stared back at the hypnotic trio of eyes, a shadow emerged from behind the tree and materialized into Gustav Werner.

"Miss Beary—may I call you Philippa? I am so sorry that you have been drawn into this sad affair."

Philippa had a sudden vision of the portrait of Bianci in the entrance hall of the castle and she found her eyes filling with tears.

"If only I could have done something to help," she said sadly. "I feel terrible about what happened."

"Don't blame yourself. Giordana was beyond help. No one could have done anything to prevent her. She was determined to die."

"What drove her to such despair? She had everything. It doesn't make sense."

Werner sighed.

"She was despondent about her voice. The love affairs were nothing—she and I understood one another, and she always came back to be consoled when one went sour—but the voice was everything. Her problems started when she took on the role of Lady Macbeth. It was too much for her."

Philippa was surprised.

"How can you say that?" she asked. "She was wonderful. I heard the live broadcast. It was an incredible performance."

"Yes, but the high D-flat put a strain on her—she was ill, though we didn't know it at the time—and she insisted on doing the off-stage scream—she pushed herself too hard, and the damage was done."

"But she was making a comeback."

"Yes, as Tosca. Not such a demanding role and one she knew well. She would have been fine, but she knew she couldn't sing it the way she did ten years ago. Ultimately, she couldn't accept not being the best any more. I tried to make her understand that it didn't matter—that she was still far better than most of the singers on the circuit—but it wasn't enough."

Philippa was struck by the conductor's reasonable tone, the absence of passion in his voice, and she had a sudden flashback to Bianci's words at the edge of the precipice. *He will break your heart.* Had her husband's practical attitude towards the inevitability of her decline caused her depression? With a start, she came out of her reverie. Werner was still speaking to her.

"I just wanted to tell you how much I appreciate your kindness and patience," he told her, taking her hand firmly in his own, "and of course, assure you that we will, for another time, reschedule. You do understand."

"Yes, of course," Philippa replied. With a rush of unease, she saw that his eyes were the same cold blue as his sister's. *I understand*, she thought, *and I don't believe you. So why did you bring me here?*

Werner gave a short bow and moved away. Philippa watched him walk past the Italian garden and disappear into the network of paths that led to the gazebo. Then she turned and headed back. In spite of the heavy wool coat she was wearing, she felt cold.

She emerged from the gardens and crossed the lawn towards the amphitheatre that had been constructed at the side of the courtyard. The castle towered above her, grim and forbidding from the north side, and she suddenly realized how powerful the production of *Macbeth* must have been in this stark setting. She moved into the courtyard, and as she stepped over the flagstones, she visualized Bianci's body, wet and broken, and something about the picture troubled her. She thrust the image from her mind and thought of the soprano as she had been, alive and vibrant, performing in this magnificent space, her voice floating ethereally into the night sky.

Philippa paused at the centre of the courtyard and stared up at the castle walls. She had heard the *Macbeth* broadcast and had listened avidly as the announcer had tried to depict the setting for the radio audience, but now she could put sound and sight together. In her mind's eye, she saw Lady Macbeth gliding across the ramparts, pale and ghostly, washing the blood from her hands. The sleepwalking aria resounded in her ears, and the offstage scream seemed to reverberate around the walls.

Suddenly, she recalled Bianci's words: "For love and art I have lived." And then she remembered. She had heard that scream before. In a flash, she realized what had troubled her about the diva's body—and she knew how Werner had murdered his wife.

◆   ◆   ◆

"I don't think you'll ever get to sing at the Ballantine Festival now," said Constable Hillerman sympathetically, after Werner and his sister had been arrested and led away. "What's that saying about killing the messenger who brings bad news? Grohman will be grateful that you brought his idol's murderer to justice, but he won't want you around as a reminder."

"I know," muttered Philippa, feeling a rush of rage against the conductor. "The reality is I wasn't ready for that league yet, but one day I could have been—but of course, he chose me for other reasons, didn't he?"

"Yes. You were the perfect witness—the sister of an RCMP detective, the daughter of a politician. Werner knew any investigating officer would take your story verbatim. What an incredible scheme—he must have gone with her to the tower as soon as you called to say you had turned off the highway. That's when he murdered her, but of course, there was nobody around to hear her scream. The only person on site was the technician, and he was under a headset in a soundproof studio. Werner knew you had never met his wife, but given her signature outfits, it was easy for his sister, who was a large woman herself, to disguise herself well enough to take you in. Fortunately for their plan, Bianci had several of the distinctive leopard coats, and because of the bout with cancer, she also had a variety of wigs."

"Yes," reflected Philippa. "Hilde Brandt must have left for the viewpoint after I called. She waited for me, put on the show of a suicidal, despondent woman, then raced back to the castle and staged a scene with her brother when I arrived. I wonder how she got rid of the disguise so quickly. She ran inside, but she was out again in a flash."

"The dumb waiter," said Hillerman. "It's electric and it goes to Bianci's private apartment. We found traces from the wig and the coat inside it. She must have thrown the disguise in and pressed the switch to send it up. Werner will have gone up to the room and put everything back in his wife's closet after he called the ambulance."

"I suppose Hilde Brandt also sent the elevator up to the tower. No wonder I kept getting the feeling that the whole situation was totally unreal. It was. It was a staged performance for my benefit—complete with the scream. I recognized it, you know. It was from the recording of *Macbeth*. One thing puzzles me, though. I can see how they could have put the scream onto an individual CD, but I wonder how they managed to play it over the courtyard speakers. The sound booth was on the fourth floor."

"They didn't use the booth. We checked the wiring from the speakers. One of them had been connected to a computer in the office, so I suspect Werner had cut and pasted the scream onto a file—maybe set it ten minutes from the start—and simply pressed play when he saw your car coming onto the drive. He'll have deleted it now, of course, but we'll convict them. A computer expert will be able to retrieve the file, and there'll be DNA from the articles the sister wore. Your statement about the weather will be significant too."

"Yes, I kept wondering why I was bothered about the condition of the body, and then I remembered. The rain had stopped when I arrived at the castle. She shouldn't have been so wet. And there's something else that struck me. Tosca's most famous aria is 'Vissi d'arte'—'I have lived for art, I have lived for love'—but when Hilde Werner quoted those words at the waterfall, she said the lines backwards with the verbs at the end of the phrase. It was a German construction. Werner himself said something similar later when I talked to him in the grounds and that reminded me of the anomaly. It didn't ring true. Bianci would never have spoken the words that way."

"It's a bizarre case," acknowledged Hillerman. "I still can't figure out his motive. Why kill her? From what one hears, she was the goose that laid the golden eggs."

"Yes, that's true. Werner was a mediocre conductor. He'd never have achieved the status he did without his wife. But Justin Williams said something significant and I think he may have hit on the reason."

"Williams? The technician?"

"Yes. I think Bianci may have been far more philosophical about a declining career than any of us believed. According to Williams, Howard Grohman has been in love with Bianci for years and would marry her at the drop of a hat if she ever left Werner. Her relationship with Werner had deteriorated into purely a business arrangement, witness the infidelities on both sides, and I suspect Bianci was starting to consider the advantages of a comfortable and pampered retirement with her multi-millionaire. Werner's career would have ground to a halt. With his wife dead, he could retain his status, if only through sympathy, but if they separated, he and his sister would have been sent packing. Bianci may have been charming and fascinating, but although Williams loved her, he admitted that she was ruthlessly self-centred. I think Werner decided to get rid of her before she decided to get rid of him."

"Good Lord!" said Hillerman. "And you want to make a career in the world of opera."

He shook his head sadly as he escorted Philippa to the main portal.

◆　　　◆　　　◆

The sky was dark when Philippa left. She said goodbye to Hillerman and stepped out into the bitter evening air. The light from the castle windows spilled onto the driveway, creating a yellow flood to illuminate her way to the car. The night was clear and a cool winter moon cast a pale ghostly light onto the grounds

so that the stunted pines with their skeletal branches appeared like a row of spec-
tral soldiers waiting to march on the castle. Philippa shivered as she passed by.
Quickly, she got into her car and pulled away. As she approached the stand of
alders, she glanced in her rear-view mirror. Ballantine Castle was a black silhouette flecked with dots of gold, stark against the evening sky. It hovered in view for
a brief second; then disappeared as the car followed the road into the woods. The
trees closed behind her, like the curtains of an opera house sweeping together and
signalling the close of the scene.

Somehow Philippa knew she would never return.

The Mephisto Waltz Jump

Sylvia Beary stared at the coach in horror.

"You expect me to sew?"

Julie Jones was firm but diplomatic.

"This is a club. You're not simply paying for a weekly class. All the mothers help with the carnival."

"Chelsea is four. She's had three skating lessons. How can she possibly be in a show?"

"The beginners are in the *Sleeping Beauty* sequence," Julie explained patiently. "The girls are roses, the boys are thorns, and they make one circle around the ice in the forest scene. It's very easy."

"And for that I have to make a costume!"

"We'll provide you with the pattern and fabric. It's quite straightforward."

Sylvia glanced toward the stands to make sure Chelsea was safely ensconced on the bleachers with her nanny, Mai Ling, then turned back to do battle with Julie. However, before she could resume the argument, there was a noise like a sabre being whipped through the air as the flying figure of the British Columbia champion flashed past the boards. Sylvia flinched, then recoiled a second time as the senior coach bellowed from the bleachers behind her.

"You're cutting it too wide, Jenny. Keep in tight."

The skater swung into a position that Sylvia recognized as the preliminary to a jump, but even to her inexperienced eyes, it was apparent that a fall was imminent.

Wendy Marshall moved to the ice as the skater tumbled. "Come round again, Jenny," she commanded. "You've got to keep the speed as you go into the jump. You're losing momentum."

"What is that jump?" Sylvia asked Julie.

"It's a triple Axel. Very few of the women do it. That's one of the reasons Jenny won the B.C. Championships. A triple Lutz is usually the hardest jump for the women's program." Julie pointed towards a muscular girl dressed in brilliant pink spandex who was skating rapidly backwards up the ice. "That's what Andrea Burke is practising."

"I can't tell the difference."

Julie elaborated.

"The Axel is like a waltz jump with extra spins thrown in. You've seen skaters in competition when they lose their nerve and fail to do an Axel. They're basically doing a high, wide waltz jump—entered forwards, but landed in the backward position. The Lutz is both entered and landed backwards. They're both powerful jumps."

Julie joined Wendy at the boards and watched anxiously as Jenny Wong picked herself up and began another circle around the ice. The tension was contagious.

"What's wrong with Jenny?" Julie asked Wendy. "She's been off her form for weeks."

"She's been off her form since she won the B.C. Championships," said Wendy shortly, as Jenny made another attempt at the triple Axel and fell on landing. "Watch where you're going, Andrea," she called sharply, as the skater in pink narrowly avoided the fallen girl. Without missing a beat, Andrea continued up the ice with a dazzling display of fancy footwork, cutting equally close as she passed Marina Milovich who was spinning at the far end of the rink. The solitary male on the ice glided over and gallantly helped Jenny up. Sylvia recognized him as Jason Moore. He had placed third in the men's free-skate.

"Never mind the chat, you two," called Wendy. "Jenny, get your breath and focus. Take a moment, then try again." She turned back to Julie. "Andrea may have been second in B.C.," she continued, "but she's going to be the club's best hope for a win at Canadians if Jenny doesn't get her act back together."

"It's too bad Marina blew her short program," said Julie. "She wasn't well before the contest, and her nerves got the better of her. If she'd made the final flight, she would have had a good chance at Canadians, and I'd much rather see her representing us. Andrea's a wonderful skater, but she isn't the nicest girl in the club."

Jenny Wong remained still at centre ice, her head down and her hands on her knees. She was an extremely pretty girl, tiny, with sculpted black hair and a dazzling smile, but today she looked strained, and her normally glowing complexion had faded to an unhealthy pallor. After a moment, she pulled herself upright, turned, and headed back up the rink.

"You need more speed, Jenny," Wendy called across the ice. "Look at her," she muttered. "She's tired. She insists she's eating properly and getting enough sleep, but she's flagging. Even Christie Knotts is out-skating her."

To Sylvia's eyes, every one of the young athletes was magnificent. Sylvia's daughter was new to the club, and the beginners' lesson came at the end of the school day when the senior skaters were finishing their afternoon ice-time, so the little ones and their parents were regularly treated to a spectacular show of skating while they laced up. It had not taken Sylvia long to realize that Wendy Marshall was a top coach, and that the best skaters in the Lower Mainland flocked to her club. She was astounded at the free-skaters' power and speed, which never seemed as apparent when watching competitions on television, and she marvelled at the skill that enabled them to carry out intricate manoeuvres without colliding with each other or coming to grief on the boards.

She watched in awe as Jason Moore shot down the ice, suspended his body into take-off position, executed a breathtaking jump and immediately began the acceleration up the rink to begin the process again. Christie Knotts was performing a series of graceful turns on the far side of the rink, and as her movements seemed to coincide with the Cole Porter melody that was emanating from the overhead speakers—in a tinny tone that would have deeply offended its composer—Sylvia assumed she was going through her routine. The other girls appeared to be practising individual elements. Marina Milovich, willowy and elegant in black and purple, was spinning like a top at centre ice, and Andrea Burke was circling around her in a graceful backwards spiral. Jenny Wong had regained her equilibrium and was moving up the ice to try her jump again. As she reached the far end of the rink and curved round to begin the downward skate, Andrea came out of her spiral and began to accelerate, skating backwards in the opposite direction.

Sylvia tensed as the two skaters approached each other, but the coaches appeared unconcerned, and she reminded herself that the athletes always appeared to know the path of the other skaters and that they would whip past each other, carrying out their individual program components as if they were the only ones on the ice.

As Andrea continued to gain speed, Jenny glided onto one foot in preparation for the Axel.

"Damn, she's going to pop the jump," snapped Wendy.

Sylvia was not sure what happened next, whether Andrea misjudged her course, or whether Jenny lost control and veered. Andrea executed a perfect triple Lutz, but Jenny elevated into the air, swung round in a slow loop, and landed, leg swinging wide, in Andrea's path. Andrea appeared to jolt and stagger. She stayed upright for a moment, then spun out of control and buckled at the knees. Jenny drifted in a slow circle, both feet on the ice; then she gently revolved downward and lay prone and still. Marina circled back to where Jenny had fallen. Jason skidded to a halt between the two girls, then glided towards Andrea and helped her to her feet. Christie Knotts was spinning at the top end of the rink, but as the sudden clamour of voices rose over the piped music of her dance number, she stopped her spin and stared in bewilderment at the confusion at centre ice.

As Wendy and Julie hurried onto the ice, there was a loud cry from Marina.

"Jenny's been cut! You have to call an ambulance."

Sylvia watched as coaches and skaters converged on the figure that was lying ominously still at the centre of the rink. She saw Wendy pull out a cell phone and dial, while Julie, white-faced and tight-lipped, tugged off her scarf and fell to her knees beside Jenny. As Wendy talked on the phone, she kept her eyes on the girl on the ice, and even though her head was turned downwards, Sylvia could see the tension in her expression. Suddenly Marina gave a shriek and put her hands to her mouth.

At first, Sylvia could not see what had caused the second outcry, but as the figures on the rink shifted position, she followed the direction of their eyes.

They were standing in a widening pool of red that was slowly and steadily spreading across the surface of the ice.

◆   ◆   ◆

Two weeks later, Sylvia marched into her husband's office and slapped a file on his desk.

"Rat poison," she announced. "I've just got the report. Jenny Wong had been receiving continuous doses of warfarin. That's why she died before the ambulance arrived. Her blood was so thin she had a massive haemorrhage and went into shock."

Her husband, who was a criminal lawyer in the same firm where Sylvia handled civil cases, thought for a moment before responding.

"That should let your client off the hook," he said finally. "If Jenny Wong was on blood-thinners, that will be considered the major contributing factor in her death."

"That's the problem," Sylvia said shortly. "She hadn't been prescribed blood-thinners. Her parents are adamant that Jenny was not taking the medication voluntarily. What's even more alarming is that the police found traces of warfarin in Jenny's hot chocolate. She always had a thermos at the rink, and it seems abundantly clear that someone was doctoring it on a regular basis."

"Wouldn't that be hard to do? I thought rink-side mothers watched their off-spring like hawks."

Sylvia looked impatient.

"Honestly, Norton. You've never been to a skating rink in your entire life. What do you know about skating mothers?"

"Nothing, obviously." Norton knew better than to argue with his wife.

"Actually," Sylvia continued, "Jenny's mother did attend her daughter's practices, but often as not she was playing music in the box above the rink, so Jenny's gear would have been sitting unattended on the bleachers. There would have been lots of opportunity for someone to slip the pills into the flask."

"Not without taking an awful risk of being seen. Anyway, how can the police be sure that the drug was added to the drink on more than one occasion?"

"Because Jenny had been suffering health problems ever since the competition and her symptoms are identical to those of a person who is on high doses of blood-thinners. The trade name of the drug is Coumadin, and it's an anti-coagulant. People are put on it to deal with blood clots, but even then they have to have regular tests to ensure that their blood doesn't become dangerously thin—and of course, Jenny's was off the chart."

"What were her symptoms?"

"She had a decreased appetite, so of course, she lost weight—not a good thing since she was a tiny little thing to begin with—and her parents were worried because she was getting headaches and dizzy spells. She also complained about excessive menstrual bleeding, and her mother had noticed that her gums bled when she flossed her teeth and that she seemed to have an unusual number of bruises. Also, her skating coach had expressed concern because Jenny had complained about getting sudden leg cramps. These are all classic symptoms. It's pretty obvious the girl was being systematically poisoned."

"How long would it take for these signs to show up?"

"A few weeks. There are other factors too. Some nutrients slow the effect of the drug—greens like broccoli, spinach or kale, for example, because they're high in vitamin K which is a major inhibitor. Antacids also tend to counteract the drug. But vitamins C or D may increase the effect, and unfortunately for Jenny, she didn't like green vegetables and she drank lots of orange and grapefruit juice, so her symptoms would have become severe more quickly."

Norton shook his head.

"Poor kid. So the collision turned out to be fatal. With a sliced artery, she didn't have a chance."

"That's right. And that means Andrea Burke may not only face a civil lawsuit, she's also in the front line when the police lay criminal charges."

"Criminal charges require a motive," said Norton firmly.

Sylvia looked glum.

"The world of figure skating is incredibly competitive," she said. "Look at the Harding/Kerrigan fiasco a few years ago."

"You mean we've got that sort of scenario at our rink?"

"Wendy Marshall is one of the top coaches in Canada, so she attracts the most ambitious skaters. Quite a few champions have come from our club."

Norton looked anxious.

"I didn't realize our club had big-league coaches. I thought we'd put our daughter into a low-key community class."

"It is a low-key class—the beginners are taught by a twelve-year-old pre-novice. What on earth are you worried about?"

"Money," said Norton flatly. "Figure skating has to be the most expensive sport in existence. And don't the serious skaters practice at all sorts of horrible hours in the early morning? What if Chelsea decides she wants to continue to the higher levels?"

"Well, if she does, you'll just have to give up your impractical notions about defending criminals and go into something sensible like corporate law," Sylvia said unsympathetically. "And it won't hurt you to get up early to drive your daughter to the rink. You'll be able to get a head start on your cases. Oh, for heaven's sake," she retorted, seeing Norton's horrified expression, "Chelsea is four. She can barely walk on the ice, let alone skate. I don't think you have to worry about her dreaming of the Olympics just yet. Now, can we talk about my case?"

"Sorry," said Norton. "OK. Explain to me how these young skaters progress from the local club to the big time."

"I'm only just learning myself, but I gather that the first big challenge is the B.C. competition, and from there, the best four skaters move to Canadians, which is the next hurdle before the World Championships. The number of skaters sent from each country to the Worlds is governed by the number that placed in the top ranks the previous year."

Norton held up a hand to stop the flow.

"Slow down. Tell me how this relates to the skaters at our club."

Sylvia pursed her lips.

"Well, if you ever bothered to come to Chelsea's skating class, you'd understand what I'm talking about. We had four senior skaters in the female free-skate category, though only three of them were serious contenders. Jenny Wong and Andrea Burke attained first and second place respectively at the B.C. Championships, and therefore, they would both have moved on to Canadians."

Norton shook his head.

"So what's the big deal? They were both going, so what's to say they wouldn't both have had the opportunity to move up the next step of the ladder. Why try to nobble a competitor at this stage of the game?"

"Because Canada is only going to be allowed to send one female free-skater to the Worlds this year, so if Jenny had won at Canadians, Andrea would have been out of the picture."

"Is Andrea the only skater to benefit from what has happened?" Norton asked curiously.

"I hadn't thought about that," said Sylvia. "Andrea is the only obvious one."

"Well, it should be considered. I'd like to know what will happen now Jenny's dead. Will another skater go to Canadians in her place?"

Sylvia paused and thought for a moment.

"Marina Milovich came in fifth at the B.C. competition, so it's now conceivable that she'll be given the opportunity to go to Canadians—but she can hardly be held accountable. She was on the other side of the ice when Jenny and Andrea collided."

"Did you see the collision?" asked Norton.

"Yes. That's why the Burkes asked me to represent their daughter. They realized they'd be dealing with a civil lawsuit, and they wanted someone on-side right away."

"How did the accident happen?"

"Nobody is sure. Jenny was having trouble with a jump, so it's possible that she veered into Andrea's path as she landed. She did what they call 'popping' a jump and turned what should have been an Axel into a waltz jump. Her leg swung out just as Andrea landed a triple Lutz, which is a high-speed, powerful jump that lands with the skater's leg extended behind, and it seems that Andrea's skate must have sliced Jenny's out-flung leg. It was impossible to see, though. All that was visible to the eye was that the two skaters were very close, but there was some kind of contact as they passed because Andrea appeared to jolt as if she'd been jarred and Jenny just seemed to spin slowly round and fall."

"Was there a trail of blood to indicate the path she'd followed?"

"No. There was so much blood pooling on the ice that it was impossible to identify the spot where the cut had happened. And the skaters gathered round her, so they all had blood on their blades. But the cut must have occurred as they collided, and the general buzz is that Andrea deliberately staged the accident, having first doctored her rival's thermos with blood-thinners, thus ensuring that she was eliminated from the competition. That's why I believe the police are getting ready to lay charges."

"Surely they'd have to have some grounds to do that?"

Sylvia frowned.

"Unfortunately, they do. A year ago, Andrea's father was prescribed Coumadin as a result of a thrombosis he'd developed after a flight from Australia. He had a six-month prescription—ten-milligram pills which is the highest dose you can take—but the doctor took him off the drug after three months."

"That doesn't mean anything. Presumably he used all his pills."

Sylvia shook her head.

"No, he'd just refilled his prescription so there was a bottle left—and it's disappeared."

Norton was astounded.

"He was silly enough to admit that to the police?"

"He didn't have any choice. Just before Christmas, one of the parents came to Andrea's house to drop off a form, and she heard him asking his wife and daughter about the missing pills. So unfortunately for Andrea, there's a direct link between her and Jenny's debilitated condition."

Norton eyed the file on his desk.

"And that's why you barged in here to discuss the case. You think this girl is going to need a defence lawyer as well as a civil litigator."

Sylvia nodded.

"I can tell from the attitude of the constable running the investigation. He's the quick-fix, one-scenario type of detective. He's already got his mind made up. It's too bad the club is downtown. If it were in an RCMP jurisdiction, I would at least have Richard to deal with."

Norton looked skeptical.

"Your brother would hardly let a family connection interfere with his investigation of a case," he said. "He's too good a detective for that."

"No, but at least he'd keep an open mind. Detective Constable Baron took one look at Andrea and decided she was guilty. End of story."

Norton raised his eyebrows.

"One look? I take it the girl does not make a good impression."

"She's the least popular girl in the club. And it doesn't help that the silly idiot threw a tantrum when the scores came up at the B.C. Championships and said for all and sundry to hear, 'I wish Jenny would drop dead!' That's why everyone is prepared to believe the worst."

"Trial by teenage gossip?"

"About that. The parents are wealthy too, so they're an ideal target for a lawsuit. Robert and Carey Burke are loaded."

"Carey Burke? Don't I know that name?"

"She hosts a cooking show. She's a celebrity chef."

Norton visibly perked up.

"'Fables and Feasts'—she does all those ethnic dishes and gives the historical background behind them. She's very good-looking," Norton added enthusiastically. "I love her show."

Sylvia scowled.

"Yes, well you and lots of other men—and it's not her dishes that catch your attention."

"She has a nice personality," protested Norton.

"Not off the screen. According to the mothers I've talked to, she's an absolute bitch. She's much younger than her husband. Robert Burke is sixty-five, and he's the one with the money. Carey is thirty-nine."

"Ah, a trophy wife," nodded Norton.

"Yes. I gather she weaselled him away from his first wife and used his money and influence to advance her career."

"So she isn't Andrea's real mother?"

"Oh, yes. Robert and Carey have been married for nineteen years. Andrea has been described as a product of his lust and her indifference, which might explain some of their daughter's personality problems—along with the fact that Carey Burke isn't exactly a good role model when it comes to getting along with people. I'm told she was scathingly nasty to Georgia Milovich the first time they met. Georgia is the mother of another senior skater. She's very artistic, but she's also stayed at home to raise a large family—nine children, I believe—and Carey looked her straight in the eye and said, 'Oh, you're the one who sings, writes, paints and …" Sylvia paused. She was extremely ladylike by nature. "Well, I refuse to use the word she used, but it was the popular vernacular term for intercourse."

Norton blinked.

"Good heavens," he said. "She's so sweet on TV. What did the other mother do?"

"I have no idea. It sounds as if the Milovich family has not had an easy time in this country. They emigrated from Croatia six years ago, and the coach told me that the Wongs, who are the longest-established, most influential family in the club, have tended to be condescending towards them, and others have followed their lead. However, it sounds as if Marina always takes the high road and she has gradually won people over—except, of course, for the Burkes, who don't seem to like anyone."

Norton sat back and looked gratified.

"You know, Sylvia," he said, "you've just described an extremely unsympathetic group of characters, along with a scenario which sounds depressingly damning, and yet you seem prepared to go the extra mile for these people. Don't tell me my influence is finally rubbing off and you're realizing the principle that everyone is entitled to a defence?"

Sylvia snorted. "Don't be ridiculous," she said curtly. "I've always taken the position that people deserve to be considered innocent until proven guilty."

"Not really," Norton pointed out. "You're a civil lawyer, and that's more like Napoleonic law. You have to prove innocence, and that's much harder to establish. Do you really believe this un-likeable girl is innocent?"

"Yes, I do."

"Why?"

Sylvia paused and thought for a moment.

"I think it has to do with her pride," she said. "She's arrogant and aggressive and competitive, but she genuinely believes she's the best. I get the impression that she thinks the adjudicators were prejudiced in Jenny's favour because of personal connections with Mrs. Wong, who has worked the judges' circuit herself. Andrea believes she can win at Canadians on her own merit. Whether she's right or not, I don't know, but even though I don't like her, I don't believe she'd stoop to cheating in order to win. And if that's the case, I don't want to see her convicted for something she didn't do because the other skaters don't like her, or because Carey Burke has offended the other mothers."

"You mean she's rude to all of them?"

"Pretty well. She's catty and hypercritical, and she's also apt to throw out racist remarks, which doesn't sit well these days. She made some remark about the club having an oversized Chinese contingent. I believe the term she used was 'a ton of little Wongs and Wings'."

"That sounds like something your father would say."

"Yes, well father has never been known for his political correctness. I'm amazed he continues to get elected."

"You know," suggested Norton, "speaking of your father gives me an idea. Why don't you get him down to the rink—and your sister too? They're both pretty sharp. They might pick up something useful amid the gossip—the sort of thing you might miss because people know you're representing Andrea. You could invite them down to watch Chelsea's class."

Sylvia sniffed.

"I've already asked them," she said. "Philippa is always too busy with her singing, though to be fair, I think she is planning to come down when she has a break—she's very fond of the children—but Dad's only comment was that he had no desire to get frostbite in the course of pretending that his granddaughter could skate when she's lucky if she can waddle five steps before she lands on her backside."

"I bet they'd be a lot more interested if they knew there was a mystery to be solved."

"Yes, you're right," said Sylvia. "I'll call them. In fact, they can take Chelsea to her lesson and I'll get a chance to start on that silly costume."

Norton looked at his wife in astonishment.

"You're actually going to sew?"

Sylvia looked shocked.

"Of course not," she said. "I'm going to give the pattern to Mai Ling and explain to her what has to be done."

◆   ◆   ◆

Philippa finished lacing Chelsea's skates, fished in her niece's Barbie bag to find her a juice pack, then stood to watch the end of the seniors' practice. She had been well briefed by her sister on the events at the rink, and Sylvia's descriptions of the major players had been clear and accurate. Philippa had no difficulty identifying each of the girls on the ice. Andrea Burke was a dynamo. Her speed was phenomenal, and the power behind the jumps breathtaking, but in spite of the brilliant technique, her face was pinched and her visible anger made her uncomfortable to watch. Marina Milovich, on the other hand, was the epitome of grace and charm, *melody in motion*, thought Philippa, her professional instinct identifying a consummate performer in action. Christie Knotts was a good skater too, solid and competent, but Philippa could see why she was not considered a contender. She lacked the speed of the other two, which made her appear cautious, and although she landed her jumps, she had no sense of showmanship, so the end result was rather bland.

The mother who was lacing her own daughter's skates on the adjacent bench noticed Philippa watching.

"Christie's not bad," she commented. "She'll never get anywhere in competition, but she doesn't care. She only enters because the coaches say it will give her good experience. Her goal is the chorus line in Ice Capades, and she'll easily make that."

"I'd never thought of that," said Philippa. "One tends to think of figure skating as the field of champions, but I suppose there are other opportunities."

The mother nodded.

"Lots of potential jobs. Ice shows are fun for those who want to travel, but there are coaching positions too. Every local rink has community classes for beginners. It's a useful skill. I'm Ginny Wu, by the way," she added, tying the last knot on her daughter's skates and straightening up. "You must be Chelsea's aunt—the one who sings."

Chelsea extracted the straw from her mouth.

"I told my friends about you," she said proudly.

"That's very sweet," said Philippa. "I tell my friends about you too, darling."

Chelsea hopped down from the bench and hobbled across the aisle to join a trio of little girls on the next set of bleachers. Philippa turned back to watch the senior skaters. Christie Knotts was coming off the ice, but Andrea Burke showed no signs of slowing down, and Marina Milovich was still practising elements from her routine. Philippa pointed towards Marina as she glided down the ice in a graceful spiral.

"What about her?" she asked Ginny Wu. "Ice Capades or competition?"

"Marina? She's an incredible skater. She may not have the triple Axel like Jenny did, but she has all the required elements, and she's lovely to watch, so she can rake in the marks on artistic merit. She wasn't well before Christmas and her confidence was low, so she didn't skate her best in the B.C. competition. Normally she would have placed much higher than the girls that came in third and fourth, but now she's going to get another chance, and if she's on her top form, she could well win at Canadians. She has the potential."

A whirring sound came from the end of the rink and the front end of a Zamboni slid onto the ice. Without missing a beat, Marina came out of her spiral and floated towards the boards, gracefully coming to a halt and putting on her skateguards before exiting into the stands and joining Christie Knotts on the bleachers. Andrea Burke defiantly completed her lap and concluded with a dizzying sitzspin before coming off the ice. She ignored the bystanders and marched past Christie Knotts, jogging her arm and nearly spilling the drink she was pouring from her thermos. Philippa eyed the sports bags at Christie's feet.

"Do all the girls have bags like that?" she asked Ginny.

Ginny looked surprised.

"Well, yes. They all need sports bags."

Philippa pointed at the one beside Christie.

"Like that one? The holder for the thermos is on the outside of the bag."

"I suppose some are like that—not all, though."

"What about Jenny Wong, the girl that died?"

Ginny was quick on the uptake.

"Oh, yes, I see what you mean. Jenny did have a bag like that—and of course, it would be easier to tamper with the thermos if it were outside, wouldn't it? It's too bad. One of us might have noticed if Andrea had been rummaging inside the bag."

"Surely it hasn't been proved that Andrea Burke was the one who drugged Jenny's hot chocolate?"

Ginny raised her eyebrows.

"Who else? Andrea's not a nice girl. The whole family is horrible—loads of money, and totally stuck-up."

"They don't mingle with the other club members?"

Ginnie sniffed.

"Andrea's mother hosted a fundraiser after the B.C. competition, but it had nothing to do with being friendly. She had cameras there because she was using the event as the basis for one of her programs. We got to see her expensive house and eat her gourmet dishes, but she barely said a word to any of the mothers. She was too busy hobnobbing with the celebrities. And Andrea's father wasn't any better—all he did was yak about how he got blood clots after one of his fancy business trips and how ill the drugs made him feel. That's probably what gave Andrea the idea."

Philippa stared wide-eyed at Ginnie.

"Was this just for parents, or were the skaters there too?"

"The senior skaters were there by invitation, of course, because they're potential champions and people outside the skating world want to meet them, but otherwise anyone could go who bought a ticket."

"When was this event?"

"Last November."

"Two months ago." Philippa frowned thoughtfully.

"What was two months ago?" asked Bertram Beary, materializing at his daughter's shoulder.

"A party at the Burke residence," muttered Philippa. "Sounds as if everyone in the club had the opportunity to take Robert Burke's pills."

"Interesting," said Beary. He turned towards Ginnie and assumed his smoothest politician's manner.

"And which charming tot is yours?" he purred.

"Oh, sorry," said Philippa. She introduced her father to Ginnie.

Ginnie responded with delight.

"I know who you are. You're the city councillor. Chelsea has told us all about her grandpa. She says you're really funny."

"So the members of the Planning Department tell me on a regular basis," said Beary. He turned back to Philippa. "Is there a radiator anywhere in this building? I've been standing at the edge of the rink, eliciting information from a very charming ice maiden who I gather churns out champions the way my vegetable patch produces zucchinis, and my extremities are frozen."

Philippa excused herself and led her father up the steps to a row of bleachers below a large, overhead heater. They settled on the bench and watched as the Zamboni left the ice and a small line of infants trailed after the junior coach to the centre of the rink.

"Why does Sylvia think we should come to watch Chelsea's class?" grunted Beary. "Those aren't skaters—more like a row of waddling ducks—except that ducks don't wobble that much. What on earth does Sylvia expect in the way of comment?"

"It means a lot to Chelsea if we come to watch her," Philippa said firmly. "See," she added, pointing to the ice, where a small figure encased in a pink snowsuit was twisting round to peer up at the bleachers.

"They all look the same," said Beary. "How do you know that one's Chelsea?"

The pink snowsuit suddenly stopped and waved frantically in their direction.

"Because I put her skates on." Philippa looked exasperated. "Honestly, Dad. Show an interest."

"I am showing an interest," said Beary. He dutifully waved back toward the ice. "Now, tell me what you've found out."

"You first."

"All right. The head coach is leaning towards a solution—any solution—that would implicate someone outside the rink because she is naturally anxious about the possibility of lawsuits against the club. She doesn't believe Andrea would do anything so underhanded as poisoning an opponent's thermos, because although she agrees that Andrea is not the most pleasant of personalities, she says that her aggressive behaviour is always overt—what you see is what you get—and since she doesn't care what other people think, she would be unlikely to sneak around and do things behind people's backs. I," added Beary, "am inclined to agree with her. Poison is a coward's weapon, and whatever anyone says about this girl, she's certainly not cowardly."

"I agree, and that's what Sylvia thinks. It's not in character."

"True. However," Beary continued, "the coach doesn't rule out the possibility that Andrea would indulge in some kind of body-check against a rival on the ice, though she doesn't think she'd do it in cold blood—more likely, it would happen during a fit of temper. I must say Andrea Burke sounds extremely volatile and domineering—a real king complex. If she had any acolytes," said Beary, "I'd consider a *Beckett* scenario. I gather, after the B.C. Championships, she expressed a wish that Jenny Wong would drop dead, but according to Wendy Marshall, she doesn't have a single friend, so there's obviously nobody in the picture who would have been willing to go out and *rid her of the meddlesome priest*, so to speak."

"Wendy seems to have a good understanding of the girls she coaches."

"Of course she does. She's a teacher—and, from what one hears, an exceptionally fine one." Beary spoke with authority, having had a long and satisfactory career as a high-school teacher before he embarked on a life in civic politics. "After all," he continued, "she'd have to be able to analyze her pupils to get the best from them." He paused. "You know," he said, "it was rather ironic. She gave me a list of Andrea's character defects a mile long, yet I had the feeling she actually liked her."

"That makes sense. She's trying to produce champions, and from what one hears, Andrea is the only one of these girls with the killer instinct that could take her to the top."

"Not necessarily. It sounds as if the Milovich girl has what it takes. And she's well liked. She's quiet and unassuming off the ice, and she never lets people see if she's upset, so she comes across as a good sport. I gather she was even gracious after she blew her program in the finals. She expressed regret that she couldn't have another chance, but acknowledged that the results were fair."

Philippa raised her eyebrows.

"She sounds too good to be true."

"Not according to Wendy Marshall. She says Milovich is a top-notch skater and very hard-working. Her mother is extremely ambitious too. She's devoted all her energies to helping Marina achieve success. Wendy Marshall spoke very highly of both of them. Marina is the one everyone would like to see win. I gather she was even more popular than Jenny Wong."

"Really? That's interesting."

"Jenny Wong was pleasant and polite, but totally focussed on her skating. She didn't have Marina's social graces."

"It's amazing the poor girl could even be civil, given what she was going through."

"Yes," agreed Beary. "The coach was very upset about Jenny—especially knowing in hindsight that she'd been pushing her and feeling exasperated at her lack of performance when the poor kid couldn't help what was happening to her. The only one the coach didn't have much time for was Christie Knotts."

"That's understandable. I gather Christie isn't going anywhere, beyond a cho-rus line in an ice show. She's not one who's going to win medals and cover the club in glory."

"No, I don't think it was that. She says Christie's performing to her personal best. I just got the impression she didn't really like her. The girl's a bit of a toady—not too bright, not very well liked and desperate to be popular."

"These days it's called a 'suck', Dad," said Philippa.

"Is it? How offensive. Anyway, Christie likes to get her glory vicariously, so she's always *sucking*, as you so inelegantly put it, to the other girls, or imitating them. She's a bit of a copycat—would go out and buy the same outfit as another girl if she admired it—that sort of thing—which used to irritate Jenny and infuri-ate Andrea, both of whom have been quite unkind to her on occasion. The only one who didn't seem to mind was Marina. I gather she managed to be kind to the girl."

"Then I guess Marina *is* the nicest of the bunch."

"That's the impression I got from the coach. The Milovich girl also has the acting ability that makes for a strong performance. I gather that's what Christie Knotts lacks. Christie is very dramatic off the ice—she makes a big thing about her feelings, and the importance of friendship and camaraderie—but for all her talk of emotion, she can't translate it into something tangible to communicate to an audience. Marina says little, but every movement speaks volumes, and Andrea may not communicate emotion, but she generates power and excitement. And there's the difference. That's what makes two of them potential stars and leaves the other one a mere satellite."

Beary paused as a pale, angular woman came down the steps between the bleachers and passed close to them. She was carrying cassette tapes, and she pro-ceeded to the front bench where the senior skaters were packing their bags. Once she had distributed the tapes, she helped Marina Milovich gather her belongings; then she picked up a skate bag and started towards the lobby. Marina and Christie followed her.

"That'll be Marina's mother," said Philippa. "She'll have been playing music for the seniors' routines." She swivelled and pointed to the top of the stands where a glass booth loomed above the bleachers. "The mothers sit up there and play the tapes and the skaters take turns running their routines. The common theory seems to be that Jenny's thermos was tampered with while her mother was in the booth and her bags were left unattended at the rink-side."

"There's a flaw in that theory," commented Beary. "Look at the sight-lines."

"I see what you mean," nodded Philippa, following his glance. "The person in the booth would have a clear view of anything that was going on in the stands as well as on the ice."

"There's another problem too," said Beary. "Wendy Marshall told me that Jenny has been so off-colour that she's not only been slow getting on the ice, but she's been the first one to quit—so you tell me how any of the other girls could have doctored her flask. In fact," Beary went on, "I don't see how anyone could have tampered with the thermos. That coach has an eagle eye, and she stands at the boards right where the girls set their gear. She notices everything that goes on, on or off the ice."

"Well, if the drink wasn't laced with warfarin *at* the rink, Jenny's thermos must have been tampered with *before* she arrived. So we'd better find out who rode with who," Philippa concluded.

"Good point. Wendy Marshall will know if anyone will. She appears to be omniscient in matters that relate to her pupils."

Philippa peered around the arena. "I wonder where she's disappeared to."

"She was going outside for a cigarette. Sensible woman. Says she's past the age where she has to keep in shape."

"Well, come on. What are we waiting for? Let's go ask her."

Beary pulled his scarf more snugly round his neck.

"Are you kidding? The conditions out there are even more arctic than in this building. Anyway, you told me I had to watch Chelsea's class."

"Dad!"

Beary fixed his eyes firmly on the line of snowsuits teetering along the boards on the far side of the rink.

"You go ask her. I'm staying under the heater."

Philippa glowered at her father but he ignored her. Realizing a lost cause when she saw it, she made her way to the exit and emerged into the winter daylight. Sure enough, Wendy Marshall was standing outside the door, a trail of smoke snaking from the end of her fingers into the frosty air. On the far side of the parking lot, Georgia Milovich was loading skate bags into the back of a jeep. Christie and Marina were already inside the vehicle.

"Aren't the senior skaters old enough to drive themselves?" Philippa commented.

"Actually," Wendy replied, "most of them only turned sixteen last year and they've been so busy skating they've not had time to learn. Jason has his own car—it's a boy thing, isn't it?—and Andrea's parents send her in a cab—they have lots of money and they never come to see her skate—but the others car-pool. Christie has her licence, so she drives one day, and Georgia Milovich drives when it's Marina's turn because she's coming to play music in the sound booth."

"Did Jenny drive?"

"No. Her mother drove. They car-pooled with Christie and Marina."

"What was the order of pick-up?"

Wendy thought for a moment. "Christie lives closest, so when the other girls' mothers were driving, she'd be picked up last. If Christie was driving, she'd probably get Jenny first, as Jenny lived halfway between the other two."

"Andrea Burke never rode with them?"

"No." Wendy sighed. "Poor Andrea. She's such a difficult girl, and having the weight of Jenny's death on her conscience is going to be a heavy load for her."

"Are you absolutely sure that Jenny was cut when she collided with Andrea?"

"Of course I am. There's no other way it could have happened—and in spite of what anyone says, I'm convinced it *was* an accident. Andrea didn't slice Jenny on purpose, and now that we know about Jenny's condition, I'd say it was most likely that she lost control and veered into Andrea's path."

"Yes, you're probably right," agreed Philippa. "Did Jenny say anything before she lost consciousness?"

Wendy shook her head.

"No. Marina reached her first, but she says Jenny had already blacked out."

Philippa fell silent and watched the red jeep on the far side of the lot. Georgia Milovich had finished loading the skaters' gear and had got into the driver's seat. As the jeep reversed out of its parking space, Philippa turned back and resumed her attempt to elicit information from the coach. She was very curious about the skate bags. They provided a common thread between the three girls.

"I was talking to Ginnie Wu earlier," she said. "She told me that Jenny had a skate bag like Christie's with the thermos holder on the outside of the bag."

"Yes, she did—exactly the same, actually. There was a sale at the sporting-goods store, and Georgia Milovich offered to pick up bags for Jenny and Christie when she got one for Marina."

Philippa stared at Wendy, her eyes wide.

"You mean the three girls had identical bags and thermos flasks?"

"Yes. They had to stick labels on their bags so they didn't get mixed up."

"Did Andrea Burke have the same sort of bag?"

"No. She had a much more expensive model. And Andrea never bothered with a thermos. She always had money, so she bought her snacks and drinks from the coffee shop or the machines in the lobby."

Wendy dropped her cigarette butt and ground it out with her foot. Then, conscious of the sudden silence, she looked up at Philippa.

"Did I say something significant?" she asked.

"Very," said Philippa. "Excuse me. I have to make a phone call."

Without another word, she returned to the arena, found a quiet corner, pulled out her cell phone and dialled her sister's office.

"Sylvia," she said. "Do you have a number for Constable Baron? I want to give him some information before he serves his warrant."

◆   ◆   ◆

The ice rink was even colder at six o'clock the following morning. Philippa and Sylvia huddled under the heater and watched the senior girls go through their early morning practice. Philippa hunched down into her quilted jacket and held a steaming cup of coffee close, so that the heat filtered through her clothing and warmed her hands and body. The speakers overhead were playing the love theme from Prokoviev's *Romeo and Juliet,* and on the ice, Marina Milovich floated with arched back and liquid arms, forming a heartbreakingly beautiful line, while Christie Knotts drifted around her with the predictable steadiness of the earth around the sun. Like a malevolent sprite, Andrea Burke darted back and forth between them, tossing off challenging program elements with an air of defiance that could have been interpreted as indifference, though Philippa suspected it was the result of a combination of anger and pain.

Suddenly Philippa became aware that the music had acquired a rhythmic variation. Listening intently, she realized that the extra beat was the sound of footsteps echoing in the passage below. She turned towards her sister.

"Here he comes," she hissed.

Detective Constable Baron appeared below the bleachers. He was accompanied by a uniformed WPC, and the two continued to the edge of the boards and stared at the group on the ice. The skaters on the rink seemed oblivious to the entrance of the two newcomers, but Wendy Marshall, who was on the far side of the boards, turned and approached the policemen. After a brief, and what looked like an uncomfortable exchange, she called to the skaters and beckoned them to the side. Then she turned and waved in the direction of the booth. The music stopped, and the abrupt silence echoed eerily around the cavernous arena.

"Come on," said Sylvia. "Let's go down."

By the time Philippa and Sylvia reached the bottom of the steps, the three skaters were gathered at their coach's side. Andrea Burke was white, and she did not attempt to disguise her hostility as she stared at the two constables. Wendy Marshall stood beside her and put an arm around her shoulders, but Andrea seemed oblivious to her touch. As Constable Baron pulled out his warrant, Sylvia moved to Andrea's other side. Christie and Marina drew closer together and shrank back against the boards.

For a moment, time seemed suspended; then Constable Baron turned away from Andrea and looked straight at Marina Milovich.

"Marina Milovich," he said solemnly, "I have a warrant for your arrest. You are charged with the willful murder of Jennifer Wong, through the administration of poisonous substances, and by deliberately slicing open the victim's artery after she had fallen on the ice."

Marina appeared stunned. She remained silent as the policeman read her rights. At her side, Christie Knotts stood frozen, her face expressing shock and disbelief. When the constable finished speaking, there was a hush, and the only sound in the vast arena was the ticking of the huge clock that hung from the central beam high above the ice.

Marina did not respond, but her eyes moved from the officer's face, and with an expression like a terrified deer, she looked towards the stands. Philippa followed her glance and saw Georgia Milovich on the bottom step.

The first person to break the silence was Andrea Burke.

"This is crap," she said. "Marina's no more likely to knock off a rival than I am. You're crazy. How on earth do you figure any of us could have put that stuff in Jenny's thermos? We were all on the ice before her, and she was always the first to pack in. Anyway, whoever was in the booth would have seen what was going on."

Philippa decided it was time to step in.

"Marina and Jenny had identical thermos flasks," she said, "and they carpooled together. Jenny always drank hot chocolate, so it was easy to make sure the contents of the flasks were the same. Marina put the Coumadin in her own flask before she left the house, and simply switched the thermoses when she put her gear in the back of whichever car was driving that day. She knew the effect that the pills would have, and when Jenny collapsed after her collision with Andrea, she saw an opportunity to put both rivals out of the picture permanently. With Jenny eliminated, Marina was able to move into the fourth slot and go to Canadians, and if Andrea had been arrested, then Marina was almost certain to win the competition and move on to the World Championships."

Andrea stared incredulously at Philippa.

"I don't believe a word of it," she stated flatly.

Marina continued to stand like a deer frozen in headlights. She neither moved nor spoke. The WPC stepped forward and took the stunned girl by the arm, and with a beseeching glance towards her mother, Marina allowed herself to be led towards the exit.

Then, as the officers and their detainee reached the tunnel that led to the parking lot, a shrill cry stopped them in their tracks.

"No! It wasn't like that at all."

Christie Knotts broke away from the group by the boards and ran up to Constable Baron.

"It wasn't Marina. It was me!"

Christie clawed at the policeman's wrist and pulled him round to face her.

"I didn't mean to kill Jenny," she cried. "I just thought the pills would make her ill. I didn't know she was going to die. I just wanted Marina to have another chance."

As Detective Constable Baron nodded to the WPC to release Marina's arm, Christie broke down and sobbed as if her heart would break.

◆   ◆   ◆

Sylvia returned home to find Norton busy in the kitchen. She took off her coat and gave him the news of Christie's arrest.

Norton shook his head sadly as he emptied a bowl of prawns into the frying pan.

"I told you your kid sister would figure it out," he said. "Her powers of observation were such a nuisance when we were courting—remember how we used to call her 'big ears'—but now that she's grown up, those skills are quite useful. How did she manage it?"

"She wasn't sure, but she realized it had to be someone from the carpool. Both Marina and Christie had the same flasks as Jenny, so it could have been either of them, or even Marina's mother. She was very ambitious for her daughter."

Norton added chopped garlic and butter to the prawns on the stove and, with professional élan, swirled the contents of the pan.

"So why did Philippa suggest Detective Baron single out Marina?" he asked. He poured Sylvia a glass of wine and set it on the kitchen table.

"Psychology," said Sylvia. She sat down and took a sip from the glass.

Norton whisked a saucepan from the back burner and took it over to the sink.

"Go on," he encouraged, as he drained the pasta and flipped it back into the saucepan.

Sylvia explained.

"If, under Marina's calm surface, there really existed a ruthless killer who had set out to make Jenny ill, then cold-bloodedly murder her, she wouldn't have blinked if either of the other two had been arrested. But if Georgia or Christie had been guilty—and of course, in their case it wouldn't have been attempted murder, just a cruel attempt to make the girl so ill that she had to drop out of the competition—there's no way they would have stood aside and let Marina take the blame. Georgia loved her daughter too much, and Christie idolized Marina."

Norton shook his head.

"It seems incredible. No matter how much Christie Knotts worshipped Marina, why would she do something so wicked?"

"She didn't see it as wicked. Remember, she was a rather stupid girl, very emotional, and desperate to be liked. Philippa said Dad almost hit on the solution when he talked about a *Beckett* scenario, but of course, he was talking about the wrong girl. After the B.C. finals, Marina made the comment that she wished she could have another chance, and when Christie heard Andrea's father describing how ill the warfarin tablets had made him, she suddenly saw an opportunity to place her idol forever in her debt. Robert Burke had been taking anywhere up to six ten-milligram pills a day, so Christie figured it was safe to slip a few pills into Jenny's thermos whenever she had the opportunity—but not being very bright, she didn't pause to consider the fact that Robert Burke was a large, heavy man, whereas Jenny was tiny, and the medication would have had a far more drastic effect on her." Sylvia paused. "The reality is," she continued sadly, "that the accident really *was* an accident, very likely through Jenny's loss of control, and her death is a tragedy for all three families. The Wongs have lost their daughter, Christie Knotts is devastated by what she's done, and Andrea will have to live with the fact that it was her skate blade that made the fatal cut. Even Marina is going to suffer, because she knows Christie did it for her, and any success she achieves will be marred by that knowledge."

Norton nodded as he served up the pasta and piled a generous helping of garlic prawns onto each plate.

"It's a tragic case, isn't it?" he said. "Will the lawsuit continue against Andrea Burke, do you think?"

"The Wongs are very angry, justifiably so, and their present mind-set is to lay blame and hurt the other families the way they've been hurt, but since the prime culprit is Christie Knotts, and her family has so few assets, a case against her will simply become a punitive vengeance against her parents. I'm hoping the Wongs won't do that, but there are no guarantees. They won't be able to win a case against Andrea, and I hope their lawyer explains that to them. If they proceed, they could end up losing a lot of money because they'd have to pay costs. And given the nature of Andrea's mother, I don't think the Burkes would give them any quarter. Everything about that woman is pure poison."

"Oh, come," said Norton. "She can't be that bad."

"Yes, she can. Carey Burke is the reason Andrea has so many problems. For Andrea's sake as much as anyone's, I'm hoping the whole mess will stay out of the courts. No one is going to win except the lawyers if the lawsuit goes ahead."

Norton looked up from his dinner and stared at his wife in amazement.

"Did I hear you correctly? Is this the woman I married? The one who said she went into civil law because in today's litigious society, it was the equivalent of the mythical pot of gold at the end of the rainbow?"

"Yes," said Sylvia shortly. "And before you blab at me any more, I have only one more thing to add. The case is closed, and the defence can bloody well rest."

"Well," said Norton, wiping his mouth with his napkin, "I deserve a rest. I hope you appreciate the fact that I got the children tucked up early and slaved in the kitchen producing a gourmet meal for you."

"Of course I do—and it's delicious. This is a wonderful sauce on the prawns."

"Glad you like it."

Sylvia savoured another mouthful and followed it with a sip of wine.

"What a marvellous recipe!" she said. "What is it?"

Norton refilled his wine glass and gave a self-satisfied smirk.

"Are you sure you want to know?"

His wife looked at him suspiciously.

"Yes, of course," she snapped. "What's in it?"

"Well," said Norton slowly, "I hate to have to admit it, but you might as well know. The ingredients are pure poison."

Sylvia sputtered and put down her glass. Her husband smiled and offered her a napkin.

"It was Carey Burke's special of the week," he said.

Through a Lagoon, Darkly

The lagoon was dark green, opaque, and rippled from the wind and the cross-movement at its centre, where the current was starting to flow as slack water ended and the tide turned towards the narrow arm that connected pool with ocean. Philippa and Juliette walked along the perimeter road, squinting in the winter sunlight and red-cheeked from the biting cold. They crossed the foot-bridge that stretched over the channel and shivered as they moved into the shade of the fir-covered cliff. The sun never shone on this side of the lagoon and the hoarfrost was thick on the grassy verge. Juliette's Labrador puppy raced back and forth, exhilarated by the icy February air and the intriguing smells amid the brambles.

As they walked, Philippa found herself staring more closely at the lagoon, and she realized that the dark hue of the water was merely a reflection of the evergreen trees that surrounded the pool. After a while, other colours appeared: nightshade where ivy blanketed the retaining wall; light green from the ferns at the water's edge; the deep pink of rosehips; patches of orange where fronds remained on alder trees; and ribbons of rusty-brown from the bare, stick-like branches of salmonberry bushes. A patch of white and crimson materialized, reflecting the walls and roof of the nineteenth-century heritage house that now served as a bed-and-breakfast hotel, and Juliette's house loomed from the depths, mirroring its position on the far shore. The grey walls of the store were replicated beside the entrance to the channel, and the bridge, duplicated by its own image in the pool, became two parallel rows of cedar railings connected by elongated pilings. Beyond it, the water was transformed into a pale aquamarine circle where the outfall entered the channel. In the middle of the lagoon, a stretch of gleaming blue mirrored the winter sky. It was like a patchwork quilt, Philippa thought, amazed that she had initially seen nothing but a dark, brooding expanse without life or character.

"There's Margaret Witherspoon," Juliette said, abruptly bringing Philippa's contemplations to an end. She pointed across the water. A woman was approaching the curve at the far end of the lagoon. The walker was tall, but Philippa could make out little else as the angle of the sun had transformed the figure into a silhouette. A second silhouette loped along the shore. It was a large dog with pointed ears, probably a German shepherd, Philippa decided, assessing the gait and the line of the tail as the animal darted towards the path that led to the adjacent bay. A sharp command from the woman caused the dog to turn and run back to her side.

The two figures continued towards Philippa and Juliette, and as they emerged from the shadows, Philippa saw that her assessment of the dog's breed had been correct. It was a magnificent black and tan Alsatian with dancing eyes and a king-of-the-world stance. The woman was still hard to make out, for she was huddled into a heavy wool coat and wore a black toque that concealed her hair.

"Poor thing. She's coming this way," said Juliette. "We'll have to stop and chat. Be nice when we talk with her. She's had an awful time of late."

Philippa stared at her sister in surprise. "When am I ever not nice?"

"You know what I mean. Just be careful what you say. Her husband ran off and left her three weeks ago, *and* took a pile of money with him. She's gone through a lot."

"Another woman?"

"I haven't dared ask, but that's what everyone seems to think."

"Do you know them well?"

"Not really. Margaret is what I call a dog-walking acquaintance. We chat when we meet and give cookies to each other's pets. I adore Quasar. He's the most wonderful dog. If she ever wanted to give him up, I'd take him like a shot."

Juliette was the animal fanatic in the Beary family. Philippa steered her back to the subject of humans.

"Has she talked to you about her husband's disappearance?"

"No. I haven't seen her since it happened. I sent her a note, so she knows I know, but so far she hasn't replied."

"How did you find out?"

"From Steven. Nicholas Witherspoon teaches—or rather, taught—at the high school. He and Steven weren't in the same department, but they used to see each other in the staff room."

"What's Steven's theory?"

"He doesn't have one. He didn't particularly like Nicholas Witherspoon—thought he was a bit smug—but he didn't strike him as the type to have a mid-life crisis. It's inexplicable."

"Financial troubles?"

"No, nothing like that. Margaret inherited a pile from her father, and Nicholas did well on the stock market. They have lots of money and a beautiful waterfront home. Margaret is the sweetest lady and still very attractive. It just doesn't make sense. Her husband simply set off in his boat for his regular pub night at Rumrunners' Point, and he never came back."

"If he took off in a boat, surely there's the possibility that he had an accident."

"The night was dead calm and there wasn't a distress call. Anyway, afterwards, Margaret found that he'd been withdrawing large sums of cash for the past four years, and just before he disappeared, he'd transferred over a quarter of a million dollars into an offshore account."

"How on earth do you know all that?"

"School gossip. The office secretary is the wife of the local banker. Anyway, you know what small towns are like. News spreads like wildfire. There's no question about it. Nicholas Witherspoon set himself up financially and deliberately disappeared."

Philippa sniffed disapprovingly. "Just one more middle-aged rat."

"Ssshhh! Here she comes." Juliette scooped up the puppy as the German shepherd bounded forward. "Down, Quasar," she commanded.

Margaret Witherspoon hurried forward and clipped a leash on the dog's collar.

"Sorry, Juliette," she apologized. Her voice was soft and mellow. "I was miles away."

Now that the woman was in front of them, Philippa saw that Juliette's description was accurate. Margaret was attractive. Her clothes were casual, but expensive and stylish. She was dressed entirely in black, except for two bright splashes of red wool where her gloves peeked out from the long arms of her coat, but even with her hair covered with the dark velvet toque, her face was still quite beautiful. The lines of middle age added character rather than detracted from her charm. But in spite of her attempt at a smile, her eyes were sad and her expression was strained.

"It's good to see you out walking," said Juliette. "How are you doing? We've been thinking about you."

"I'm all right." Margaret spoke slowly as if each word took a deliberate effort. "It's kind of you to worry, and thank you for your card and invitation. I would have come by, but there's been so much to see to ... so much ..." She faltered and her voice quavered. Quasar nuzzled her hand, and she reached in her pocket and pulled out two dog biscuits. Quasar gobbled one down and watched patiently while the other was presented to the puppy.

"You dropped a glove," said Juliet, bending to pick up a black glove that had come out of Margaret's pocket along with the biscuits. She looked around to see if anything else had fallen. "Have you got the other one?"

Margaret fished in her pocket and drew out the matching glove. With it, came a set of keys. She seemed puzzled. "Oh dear," she said. "These belong to my neighbour. I found them in my kitchen and I meant to return them; then I started my walk and completely forgot."

"It's understandable," said Juliette. "You're distracted."

Margaret paused and took a deep breath. "I am coping," she said, looking anxiously at Juliette, "but I'm very confused. I keep forgetting things. I know it's stress, but it's still frightening."

Juliette posed the question that Philippa had been willing her to ask.

"Have you heard from your husband yet?"

"No. Not a word." Margaret sighed. "My life was so orderly, so perfect—then suddenly, a bolt from the blue and everything's gone."

"He didn't say anything to you?"

Margaret's voice caught and her eyes filled with tears. "He left for the pub that evening and never came back."

Juliette handed Philippa the puppy and stepped forward to comfort the distraught woman. She put an arm around Margaret's shoulders.

"I'm sorry," she said softly. "I shouldn't have asked. I didn't mean to upset you."

"It's all right. I need to talk, but …" Margaret gave a sob and bowed her head. "I'm sorry. It's all been too much …" She gave up trying to maintain control and broke down in tears.

Embarrassed, Philippa fondled the puppy and took refuge in staring into the dark waters of the lagoon. At this end of the pool, the water was almost black, mirroring the shadowy evergreens at the base of the cliff. As Philippa watched, the reflection of a gull flying overhead shot across the surface, and at that moment, the sun went behind a cloud. As if in keeping with the grief of the sobbing woman beside her, the scene darkened.

To her horror, by a cluster of sea-grass, Philippa saw the reflection of Margaret's contorted face in the water. The features under the black toque were a mask of agony. Philippa drew her eyes away and fixed her gaze on a school of shiners that were gliding slowly across a rock. Suddenly she noticed a perch dart out from the shore, and with a start, she realized she was now seeing into the depths of the lagoon. As she peered below the surface, the rocks and sea-grass stared back at her, as crystal clear as the previous patchwork quilt of trees and sky and buildings had been before.

She was sub-consciously aware that the wind had subsided and the sobbing of the woman beside her had ceased. The day had become as quiet as the lagoon was still. Her eyes were drawn back to the cluster of sea grass drifting back and forth at the bottom of the pool. With a coldness inside that caused a chill far greater than the freezing winter air, she saw that the face still stared up through the surface of the water.

Beside her, Margaret started to scream.

◆   ◆   ◆

Billy Brown's eyes narrowed as he stared at the bridge that spanned the mouth of the lagoon.

"The body must have drifted in on the high winter tide," he stated firmly.

Detective Constable Adrian Wright looked sharply at the weather-beaten man at her side. Billy Brown owned the store and marina, and was an authority on matters local and nautical. Billy frowned and tugged down the quilted vest that tended to ride up over his ample beer-belly. He was a regular at the Rumrunners' Pub.

"As a rule, the remains of the old dam would stop anything large coming into the lagoon," Billy went on, "but last night was an abnormally high tide. You'll get them in winter."

"You're sure the body wasn't here yesterday?" Adrian asked.

Billy glared at her. He was seventy years old and disapproved of female policemen.

"I just said so, didn't I? There's no way he'd have drowned in the lagoon. The body would have been found within hours. At low tide, it'd have been completely exposed. No, he'll have gone overboard in the bay, and that fifteen-foot tide will have brought him in during the early hours of the morning. What I can't figure is why he didn't wash ashore out there." He gestured to the ocean beyond the bridge. "The body might have sunk initially, but it would've risen up with the gases, and the tide should have either washed him across the harbour or carried him in by one of the big fancy houses on the far side of the bay." Billy scowled. "But that should've happened within a few days. After this amount of time, the gases would have dissipated and he'd have sunk again, and the crabs would've got at him on the bottom. Even if the shifting tides had moved him, he'd have been a lot more chewed up than the remains I saw before your crew carted him away."

Adrian waited patiently. She was too good a policeman not to recognize an expert witness, even if it did come in the form of a misogynistic amateur patholo-gist.

Billy obliged. "You'd better ask those forensic people that get big fat salaries on my tax dollars why his face was in such good shape after all that time in the water. Something was protecting him. You mark my words, there's funny busi-ness afoot."

Billy plodded away and headed back over the bridge to his store. Adrian looked after him thoughtfully. Clever old rum-pot, she thought to herself. She had looked closely at the body before it was taken away. Billy was right; the crabs had done some work. They had started to peel away the layer that had been pro-tecting the corpse's face, but there had been enough pieces left to be recognizable. Nicholas Witherspoon's head had been encased in a tightly tied plastic bag.

◆   ◆   ◆

Curiously, Philippa watched the interchange between Billy and the local con-stabulary. From Juliette's deck, she could see over the garden fence, and as the driveway led straight down to the perimeter road, she had a clear view of the two people at the edge of the water. She had recognized Adrian Wright immediately.

The French doors opened and Juliette came onto the deck. She looked tired and harried. Leaving the doors ajar, she joined Philippa at the railing.

"I had no idea our cousin had been posted to the Sunshine Coast," said Phil-ippa, continuing to watch as the RCMP constable listened attentively to what-ever the marina owner was telling her. "When did she transfer?"

"Adrian has been here for two years," said Juliette. "I'd lost touch with her too, but I ran into her one day down at Sechelt. She said Richard knew, but of course I hardly ever see him so it was a complete surprise."

"I see Richard quite often, but it's a surprise for me too. Typical older brother—he couldn't be bothered to tell us."

Juliette was charitable by nature. "It probably slipped his mind. He's busy try-ing to break drug rings and stop gang shootings, poor dear."

"I suppose." Philippa pointed towards the lagoon. "What's Adrian doing now?" she said.

Billy had moved away and Adrian appeared to be examining the broken dam that jutted out of the water beneath the bridge.

"Probably trying to see where the body washed in. It certainly wasn't there before today. I'd have seen it at low tide. I walk round the lagoon every day."

"I'm not surprised," said Philippa. "I would too if I lived here. This is such a glorious spot." She leaned back and took in the panoramic view. The lagoon gleamed silver in the winter sun, and since it was set between two bays that were separated by a high wooded peninsula, the ocean was visible on either side of her sister's property. "You and Steven really knew what you were doing when you decided he should apply for a teaching post on the Sunshine Coast," she said. "You could never afford anything like this in town."

"Certainly not with me staying home to raise the children—still, we were lucky. This house was a small, run down cottage with no foundation, so it was within our reach, but I worry about it being too much for Steven. He's worked like a Trojan to upgrade the property and build the addition, but there's still a lot of maintenance—and he's teaching all day, and doing gigs with his band on weekends, plus he's taking on recording jobs. He doesn't complain, but he does get a bit tired and cross sometimes."

"He *does* complain—all the time," Philippa said acerbically. Her brother-in-law was a fireball of energy and enthusiasm, but not the most patient man in the world. "But don't let him make you feel guilty. He loves everything he does."

Juliette sighed and leaned over the railing so that her long brown hair swept forward and hid the anxious frown on her face. "I know, but I wish I could be more like Sylvia. Then I could contribute more. She's a partner in her law firm, and she still runs an incredibly efficient household—*and* her children are far better behaved than mine."

Philippa looked affectionately at her sister. Privately, she was much fonder of Juliette than she was of her oldest sister. "Sylvia takes after Mother," she pointed out, "and Steven would loathe it if you emulated her. I'm quite sure he has no desire to be hitched to a high-powered career woman who takes pride in being a superwoman in the home and the office. Sylvia's utterly exhausting. Don't downgrade yourself," she added. "You've been taking in marking to earn extra money, and that's pure drudgework. Besides, you've started the puppet company now, which is a fabulous family enterprise—fun for the children to boot. You're a wonderful wife and mom. Steven thinks the world of you."

Juliette glanced nervously towards the French doors.

"Steven isn't going to think the world of me if we don't get your show numbers recorded this weekend." Philippa's contribution to her sister's marionette company was to provide the voice for Shannon, the Sheepdog, plus any other character that required a classically trained soprano.

"It's hardly your fault that there's a body in the lagoon."

"Well, no—and I had to bring Margaret back to the house. She's in such a dreadful state. I feel I should offer to let her stay the night."

"How is she doing?"

"Still in shock. She isn't crying any more, but she's either babbling non-stop, or completely silent. I've had to wrap her in two blankets, and I've been giving her cups of hot, sweet tea. But she's still having fits of the shivers. She really can't be left on her own."

"Is there any other family member who could be called?"

"No. Her parents are both dead, and there are no siblings."

"Perhaps a neighbour? She must have some close friends."

"Of course—there's Ann Sotheby! She lives next door to them. She's a widow and a lovely person. She and Margaret are good friends. I'll phone her."

Juliette started for the French doors and Philippa turned back towards the lagoon. She saw that Adrian was approaching the driveway.

"You'd better hold that phone call," she said. "Adrian is coming. We should warn Margaret. I imagine she's going to have to answer a lot of questions."

◆   ◆   ◆

"He left on the twenty-ninth of January," said Margaret. "It was a Friday evening. He always went to the pub on Friday nights."

"Which pub?" Adrian asked. "There are several in the vicinity."

"Rumrunners' Tavern. The one on the point."

"Why there? Surely the pub in Pool Bay is closer."

Margaret looked blank.

"Friday's the big social night at the tavern," Juliette interjected. It was her nature to be helpful. "The owner brings in entertainment, and there's a darts tournament too."

Adrian silenced her with a brief gesture and continued to address her questions to Margaret.

"Doesn't your local pub do something similar?"

Margaret blinked and made an effort to focus.

"Yes, they do, but the big night at Pool Bay is on Saturday, and that was the evening Nicholas and I would go out together—or sometimes we'd take Ann to dinner or a movie. She lives next door and she's on her own, so we've become good friends. Anyway, Friday was the end of the school week. Nicholas liked to go out and unwind."

"You didn't ever go with him?"

"No. I don't enjoy the pub nights. The main subjects of conversation are fishing and boating, and the music is so loud you can't hear what people are saying. I preferred to stay home and watch 'Classic Theatre'."

"You're not interested in fishing or boating?"

"Not fishing. I liked going out on the boat. We used to take a two-month cruise up the coast every summer. We were both teachers, you see. Well, I retired some years ago as we didn't need the extra money, but even in the early days when we were both working, we had the whole summer to get away together. We were so happy …" Margaret faltered and her voice trailed off.

Adrian was a sympathetic woman, and she paused to let Margaret recover her composure.

"Are you all right to carry on with these questions, Mrs. Witherspoon? I can come back later if necessary."

Margaret pulled herself up straight. "No. It's all right. I know you have to do this. Go on. I can cope."

Adrian glanced down at her notes and resumed her questioning.

"Did you ever have any inkling that your husband was worried about anything? Had his behaviour changed in any way, however slight?"

"He had seemed a bit worried at times in the last few years, but I knew he was preoccupied with the ups and downs of the stock market. Ever since 9/11 things have been volatile and the possibility of another downturn preyed on his mind. It never occurred to me that there could have been anything more serious."

"Did you ever meet any of your husband's associates—financial contacts or friends from the pub? Did any of them come to the house?"

"No, the pub acquaintances weren't part of our social circle and his stockbrokers were all in town." Margaret paused and reflected. "There was one man who came to the house last year. I didn't like him. He wasn't local and he seemed a very unsavory sort. Nicholas took him into the garden and talked with him there. I was leaving to go shopping with my neighbour and when we returned, the man had gone."

"You'd never seen him before?"

"No." Margaret hesitated. "He seemed familiar, but I couldn't place him—neither could Ann—and he acted as if we'd never met."

"Did your husband tell you who he was?"

"Nicholas said he was someone who had borrowed money from him at the pub. He didn't tell me his name … and I never saw him again."

Adrian switched to another subject.

"Why did your husband go to the pub by boat? Wouldn't it have been easier to drive?"

"Not really. We have waterfront property with our own dock. To go by road, we have to drive all the way out to the highway and then it's another fifteen minutes round to the point, but in the boat, it takes less than five minutes."

"What time did he leave for the pub?"

"Around seven o'clock."

"When did you realize he hadn't come home?"

"Not until the morning. He often stayed until closing time. I'm a sound sleeper and he always came in quietly so as not to wake me."

"What did you do when you woke up and found he wasn't there?"

"I went down to the dock to see if the boat was in."

"And then?"

"I saw it wasn't there so I came up to the house and phoned the marina."

Adrian glanced up from her notebook.

"Why the marina?" she asked.

"I thought Billy Brown might be able to tell me where he was. Billy always goes to the tavern on Fridays."

"And what did he tell you?"

"That Nicholas hadn't shown up that night. No one had seen him."

"What did you do next?"

"I talked to Ann to see if she'd heard or seen anything—then I called the coastguard to see if there had been any distress calls—and I called the hospital ..."

"But not the police?"

"What was the point? The RCMP isn't interested in calls from wives whose husbands haven't come home."

Adrian had to concede the point.

"So what led you ultimately to the conclusion that he had left you?"

"It was his travel kit. I was frantic, and I didn't know what to do. Ann came over and made me a cup of tea. We were trying to think of places I could call. Then she suggested that I should look and see if any of his things were missing, so I thought of his kit. It's a brown zip-up case with shaving gear—personal things. He always took it if we went on a trip."

"And it wasn't there?"

Margaret looked down. "No. It had gone. And when I looked in his closet, I saw that half his clothes had gone too—along with one of our suitcases."

"Then what?"

"I was numb. I couldn't think straight. Ann was the one who suggested I check the bank accounts. That's when I found out about the missing money."

"How much was missing?"

"Nicholas had been withdrawing twenty-five hundred dollars in cash every month for the past three years, and then last month, our largest term deposit had been closed and the money transferred to a series of accounts at eight different banks and credit unions. When I checked with the other banks, I discovered that Nicholas had emptied every one of these accounts. They were all in his own name and two days before he disappeared, he'd cashed them all in."

"How much was that?"

"Three hundred thousand dollars."

"So he basically cleaned you out?"

"No. He mustn't have intended to leave me penniless. We had that much again in two other term deposits, and our property is worth more than a million dollars. I wouldn't have had to worry about money."

Adrian looked surprised.

"That's a lot of assets on two teachers' salaries."

"I inherited money from my father," said Margaret. "That's what paid for our waterfront home and the boat—and Nicholas was clever with stocks. We were very comfortably off."

"And you didn't know that money had been disappearing regularly from your joint accounts?"

"No. Nicholas dealt with all the banking and looked after our investments. I had a personal checking account, but other than that, I left everything to Nicholas and our financial advisor at the bank."

"The advisor didn't contact you about the closing of the investment account?"

"No. I talked with him later and he told me the form authorizing the collapse of the account had both our signatures. He was used to dealing with Nicholas so it didn't occur to him to question the transaction."

"So your husband forged your signature?"

Margaret bowed her head.

"He did it all the time. It was a joke between us. If I was downtown and he needed a signature for a stock transaction, he'd write my signature for me. He always told me, and I didn't care." Margaret looked up at Adrian and her face was a mask of utter despair. "I trusted him, you see. I trusted him completely."

"Did you ever suspect him of having a relationship with another woman?"

Margaret's voice quivered. "No. I know that's what everyone is assuming, but I never believed there was anyone else. And after what happened, you must see that too. He must have been in some kind of trouble. That's the only possible explanation."

◆   ◆   ◆

"Are you sure Nicholas Witherspoon wasn't a womanizer?" Philippa asked, after Margaret's neighbour, who had turned out to be a voluptuously glamorous brunette, had picked up Margaret and taken her home. "I wouldn't want Ann Sotheby living next door to my husband. That white wool sweater that she was filling out so obscenely was cashmere. It must have cost a bundle. Sex and money—Margaret's husband couldn't have been impervious to a package like that."

"According to village gossip, he wasn't the sort to play around," insisted Juliette. "Anyway, rumour has it that Ann Sotheby has a virile toy-boy tucked away somewhere further up the coast."

"Oh, that I can believe."

"I think that's why Margaret enjoyed her company so much. Ann does all the things Margaret would never dare. To be fair, I don't think Margaret ever wanted to live any other way, but she isn't a prig and she finds Ann great fun. Nicholas didn't mind the friendship. According to Steven, he seemed a perfectly contented man. He was financially secure and set to take early retirement. He had an attractive, docile wife who allowed him to live as he pleased and make all the important decisions while she ran the home. She went along with whatever he wanted, even to the extent that they didn't have children, though I think she'd have liked them. No, Margaret has to be right. He was in some kind of trouble, and rather than bring her into it, he chose to disappear."

"Except that he didn't. Whoever he was trying to get away from obviously found him."

"Yes," said Juliette soberly. "Adrian isn't treating this as an accidental drowning, is she?"

"You don't think Margaret is too docile, do you?" said Philippa suddenly. "She does seem to have been the perfect wife, but then some men get bored with perfection."

"Not Nicholas Witherspoon. Steven says Margaret's dependency made him feel important."

"She wasn't exactly liberated, was she? She couldn't have been the typical young woman of the sixties. Can you imagine letting a husband take control like that?"

Steven strode into the room and answered before Juliette could respond.

"Margaret needed a father figure," he said shortly. He held a daisy-chain cable with his right hand, the puppy with his left, and his expression was mildly impatient. "And if you two girls don't stop playing detective, we'll never get the tracks laid for Philippa's songs. We've got three numbers to record, plus dialogue. And for heaven's sake, shut this animal in the kitchen so he can't sneak in and chew my cables." He thrust the puppy into Juliette's arms. "Where are the girls? He's supposed to be their dog. Why aren't they looking after him?"

"Jennifer and Laura are sleeping over at the Browns," said Juliette patiently. "I already told you that." She fondled the puppy's ears. "And this little fellow does have a name, you know."

"Yes. Purdy. Ridiculous moniker, just because he's a chocolate Lab. Now, could we please get started?"

Steven turned and headed back to the studio. Philippa made a face behind his back, but obediently got up and followed him. However, her mind was still preoccupied with the bizarre events of the morning, and as Steven set up for the recording session, she persevered with her questions.

"Why did Margaret want a father figure?" she asked curiously, as Steven connected the cable to his microphone.

"She was an only child and her mother died when she was small, so she was raised by a father who she absolutely adored. He tended to be over-protective, but because she's such a placid soul, she didn't mind him running her life. She was still quite young when she married Nicholas, and after her father died, she was in a terrible state—shocked and grieved, totally distracted—and all that dependency settled on her husband. Stand here," he added, moving Philippa to the center of the studio. "Not too close to the mike. Now give me a couple of lines from one of the songs. I need to set the levels."

Philippa obliged with a passage from her first solo.

Steven nodded. "OK. Now a dialogue line."

Philippa decided to combine curiosity with practicality.

"Why was Margaret in such a state when she lost her father?" she enunciated.

Steven rolled his eyes.

"I told you—she adored her father. He was a very important part of her life and the way he died was incredibly traumatic." Steven pulled two headsets from the cabinet and plugged them into the eight-track that he reserved for puppet recordings. "There was a huge mudslide at Lions Bay in 1981," he continued. "I was only a little boy at the time, but I remember my parents talking about it because one of my father's co-workers was George Brent's neighbour and he knew all the catastrophic details."

"George Brent?"

"Margaret's father. He lived in Lions Bay. Evidently Margaret and Nicholas were visiting him at the time of the disaster and they were nearly wiped out when the slide started. Nicholas managed to get Margaret to safety, but he couldn't save her father. Now, does that satisfy you? Can we concentrate on the job at hand?"

"In a minute. I just want to ask—"

"Not another word," Steven said firmly, "unless it's set to music."

He put one headset on himself and plopped the other one around Philippa's ears.

"Come on, Shannon, the Sheepdog," he said. "Time to sing."

◆   ◆   ◆

The next morning, Philippa and Juliette set off for a walk. Jennifer and Laura raced ahead, with Purdy pulling exuberantly at the end of his lead. Philippa followed the others around the pub path, which wound through a tunnel formed by ivy-covered rocks and twisted vine maples. The sun was still hovering on the horizon and the day was cold. Philippa noticed that her breath was creating patches of mist in the winter air, and she wrapped her scarf around her mouth to protect her vocal cords. At the end of the tunnel, the path curved round a bank of rocks sparsely dotted with the skeletal, rime-coated branches of sowberry bushes. Below the path, the sea was covered with a thin layer of ice, and as the light caught the waves and the ice flexed with the water, it appeared that a row of horizontal dark stripes moved continuously shoreward.

The trail circled back to the lagoon road, and the children jumped over the chains by the yacht club and tried to get Purdy to follow suit, but he stubbornly refused and wriggled below the barrier. Giving up the battle, Jennifer and Laura pulled him through and continued around the lagoon. Philippa and Juliette followed at a more leisurely pace. As they approached the store, they saw Billy Brown standing by the fuel pipes that stretched from the asphalt to the top of the cliff where the tanks were kept. Billy was bent over the valves at the base of the pipes. His expression was more dour than usual.

"Trouble, Billy?" asked Juliette.

Billy nodded. "You name it, I've had it." His piercing blue eyes glittered in his coarse, weather-beaten face. "All day yesterday I was answering fool questions about Nicholas Witherspoon. The RCMP has put out a bulletin to trace his boat, but there haven't been any sightings. Whoever finished him off and dumped him overboard seems to have vanished into thin air. Then this morning I had Fisheries on my case. There's been the odd patch of oil in the bay, and right away they're on about my fuel pumps. I've had to check all the lines, even though I know damn well the spill isn't coming from here."

Philippa was curious.

"How do you fill the tanks?" she asked. "They're at the top of the cliff."

"The truck comes in here and pumps the fuel up these pipes, and while the tanks are being filled, we shut off the valves to the dock lines. See." Billy pointed to the other side of the road and Philippa noticed that the pipes continued alongside the ramp to the docks. "The lines go under the road and come out by the gangway. Then they run down and along the side of the dock to the pumps."

"Why are there three pipes?"

"Different types of fuel. There's gas and diesel, and some of the older boats take a mixture of fifty-to-one gas and oil. If there was a leak, it could be responsible for the sort of minor seepage they're talking about, but I've checked everything. It's not coming from here."

Philippa felt a surge of excitement.

"Could it be from a boat? What if Nicholas Witherspoon's vessel is sunk in the bay? Maybe he really did have an accident."

Billy snorted. "Not a chance. Witherspoon had a twenty-five-foot, fiberglass Bertram. I've worked on it myself. If that thing had gone down, there'd have been a lot more than the few patches the environmentalists are beefing about. No, you mark my words, whoever went with him on that boat popped him off."

"So what's your theory, Billy?" Philippa challenged him. She was very taken with the crusty old marina owner, with his forthright tongue and his king-of-the-peninsula attitude. She considered him a wonderful source of information. "Do you think Nicholas Witherspoon had a mistress who turned homicidal?"

"Not likely. Witherspoon wasn't a womanizer. Money was what turned him on. I think he was up to something shady and he needed to disappear. He had at least one sleazy acquaintance who was into drugs. Your lady-cop cousin was back here yesterday asking a lot more questions, and she started quivering like a jellyfish when I told her about him."

Philippa caught Juliette's eye and she could tell they were sharing the same thought. *That must have been the man that Margaret saw at the house.* She turned back to Billy.

"Who was he? Did you know him?"

"His name's Logan. He shows up at the pub periodically. I don't know where he lives, but I've seen him smoking pot on the trail behind the tavern. He wasn't there every Friday—maybe every third week or so. He was there the night Witherspoon disappeared, but he didn't stay around long, and I haven't seen him since."

"I know who you're talking about," said Juliette suddenly. "I've seen him at the pub. I go to the tavern whenever Steven's band is playing. Logan was a tall, seedy-looking fellow with greasy, shoulder-length hair. He was always sitting with Margaret's husband."

"That's him. Useless scum-ball as far as I could see, but for some reason, Witherspoon put up with him. I'll tell you one thing though—our Nick was a lot edgier once this character started appearing."

"I guess it's too much to expect you to remember how long it is since Logan first started coming to the pub," said Philippa.

"Well, you're wrong, young lady." Billy spoke with satisfaction. "I remember the date exactly because it just happens to have been my sixty-eighth birthday. It was the twelfth of February, 2005. Three years ago almost to the day."

◆   ◆   ◆

Constable Adrian Wright drank a much-needed mug of coffee as she sat at her desk and pored over the forensic report. Billy Brown might not have been entirely accurate in his theories about the body's movements in the ocean, but he had been on the right track. There had definitely been foul play. Nicholas Witherspoon had died from suffocation. He had been stunned with a blow to the back of his skull and a plastic bag had been pulled over his head and secured tightly around his neck. His body had been in the ocean for at least a week, and he had more than likely been killed and dumped overboard on the night he disappeared. That part was straightforward. But there was something that did not make sense.

Adrian studied the facts listed by the pathologist. Salt water was denser than lake water, so bodies in the ocean were more likely to float. Fat floats, muscle doesn't, and Nicholas Witherspoon was definitely on the portly side. Bodies with air in the lungs will float, but drowning victims sink. So Nicholas Witherspoon should have been a floater, and if he had been killed on the night he left, his body should have washed ashore much sooner.

The condition of the body was a puzzle too. The water in the bay was around fifty-five degrees in winter. At that temperature, it would take one to three weeks for a corpse's tissue to convert to adipocere, the compound that stopped the activity of bacteria, and then the skin would turn white and soft. If there were crabs or small fish present, the decomposition process would be faster. So why was the face so well preserved? Even with the protection of the plastic bag, surely the crabs would have done their work faster.

She set the report aside and took another sip of coffee before turning to the files from Margaret Witherspoon's financial manager. Her first thought had been that Witherspoon's fortune had been acquired through fraudulent means, which would certainly explain the deliberate nature of his attempted disappearance. But it was evident from details from the bank and stockbroker's office that every penny made by the Witherspoons had come legitimately, either through earnings, inheritance, or careful and well-advised trading. So there had to be some other explanation for the disappearance of large sums of money from the joint accounts.

The cash withdrawals had started in March of 2005, she noted, which meant that over the past three years, Nicholas Witherspoon had filtered off more than ninety thousand dollars from the joint accounts. The amounts were always withdrawn on the last Friday of the month and they were always for identical amounts. In Adrian's experience, the need for large amounts of cash was often connected with drug deals or gambling. Billy Brown had been adamant that Witherspoon had been involved in something of the sort with the elusive Logan, who also seemed to have disappeared, but there was a third option that was far more likely when such a regular pattern of payouts was involved. She had a hunch that Nicholas Witherspoon was being blackmailed.

◆　　◆　　◆

The following Friday, Steven's band was playing at Rumrunners' Tavern. Philippa had dutifully recorded songs for Shannon, the Sheepdog, and Molly, the Milkmaid, and was ready for a night out before she returned to town. Steven and his troupe had to drive around early and set up their equipment, so Juliette offered to take Philippa over by boat. She and Steven had the use of her father's twenty-foot runabout, and Juliette was quite adept at operating the old tub, having been drilled in the rules of the sea from an early age. She was the only one of the Beary girls who had shown an interest in fishing, and she had accompanied her father on many lake and ocean expeditions.

"Wrap up," Juliette dictated, coming out of the kitchen with a large casserole dish in her hands. "It's freezing on the water this time of year."

"Don't worry," said Philippa, who was already encased in enough layers to triple her normally diminutive girth. "Remember, I'm a singer." She donned one of Steven's heavy woollen toques and wrapped a long scarf around the bottom of her face until she looked like a miniature Pavarotti.

Juliet smiled indulgently.

"I have a ski mask if you'd like that."

"No. I have to draw the line somewhere." Philippa nodded towards the casserole dish. "What's that for?"

"I thought we'd drop by Margaret's on the way over. Just something to let her know we're thinking of her."

Juliette issued some final orders to the babysitter; then she led Philippa down to the marina where the *Optimist* was moored. Although it was already dark, the dock lights made visibility easy, and as Philippa stepped on board, she noticed Billy by the fuel pumps. He was holding his cell phone and his expression seemed worried. He noticed Juliette untying the lines on the *Optimist* and he hurried over to speak to her.

"I've been trying to get hold of your cop cousin," he said, stooping to get the bow line. "They've paged her but she still hasn't got back to me, and I have an idea that ought to be passed on to her."

Juliette had been about to start the engine, but she paused. "If the dispatcher has paged her, she will get back to you, Billy. She's probably out on a call."

"What's the information?" asked Philippa. "Has something new come up?"

"No, but I keep wondering why the *Seagull* hasn't been sighted anywhere on the coast, and I've been thinking some more about that oil slick. You might be right, young lady. That boat could have sunk in the bay." He pointed to the waterfront homes on the far shore. "That's the Witherspoons' house over yonder. If you take a direct line from their boathouse to the mouth of the bay, it passes only a hundred yards from the end of my docks. If the boat had gone down on its way out of the bay, it could quite conceivably be sunk where the oil slicks were appearing."

"But I thought you said a shipwreck would produce masses of oil."

"Yes, if it had been an accident, but what if the boat had been deliberately scuttled?"

"What difference would that make?"

"Well, suppose Logan was on the boat with Witherspoon and he intended to kill him and make off with the money. He could scuttle the boat and row ashore in the dinghy, but he'd want to avoid people knowing the boat was there, so he'd have turned off the valve to the fuel line and then used vice-grips to clamp the vent line for the diesel tank so none of the fuel would escape."

"I still don't see," said Philippa. "If he took those precautions, how could there be any oil coming to the surface?"

"Because the *Seagull* had been damaged. He wouldn't have known that, but I do because I did the repair job. You see, if the oil filter plugs on that boat, there's a bypass so oil can circulate through the engine, but if the bypass plugs, it blows the gasket on the oil filter and spews the crankcase oil into the bilges. That happened to the *Seagull* last year, and although the boat was repaired, there would still have been traces of oil in the bilges. Just enough to explain the small slicks that have been surfacing offshore. That's what I want to tell the PC. The police may be wasting their time searching the coast for Witherspoon's boat. Maybe they should send down a diver to see if the boat is there."

Billy's cell phone rang, and he dropped the line and waved them off. He was already talking earnestly to the person on the other end as Juliette started the engine.

The *Optimist* pulled out into the bay and Philippa stared down at the black water, shivering as she remembered that it was this time of evening that Nicholas Witherspoon had set off on his final voyage.

"Should we say anything to Margaret, do you think?" she asked Juliette. "Shall we tell her about Billy's theory?"

Juliette kept her eyes on the lights on the far shore.

"I don't think so," she said. "Billy could be wrong. There's no point in tormenting her with possibilities."

It took less than five minutes for the *Optimist* to churn its way across the bay. Juliette steered towards a bright halogen light that towered at the end of a wooden jetty, then veered to port and headed along the shoreline. The boat cruised past a series of floats and slowed as an empty boathouse loomed ahead of them.

"Big," Philippa commented.

Juliette nodded. "Treated hemlock and well maintained. The Witherspoons were loaded."

Juliette turned towards land, brought the *Optimist* neatly alongside the float, and stopped the engine. Taking the spring line, she hopped onto the dock and tied up. Philippa handed her the casserole, which had been nestled in one of the children's life-jackets, then grabbed her shoulder bag and stepped ashore. She was pulled back abruptly by a tug on her arm, and she looked down to see that the strap of her bag had caught on the cleat at the edge of the dock. She bent to unhook the strap.

"Damn," she said. "Now I've caught my sleeve on a nail."

Juliette laughed. "You wouldn't get hung up like that on a stage set. Come on, city girl, extract yourself."

Philippa did so with dignity.

"I'm not the only one who did that," she said. "There's a chunk of white wool on the nail and it didn't come from my sweater."

She crossed the ramp and followed Juliette to a series of rocky steps that zig-zagged up to the top of the cliff, where a wide deck, that must have had a breath-taking view of the bay during the daytime, extended along the width of the property. Beyond the deck was an expanse of lawn that stretched across to a large, split-level home. The high, plate-glass windows of the house were dark, but the patio light was on, and it spilled across the grounds, illuminating an assortment of tools, fishnets, oars, and assorted garden implements stacked in an open shed at the edge of the property. Juliette led Philippa across the grass and round the path at the side of the house.

"I hope you called and said we were coming," said Philippa. She had an adventurous spirit, but was a stickler for common courtesies.

"Of course. Margaret's always home on Fridays. Remember—'Classic The-atre'. As long as we leave by eight, there's no problem."

Juliette knocked on the side door and a bark erupted from inside the house. The door opened and Margaret greeted them with a wan smile. Quasar stood behind her. Margaret gestured them inside and they entered to find themselves in a spacious kitchen. The room was white, angular and modern. Margaret took the dish from Juliette, thanked her, and put it in the refrigerator. She looked as if she had not slept in days, and her navy sweater made her skin appear jaundiced in the fluorescent light of the kitchen.

"Would you like coffee?" she asked. "I'm just making some."

Juliette nodded. Margaret ushered them through into the living room and returned to finish making the coffee. Quasar padded in and settled by the fire-place. Philippa gave him a pat, and then stood up to examine a photograph of a handsome middle-aged man, which stood in gold-framed isolation on the man-tle.

"Is that Nicholas Witherspoon?" she whispered to Juliette.

"No. That's Margaret's father. Handsome, wasn't he? There used to be one of Nicholas right beside it."

"I had to put it away." They turned to see Margaret re-entering the room with a tray set with coffee mugs. "I can't bear to look at it. Every time I do, it turns into the face I saw staring out of the lagoon."

Margaret's knuckles were white as she gripped the handles of the tray. "I don't know how I'm going to go on," she said. "I'm trying to keep busy, but I'm just going through the motions. There's not much point in anything anymore." She set the tray down on the coffee table, which was bare except for a large scrapbook. She poured the coffee and served her guests. Then she opened the scrapbook and turned it towards the sofa where Philippa and Juliette sat side by side. "Remember that day we walked by the lagoon?" she said.

Juliette nodded.

Margaret continued wearily. "I talked about bolts from the blue—things that completely change one's life. It's happened to me twice now—I've lost the two people I most loved in the entire world. I think I'll go mad thinking about it." She stabbed a finger at the scrapbook. "That was the first time. Now it's all come back again. All the pain is as fresh as if it happened yesterday."

Juliette nodded sympathetically. "They say that happens. When tragedy strikes, the anguish from old wounds flares all over again. Margaret, I really don't think you should be on your own right now. Couldn't Ann come and stay for a while?"

Margaret shook her head.

"Ann's away for a month. She said she was going to Victoria with her gentleman friend. I'm all right … really. You're not to worry. I prefer to be on my own."

"Then you should get away for a while," Juliette insisted.

Philippa was peering at the album. It contained a series of newspaper clippings about the collapse of the mountainside in Lions Bay. She turned the page and found a trio of photographs, two men and a woman, and an article detailing the tragedy. Right away, she recognized the first photograph. It was the same picture as the one on Margaret's mantelpiece. With a start, she realized that the centre photograph was of a much younger Margaret. She looked curiously at the third picture. The caption underneath confirmed her suspicion. It was Nicholas Witherspoon. Juliette and Margaret were still engrossed in their conversation, so she started to read the article. When she finished and looked up, she saw Margaret staring at her.

"Your husband was a hero." Philippa said simply. "It must have taken incredible courage to go back across that bridge."

"Is that what happened?" asked Juliette. "I never heard the details."

"It's all here," said Philippa. "Margaret's father hurt his ankle as the three of them were trying to get to the footbridge that crossed the creek. He insisted Nicholas take Margaret ahead and get her up to the road, but once Nicholas had got her to safety, he went back."

"I begged him to," said Margaret. "I knew Father needed help. Nicholas left me with the emergency crew and ran back down the trail."

"What happened?" asked Juliette. "Did the bridge go before he could get there?"

Margaret was staring at the tray. She picked up a cup, then put it down again, as if she were not sure what to do with her hands. Philippa answered Juliette's question.

"It was much more dramatic than that," she said. "It must have been horrific. By the time Nicholas Witherspoon went back, Margaret's father had managed to drag himself onto the bridge. Nicholas went over and brought him across, but as they reached the other side, a whole chunk of the mountainside came down and swept the bridge out. They were both caught by the edge of the slide and swept down the bank, but Nicholas was hurled sideways and landed against a tree. His father-in-law wasn't so lucky."

"No," said Margaret bitterly, suddenly regaining her focus. "My father was swept out to sea. One of the paramedics who had been standing on the highway bridge heard Father calling to Nicholas for help. He saw the whole thing. He told me how he'd seen Nicholas cross to my father and lead him back … how they'd both been swept away when the footbridge collapsed. He said … he said it was a miracle that Nicholas had survived …"

Her voice petered out, and she rocked back and forth in her chair. "I was so proud of him," she sighed. She gasped and bit her upper lip. "Oh, Juliette, how do I go on? I've lost them both—everything I cherished—it's all gone."

Quasar got up and padded across the room to his mistress. He set his head in her lap, but she seemed oblivious to him.

Juliette was good at comforting people in a crisis, but in the face of Margaret's despair, she felt utterly at a loss. Unsure what to do, she stared at the pages of the album, at first not seeing its contents, but after a moment, the pictures came into focus. She leaned forward, suddenly caught by a photograph at the head of a full-page article.

"Who is that?" She pointed her finger at the headshot. "I've seen that man somewhere."

Philippa scanned the article in the album. The man in the headshot was named Peter Hoffman and the article had been written ten years after the catastrophe. It was less about the mudslide and more about the miracles of therapy and modern medicine. Peter Hoffman had been one of the lucky ones. He'd been swept down the hillside and suffered major injuries, including some brain damage, but he had survived. Philippa finished reading the article and looked up.

"Do you know this man?" she asked Margaret. "Did you ever meet him?"

Margaret's eyes were miserable and confused. "He's … he looks like the stranger who came to our house," she said finally. She sank back down in her chair. "He was such an odd man—so pathetic. He'd had a very difficult life."

"Could it have been the same man?" Philippa asked.

Margaret's voice trailed off to a whisper and she appeared to be drifting into a trance. "He wasn't the man I thought he was," she murmured sadly.

◆   ◆   ◆

Two days later, divers found the *Seagull* at the bottom of the bay. Now Adrian realized what had protected Nicholas Witherspoon's face. His body must have floated up and caught against the cabin roof, but because the door of the cabin had been hooked open, the movement of the water had worked him loose and a particularly high winter tide had carried him over the dam and into the lagoon.

Adrian waited on the dock and stared towards the islands in the mouth of the bay. A tug had been contracted to raise the boat, and the search was on for the dingy that had carried Nicholas Witherspoon's murderer ashore. The search was also on for Peter Logan Hoffman, a casual labourer who had been living at the Anchor Bay motel but who had not been seen since the night Nicholas Witherspoon died. Billy Brown was feted as the hero of the day, and had yet another story with which to regale the regulars at the pub.

The weather had warmed up and the sky had clouded over. The day was grey and promising rain. As Adrian stood at the marina and watched the zodiac returning to the dock, she heard her name called. She turned to see Philippa and Juliette coming down the ramp. From past experience, she knew that her cousins could be valuable sources of information, and she was always ready to listen to whatever facts or theories they could provide. She moved to meet them as they stepped onto the dock.

"You look like you have something for me," she said.

Philippa nodded.

"Adrian, have you considered the possibility that Nicholas Witherspoon was being blackmailed?"

"We're investigating every avenue. That's certainly one of the scenarios."
Adrian dropped her official caution and expanded a little. "So far, he seems to
have led a blameless life. If he was being blackmailed, there's something in his
background that we have yet to uncover."

"It may relate to an incident that happened a long time ago," said Philippa.
"Have you looked into the details of Margaret's father's death?"

"No. That hasn't come up at all. What's the connection?"

"A man called Peter Hoffman," said Juliette. "We saw his photo in a press cutting in Margaret's album. There was an article about him too."

Adrian looked alert. "All right, now it's making sense. Tell me about it."

Juliette turned to her sister.

"You explain," she said. "You read the article."

Philippa took a deep breath and related the details of the Lions Bay disaster of
1981. Adrian listened attentively.

"Peter Hoffman was also injured in the mudslide," Philippa concluded, "and
according to Margaret, the stranger that showed up at her house resembled the
man in the photograph."

"And," added Juliette, "the photo looked just like the man I used to see with
Nicholas Witherspoon at Rumrunners' Tavern."

"It fits," said Adrian. "Hoffman's middle name is Logan, so chances are it was
the same man. Logan moved to the coast in 2004. He's been working here as a
casual labourer for the past three years—but what sort of hold could he have over
Witherspoon?"

"What if during the attempt to rescue Margaret's father, Nicholas Witherspoon had somehow been responsible for Hoffman's accident?" said Philippa.
"What if it were a case of criminal negligence? Wouldn't that result in him feeling
compelled to pay Hoffman off?"

"Very likely, but you're talking about something that happened twenty-five
years ago. The cash withdrawals only started three years ago. If Witherspoon had
caused a catastrophic injury to Hoffman, why would the man wait all these years
to start kicking up a fuss?"

"He suffered brain-damage," Juliette pointed out. "Massive trauma would
have affected his memory. It took several years of therapy before he recovered
enough to function, and quite honestly, from what I saw of Logan, I suspect he
didn't ever function very well."

Adrian nodded.

"Post-traumatic stress. Yes. He could well have forgotten everything leading
up to his accident—but something must have happened to trigger his memory."

"I think it was as simple as his move to the coast," said Philippa. "He was the sort of man to hang out in bars and pubs, so it was only a matter of time before he ran into Nicholas Witherspoon. Seeing him face to face would have brought it all back."

"That might explain Witherspoon deciding to stage his own disappearance," argued Adrian, "but it doesn't explain his murder. Why should Hoffman kill him?"

"Juliette and I have a theory," said Philippa. "Billy said Hoffman left the pub early the night Margaret's husband failed to show up. What if he caught him trying to get away? Remember, Witherspoon was probably carrying a quarter of a million dollars in cash."

"Well," Adrian agreed, "it's possible. I'll have to talk to Margaret again and get a statement to the effect that Hoffman came to her house. Was she definite that he was the visitor?"

"No," Philippa admitted. "She acknowledged the resemblance, but she said it wasn't the same man. Still, she could have been wrong. Newspaper photographs aren't always that accurate."

Adrian's cell phone rang. "We'll know more when the boat is raised," she said. She gestured to Philippa to be silent while she answered the call. Her eyes grew wider as she listened to the person on the other end. The one-sided call went on for several minutes, but finally, with a brief word of thanks, she rang off and tucked her cell back into her belt.

"They've traced Hoffman," she said. "He's in a motel in Burnaby."

"Well, go on," Philippa urged. "Tell us what's happening. Did you discover the connection between him and Nicholas Witherspoon?"

"Yes," said Adrian, "and it's pretty grim. You were right about the blackmail, but Witherspoon was guilty of far worse than causing Hoffman's accident. He was responsible for his father-in-law's death."

Juliette looked stunned.

"But he couldn't be!" she cried. "One of the paramedics saw him helping George Brent across the bridge."

"The paramedic could only see one section of the bridge. He looked down and had a distant, bird's-eye-view of a man coming over the footbridge and helping Brent across, but the man he saw wasn't Witherspoon. It was Hoffman. Hoffman was a repairman in those days. He was on a job at a house on the opposite side of the ravine. He was making his way up the slope when he saw Brent calling for help. He also saw Witherspoon standing at the end of the bridge. There was a raging torrent in the creek below, and the hillside had already destabilized so badly that the bridge was starting to shift and an end-brace had broken away."

Philippa shook her head in disbelief. "You mean Margaret's husband was just watching—deliberately ignoring the call for help?"

"It's worse than that. He had picked up the end-brace and was using it to pry the base of the footbridge away from the bank."

Philippa gasped. "He was trying to murder his father-in-law?"

"Yes."

"But why would he want to kill George Brent?" Juliette was horrified. "Margaret told me her father was wonderful to them."

"I'd say it was a straightforward case of murder for money," said Adrian. "George Brent was wealthy, and at that time, Witherspoon and Margaret were young teachers with no assets and working on minimum salaries. Brent was in his fifties, so they'd have waited a long time for Margaret's inheritance."

"That's diabolical," said Philippa. "What a nasty, opportunistic rat."

"That's what Hoffman thought. He says he knocked Witherspoon down and raced over the bridge to help Brent. He managed to get him across, but Witherspoon tried to block their way off the bridge. Then, at that moment, the whole mountainside started to come down the ravine. Witherspoon saw it coming and moved back in time to be clear of the slide, but Brent and Hoffman were caught. Hoffman was the lucky one. He was hurled clear and landed against a tree. Brent, as we know, was swept out to sea. His body was never recovered. Witherspoon staggered back up the hill. He was covered in mud, and as he thought both his father-in-law and the unexpected witness were dead, he figured he was safe. He told Margaret he'd tried to save her father and had failed, and his lie was reinforced later by the paramedic who came round to tell Margaret of his heroism."

Juliette had fallen silent and her face was white, but now she spoke and her normally gentle voice was bitter. "No wonder Hoffman was able to force him to pay," she said. "Can you imagine what this is going to do to Margaret when she finds out?"

"Does Hoffman have the missing money?" asked Philippa.

"His room has been searched. The money isn't there. He admits to receiving the monthly payouts, but he denies knowing anything about the missing investments. However, his bank account has a recent deposit of one hundred thousand dollars."

"How does he explain that?"

"He won't talk. He's obviously covering up something."

"What about his movements on the night Nicholas Witherspoon disappeared?"

"Hoffman says he left the tavern when Witherspoon didn't show. He was angry, and he went to the house to confront him, but the house was dark and silent, and nobody answered when he knocked."

Juliette frowned.

"That can't be right. It was Margaret's 'Classic Theatre' night."

The conversation was interrupted as the zodiac returned to the marina. It pulled in by the fuel pumps. Billy Brown was at his station, and he bent down to tie the lines as the divers climbed ashore.

"Hold on a sec," said Adrian. She waved to the diver who appeared to be in charge of the operation. He left his colleague and came over to join them. "What did you see down there?" Adrian demanded.

The diver looked warily at Philippa and Juliette, but Adrian nodded to him to go on, so he elaborated.

"Not a lot. There was a suitcase in the cabin. We brought it up, but it contained clothes, not money. The boat was definitely scuttled, though. Someone cut the salt-water intake pipes to the engine. It would have gone down in less than ten minutes. You'll be able to see more when the boat is out of the water, but it looked to me as if someone was also tampering with the valves that control the engine fuel."

Another point for Billy, thought Adrian.

"How can you tell?" she asked.

"There was a piece of black leather caught in the valve. It looked like it had been torn from a glove."

"Oh, my God," whispered Juliette. She clutched at Philippa's wrist. "*She already knew.*"

Philippa felt a chill run down her spine as she saw the look of naked terror in her sister's eyes. Juliette's face was ashen.

"You've lost me," said Adrian. "What are you talking about?"

Juliette looked close to tears.

"Margaret's black leather gloves … the ones she usually wears … they were in her pocket."

Philippa nodded thoughtfully. "That's right, they were." She turned to Adrian and explained. "We met Margaret by the lagoon the day the body was found. Everything about her outfit was immaculately matched, except for her gloves. She was wearing red woollen mitts, yet she had the other pair with her. That doesn't make sense, does it?"

Adrian frowned.

"No, but what you're suggesting doesn't make sense either."

Juliette cut in: "Don't you see? She must have found out what happened to her father. That's why she's been so distraught. The discovery would have devastated her."

"Now just a minute," said Adrian. She looked hard at Juliette. "This is a pretty startling change of direction. What makes you think Margaret learned the truth about her father's death?"

"Because she told us," said Juliette sadly. She turned towards Philippa. "Remember what she said when we asked if she recognized the photograph of the man in the newspaper article. '*He wasn't the man I thought he was.*' She wasn't talking about Hoffman. She was talking about her husband."

Juliette's eyes misted over and she bit her lip. Philippa put her arm round her sister's shoulders and drew her away. As they moved towards the ramp, Billy came hurrying across the float to speak to Adrian. He had clearly had another of his inspired brainwaves.

"Hey, Constable, I need to speak with you. I've been talking with your diver and he says I was right about the fuel lines, but something else has occurred to me. That Logan fellow wasn't a boater, but even if he had been, he wouldn't have known where to find the fuel lines on someone else's boat. Your killer has to be someone who had intimate knowledge of the *Seagull*."

Adrian's face was sombre. She turned to Billy and nodded.

"Thank you, Billy. You've been very helpful."

Billy shook his grizzled head and his leathery face looked sorrowful. "That was one hell of a good boat," he said. "What a tragic business all round."

"Yes," agreed Adrian, "you're right about that too."

◆   ◆   ◆

The rain started in earnest as they reached the footbridge. The tide had turned and the water was rushing over the dam, causing a series of rapids and whirlpools that made the channel resemble a miniature Skookumchuck. On the far bank, the wet bark of the arbutus trees gleamed a vibrant orange and the blackberry brambles drooped in the heavy shower. The lagoon was opaque again, but there was no reflection, for drops of rain were creating a pattern of circles in the water, making it appear like frosted glass. Only at the extreme edge of the pool were the rocks on the seabed visible. Philippa and Juliette followed Adrian across the bridge and onto the perimeter road.

They found Margaret at the end of the lagoon. She was staring into the water where her husband's body had been found. She was dressed exactly as Philippa had seen her the first time they met, except that she now wore her leather gloves, not seeming to care about the missing strip that revealed the palm of her right hand. Quasar sat at her side, looking as sad as his mistress, as if he sensed her misery and realized that his life was somehow about to change.

She made no resistance as Adrian informed her of her rights.

"It doesn't matter," she said. "I want to talk. I can't bear keeping it to myself any longer. He deceived me for twenty-five years, you know." She stared into the depths of the lagoon. "It was all about money and control. Father and I were just a means to an end." Margaret turned and faced Adrian. "I think I went mad when I found out. I spent my whole life loving someone who didn't exist."

"How did you find out?" Adrian asked gently.

"He did his banking on the computer in his study. I was taking in tea, when the doorbell rang. He'd called a painter for an estimate—we were planning to renovate the top floor—and he left the room to speak with him. As I put the tea down, I noticed the screen. I'm not as stupid about money as everyone seems to think. I saw the withdrawals, and when he came back, I asked him about them. He finally broke down and told me that he was being blackmailed." Margaret's face became suffused with anger. "But even then he lied," she said. "He said Logan had found out about an illegal financial transaction, and that I was going to have to help him get out of the mess he'd got into."

"He wanted you to help him disappear."

"Yes. He said I could sell up and join him later."

"So it really was your signature on the documents that shut down the investments."

"Yes. For once he didn't have to forge my name. I even helped him bundle the money into five packages so it would be easy to take with him."

"How did you find out the truth?"

Margaret smiled bitterly.

"I could tell he was lying. I'd always trusted him—believed him honest and ethical—but suddenly, I saw his cunning side, and it shook me. So I tracked down Logan and asked him what he knew about my husband. He didn't want to tell me—he was afraid I'd be angry about the blackmail—but he finally broke down. I didn't believe him at first. I was stunned. But then I realized if he was telling the truth, he had suffered massive injuries in a heroic attempt to save my father. How could I be angry with him if that were true? How could I begrudge him the money? So I told him I would check into his story, and if it were verified,

I would pay him a lump sum of one hundred thousand dollars as compensation for his injuries." Margaret paused and sighed; then she looked sadly into the dark waters of the lagoon. "He was pathetically grateful, poor man," she continued finally. "I told him to keep meeting Nicholas to collect the payments in the interim—and then I returned home."

"You confronted your husband?"

Margaret nodded.

"Yes. He tried to deny it at first, but he finally broke down and admitted that Logan was telling the truth. He actually had the gall to say he'd done it for me. He didn't seem to comprehend what I was feeling. He just assumed I would go along—the way I always did." Margaret's eyes glinted. "And I did cooperate—right up until the night he left."

"Oh, Margaret," said Juliette. "You couldn't have meant to kill him. It must have happened on the spur of the moment."

Margaret looked defiant. "Oh, no. I planned to kill him as soon as I realized what he'd done. I replaced two of the money packages with bundles of paper, and the day before Nicholas died, I mailed two of the original packages to Logan. Then, on the night Nicholas was leaving, I helped him take his gear to the boat. When he took his suitcase into the cabin, I picked up the oar of the dinghy; then I waited until he came out and knocked him out. After that, I put the bag over his head and waited for him to die. It was amazingly easy."

"Then it was you who took the boat out into the bay?" Adrian said quietly.

"Yes. I scuttled it well off the shore and rowed back in the dinghy. It's fiberglass and very small, so it was easy to sink. You'll find it on the bottom under the boathouse. The oars wouldn't go down, of course, so I put them in the shed. Then I went back to the house. I was in time for my show. I'd planned it all so well, but I couldn't focus. I thought I'd go crazy. I took Quasar out and we walked. We walked until I was exhausted—but I couldn't sleep even then—I still can't sleep. You see killing him hasn't stopped my anger. I wasted so many years. I wasted my entire life."

Margaret looked at Juliette and her face was ashen. "I told you, Juliette, that I'd lost both of the men I loved. One of them died, and the other didn't really exist. And the truth is I don't care any more. I think I died with both of them."

She handed Quasar's leash to Juliette. "Look after him for me," she said.

Without looking back, she allowed Adrian to lead her away.

A Political Tail

Early in his political career, Bertram Beary learned that there were two issues that should be avoided if one wished to stay out of trouble with the electorate. One was garbage, for local residents tended to become extremely hostile if the powers-that-be threatened to enact changes to the customary procedures for picking up refuse; the other contentious and inflammatory subject was man's best friend.

Beary was a dog-lover—MacPuff, the Siberian husky, being a cherished member of the Beary household—so he had vigorously championed the dog people during the raging debate over leash laws during the 1980s, and had been delighted when finally, a decade later, Burnside Council, of which he was a member, had become sufficiently enlightened so as to dedicate certain areas of parks where well-behaved canines could run free if under the control of their owners. One such area, fifty acres in size, had been designated in the lower section of Fernie Park, which was only a few blocks from the Beary home, so for many years, MacPuff had enjoyed daily forays along the paths and through the creeks of this picturesque woodland.

Therefore, it was with a great deal of annoyance that Beary arrived at city hall to pick up his agenda one Friday afternoon and found a report from the manager's office requesting a review of the off-leash policy in general, and the Fernie Park location in particular, due to complaints from canine-phobic residents.

"I see Sherry Gordon is on her ban-all-dogs kick again," said Beary. "One of these days, someone's going to murder that woman."

Harry Salai, who had just emerged from the clerk's office, paused in the hallway and looked over Beary's shoulder.

"You don't pop people off because they don't like dogs," he said.

"Why not?" said Beary. "You'd probably be glad to exterminate all the computer-illiterates on the planet." Harry was city hall's resident computer genius. He solved everyone's problems, from installation of software to elimination of viruses. Beary, who knew nothing about computers, was in awe of Harry's prowess.

"I wish!" said Harry amiably, and quite untruthfully, since he was a good-natured individual who couldn't swat a gnat without suffering an attack of conscience. "You'd have known about that item if you hadn't been out of town," he added, nodding towards the report. "Sherry had Councillor Borelli give notice of motion on the subject at the last meeting."

Harry ambled down the hall in the direction of the finance department, and Beary turned and marched purposefully toward the stairwell. *And that would be why the notice of motion was given last week*, he thought furiously. Sherry Gordon was the city's assistant manager, and she always slipped items onto the agenda when she knew the strongest opponents would be absent. Beary wheezed up the flight of stairs to the top floor, then, with the sense of drama that he used to employ when attempting to stimulate apathetic students who were struggling with the text of *Julius Caesar*, he stormed into the manager's office, flailed his agenda, and planted himself in front of the receptionist's desk.

"Where's Sherry Gordon?" he demanded. "I wish to speak with her."

Paula Trentini looked up, startled.

"Sherry hasn't come in yet," she informed Beary.

Beary was surprised.

"But it's after lunch. She's usually here before nine."

"Actually," said Paula, "I'm rather concerned." Paula was one of the sweeter members of the secretarial staff, unlike some Beary could think of who had been hired for their ability to quell recalcitrant councillors and repel hostile members of the public.

Paula elaborated. "There have been complaints about a vicious dog running loose in Fernie Park—"

"I know. That's why I'm here. I don't trust Sherry Gordon's definition of a vicious dog. She'd equate an unleashed chihuahua with the Hound of the Baskervilles."

"That may be," said Paula, "but Sherry said she was going to visit the area last night and see first-hand if the complaints were justified—and nobody has heard from her since. Jeffrey," she continued, naming the city manager, "telephoned last night to see what she'd discovered, but the answering machine took the message, and when he tried Sherry's cell, he just got her voicemail. He left a message on both, but Sherry didn't call back."

"Did anyone try to contact her this morning?"

"Yes, I called to see why she was late—I mean, it's so unusual; Sherry always phones if she's ill or delayed—but I still got the voicemail." Paula furrowed her pretty brow. "I can't help wondering if something has happened to her. Do you think I should call the police?"

"Grown adults have to be missing for a lot longer than fourteen hours for the RCMP to take an interest," said Beary. "Besides, Sherry can take care of herself. Unlike the canines she takes such pleasure in defaming, her bite is definitely worse than her bark."

"Oh, Councillor Beary, please don't joke about it," said Paula. "I really am worried. No woman should walk the park trails alone, especially when it's getting dark. I told Sherry she shouldn't go—"

"Certainly not without a dog to protect her," Beary interjected.

Paula quelled him with a reproving stare. "But she was quite determined," she finished.

"Did anyone else know what she was up to?"

"The entire dog-owning population must have known. The subject was raised at the last council meeting, and that Jones woman was on the phone the very next day, so I imagine she's alerted every dog-walker in the neighbourhood that there's a battle brewing."

"Trixie Jones." Beary beamed. "I remember her back in the mid-eighties. What a fighter! Winston Churchill would have loved that woman. If he'd had her leading a regiment in 1939, Hitler would have been hiding in his bunker by Christmas."

"She's rather overwhelming," said Paula. "She marched in yesterday, complete with that cross little black terrier of hers, and gave Sherry an earful. Sherry was already late for the Advisory Planning Commission because Jack Canterbury had come in to pressure her over his rezoning, and then Mrs. Jones appeared."

"So Sherry agreed to inspect the situation just to get rid of her."

"Not really. Sherry agreed because she was trying to be fair."

"Paula," said Beary firmly, "you are very young, very sweet and very naïve. Sherry Gordon doesn't know the meaning of the word, *fair*. She is a career bureaucrat whose only function is to manipulate politicians and the public, and the only operative word she understands is *expedient*. If she has gone down to the dog park, it will not be to make an accurate assessment of the situation, but simply to ensure there is some kind of incident that will put a kybosh on the area once and for all."

The phone on Paula's desk rang, and she excused herself to answer the call. Beary fidgeted impatiently while he waited, and glowered at the exotic lady in the Daniel Izzard reproduction on the wall behind the desk. The call seemed to be taking some time, and suddenly becoming aware that there was very little input from Paula, he glanced down and saw that her face had paled until it matched the cool ice blue of the paint on the walls. Her eyes were wide and suspiciously damp.

After what seemed an interminable silence, Paula muttered a semi-intelligible acknowledgement, put down the receiver and looked tearfully at Beary.

"That was the police." There was a tremor in Paula's voice. "Sherry was found in the park this morning. A dog-walker saw a car with a broken window in the parking lot, and when he went further down the path, he discovered a shoe on one of the trails, and ... and then he saw a foot sticking out of the bushes ..." Paula caught her breath and gave a little cry. "Sherry's dead," she sobbed. "Her body was there all night."

Beary pulled a tissue from the box on the desk and handed it to the distraught girl. Paula took it from him, and her crying began in earnest. Beary genuinely liked Paula and was sorry to see her so distressed. He gave her a fatherly pat on the shoulder, but curiosity forced him to ask the question that was foremost in his mind.

"How did she die?" he asked.

Paula looked up between sobs and managed to reply.

"She was mauled to death by a dog."

◆   ◆   ◆

The following Tuesday, the pound patrols ran rampant in Fernie Park, for Council, predictably, had abandoned the proposed review of the off-leash area and simply used the Monday-night meeting to repeal the bylaw. The immediate crackdown resulted in more than a dozen tickets issued to indignant owners of assorted good-natured mongrels who were taking their morning exercise in the park. Three days later, a rebellious group of dogs and dog-owners congregated in Trixie Jones's living room to discuss a strategy for rectifying the situation.

Trixie sat on a Queen Anne chair taken from the dining room. With pen in hand, the council report in her lap, and Nisha, the cross black terrier, glowering at her feet, she assumed her natural position as leader of the debate.

"There are two issues we have to address," she announced. "First, we have to take measures to ensure that we can enjoy our walks without having to worry about fines because our dogs aren't leashed, and secondly, we have to track down the beast that killed the wretched woman. It'll be a pit bull from a grow-op house," she stated peremptorily. "There's no way any of the regular walkers' pooches would have done any such thing, but until we prove that, we're up dog-pooh creek, and there isn't a paddle or shovel in sight."

Millie Jenkins raised her hand tentatively. She was a shy lady of indeterminate age, whose husband had either died or left her some years previously. She lived in a small house on the edge of the park, accompanied only by an equally gentle Doberman named Beanie.

"There were rumours a few months back about a bear in the park," she said timidly. "Could Mrs. Gordon have been the victim of a bear attack?"

"Unlikely," rebutted Trixie firmly. "There was only one sighting, and it was never confirmed."

"There was a cougar two years ago," said Trixie's husband, who had been relegated to making the coffee but had overheard the conversation as he was entering the room with a tray.

Trixie gave him a scathing look.

"Don't be ridiculous, Henry. The cougar was caught and returned to the mountain. Anyway," she added, "there wouldn't have been much left of Sherry Gordon if a big cat had got hold of her."

"So we're definitely looking for the Hound of the Baskervilles," said Jimmy Burgess.

Jimmy was a retired widower, and his life revolved around his garden, his misbehaved mongrel, Maverick, and his library of mystery novels, although some of the dog-walkers speculated that his carefully timed morning perambulations were calculated to coincide with those of Millie Jenkins, and not because Maverick wanted to play with Beanie.

"Who complained about this dog?" asked Carrie McVey. She puffed her ample bosom out indignantly so that the slogan on her T-shirt—*Multiculturalism includes Mutti-culturalism*—expanded by at least three font sizes.

"Who do you think?" said Trixie dryly. "Janice Goodyear, of course. She was the leader of the anti-dog brigade back in the 1980s. If it hadn't been for her, we'd have got the dog park much sooner. And it doesn't help that her husband served with Sherry Gordon on the Advisory Planning Commission. They were as thick as thieves, always voting the same way and seconding each other's motions."

"Can't stand the man," snorted Carrie. "Howard Goodyear talks a great line about liking animals, but he's a duplicitous donkey's-rear-end, as far as I'm concerned. He'll never do anything to oppose his wife because she's the one with all the money."

"The Goodyears live on Grant Street," said Jimmy. "It goes into the trail on the west side of the park—and that's where the incident occurred."

"What exactly happened?" asked Millie.

Trixie enlightened her.

"An elderly couple was strolling along the edge of the baseball field, and the dog lunged out of the bushes and snapped at the man's hand. The wife screamed and her husband yelled at the dog—from their description, I'd say the animal is some kind of pit bull cross—and then they heard a shrill whistle, and the dog turned and ran off."

"So the owner was nearby," said Jimmy thoughtfully. "Do we know which way the dog ran?"

"That's a good question," Trixie acknowledged. "I'll ask Bertram Beary. He might be able to find out. The problem is there have been several more sightings of this so-called monster dog, always around the same time in the evening, and always at the top, westernmost side of the park."

"Well," said Jimmy decisively, "we need to find out where the animal comes from, so let's set up shifts to keep watch. How about it, Millie?" he added, looking across the room. "Are you on for tonight?"

Millie flushed and nodded.

"No," said Trixie. "It's too soon. The park is a crime scene at present. The area will be crawling with RCMP, so whoever is letting this troublesome dog run won't risk it at the moment. You can start the vigil next Tuesday. Henry and I will do Wednesday evening, and Carrie, you and Ralph Johnson can do the next night."

"Who?" asked Carrie.

"Sammy's owner."

"Oh, the nice old gentleman with the white Samoyed. Excellent. Brandy likes them." She patted the sheepdog lying at her feet.

"Once we get to the root of the problem," Trixie continued, "we'll re-approach Council. We should start lobbying right away though, so get your friends to write letters and make phone calls. We need to make the media aware that dog-owners are a presence in the community."

"How about T-shirts?" Carrie suggested. "I could get a batch made up."

"Good idea."

"Placards shaped like dog biscuits?" ventured Millie Jenkins.

"Excellent," said Trixie.

"We could leash ourselves to the railings outside city hall," Jimmy added flippantly.

Trixie took him seriously.

"If all else fails," she agreed. She paused to rebuke Nisha, whose nose was inching towards the cookie plate. Then she continued.

"Now, to the matter of organizing our daily walks. Since the pound patrols are going to be a constant presence until the matter is resolved, it will be impossible to have a decent walk on the park trails, so," she announced, looking defiantly around the room, "we will have to cut some alternate routes."

"Where?" asked Carrie.

"In the park, of course. There's lots of bush between the main paths. All it will take is a crew with machetes, and some forks and garden gloves for pulling up the ground cover. We'll have new trails in no time."

Millie gasped.

"You can't hack up park property," she protested. "Isn't that illegal?"

"It is one's civic duty," Trixie pointed out firmly, "to oppose an unjust law. Now," she continued in a tone that clearly brooked no opposition, "my proposal is that we start two trails from the grassy field at the bottom of the park, link them across the top, and then cut a second loop so that we end up with a figure-eight configuration. The new trails will be a bit rough and they won't be wide like the main paths, but they'll serve as an interim dog park until we get our off-leash area back, and they'll enhance the area once the bylaw is reversed."

"But what's to stop the pound officers from nailing us on the new trails?" asked Henry practically.

Trixie gave him a withering glance.

"We won't cut the trails right to the edge of the grass. We'll leave a small section of bush covering each entrance. That way, the dog-walkers will be the only ones who know about the paths and they'll be able to appear and disappear as stealthily as the Viet Cong. We'll start at the bottom of the ravine. There's a natural trail along the edge so there will be less underbrush to clear."

"There's fifty feet of long grass to plough through before you reach the ravine," Carrie protested.

"I've thought of that." Trixie nodded towards her husband. "Henry can take the lawnmower down tonight in the back of the car. Well, you do need the exercise, dear," she added, as her husband started to protest. "And that," she concluded, closing her notebook, "should be sufficient to get us started."

The phone in the kitchen rang and Henry went to answer the call. Sensing that the serious business of the evening had ended, Maverick uncurled himself, stretched, eyed the cookie plate and looked expectantly at Jimmy. Beanie sprang up and padded across to Carrie's sheepdog, and gradually, the owners stood and began to gather leashes and pets. As the exodus to the front door began, Henry reappeared from the kitchen.

"Hold on, everyone," he announced. "Here's something you'll want to hear. That call was from Councillor Beary. His son is on the case and he just gave Beary a heads-up on the pathologist's report. Sherry Gordon didn't die as a result of a dog attack. She was stabbed to death. The so-called mauling must have occurred after death, probably a coyote during the night."

"Well," said Trixie heartlessly, "that *is* good news. Now we just have to find some hard evidence to show that the Hound of the Baskervilles has nothing to do with the off-leash area. Once that's done, we should get our dog park back in no time. After all, if there's a homicidal maniac running loose, we need our dogs to protect us. Any councillor worth his salt will understand that." She paused and looked down at the plate on the coffee table.

"And what," she demanded, "happened to the rest of the cookies?"

Maverick licked his lips as he followed Jimmy out the door.

◆   ◆   ◆

One week and many interviews later, the police appeared to have reached a dead end. Richard Beary had spent the morning poring over the pile of reports on his desk and he still had not come up with a definite lead. Sherry Gordon was an enigma. Her private life seemed virtually non-existent, and from the descriptions given by her colleagues at city hall, Sherry could have been half-a-dozen different people. Her only regular engagements were a twice-monthly visit to her mother, who had nothing to tell except for the fact that Sherry was an exemplary daughter, and a weekly business lunch at Haversham House with her boss, Jeffrey Arlington. The contents of her home and workspace, including all the files and emails in her office computer, had been examined, but these revealed nothing other than the multitudinous details of various committees and city re-zonings.

The door opened, and Detective Sergeant Bill Martin appeared. Martin, who had been born and raised in London during the Beatle era, had just returned from a visit to his mother in England. Richard was glad to see him back. Martin entered the office, a coffee in either hand. He planted one mug in front of Richard and sat in the chair on the other side of the desk.

"So what have we got on this Gordon woman?" he asked.

"A lot of conflicting information," said Richard, "and it's hard to sort between rumour and fact. Have you had a chance to look at the file?"

"Only enough to know that the victim was a high-powered employee at city hall and that she was forty-two years old and single. I talked with Jean Howe on the way in—I gather you've got her working on the case—and she told me that

Sherry Gordon was pretty hard-nosed and had put up the backs of a couple of local developers, plus the entire dog-walking population of the community, which," he added with a grin, "I gather includes your father."

Richard nodded.

"Yes," he said, "my father has been quite vocal on the subject."

"Surely the woman didn't get murdered by an irate dog-lover or a thwarted developer," protested Martin. "That would be pretty extreme."

"Yes, but the possibility can't be ruled out. The woman didn't appear to have any close relationships, so it's hard to dig out motives in her personal life. Apart from visits home, lunches with her boss and attendance at civic functions, her only outings were to the theatre, usually in the company of a lady who works in the Planning Department. Evidently Sherry Gordon was a great Shakespeare enthusiast—never missed a performance at Bard on the Beach, and always took her annual holiday in Ontario so she could take in the Stratford Festival."

Martin looked at the photograph that lay face-up on the desk.

"Was she gay?" he asked. "She was very attractive. It's hard to believe men wouldn't have been interested in her—unless, of course, she was such a harridan that she scared them all away."

"She didn't go out with men," said Richard, "which prompted talk among some city employees that she was a lesbian, but according to Paula, the manager's secretary, Sherry had recently dropped a couple of crashing hints that there was a man in her life."

"Does the secretary know who he was?"

"No. She had wondered, given all the secrecy, if the man was married."

"What about the other people Gordon worked with? Had they heard anything of the sort?"

"Nothing specific. There's a junior planner who worked with her on the Advisory Planning Commission—Mark Hudson is his name—and he reiterated the fact that she was a workaholic and didn't have much personal life, other than being pretty cozy with her boss, Jeffrey Arlington. I think there may be a bit of professional jealousy there—Hudson strikes me as the ambitious type. However, Hudson thought it was conceivable that Gordon had a man in the background somewhere—just an air she had—and that if we dug around we might find something. But Jeffrey Arlington dismissed the idea completely. Mind you, I got the impression he considered Hudson an arrogant young upstart and on principle would say the opposite of anything that Hudson suggested. Still, Arlington seems to have known Gordon better than most. He met her in Ontario when they were attending a planning conference. She was with the city hall in Nelson at the time, and he was sufficiently impressed by her that he offered her a job here. He's pretty well been her mentor, so they're very close. He was adamant that Sherry was not interested in men and that her life revolved around her work."

"Do you think he's reliable? After all, he's the one who had regular lunch meetings with her. Maybe *he* was the man in her life."

"He has a reputation for being a prudishly Victorian family man, and everything one hears about him suggests his reputation for being a model of propriety is justified. He's from a very old, well-to-do family who are so much a part of the Ontario establishment that they have buildings and streets, and even the odd body of water, named after them. And his wife is a Burgess—you know, the steel millionaires. The Arlingtons are the proverbial pillars of the community."

"So were the Borgias," muttered Martin. "You never know what's under the surface. Did you tell Arlington that his secretary had agreed with Hudson's suggestion about Sherry Gordon's love life?"

"Yes. Arlington looked shocked, and then he suggested that Sherry Gordon's hints about a lover were simply a ploy to counteract the lesbian rumours. Mind you, when I suggested that to Doreen Doerkson—that's the theatre-going lady from the Planning Department—I got a very indignant response. Mrs. Doerkson informed me in no uncertain terms that if Sherry did happen to be that way inclined, it certainly wasn't with her."

"Did you believe her?"

"Yes, actually. She had a certain look in her eye, and my father tells me that Mrs. Doerkson is very much the merry widow and makes merry every second weekend with a gentleman in the Engineering Department. Her read on Sherry Gordon was that she was a frustrated career woman who wanted a man but didn't want to change her lifestyle. Harold Goodyear said the same thing. He's a citizen representative on the Advisory Planning Commission. He completely dismissed the idea of a lover in the background—told us in no uncertain terms we were wasting our time barking up that particular tree. The metaphor was rather appropriate actually. He's married to the woman who's been stirring up the dog controversy in Fernie Park."

"That would be Janice Goodyear," said Martin, thumbing through the papers on Richard's desk.

"Yes, a wealthy and influential lady. She's good friends with Gwendolyn Pye."

"Is she indeed? Nothing like being pally with the mayor to help push a personal agenda."

"Exactly. Mrs. Goodyear gives generously to Mrs. Pye's campaign, so she expects to be listened to. I gather the Goodyears are not only up in arms over the dogs, but are also trying to obstruct the re-zoning of the woods at the foot of their street. Harold Goodyear was actually the last person to report seeing Sherry Gordon alive. After the planning meeting, he remained chatting with Mark Hudson. They were discussing ways to deal with Jack Canterbury—that's the developer who was putting the heat on—but Hudson had to leave to supervise his son's ball game, so Sherry took over."

Martin looked alert.

"Ball game? Wasn't Gordon murdered near the baseball diamond?"

"Good thought, but wrong park. We checked on that. Hudson's son's game was in Central Valley on the other side of the freeway. Anyway, Sherry Gordon took Goodyear to her office to show him a district map, and Hudson was gone by the time they returned to the meeting room. Goodyear escorted Gordon to the parking lot and, hearing that she was going to investigate the dog-biting incident, he arranged to meet her at Fernie Park. Then he drove home and walked round to the ball diamond where Gordon had parked. He showed her the entrance to the trail where the incident had occurred, after which she set off down the path and he returned home."

"He didn't offer to escort her?"

"He says he would have gone with her, but he and his wife were expecting dinner guests, and Sherry insisted that she'd be fine on her own."

"So we have a married man on site at the appropriate time?"

"Yes, but other than their committee work, we haven't found anything to connect Goodyear to Gordon."

"And there was nothing on her voicemail or in her daybook to hint at an assignation?"

"No. There were messages from Jeffrey Arlington asking if anything interesting had come out of her trip to the park, and a message from Mark Hudson regarding the planning meeting—other than that, just a call from the secretary to see why she hadn't come in that morning. Her daybook listed nothing but routine appointments."

"So it's a dead end?"

"Seems to be. If Sherry Gordon had a secret life, she was as efficient at keeping it secret as she was about everything else she did."

◆   ◆   ◆

Sydney Broom steered his truck towards Fernie Park and smiled a beatific smile. He was greatly enjoying the bylaw amendment. His job as pound officer had been relatively boring when the dog park was legal, and it had been virtually impossible to get a conviction if an animal was troublesome because the off-leash bylaw had taken away the most specific clause that could be used to nail the owners. But now Sydney could enjoy the challenge of the chase. Every dog-walker was fair game, so each shift was sure to provide some action and a few tickets. There had been a lot of rain for the past two days, but now the sun was shining, and it was the kind of glorious Sunday morning guaranteed to inspire the locals and their canines to brave the great outdoors.

Sydney whistled as he drove down the hill to the parking lot at the bottom of the park. As he pulled round the corner, he saw an unmistakable sight—three in-the-bag citations—a trio of two-legged walkers steadily progressing across the grass, circled by a lean Doberman who was racing after swallows, a lithe sheepdog chasing a ball, and a black and white mongrel thundering alongside, running interference and barking hysterically.

Millie Jenkins and Jimmy Burgess did not hear the sound of the pound truck because the roar of the cars on the freeway drowned out all other noises, and they were intent on listening to Carrie MacVey's update on the progress of placards and T-shirts, but suddenly sensing another presence, Millie glanced across the parking lot and saw the officer climbing out from his vehicle. She grabbed Jimmy's arm and pointed.

"Damn," said Jimmy. "Quick, call the dogs."

Carrie, with great presence of mind, hurled her ball towards the bushes. Brandy shot after it, with Carrie in hot pursuit. Sydney sprinted in the same direction, for he could see that the others were having trouble retrieving their dogs and would have nowhere to retreat except the freeway, but by the time he reached the bushes, Carrie had most mysteriously disappeared. Irritated and perplexed, he turned towards Millie and Jimmy, but to his surprise, they too had vanished.

Sydney walked back to the field and scanned the area, but there was nobody in sight. By now thoroughly annoyed, he hopped back into his truck. *OK*, he thought, *this is war*. Normally, he didn't stoop so low as to drive the truck on the park trails, but his blood was up. He steered onto the gravel path and started up the main trail.

Hidden inside the culvert that ran below the freeway, Jimmy and Millie watched him leave.

"Look at that," hissed Jimmy. "Rotten sod. He's actually going to drive the trails. That's really hitting below the belt."

"How long do you think he'll be?" asked Millie, patting Beanie, who was getting restless, and making her sit.

"At least five minutes. Come on, we've got time to make it to the bushes. We'll cut up the ravine and go out via the top parking lot. Leave that," he added sharply to Maverick, who had unearthed the remains of a McDonald's chicken-burger. He nodded to Millie, and with the dogs at their side, they loped across the grass, plunged through the huckleberry bushes that covered the new trail, and disappeared from view.

Sydney continued his tour of the trails, his blood pressure steadily rising, for there was neither dog nor dog-walker anywhere in sight. Utterly frustrated and bewildered, because he knew that his quarry could not possibly have evacuated the hundred-acre area, he made another circuit, finally proceeding along the precipitous trail at the upper end of the park. To add to his annoyance, the gate was closed at the top entrance, so he was forced to go back. Slowly and carefully, for the two days of rain had made the area muddy and slippery, he reversed down the track, making sure that he stayed well in the centre and clear of the ditch that ran alongside the path. Sydney was not having a good day.

◆   ◆   ◆

The following Monday, Beary cornered Cindy Chan before the council meeting. Cindy was a good-natured councillor who had been elected on the basis of her volunteer work with the hospital. She had no party affiliations, no political axe to grind, and was also the possessor of a nippy and obnoxious Pomeranian—in Beary's eyes a mere appetizer dog and not worthy to be considered a canine—but Cindy doted on the little beast, so Beary regarded her as an ally.

"Look, Cindy," said Beary firmly, "now that we know Shelly's death was not the result of a dog attack, I'm going to ask Council to reconsider the repealing of the dog-park bylaw, so I need you to second the motion."

"No problem," said Cindy agreeably, "but do you really think you stand a chance? After all, there's still the complaint about the vicious dog. You know how nervous our colleagues are over the controversy."

"Once the motion's on the floor, I'll ask for the vote to be tabled for two weeks. The dog-walkers are going all out to try to get to the root of the problem, and in the meantime, I'll work on the rest of the councillors. We have three certain votes: you, me and Bob Green—he never walks in the park, but he has that unmanageable wolfhound that runs all over the place, so he hates leash bylaws because he's always getting tickets."

"Yes, but there's also strong opposition. The mayor has always been dead set against the dog park, so she sees the current furor as the perfect opportunity to get rid of it—so do Carlo Borelli and Janet Smith. They both hate dogs."

"That's the only thing those two agree on," grunted Beary. "The extreme left and the extreme right. There's a message in that," he mused. "Nice, reasonable people love their four-footed friends, but fanatics lack the necessary humanity to care about the animal kingdom."

"Well," said Cindy practically, "if we're three and three, you'll have to work on the ones who could go either way."

"Corinne Howe and Glen McNair are fair-minded. If it's proved that the hound terrorizing the park is an escapee from an adjacent property, they'll reconsider. That will be enough to take us over the top."

"Councillor Beary, you really should pay attention to the notices in your letter tray," sighed Cindy. "Corinne will be at a conference in Seattle in two weeks, and when she comes back, she's going to be off for another month because she's scheduled for hip surgery. So even if you get Glen on side, it'll be four-four, and a tie vote fails."

"Damn," said Beary. "That means I'll have to lobby Merve Billings, and he's such a wishy-washy wimp, he never takes a courageous stand on controversial issues."

"According to Mark Hudson, if you want to get around Merve, you have to make him believe he stands to lose a ton of votes unless he supports your cause. Merve gets elected on a very narrow margin, so it would only take the loss of one group of supporters for him to lose his seat. Mark threatens him with the wrath of the real-estate network when he wants to get a rezoning through. It works every time."

"Mark Hudson is too smart for his own good," growled Beary.

"Maybe," said Cindy, "but his tactics work. Janice Goodyear will be bombarding Merve with petitions and phone calls from the anti-dog brigade, so you'd better start thinking up a way to counter her manoeuvres or your dog park will be gone forever."

◆   ◆   ◆

The rain came back on Tuesday morning, but bad weather never deterred the dog-walkers. As Trixie Jones said, there was nothing as nice as a wet, windy day in the park when the joggers and fair-weather wimps stayed home and the dog-walkers had the place to themselves. This morning, the group that congregated by the footbridge was particularly euphoric because word had spread about the dogcatcher who had got stuck in the ditch on the weekend, requiring a tow-truck to extricate his vehicle.

While Jimmy Burgess and Carrie McVey crowed about their adventures evading Sydney Broom, Millie Jenkins watched the dogs playing on the field. Beanie and Sammy lay companionably side by side, each chewing on a stick, while Brandy and Maverick frolicked in and out of the creek. Millie sighed. It was such a happy scene, and being a gentle soul, she felt genuinely grieved that it was necessary to battle in order to keep something that was so obviously good.

A hail from Trixie Jones, who had materialized at the edge of the ravine trail, caused the others to pause in their conversation, and they turned to greet her as she approached. Nisha, unlike her owner, detested the rain, and she plodded across the grass, head drooping, and every ounce of her body language saying *is this journey really necessary?*

"Any word from Bertram?" Carrie demanded, as Trixie reached the bridge.

"He's down at the hall this morning. He's trying to talk sense into the Ubiquitous Vacillator." Trixie had so named Merve Billings because she considered him an incurable fence-sitter and abhorred the way he regularly weaselled his face into press pictures at community events.

"Good luck," said Jimmy. "That man won't come down in our favour, even if we do prove the vicious-dog incident wasn't connected to the dog park. He's totally gutless."

"It doesn't look very good, does it?" said Carrie.

"Don't lose heart," urged Trixie who, in spite of her brave words, was feeling rather despondent. "We have a game plan, so let's stick to it. The ravine path and the trillium trail are finished, and you and Ralph have worked like Trojans to get the connector through between them—and the other trails are well underway. Now we just have to track that wretched dog." She turned to Jimmy. "You and Millie are on tonight, aren't you? Let's hope you can find out something concrete so we can give Bertram some ammunition."

"What will you do if Council votes against his motion?" Millie asked.

"Well," said Trixie philosophically, "I'll give a rip-roaring speech that will appeal to their consciences and prime them for us to try again in a few months. When you have right on your side," she added, hitting her stride and taking on the militant tone that caused the heartiest politicians to quail, "you have to persevere in the hope that one day, you'll get your message through."

Ralph Johnson was feeding cookies to Beanie and Sammy, but he paused and looked up when Trixie raised her voice.

"What sort of rip-roaring speech?" he asked.

A solitary swallow swooped down and darted in front of Beanie's nose. Her head jerked up, and in one smooth movement, she pulled herself upright and went hurtling across the field. The swallow soared and dived, elatedly scooping up bugs from the grass, and the dog leapt and circled, completely caught up in the thrill of the chase. The exhilaration of both creatures was a joy to behold.

"Well," said Trixie, after watching Beanie's indefatigable determination to catch the bird, which always stayed just out of reach, "I shall call it 'In Search of the Swallows', because it seems to me that in the current political climate, justice is as elusive as that wretched bird."

◆   ◆   ◆

As Merve Billings left the Board of Variance meeting, he was surprised to see Beary waiting in the hall outside the council chamber.

"Be reasonable, Beary," said Merve, when he heard why Beary had waylaid him, "whenever there's a vicious-dog scare, the public always gets up in arms. And, by the way, Mrs. Goodyear isn't satisfied with the closure of the dog park. She's pushing for a total ban on dogs within the city limits—period. You dog-walkers will just have to compromise on having your pets but keeping them leashed."

"Don't be bloody ridiculous, man!" snapped Beary. "Dogs need exercise. How would you feel if Council put a ban on squash courts and tennis clubs?" Merve prided himself on his trim figure and his prowess with a racket.

"It's not the same," insisted Merve. "Besides, dog-owners are a relatively small segment of the community. As a councillor, I have to consider the sentiments of the rest of the population."

"By sentiments, of course, you mean votes."

"Well, one does have to be practical," said Merve prissily. "And," he added firmly, "the mayor has made her feelings quite clear on the subject."

"Yes, well, we wouldn't want to upset Queen Gwennie, would we? She might crown you with her gavel—not to mention oppose your nomination at your voters' association in the fall."

"That's most unfair, Beary. You know perfectly well that I respect Gwendolyn's opinions. She's a highly perspicacious woman."

Merve also prided himself on finding new words in the dictionary and using them on a daily basis until they became part of his vocabulary.

"Only when it comes to politics."

"Well, that's what we're about, isn't it?" purred Merve. His eyes lit up as he saw Paula Trentini come forth from the manager's office. Merve also fancied himself as something of a gallant. He ran his fingers through his chiselled curls. "Oh, Paula," he crooned, "could I have just a teeny moment of your time? You will excuse me, Beary, won't you?"

"No," said Beary, but Merve was already trotting down the hall at Paula's side.

The door of the council chamber opened and Jeffrey Arlington emerged, closely followed by Mark Hudson. The city manager was a handsome man in his mid-fifties, distinguished, meticulously correct in his manner and normally able to pull off the difficult feat of exuding bonhomie as well as authority, but today he looked tense. He noticed Beary and approached him directly.

"Councillor Beary, is there any further news on the investigation? My staff members keep asking me questions and I don't know what to tell them. Everyone is dreadfully upset."

"I haven't talked to Richard since last week," Beary told him. "I'm sure I'd have heard if there were any developments."

Arlington nodded.

"So no more nonsense about a married lover and a secret life. I find it appalling the way everyone gossips about Sherry now that she's dead."

Mark Hudson overheard and joined them.

"Come on, Jeffrey, be fair," he said. "All those lunches you had together—you must have noticed what an attractive woman she was. Is it not conceivable that she was murdered by a jealous lover?"

Arlington's brow darkened.

"It is far more likely that her death was a random attack due to the fact that she was in the wrong place at the wrong time. It all comes back to this situation with the dogs."

"Now wait a minute," objected Beary. "You can't be serious. There's no way the dog-walkers—"

"No, of course not," Arlington reassured him. "I'm not suggesting an irate dog-walker killed Sherry, but what about your theory that the vicious dog came from a drug house? What if during the course of her investigation in the park, Sherry inadvertently came across some thugs in the process of a drug deal?"

Beary acknowledged the validity of the point.

"Now, that is a possibility."

Mark nodded.

"Yes, but I'm still surprised that the police haven't come up with anything about her private life."

"They're trying," said Beary, "but the fact is, there's nothing to indicate that she had much of a personal life."

"Sherry kept a journal. Haven't the police looked through that?"

Arlington stiffened. "You mean her daybook. Of course they looked through it. The police took everything from her desk, plus all the files from every computer in the manager's office, including my own."

"This was on her laptop," said Mark. "Sherry used it to take notes at meetings, and I remember once seeing an item on the desktop labelled 'personal diary'. I asked her about it and she looked rather secretive and said it was a record of her private meetings. The police must have read the file."

"No," said Beary. "According to Richard, the only computers they checked were from the manager's office."

"But the police must have the laptop," insisted Mark. "She always took it home with her. I know she had it at the planning meeting because she left it in the council chamber when she took Harold Goodyear to look at the area maps. I have to admit I was itching to open the journal and take a peek."

Jeffrey Arlington looked shocked. His face had gone very pale.

"You didn't, did you?"

"No, of course not," said Mark. "But it was rather tempting."

Beary struck his forehead and swore.

"Damn," he said. "That's why Sherry's car was broken into. The bloody laptop was stolen—along with the evidence."

"Then it'll be trashed," stated Arlington decisively.

Mark Hudson shook his head.

"I doubt that," he said. "Computers have market value, and even if Sherry's laptop is sold, the original material can be lifted from the hard-drive. Therefore," he continued logically, "if the police trace the laptop, they'll not only have the local thugs who stole it, they'll also know the name of the lover. So it's really only a matter of time," he concluded. "Once they have that information, forensics should do the rest to determine whether Shelly's death was the result of 'crime of passion' or 'crime of pushers'. I'm going to call the cop shop and let them know the significance of the missing laptop."

He adjusted the papers under his arm, nodded to his boss and set off down the hall.

Jeffrey Arlington looked grim. "That young man is too clever for his own good. One of these days I'm going to have to do something about him."

◆   ◆   ◆

By seven o'clock the sun was setting, and on the trails of Fernie Park, the light was dim. Feeling guilty, because they were in the park without their dogs, Jimmy Burgess and Millie Jenkins huddled behind a salmonberry bush, twenty feet back from the trail that led into the park from Grant Street.

"It's eerie in the dark." Millie felt apprehensive. "I really don't like it here without my dog."

"I'll protect you," said Jimmy gallantly. "I've come equipped." He patted his pocket, which contained pepper spray and a Swiss army knife. "And you can whack the Hound of the Baskervilles with your umbrella if it charges."

"The umbrella isn't to hit the dog with," said Millie firmly. "I talked with the director of the SPCA, and he told me that pepper spray can actually incite an aggressive pit bull to attack because fighting dogs are trained in such a way that pain can make them even more determined. He told me that the best defence was to open an umbrella as they run at you, and they become confused because the target has suddenly disappeared."

"That's clever," said Jimmy. "Are you cold?" he added, noticing that Millie was shivering.

"A bit. I'll be all right."

Jimmy pulled off his scarf and slipped it solicitously over Millie's shoulders.

"Here," he said, "this should help."

Millie felt an instant warm glow, which was partially attributable to the scarf, and partly due to the fact that Jimmy's hands lingered a few seconds longer than necessary as he arranged it around her neck. She flushed, and murmured, "Thank you," but the magic of the moment was interrupted by a rustling overhead, and then, suddenly, wonderfully, the enchantment returned with a thrill of a different kind, for in a patch of light that filtered through the foliage, they saw an owl, majestically perched on the branch of an alder tree, its eyes gleaming and golden as it peered solemnly at the two humans huddled in the bushes below.

"Oh, look," exclaimed Millie. "How beautiful!"

"Very," agreed Jimmy, looking fondly at his companion. Millie's appreciation of simple pleasures gave her a glow that would have been worth millions if it could have been patented by the beauty industry.

Suddenly the owl stiffened, and with a flourish, it spread its wings and sailed away through the treetops. At the same moment, a faint sound from the path signalled the presence of another creature nearby.

"What's that jangling noise?" asked Millie. "It sounds almost metallic."

"It's a choke chain." Jimmy peered into the gloom. "Come on. I bet this is him."

"Be careful."

They crept forward; then Millie clutched at Jimmy's arm and pointed towards a gnarled, twisted hemlock further up the trail.

"Look," she whispered.

The light was fading rapidly and the wood was already bathed in shadows, but another ominous silhouette had materialized at the curve in the path. Then, without a sound, the shadow became fluid and began to glide eerily along the edge of the bushes.

"God, it's huge," grunted Jimmy. "That's no ordinary pit bull. It must be crossed with some kind of mastiff."

"Careful. He's seen us," hissed Millie.

The dog had paused and fixed its gaze on the salmonberry bush that shielded the two watchers. Millie shuddered inwardly, for in the last traces of sunlight trickling through the leaves, the beast's eyes burned red and glittered balefully, and though its body was a mere black outline against the dark bushes, she could tell that the animal had stiffened. Suddenly, a low growl emitted from the dog's throat.

"Oh, shit!" said Jimmy. "Get your brolly ready."

"If we don't move, it probably won't charge," Millie reassured him, but Jimmy had already shifted position, and the dog erupted into a volley of barks.

"It's OK, boy, calm down," urged Jimmy, inching slowly forward.

The animal retreated a few paces, but the barks became snarls as he lowered his body into a crouch.

"I think he's scared of us." Millie recognized fear in the animal's body language. "He's probably been abused."

"He can still turn our backsides into hamburger," retorted Jimmy. "Don't start feeling sorry for him. Watch out!" he yelped, as the dog lunged forward.

Millie stepped in front of Jimmy and pressed the button to release her umbrella. With a whoosh, it opened into a shield between her and the angry animal. Startled, the dog darted away; then it turned back, glowering malignantly from the far side of the trail. Keeping the umbrella between herself and the dog, Millie spoke gently and calmly.

"It's all right," she said. "We're not going to hurt you."

The dog took a couple of tentative paces towards her and growled softly.

"No," Millie said firmly. "Settle down, now. We're friends." The dog stared back at her, but she held her ground and waited. Then she took a cookie from her pocket and tossed it towards him. The animal flinched, and then inched forward to investigate the thing that had landed on the path. He sniffed, glanced up suspiciously, then after a moment, he picked up the cookie and ate it. He raised his head and eyed Millie curiously. She threw two more cookies and watched the dog devour them. When he finished eating, the mastiff looked back at her, and this time his expression was expectant. Millie threw one more cookie; then she held up the hand that was not holding the umbrella and showed the dog that her palm was empty.

"All gone," she said. "Go home now." She repeated the last order several times, pointing in the direction that he had come from, and after a moment, the dog turned and started back up the trail.

"Well done," said Jimmy with admiration. "Come on, let's see where he goes."

They set off after the dog, Millie still holding her umbrella open, and the strange procession moved along the trail. The mastiff occasionally turned to check on his pursuers, and then having decided they were not a threat, continued on his way. The end of the trail opened onto a grassy expanse that stretched between the woods and a dilapidated bungalow on a double lot at the end of Grant Street, and once on the green, the dog started to run. He shot across the field, and Millie and Jimmy emerged from the trees just in time to see him lope up the steps to the rear porch of the house. There was a gleam of light as the back door opened, and then the mastiff was gone from view.

"Well, I'm damned," said Jimmy. "That was so easy it was ridiculous."

"I know," agreed Millie. "You'd think someone from the city could have traced it instead of assuming the attack was a direct result of the off-leash area. Oh," she added, wrinkling her nose. "There's a skunk in the area. What an awful stench."

"That's no skunk," said Jimmy. "Look at those boarded windows. Trixie was right. The dog does live in a grow-op. The RCMP will be very happy to be handed an excuse to check that place out."

Millie suddenly looked solemn.

"What about the dog?" She furrowed her brow. "They might shoot it."

"Millie, you can't adopt every stray with a problem. We could warn the police, I suppose, and they might bring the SPCA along with a tranquillizer gun, but it's possible that the dog may be put down anyway."

"Well, let's let them know the dog might be salvageable," Millie insisted. "I know it couldn't be allowed to run loose, given its history, but with kind owners, and a fenced yard, and nice walks, albeit leashed and muzzled, it might be OK. At least give it a chance."

Jimmy rolled his eyes.

"I know who'll be at the shelter working with the blessed animal if they do manage to get him out in one piece," he groaned. "All right," he conceded, seeing Millie's pleading expression, "I'll call them."

He pulled out his cell phone and gave Millie a big smile. "This has been a good night's work, hasn't it? We should make an evening of it and celebrate."

"Oh, yes," murmured Millie. "That would be nice. We could go fetch the dogs and bring them back for a walk."

"Actually," said Jimmy, as he dialled the police station, "I was rather thinking of something else. I have a very nice Chardonnay back at the house, and I'm sure the dogs would be perfectly happy to hang out together and watch us drink it."

"Oh," said Millie, blushing. "Well, that would be nice too."

◆   ◆   ◆

The raid on the grow-op proved rewarding, producing not only an abundance of marijuana plants, but also a sizable store of stolen goods. These included Sherry Gordon's laptop, complete with the file that revealed Jeffrey Arlington to be her secret lover. After reading the explicit details of the relationship, laid out in meticulous detail in the journal, the police searched Arlington's home and work-place. In his office, they found the evidence they needed. When the raincoat that Arlington kept at work for use in emergencies was sent to the lab, traces of Sherry Gordon's blood were found on the sleeve.

The news of Arlington's arrest swept around city hall, and staff and politicians alike were stunned. Beary himself was so amazed he called his son to get confir-mation of the news.

"Has he admitted to the murder?" he asked abruptly, when Richard came on the line.

"No," Richard answered. "He says he hasn't worn the coat in weeks. He only keeps it there in case of a sudden change in the weather. But then he would say that, wouldn't he?"

"What about the affair?"

"He denies that too. He insists he knows nothing about it. If it weren't for that damming file, I'd wonder if someone hadn't used his coat to frame him, but there's no doubt, Dad. It has to be him. He's obviously a superb actor and a very smooth liar."

"Could I have a look at the file?"

"Yes, I could arrange that. I'd be interested in your take on the situation."

"I'll come down right away."

"You'd better make it later," Richard suggested. "I'll be in a meeting this morning, and you aren't capable of finding your way around a computer without assistance."

"Not a problem," Beary assured him blithely. "I can manage perfectly well without you."

He hung up and set off down the hall in the direction of the Finance Department, and half-an-hour later, with the able assistance of Harry Salai, he was poring over the personal file in Sherry Gordon's laptop.

◆   ◆   ◆

The first time I met Jeffrey Arlington was before I came to city hall as assistant manager. I was on holiday in Ontario and I'd gone into the Arlington Bay store to get my watch repaired, and there he was, on the far side of the jewellery counter. We started chatting, and discovered we were both from B.C., and when we introduced ourselves, we laughed about the coincidence of names given the place where we were meeting. Jeffrey was so charming. He was in Toronto for a conference on urban planning, and when he discovered that I was a senior employee in the manager's office in Nelson, he suggested I come to the Lower Mainland and apply for a similar job. He told me he was married, but it didn't matter.

"Oh dear," said Beary. "That seems pretty conclusive."

"Where's Arlington Bay?" asked Harry.

"It'll be some dinky little town on Lake Ontario. Our no-longer-venerable city manager is from one of those bigwig Toronto families that have everything named after them from hospitals to mountain peaks."

"A jewellery counter in a small-town general store?"

"I guess that's why they're called general stores," said Beary. "Let's read on."

After a couple of entries, Beary spoke again.

"I just can't visualize it," he muttered. "It's obvious where they're heading. It's as if Arlington was a split personality, business-like one minute, and coming-on strong the next. Let's skip to the end. I want to read what she says in her last entry."

Harry scrolled down to the end of the document. The final entry was dated three days before Sherry Gordon's death.

Jeffrey's wife is going to Vancouver Island tomorrow, which means we can spend the night together. So it's now or never. I have to make him understand that the secrecy is at an end. We're both secure in our positions and a divorce isn't going to ruin his career prospects. It's time for me to force his hand, and if he isn't prepared to tell his wife about us, then I will. I wonder how he will react. He can be so warm and loving, but there's a cold and hard side to him under the smooth surface. Still, I know things about him that could make his life very difficult, so I think he'll understand that his future lies with me.

"Not only a bulldozer, but a very foolish woman," grunted Beary. "She apparently didn't understand that the same hard-nosed tactics she used to push her agendas at the hall wouldn't work in a personal relationship."

"Let's scroll back," suggested Harry. "We've skipped the hot stuff. Arlington seemed such a puritan. I want to see what they got up to."

"Harry, you shock me," said Beary. "I thought the only thing that excited you was computers. Yes, good idea," he added. "Run back a bit."

Harry went back several pages. "This looks promising," he said, nodding to a paragraph in the middle of the screen. "Wow," he added after a moment. "They believed in covering their tracks, didn't they? Every tryst at a different motel! I'm impressed."

"It's very surprising," Beary acknowledged.

"I never knew the old man had it in him. He sounds so young and vigorous. I must say, Sherry's comparing their affair to Anthony and Cleopatra is a bit much. I know she liked Shakespeare, but I would never have thought of Sherry Gordon as Queen of the Nile. Come to that, I'd have thought old Arlington would be better cast as an aging Caesar, but after reading about his antics in the bedroom, I have to reassess. He must be in better shape than he looks."

He started to scroll down again, but Beary stopped him.

"Just a moment. Go back. There! Stop. Well, I'm damned. Look at that."

He pointed to the words on the screen. "*How goes it with my brave Jeffrey Anthony?*"

"It's a quote," said Harry, "but she's slipped Arlington's name in by mistake—or maybe it was deliberate."

"Yes," said Beary thoughtfully. "Exactly. Maybe it *was* deliberate. Just a minute—let me think. We've both been struck by the fact that Arlington sounds so different in this document, at least in the sections about the private meetings. Could someone have tampered with the text? Is there some way that the name would have popped up in the wrong place if someone had altered the document? I mean, how would you go about it if you wanted to change the name of someone in a computer file?"

"That's easy. You use the 'edit/replace' feature. Then you hit 'replace all' and the entire document is changed."

"But why would that one error occur?"

Harry paused.

"Well, obviously the line was supposed to read 'Mark Anthony', so that means that the name that had been replaced throughout the entire document would have to be 'Mark'."

Beary nodded grimly. "Now it's starting to make sense."

Harry turned to Beary, wide-eyed. "Oh, my, I've just thought of something. Hold on, let me go back to the beginning."

He started to scroll rapidly back through the document until he reached the opening paragraph. He pointed at the first lines. "Remember how I was surprised that there was a jewellery counter in a general store. Look at that. There's nothing to indicate that Sherry met her lover in a small town; in fact the only specific location mentioned is Toronto. Now, if I'd wanted to replace a name with Jeffrey Arlington, I'd have had to use 'replace all' twice—once for Jeffrey, and once for Arlington. So if Arlington Bay doesn't refer to a general store in a dinky lakeshore town, but a department store in Toronto, you see what would it be?"

"Yes," said Beary. "Hudson Bay. Our killer is Mark Hudson."

◆　　　◆　　　◆

On the following Monday, the council chamber was full twenty minutes prior to the start of the meeting and the citizens who could not find seats were overflowing into the hallway. The atmosphere was highly charged, both from the dog-lovers, all sporting *Multiculturalism includes Mutti-culturalism* T-shirts, and from the staff and councillors who were jostling for space to talk with Beary and bursting with questions about the arrest of Mark Hudson. Even the reporters on the press table looked more alert than usual.

"Are the rumours true?" Cindy Chan asked Beary. "Was Mark Hudson taking bribes?"

"Evidently. And that's what Sherry Gordon was holding over him. When Hudson killed her, he not only eliminated a troublesome mistress, he was covering his tracks. If he'd simply deleted the file instead of using it to set up Jeffrey Arlington, he'd have probably got away with it."

Merve Billings looked appalled.

"I often wondered about Hudson's ethics," he piped indignantly, "but I never dreamed he was capable of anything so wicked—and to take Arlington's raincoat too—I mean, he could have framed any one of us. It's unthinkable."

"True," said Beary, looking towards the end of the table where Jeffrey Arlington, pale, but dignified, was taking his usual place in readiness for the council meeting. "But then, you weren't in his way. You may have wondered about the way Hudson operated, but he found it easy to control you. Arlington was upright, shrewd and utterly incorruptible, and he had Hudson sized up pretty well. He'd have cottoned onto the bribes before too much longer, so Hudson aimed to kill two birds with one stone, so to speak, and discredit him while he had the chance."

"I'm still a bit confused," said Merve. Beary bit his lip and refrained from uttering the comment that came to mind. Oblivious to Beary's less-than-complimentary train of thought, Merve continued. "I thought Mark was at his son's ball game. I know the physical distance between the two parks isn't great, but the freeway bisects them, and it was rush hour. How did Mark get to Fernie Park?"

"He was wearing a track suit and had the raincoat in his backpack. He slipped away once the game started and ran along the jogging trail. Right opposite Fernie Park, there's a culvert that goes under the freeway. It's only a short distance from the trails on either side. The coyotes go back and forth that way all the time. Hudson went through the culvert, jogged up the hill and was lying in wait, wearing Arlington's raincoat, when Sherry came down the trail. After he killed her, he took off the raincoat and ran back the same way. He'd only have been away from the game for fifteen minutes or so. No one would have noticed his absence because all the parents were intent on the game, and people were spread out around the field."

"How did the police get Mark to confess?" Cindy asked. "They didn't have any proof."

"Yes, they did. After we showed Richard the discrepancy in the file, we were wondering how to proceed, when Harry suddenly realized he had the solution back in his office. Sherry's laptop had been acting up the previous month, so she'd given it to Harry to sort out, and before he started playing around with it, he downloaded all her files onto a CD."

"So he had the original file all the time?"

"Yes ... well, up to the date of the computer malfunction, but that was quite enough. When we saw the original, we realized how clever Hudson had been. He'd taken legitimate mentions of Arlington and combined them with sections with his own name. The first paragraph mentioned Hudson introducing Sherry to Arlington at the conference and went on to say that Arlington offered Sherry the job here—so Hudson sliced out the bit about the introduction and it sounded as if the job offer had come out of the meeting with the lover. Basically he cut anything that contradicted the impression he was trying to create, then finished up by replacing his name with Arlington's, and if it hadn't been for Sherry's Shakespearean quote, we'd never have twigged."

"The Bard strikes again," said Merve, waxing philosophical. "Sherry would have been rather pleased that good old Will Shakespeare helped trap her killer. What was it he said? 'Murder, though it have no tongue, will speak.' *Macbeth*, I think."

"*Hamlet*," corrected Beary.

Cindy Chan was more interested in practicalities.

"It would have taken a couple of hours for Mark to amend that file," she said. "How did he manage? Sherry always had her laptop with her."

"Two days before Hudson killed Sherry, they spent the night together. He copied the file onto a disc while she was asleep. Then he edited it on his own computer, resaved the amended file, and replaced the original with the new version when Sherry left her laptop unattended in the council chamber after the planning meeting."

"Tricky," said Merve.

"Yes," agreed Beary. "Well, I always said Mark Hudson was too clever for his own good."

There was a flurry of movement at the far end of the hall as a cluster of people came out of the stairwell and forged their way through the crowd.

"Oh, Lord," muttered Merve. "Here comes that Jones woman. I've said I'll co-operate, but I don't need an earful from her. Good God," he added, "what on earth is she carrying? It looks like a giant dog biscuit. I'm heading for my seat." He ducked into the council chamber and made a beeline for his chair.

Beary stayed in the doorway and watched as Trixie Jones, trailed by two eager reporters who were attempting to interview her, marched down the corridor. She flashed Beary a Cheshire-cat-has-swallowed-the-mouse smirk and joined him in the doorway.

"All set, Councillor Beary?" she demanded.

"Without a doubt," said Beary.

"How on earth did you do it?" she whispered, turning her back on the two reporters who were attempting to project their ears around her placard.

Beary looked smug. He leaned in close and murmured in Trixie's ear.

"Sherry Gordon's laptop provided the solution to more than the mystery of her murder," he said. "Just as Harry was shutting it down, I noticed an icon labelled 'Sponsor List'. It turns out that Bow-Wow Dog Chow paid for the cost of the ball diamond, with the proviso that there would be a plaque with the company name on the perimeter fence. They considered the sponsorship good advertising because the facility was adjacent to the dog park."

Trixie appeared baffled.

"I don't see the connection. The diamond is in place. They can't take back their money."

"No, but they'd agreed to two more major sports sponsorships in other parks where there were off-leash areas, but of course, with the bylaw reversed, those sponsorships were in jeopardy. I simply pointed out to Merve that if the junior-league sports lobby turned against him, he'd be out on his ear in the next election, and that did the trick."

"Oh, well done," said Trixie. "Now, to the fray. I'd better join my group. They're pretty keyed up because I didn't let any of them know that our win was a foregone conclusion."

She stared at the rows of paw-imprinted T-shirts and frowned at the couple sitting at the end of the second row. "Why on earth are Millie Jenkins and Jimmy Burgess smiling like complete idiots?" she said sharply. "They don't know the outcome yet."

"Better get in," urged Beary, seeing Gwendolyn Pye emerge from the stairwell. "Mrs. Thatcher, the sequel, is coming down the hall. Woe betide anyone who detracts from *her* entrance."

Trixie nodded. She hoisted her placard, sailed into the council chamber and installed herself in the seat that Henry had saved for her in the front row. Beary straightened his jacket and adjusted his tie. Then, with a seraphic smile, and deliberately ignoring the suspicious look that Mayor Pye gave him as she approached, he strolled into the room and took his place at the council table.

There were times, he thought, that the political process was truly rewarding.

Gilda Died for Love

Natalia Petrenko had no intention of dying for love. Gilda was one of her most celebrated roles, but unlike the operatic heroine who sacrificed herself to save the man she adored, Natalia believed that the men in her life were there to serve her, and not the other way around. With a wealthy husband to provide for her material needs and a series of lovers to cater to her other requirements, Natalia's life had been as comfortable as a luxury cruise. But recently there had been a few ominous ripples on the ocean's surface. Her husband was as courteous as ever, but there was something subtly different in his manner—an absence of some hard-to-define quality, like the wind quietly disappearing before a storm—that rendered her uneasy; and her current paramour was proving tedious. The passion and intensity that made Andrei Narumoff a fine Rigoletto also caused him to be jealous and volatile, and the scene he had thrown at Luigi's studio that morning had been witnessed by far too many people. Natalia's husband had always amiably turned a blind eye to her occasional adventures, but the one thing he would not tolerate was indiscretion, and she was beginning to be concerned that his current excessive politeness might be the prelude to rough waters. *Yes*, thought Natalia, *Andrei would have to go.*

◆　　　◆　　　◆

"I can't imagine her singing Gilda," remarked Philippa Beary, as she followed Robin Tremayne down the steps of Luigi Bosci's brownstone. "The Queen of the Night, now *that* I could believe. The way she laid into that Russian basso was scary."

"She's actually a wonderful Gilda," Robin replied, "though she's spectacular in the Mozart role too."

"So what you're saying is that she can act as well as sing."

"Exactly. This way," Robin added, stepping out into the intersection. "We'll walk alongside the light-rail line and then cut down to the waterfront. There's a fabulous deli a few blocks away."

"The light's red."

"Doesn't matter. Nobody pays attention to the 'don't walk' signs. The Jersey City side is much more laid back than Manhattan."

"It's pretty," Philippa commented, observing the brick houses with vibrantly painted doors. Black wrought-iron railings surrounded miniscule gardens where pansies were already in bloom, and even the street lamps and garbage bins matched the ironwork on the buildings.

She looked around with pleasure. The weather was already warm, but where the street was lined with brownstone residences, there was shade and a cool breeze. Tiny stores nestled amid the apartments, and the pedestrians that sparsely dotted the sidewalk seemed relaxed and unhurried.

"Luigi's studio must be near where my parents are staying," Philippa mused. "They're at the RV Park in Liberty Harbour."

"That's only a few blocks back," Robin told her. "We can head that way after lunch. There's a PATH station close to the RV Park."

"No point," said Philippa. "They're already out seeing the sights. Now that my mother has retired, she's putting all her ferocious energy into travel. You wouldn't believe the itinerary she and Dad have planned. In six weeks, they're covering thousands of miles and devouring more tourist destinations than most people see in a lifetime."

"Ah well," Robin reminded her, "their trip has provided you with a wonderful holiday. I think it's great that they offered to fly you out to join them for their two weeks in New York."

"True—and it's really nice of you to put me up. Your apartment is much more comfortable than the top bunk in a twenty-two-foot motor-home."

"Don't thank me. It's lovely to have you here. Besides, you need cheering up with Adam away all year. How's he doing, by the way? Does he call you?"

"Not much," Philippa admitted gloomily. "The odd email—every message makes it obvious he's having a fabulous time."

"Then you'd better have a fabulous time in his absence."

"I intend to. And there couldn't be a better antidote for depression than New York. The best part will be getting to see you in the opera. I can't believe I'm going to be sitting in the grand tier at the Lincoln Centre tomorrow night! We really appreciate you lining up the tickets for us. Mum and Dad said to thank you, by the way."

"Not at all. There was a block of seats available for friends and family, so it was easy to arrange. You're going to love *Rigoletto*. It's an incredible cast—Petrenko, Narumoff, Marco Rubini—all top-notch."

"Rubini's wonderful. He gave a concert in Vancouver last year. What's he like offstage?"

"Total letch," said Robin. "He's right in character playing the Duke. He hits on everyone he works with. Right now he's working on Mary-Anne James—she's singing Maddalena. Not that he'll get anywhere with her—she's wildly in love with her husband, and that's hardly surprising. She's married to Daniel James."

"The newsman. He's gorgeous!"

"Exactly. Rubini doesn't stand a chance, but that doesn't stop him from trying."

"I'm surprised he hasn't made a play for Petrenko."

"Oh, he has. He and Natalia had a thing going a few years back."

"Good heavens! You mean Gilda has a stormy relationship with both leading men?"

"No. Rubini gets along with Natalia. The only thing that was hurt when she dumped him was his vanity. But Narumoff is another story. Totally different temperament—she plays him like a fish, and he storms and rages, but always comes back to her. He's so young, in spite of that amazingly mature voice. He's come up the hard way. His family was poor—his father died young and his mother worked and slaved and went into debt to pay for his training—but now that he's on the brink of a spectacular career, Natalia is destroying him. Last Friday was torture backstage. Natalia was in one of her manic-triumphant moods and she'd been disgustingly cruel to Narumoff, but then she called him into her dressing room forty-five minutes before the curtain. Her dresser was dismissed and came out looking like thunder, and according to Rubini, there were unmistakable noises emanating from the room."

"They had another fight?"

"Just the opposite. Rubini took a lewd delight in being quite graphic on the subject."

"So Natalia and Narumoff made up?"

"I suppose so, but look at the ding-dong row they had today at the studio. How long can it go on?"

"Well," declared Philippa, "it'll be quite something to see them perform as father and daughter after hearing that screaming lover's tiff. What a difference from Petrenko's public image. Everything I've read makes her sound so respectable—a brilliant artist with a blissful marriage to a billion-dollar electronics mogul. I'm amazed her husband puts up with her."

"Probably too busy to notice," Robin surmised. "Malcolm Gordon never comes to the opera. When he isn't tied up with corporate business, he's a big-time hunter and collector. Their apartment is full of all kinds of exotic artefacts and creatures he's brought back from different parts of the world. He specializes in snakes and spiders."

"Well, he certainly doesn't need a tiger," Philippa observed. "Not while he's got Petrenko. I'd be terrified working on stage with her. You must have nerves of steel."

"I stay out of her way," said Robin. "Fortunately I'm singing Countess Ceprano, so we're never on stage at the same time. Cut down here," she added. "We'll go along the waterfront."

The light-rail train rattled by as Philippa followed Robin around the corner and down to a wide promenade where the Colgate Clock overlooked the Hudson River and a cluster of fishermen lined the railings. The Goldman Sachs Tower loomed overhead, but it was the view on the far side of the river that made Philippa gasp, for as she emerged from the shadow of the tall buildings, she saw the magical, yet familiar, postcard view of Manhattan across the water.

Robin was already on the promenade, so Philippa tore her eyes from the river and caught up. The two friends strolled along the waterfront, past the heart-rending statue of the bayoneted solider that commemorated Polish victims of the Katyn Massacre, and the simpler, yet no less disturbing, 9/11 memorial, draped with personal possessions and pictures of Jersey City residents who died when the World Trade Center came down. The sun was hot, and Philippa looked enviously at an elegant blonde who paraded an umbrella that served as a parasol.

"Now there's a lady with style," noted Robin. "A modern-day Musetta. Wouldn't I love to get my hands on that part," she added wistfully.

"I hope the management gives you some substantial roles soon." Philippa spoke from the heart. "We were all ecstatic when you won the auditions and got a New York contract, but you're far too good to be relegated to the assorted three-liner maids, nuns or friends of the heroine that abound in opera. Ceprano isn't even your voice part."

"I know, but I did it for Vancouver Opera last year, so I know the part, and I've got the weight in my voice to carry it off. Unfortunately, other than Richard Strauss, most composers limit their operas to one principal soprano role. But speaking of Strauss, I've been assigned a nymph in *Ariadne* next season, and if that goes well, I'll have a much stronger foothold in the company. Besides, I'm getting coaching from Luigi Bosci, and that alone is worth the trip to New York. Can you imagine having the same singing teacher as Natalia Petrenko, not to mention the buzz from treading the boards in the Lincoln Centre? Life is very exciting."

Philippa smiled.

"I can imagine. It was a huge thrill for me just auditing your coaching session. Who was the attractive young man accompanying your lesson?" she added speculatively.

Robin blushed.

"That's Timothy Mason—he's a fabulous accompanist—one of the best. He's studying to be a conductor. He's going to be great, you wait and see. He's brilliantly talented, but unlike so many of the mega-gifted individuals in this business, he's kind and decent and a generally wonderful guy."

"Wow! You really like him, don't you?"

"Yes. A lot. Much good it does me. I only exist for him as a singing machine."

"Nothing outside the studio?"

"Oh no, we see each other socially all the time. We go for coffee or lunch at the deli, and we have a wonderful time talking opera, and we've taken in the odd show together. We're the best of friends, but that's all. Never a pass—never a hint of flirtation—he's the perfect gentleman."

"Punctiliously courteous and depressingly correct."

"Yes. The fact is," Robin explained sadly, "he's another one that Natalia chewed up and spat out. He came here from the West Coast three years ago, and I'm told he was engaged to a girl who plays violin in the Seattle Opera orchestra, but the minute he arrived, Natalia took one look at him and set to work. He was dazzled. She kept him enslaved for almost a year, and then she simply discarded him. He's had his fingers badly burned."

"And the fiancée back home?"

"Still hovering and waiting for him, according to the girls in the chorus. I gather they still keep in touch. Just up here," Robin added, pointing in the direction of the Essex Station. On the corner was a small deli. Above the glass front door hung a green marquee decorated with a design of an amiable-looking cow. Philippa followed Robin across the street and into the shop.

"You'd better incorporate some love songs into your coaching repertoire," she laughed as they entered the deli.

"Oh, I already do. I've tried Lehar and Friml and Victor Herbert. You wouldn't believe the passion and intensity I can invest into 'Some Day' and 'Kiss Me Again', but all Tim does is praise me. He never leaps off the piano stool and sweeps me into his arms."

"Good job. Luigi Bosci would have a fit."

The girls dissolved into hysterics, earning a glare from a blue-suited woman who was bent over a laptop at the table near the ATM machine and a broad smile from the handsome Italian waiter at the create-your-own-salad bar.

"Oh, my God, scrumptious!" cried Philippa, gazing at the counters laden with an enormous assortment of savouries and sweets. "How on earth am I supposed to decide between a gourmet salad, catfish, or a grilled eggplant-parmigiana sandwich? It's not even that expensive. You're going to have to bring me here every day."

"And just think," said Robin cheerfully, "you haven't even started on Manhattan yet."

◆   ◆   ◆

After lunch, Robin accompanied Philippa to the PATH Station and instructed her how to navigate her way to Times Square once she reached the far side of the river. With the aid of a friendly commuter, Philippa managed to find the right train, and having been identified as a tourist by her fellow travellers, was solicitously directed where to get off at the other end. When she ascended to ground level at the Thirty-third Street Station, her initial reaction was surprise and a strange sense of familiarity, for she found herself facing the same chain stores that line Robson Street in Vancouver. But as she continued to survey the scene, she noticed Macy's looming in solitary splendour above Banana Republic and Aldo, and gradually she tuned in to the details that differentiated East Coast from Pacific Rim. As she did so, New York came to life before her eager and receptive eyes.

The road was a sea of yellow cabs, and the ethnic variations in the milling crowds were Hispanic and Afro-American rather than Asian. She observed that there was a notable lack of panhandlers and a preponderance of cheerful-looking policemen. The architecture of the older establishments pre-dated anything she had seen in the West, and there was something in the air—perhaps it was as simple as the fact that she was on holiday—but there was a vibrancy that made her feel incredibly alive. She walked down the street, trying to orient herself and remember Robin's instructions; then suddenly she stopped short, staring at the plaque on the side of the building in front of her. Bug-eyed, she leaned her head back and strained to look upwards. She was standing in front of the Empire State Building.

The thrill of the moment was shattered when her cell phone rang. Philippa fished the phone out of her purse and answered the call.

She flinched as her mother's voice barked into her ear.

"Philippa, where are you? We've been waiting for fifteen minutes." Before Philippa could reply, her mother continued. "We're heading to the St. James Theatre to buy tickets for tomorrow's matinée. We'll wait for you there."

Philippa made her way to Times Square; then she meandered through the theatre district, negotiating the crowds where the omnipresent *Phantom* continued its inexorable run and pausing to examine the posters outside the theatre where Julia Roberts was making her Broadway debut. She stopped to purchase a set of NYPD salt-and-pepper shakers from one of the ubiquitous gift shops, the perfect gift for her brother, then cut through a poster-lined alley and emerged to find herself in front of the St. James Theatre. Delighted to see that the lunacy of Monty Python had made it to New York, she leaned back to enjoy the colourful murals above the marquee where *Spamelot* was playing. A sudden surge in the crowds on the sidewalk forced her to retreat, and as she moved back, she collided with a solid figure and turned to see her father. He was holding a camera.

"Where did they all come from?" Philippa gasped.

"The matinée just ended," explained a friendly tourist who was carried forward on the tide of humanity. "After the show, the side walls of the theatre open to become extra exits to the street."

"Interesting city, this," said Beary, his city councillor's mind stimulated by the prospect of a new and novel form of crowd control. A shrill hail from the road interrupted his deliberations.

"Was that Mum?" Philippa asked. "Where is she?"

Beary nodded toward the street. Edwina was tucked under the arm of a tall, blonde, exceptionally good-looking policeman.

"My God, what's happened to her?" exclaimed Philippa. "Am I seeing right? Mum wearing jeans and a ball cap?"

"She's gone quite mad since she retired," said Beary gloomily, moving to the edge of the pavement and raising his camera. "It's going to cost me a fortune. She's been doing her Christmas and birthday gift shopping in every tourist trap from Mount Rushmore to the Statue of Liberty, and now she's decided that the family souvenirs have to be bought from Tiffany's."

"Actually, she looks pretty good in that outfit." Philippa eyed her mother critically. "She's lost weight too. The new look might herald a more laid-back Edwina. Maybe she'll be easier to live with."

"Not a chance—she's every bit as bossy, just enjoying herself more."

Beary snapped the picture and lowered his camera. Edwina smiled graciously at her policeman, took him firmly by the arm, and led him to meet her family.

"This nice young officer is Bill Gunsen," she informed them. "He has a married sister who lives in Vancouver and she's visiting here too. She's an opera fan, so I'm sure she'd love to meet you and Robin," she told Philippa. "Maybe you young people could get together one evening."

The policeman shook Beary's hand and gave Philippa an intensely admiring gaze that sent a sudden glow rushing through her, followed by a vague feeling of disloyalty to Adam, which was immediately replaced by a surge of rebellion. She flashed her most potent stage smile at the young officer, but before she could speak, an Amazon in hiking shorts and a tent-like floral top whisked him away with a request for a photograph, and Philippa was left beaming at thin air.

"Nice job," said Beary. "Spends his whole day having pictures taken with tourists."

"Are you coming with us to Tiffany's, darling?" demanded Edwina, turning to Philippa.

"Why not?" Philippa shrugged. She could see that the line-up for Officer Gunsen was increasing by the minute, and the expression that had made her feel special was being replicated for every tourist that begged his attention.

"Come on, then," ordered Edwina. "We've bought our theatre tickets, and we've still got time to visit the Fifth Avenue stores."

"I don't want to go shopping," said Beary mutinously. "I want a hot dog. You can't go to New York and not have a hot dog."

"You can get one in Central Park. We'll go there after Tiffany's."

"That's thirty blocks away," protested Beary.

"We'll take a cab." Edwina marched to the edge of the sidewalk.

"Look at her," grumbled Beary. "Two days in New York, and she already considers any yellow car to be her personal limo—*and* she backseat drives the cabbies. And how am I supposed to afford a jaunt to Fifth Avenue when she's spending half our budget on cab fares?"

As her mother flagged down a taxi, Philippa gave her father a sympathetic smile.

"Accept defeat, Dad," she advised. "There isn't a woman in the world that would pass up a chance to go shopping in New York. You're outnumbered on this one."

Beary reluctantly followed his wife and daughter into the taxicab, and they set off Uptown. The driver deposited his passengers outside Tiffany's, glowered at Edwina's departing back and offered Beary a commiserative glance in exchange for his tip. Philippa followed close on her mother's heels, and by the time Beary entered the store, both mother and daughter were staring, mesmerized, at a spectacular display of sapphires and diamonds laid out under glass in the first counter. Beary fell back a few paces and had a brief word with the uniformed doorman, then hastened forward and took his wife's arm.

"Third floor for us," he dictated. "I asked the doorman which department carried the under-hundred-dollar items."

"You really are embarrassing," snapped Edwina. "I know the silver fashion jewellery is on the third floor, but there's no reason why Philippa and I can't enjoy exploring the main floor. Haven't you any desire to see how the billionaires live?"

"No," said Beary. "Come on, the elevator is at the back of the store."

"Don't be a spoil sport, Dad," coaxed Philippa, still siding firmly with her mother. "Look at that emerald choker, Mum. Have you ever seen anything like it?"

"Maybe the grey-haired gent over there will buy it for his lady friend," suggested Beary, nodding towards a counter near the elevator. "He looks like he's ready to throttle her."

"Good heavens!" Philippa blurted out. "That's Natalia Petrenko. I bet that's her husband with her."

"Who?"

"The soprano we're going to see tomorrow evening. She's singing Gilda."

"Doesn't look like the sort of female who'd die for love," observed Beary, noting the soprano's high colour and dangerously glittering eye.

"Come on, Mum," said Philippa, curiosity causing her to do an immediate about-face. "Dad's right. Let's head up to the third floor."

She sauntered towards the rear of the store, keeping her eyes on the elevator but her ears tuned to the clarion-clear tones of the soprano, who appeared to be berating her companion about the purchase of a diamond bracelet for someone called Mariana. A smartly attired sales attendant, clearly the culprit who had let the cat out of the bag, cowered in the background. As Philippa reached the elevator, Petrenko continued to rage, oblivious to the presence of anyone else in the store, but her companion dropped his voice, and no matter how hard Philippa strained to hear, his words were drowned by the hysterical accusations of his wife. Philippa pressed the button to call the car to the main floor, and suddenly the prima donna became aware that she had an audience. She glowered at Philippa and fell silent.

"Very uncouth," muttered Edwina, joining her daughter at the elevator. "I hope she's nicer on stage than off."

"According to Robin, Petrenko is dazzling in performance," Philippa told her, "but it sounds as if her private life is even more exciting than her operatic roles."

"I think her private life is about to come crashing about her ears," said Beary, catching up to his wife and daughter as the elevator door slid open. "As I went by, I heard hubby tell her that he was going to Washington and that things would be settled when he returned. He sounded like he meant business, because I distinctly heard the word, 'pre-nup'. It was definitely a threat."

The third floor, unlike the main floor, was humming with tourists, and with the able assistance of the friendly staff, Edwina made the rounds of the various counters, acquired a variety of pendants, earrings and money clips for children and grandchildren, and bought a particularly stylish chain-link necklace for herself. Once her purchases were complete, she demanded a plain white bag to carry them in, since she had no intention of strolling along the streets of Manhattan parading a Tiffany's bag, and then she declared herself ready to leave. Philippa grinned at her father's dazed expression as the elevator carried them back to the main floor. When the doors opened, Edwina forged ahead, sailed out the front entrance and waved her bagful of loot at the uniformed doorman.

"Breakfast," she quipped, with a dazzling smile.

"Good God!" said Beary. "She made a joke."

"She has to bust loose once in her life," Philippa pointed out.

"Bust loose? She just spent four thousand dollars in thirty minutes! How long is this insanity going to last?"

"Probably until you get back to Vancouver and the bills start coming in. Give her a couple of months and she'll be right back to normal."

"That's hardly encouraging," Beary said glumly. He turned to the doorman as they left the store. "What is there in the way of restaurants around here?" he asked. "Someplace I can afford after visiting your store."

Philippa did not hear the doorman's answer because her attention was caught by a figure that hurried past them and headed down the street. She clutched at her father's arm.

"That looked like Robin's accompanist," she exclaimed. "I heard him play at Luigi Bosci's studio."

The doorman flashed white teeth in a disarming smile.

"That's right, Miss," he said. "That's Timothy Mason. He's a fine musician, that young man."

"I'm surprised he can afford to shop at Tiffany's," said Philippa.

The doorman leaned towards her and whispered confidentially.

"It's a very special occasion. He told me so himself. He's been buying an engagement ring for the lady he's going to marry."

Philippa's heart sank. Robin was heading for heartache.

◆　　　◆　　　◆

When Philippa arrived at the Lincoln Centre the following evening, she made her way to the opera house and located her parents in the downstairs bar. She picked out her mother right away, for Edwina was resplendent in a glittering lilac cocktail dress. A moment later she saw her father, who was munching a sandwich and appeared oblivious to the crush in the bar. A large Scotch stood on the high round table in front of him. He appeared to be in good humour, unlike Edwina, whose elegant appearance was marred by a glazed expression.

"She finally found a cab driver that was her match," Beary informed his daughter. "Shaven head, cut-off T-shirt and tattoos. We were running late and there was a massive traffic jam, so she told him to get us to the Lincoln Centre as quickly as possible. I've never had a ride like it in my life—just like those car chases in the movies. Your mother was scared out of her wits."

"Back-seat driving didn't work?"

"Not at all," said Beary happily. "He ignored her completely. I gave him a huge tip and asked him if he'd done his driver training at the Indy track. He took it as a great compliment."

Edwina flushed a dark red.

"He was a maniac," she stated categorically. "He broke every rule in the book."

"He got us here on time," observed Beary, "*and* in time to get something to eat. That's another bone of contention," he told Philippa. "We were held up because your mother insisted on going shopping again, and when she tried to pay the extortionate price for that sequined straight-jacket she's wearing, she discovered that her credit card had been cancelled."

"It was ridiculous," snorted Edwina. "Because I'd made several purchases at Tiffany's the day before, the credit company assumed that my card had been stolen and arbitrarily cancelled it. It took forty-five minutes to straighten the mess out, and then I was late for my hair appointment—that was disappointing too—overpriced, and the stylist had a vibrating chair that was about as comfortable as a ride on the PATH train—and then there was no time for dinner. Now the chimes are going and I've bolted down a chicken sandwich and I'll probably suffer indigestion all through the opera."

Edwina snatched up her evening bag and propelled her way through the crowd. Beary rolled his eyes, stuffed the last portion of his sandwich into his mouth, and washed it down with the rest of his Scotch. Then he took Philippa's arm and steered her after her mother. They followed Edwina up two flights of stairs and found the seats that Robin had arranged for them at the back of the grand tier. As Philippa slipped off her coat and sat down, she recognized the young man sitting in the row directly in front. It was Timothy Mason. He was studying his program and appeared to be alone. Further down the row, Philippa noticed another familiar personage. It was the newsman, Daniel James, who was even more handsome in the flesh than he appeared on television.

Edwina's expression grew even darker as she settled into her seat.

"How are we supposed to see through that?" She glowered at the chandelier in front of them.

"It goes up, Mum," said Philippa.

"What?"

"When the lights go down. You watch. I've seen it on TV. The chandeliers rise up into the ceiling."

Timothy Mason's head emerged from his program. He turned, looked quizzically at Philippa, and a smile of recognition lit up his face.

"Hello again," he said. "You're Robin's friend, aren't you?"

Edwina, oblivious to the interruption, was staring at the stage.

"There's no screen for surtitles," she announced, criticism emanating from every pore.

"They're on the backs of the seats, ma'am," Timothy broke in. "You have your own individual translation. If you want to use the titles, you just press that button and they'll come on."

He gave Edwina a charming smile and her disgruntled expression relaxed into a mildly austere hauteur.

Beary winked at Philippa.

"Helpful young man, that," he said. "She'll be reasonably civil by the end of Act One, and once Gilda has been seduced and violated, and our ears have been assaulted by her father bellowing for revenge, your mother will be restored to a perfectly good humour. I, on the other hand, will be finding solace in the bar."

Philippa leaned forward and spoke to Timothy.

"Robin and I are going out to eat after the opera tonight. Why don't you join us?" she suggested impulsively.

The young man shook his head.

"I'd love to, but I'm only staying for the first half. I'll whip back and congratulate Robin during the intermission—that's really why I came, to cheer her on—but then I have to head for the airport. I've got an eleven-o'clock flight."

Philippa grasped the opportunity for some shameless probing.

"Robin is wonderful, isn't she?" she said. "Is your assessment the same as mine? That she's headed for the big time?"

"No question about it. One of these days, I hope to be down there conducting, and she'll be on stage singing Gilda. Robin could be Petrenko all over again, but without the volatile temperament." Timothy looked pensive for a moment. "Natalia is incredibly exciting—I've never known anyone like her—but Robin is special in a different way. She's so serene in everyday life. All her passion and intensity goes into her art."

"She does have feelings, you know."

Timothy gave Philippa a sharp look as if he realized he was being grilled, and his tone became impersonal.

"I'm sure she does," he said, "but fortunately she doesn't spout them all over the place. Anyway," he added, sounding aggravatingly casual, "she deserves some fun after the way she's been working, so I hope you girls have a great evening out tonight."

"We will. I'm sorry you can't join us. Is it a job that's taking you out of town?"

Timothy looked amused, but his face closed into a mind-your-own-business expression.

"No, strictly personal. I'm flying back to Seattle."

"That's nice," muttered Philippa, thinking the exact opposite. She was saved from further comment as a wave of applause rippled through the house. The conductor had entered the pit. Timothy swivelled back to face the stage, the lights dimmed, and the opera began.

Philippa soon forgot about the personal trials and tribulations of the singers on stage and was drawn into the drama of *Rigoletto*. As the evening progressed, she drifted into a state of euphoria. She was proud of Robin's performance and thrilled by the superb singing of principals and chorus alike. She was vastly impressed by the meticulous theatrical detail: curtains that rose and fell at varying speeds to co-ordinate with the mood of a scene; the sweep of Gilda's nightgown that mirrored the sorrow of its wearer; and an ensemble that sang as one magnificent unit but acted as individual characters inhabiting the court. It was a night to remember forever. Philippa could tell that her parents were as captivated as she was. By the time the final intermission drew to a close, Edwina was radiating good will, happily engaged in conversation with the couple beside her, who appeared to be giving her advice on museums and galleries, while Beary, having made several visits to the bar, was humming snatches of melody vaguely recognizable as Verdi.

The sparkling chandelier glided upwards and disappeared into the shadows as the lights went down for the last act. Ominous chords rumbled from the pit and the golden curtains made a smooth and measured ascent, as stealthy as Sparafucile himself, to reveal the sombre riverside dwelling of the assassin and his sister. Rigoletto, restless and overwrought, concluded his evil contract and faded into the night. The Duke wooed Maddalena and tossed off his bravura aria with cavalier abandon. As the stormy climax approached, Philippa found herself clenching her fists. The tension was so strong that the music had become subservient to the drama. She watched Natalia Petrenko closely. The soprano appeared fragile and gentle, everything Gilda should be, and her pure tones soared above the storm music, angelic and ethereal, yet strong, and Philippa wondered at the art that could transform a woman from tiger and temptress to the epitome of virtue and grace. As Gilda approached the door, Philippa held her breath, willing the soprano not to knock, and as the inevitable conclusion rolled forward, she felt a deep sorrow, as if the staging and the orchestration were peripheral and irrelevant, and only the tragedy was real. And when Rigoletto claimed his evil purchase and discovered the dreadful price he had paid in his quest for revenge, the basso's grief was heart-wrenching. Philippa's eyes misted over and she fumbled for her handkerchief.

Then, suddenly, the spell was broken. Philippa blinked and sat forward.

"She missed a note," she whispered.

"What?" hissed Beary.

"Nothing. I'll tell you later."

Philippa kept her eyes on the stage. Nothing else seemed out of place in an otherwise perfect performance, and she began to wonder if she had imagined the omission. Gilda's life ebbed away and Rigoletto sobbed the words of the curse. The orchestra ground out the final crashing chords, and the golden curtains swept down. There was a hush, no longer than a heartbeat, and then the applause began. A moment later, ripples in the fabric signalled the performers' reappearance and the five principals emerged to take their bows. The audience's response was rapturous, but as the singers basked in the cascade of 'bravos' that bombarded the stage, Philippa was struck by the demeanour of Natalia Petrenko. The soprano seemed hesitant and remote. The fragility that had so suited Rigoletto's daughter remained incongruously present in the triumphant prima donna as she acknowledged the adulation of her fans.

When the clapping finally ceased and the lights came up in the auditorium, Philippa turned to see her father taking a note from an usher at the end of the row. Beary passed the envelope to Philippa.

"From your friend," he said. He watched as Philippa pulled out the note and read it. "Problems?" he asked, seeing her disappointed expression.

"Robin went home after she finished her role," Philippa replied. "She doesn't feel well."

"That certainly didn't show on stage," said Edwina briskly.

"No," agreed Philippa, without voicing the thought that had crossed her mind. Maybe during Act One, Robin hadn't known that Timothy was heading back to Seattle.

◆   ◆   ◆

Robin was asleep when Philippa returned to the apartment, and she had already left for her singing lesson when Philippa awoke the next day. She left a note to say she would be out until five, but would call later so they could team up for dinner. Philippa showered and dressed, putting on jeans and a lightweight top. Having looked out the window at the patchwork of blue and grey that formed the sky, she stuffed water bottle, sunhat, umbrella and jacket into her backpack, and feeling ready for all eventualities, set off for the nearest deli. Then, fortified by a bagel and a latte, she headed Uptown. A walk in Central Park promised the perfect way to spend the morning.

Forty-five minutes later, she had walked around the lake and was progressing along a picturesque path which was interspersed with stone bridges as it snaked between antiquated brick edifices with ivy-covered walls. Near the concession stand on the east side of the park, she saw two familiar figures sitting on a bench in the shade of a large oak. Her father hailed her, wildly semaphoring with his hot dog.

"Want one?" he asked as she approached. "Good fuel."

"We tried to call you," Edwina admonished.

"I forgot to turn my cell on," Philippa lied. Her mother's habit of getting up at six o'clock in order to start sightseeing early was not an endearing trait.

"Sensible," said Beary. "Your mother has been dragging me round the Frick Collection." Beary's tastes in culture ran to literature rather than art or music.

"It was wonderful," Edwina enthused. "An incredible display—all the old masters."

"Po-faced ladies in oils and sadistic sculptures in bronze," grunted Beary. "The boats by Turner weren't bad," he admitted, "and I liked the clocks, but the overall effect was sore feet and semi-hypnosis from all those staring eyes. However," he went on, "we did discover something interesting."

"Yes," nodded Edwina. "You'll find this rather startling. Remember the people I was talking to at the opera last night."

"Vaguely," said Philippa. She had not paid much attention to the middle-aged couple in the end seats.

"Well, they were the ones who told me about the Frick Collection," her mother replied. "Their name is Lendl—charming people. They were planning on attending the gallery this morning, and when they described it to me, it sounded incredible, so that's why your father and I decided to view it."

"Why *you* decided to view it," muttered Beary.

"Yes, well you certainly didn't view much," snapped Edwina. "You raced through; then spent most of the time in the atrium."

"It was a very nice atrium," said Beary. "Potted palms and a rectangular pond with water features. And it's a good job I did," he pointed out, "or we would have been missing part of the story."

"Anyway," Edwina continued, ignoring the diversion, "the Lendls are visiting from Saint Louis so their daughter had arranged opera tickets for them—she's the set designer for the production—"

"And she took them backstage afterwards," Beary interjected impatiently. "Get to the point," he added to Edwina.

"The point is," his wife retorted frostily, "that we saw them this morning at the gallery. We met as we came in, and they introduced their daughter to us."

"Very attractive woman, but tense," commented Beary. "Tight as a drum. Something was eating her pretty badly."

"That nasty soprano, by the sound of it." Edwina sniffed disapprovingly. "The Lendls were quite vocal on the subject. When they went backstage after the opera, Natalia Petrenko was already on her way out of the theatre, but she stopped when she saw them and laid into their daughter—something to do with a dangerous projection on the last-act set. It sounds as if she was very unpleasant. The diatribe only ceased because her dresser appeared with a question about an alteration to a gown, and fortunately for the Lendls—and unfortunately for the dresser—Petrenko turned on her and started venting her spleen in that direction. She sounds like an awful woman. The poor dresser stood there smiling politely while the tirade washed over her, and the Lendls were stuck in the middle. Mrs. Lendl wanted to intervene, but was afraid she'd make matters worse, so they quietly slipped away. They're such a dignified couple—they must have been morti-fied. Anyway, after they told us about their nasty experience, we went our separate ways and began our tour, but towards the end, we saw the oddest scene. I was admiring the gown on one of the Gainsborough ladies, and your father had emerged from the atrium and was being annoyingly facetious about a moralistic painting of Virtue conquering Vice, when suddenly we heard a sob. We looked around and saw the Lendls' daughter. She had come out from the atrium and was staring at an Italian painting of the Madonna and Child. The poor woman was distraught. She had tears streaming down her face. Her parents went over to her and put their arms around her, but she pulled back. Her face was twisted with …" Edwina turned towards Beary. "Was it rage, do you think, or sorrow? I couldn't be sure."

"I think it was desperation," said Beary.

"Did she say anything?" Philippa asked.

Edwina nodded sadly.

"She said, 'She's a monster. She deserves to die!' Then she ran out of the room."

Philippa turned towards her father.

"You said something was going on in the atrium. What was that all about?"

"I overheard the Lendls' daughter putting a call through to Malcolm Gor-don—that's Petrenko's high-flying husband."

"I know who he is. Why was she calling him?"

"I couldn't pick up much—she was listening more than talking, and she was muttering anyway—but it was obvious from her manner that she didn't like what she heard."

"Did her parents say anything to you after the outburst in the gallery?"

"I don't think they even noticed us," said Edwina. "They were focussed on their daughter. They rushed out after her—"

"And they called out her name," finished Beary.

"What was it?" Philippa asked curiously.

"Mariana," said Beary.

◆   ◆   ◆

At six o'clock, Philippa found her way to the Greenwich Village taverna where she and Robin had arranged to meet. Robin was already seated at a secluded table at the back of the restaurant, so Philippa made her way through the sea of white tablecloths and joined her friend in the corner.

"How was your day?" Robin asked.

"Great," said Philippa. "I hiked around Central Park in the morning and did the Greenwich Village walking tour this afternoon."

"Sore feet? Or can you manage more walking after dinner?"

"My feet are fine," Philippa assured her. "They were feeling overheated, but I stopped by Macy's and told the dignified Jewish saleslady behind the counter that I was a tourist and needed comfortable walking socks. What a darling! She became instantly motherly and took so much care helping me that you'd have thought I was buying a mink coat. She told me what to wear for every occasion, took all the tags off my purchases, walked from behind the counter to hand me my shopping bag, shook hands and gave me a coupon. I must say New Yorkers are tremendously friendly. My God, I'm drooling," she digressed, peering at the menu. "White butter-beans, beets, watercress and shaved roasted almonds in lemon-garlic mayo—now that's a salad!"

The girls chattered on over dinner and coffee, and as they paid the bill and prepared to leave, Philippa suddenly remembered the aberration that had troubled her during the previous evening's performance.

"Did I imagine it," she asked, "or did Petrenko miss a note during those final phrases? I know you left early, but someone in the cast must have noticed."

"If she did flub something, it was hardly surprising," said Robin, guiding Philippa out of the restaurant and setting off down the street. "I gather she was totally out of sorts after the final curtain. Mary-Anne said she was sweating profusely and in a thoroughly vile temper. There was a corporate reception after the show that night, but evidently Natalia made her excuses and went straight home. Come on, this way," she added, taking Philippa's arm and steering her across the street.

"Where are we going?" Philippa enquired as Robin forged ahead.

"You're a tourist," Robin replied, "and you said you were prepared for another hike. I thought we could walk up to the Empire State Building. It's beautiful at night. We won't have to wait in line for hours because it's only May and it's late in the evening."

Robin's prediction proved correct. When she and Philippa reached the imposing entrance of the Empire State Building, there was a steady stream of people heading up the escalator to the first level, but there were no delays. At the top of the escalator, there was a vast concourse containing yards of ropes which delineated the route for the line-up, and also indicated the volume of people that must go through during tourist season. However, at this late hour, the rows were empty and the flow of visitors only came to a halt at the final turn. Robin and

Philippa sped through the maze and joined the tail end of the cluster of people inching towards the elevator.

While they waited, Philippa reverted to the subject of Natalia Petrenko.

"It's strange, isn't it?" she mused. "I thought Petrenko looked rather frail at the final curtain, yet for most of the performance, she was magnificent. She only flagged at the very end, but you say she wasn't ailing, just in a vile temper—maybe something happened to upset her during the performance."

"That's quite possible. She was in a chirpy enough humour earlier on—in fact, she was about the only person who was. It was an awful night backstage—I'm sorry I bailed on you, but I was so relieved to be able to leave early."

"What was going on?"

"Natalia was acting as if she was on top of the world—she'd been flirting outrageously with Daniel James when he'd arrived with Mary-Anne earlier, and that put Narumoff in a ferocious mood. He stormed through the wings to make his first entrance and nobody could get a word out of him. Rubini was in an ugly frame of mind too because Mary-Anne had finally had enough of his lecherous suggestions and told him in no uncertain terms what he could do with his ducal personage. Then to top it all, there was a big tirade from the props mistress because things had been rearranged on the props table. Sparafucile's dagger had been moved, and the sack for the last act had gone missing. I was so happy to get out of there."

The line moved ahead to the first elevator and Philippa and Robin squeezed inside with a voluble group of Japanese tourists who were chattering non-stop in their own language. Philippa waited until the doors opened on the next level before she continued.

"From what you're telling me," she observed, "nothing that was going on would have had any impact on Petrenko. It sounds as if she was the one person who was unaffected by the atmosphere. So what happened to alter her mood?"

"I don't know," answered Robin. "She was her usual self when I left. *I* was the one who was down in the dumps."

"Because of Timothy?" Philippa remembered the conversation in the grand tier.

Robin looked gloomy.

"Yes. Would you believe he came back to congratulate me during the intermission, gave me a big hug, and then told me he was off to the airport as he was flying to Seattle for the weekend—*and* that when he came back, he was bringing someone special that I simply *had* to meet? I was ready to throw up, I was so upset."

Philippa smiled sympathetically at her friend. Then a thought struck her.

"Was Natalia around when he came backstage?"

"Yes. She was there. After Tim left, she laughed at me and told me not to take life so seriously. She really is utterly heartless. Not always reliable either," Robin added as an afterthought. "Luigi was annoyed this morning because she didn't show up for her coaching session. Come on," she urged, "move ahead—we're at the second elevator. I haven't been up here since I first arrived, and before I do anything else, I'm going to get one of those little models to send to my nephew back home."

The elevator carried them up to the eighty-sixth floor. When the doors opened, Philippa was surprised to see what a crush filled the gift shop. Robin signalled her intention of heading for the souvenir counter, so Philippa forged her way through the crowd and moved onto the open viewing deck. She gasped as the gust of wind hit her. She did up her coat, braced herself and moved to the railing so she could properly look out. In spite of the misty rain that permeated the air, the city lights were spectacular. Gradually she picked out Times Square, the East and Hudson rivers and, in the distance, the ocean. Feeling another blast of wind, she looked upwards, and realized that the swirling clouds that clung to the topmost peak of the building were the same mists that surrounded the viewing deck.

"Exhilarating, isn't it?" said a voice at her side. "We're in the clouds."

Philippa looked round and saw Bill Gunsen at the railing. Next to him was a statuesque blonde who held a bulging gift-shop bag in one hand and a Sardi's umbrella in the other. She bore a striking resemblance to the young officer.

"This is my sister," said the policeman. "Karen Jacobson. It's her first visit to New York too. You know," he added, "I'm really glad we met up again. You disappeared before I could find out how to contact you."

"To be honest," murmured Philippa, "I thought my mother had put you on the spot. She's kind of pushy."

"I thought she was pretty straightforward. It'd be great if we could all go out together like she suggested—maybe a show and dinner. Is that your singer friend over there?"

Robin had emerged from the gift shop and was waving in their direction. Philippa beckoned to her, and Robin wove her way through the crowd and joined them on the viewing deck. Philippa made the appropriate introductions, but before there was time for further conversation, Gunsen's cell phone rang. As he answered the call, his face became serious, and his expression grew even graver as he continued to listen to the voice at the other end. After he had rung off, he turned to his sister.

"I have to go," he said. "Why don't the three of you team up for the rest of the evening? Trade numbers with Philippa so I can get in touch."

Karen smiled and nodded. She appeared to have as sunny a personality as her sibling.

Bill turned back to Philippa.

"I'll call you tomorrow and make that date. I'm off Wednesday. Maybe we could go to lunch—assuming this crisis doesn't affect my schedule. They'll be pulling out all the stops on this case."

"Something serious?"

"Yes," said Bill. "It'll impact you as well," he added, looking at Robin. "You'll know soon enough so I might as well tell you. Natalia Petrenko has been found dead in bed in her penthouse. There's a very good chance that it was foul play."

◆   ◆   ◆

A week later, Beary and Edwina had taken in three Broadway shows, visited MOMA and the Guggenheim, toured the Statue of Liberty, and hiked around Greenwich Village. Everywhere they went, the main topic of conversation was the mysterious death of the prima donna, but gradually the story retreated to the inside pages of the newspapers, and as the sensation died down, similarly, their enthusiasm for excursions diminished. With only a few days in New York remaining, the prospect of a morning stroll along the Hudson, followed by coffee and biscotti in the quaint, book-lined shop that they had discovered three blocks from the RV site, seemed more appealing than frenetic sight-seeing. Beary, who had far less energy than his wife, was grateful for the change in routine.

As he ordered the coffee, marvelling at the array of gourmet breads and flinching at the price on the Statue of Liberty maple-syrup bottles, he noticed a pile of newspapers on a stand by the counter.

"Good God!" he said, staring at the headlines. His wife, who was already seated at their favourite table, replied without looking up from her mystery novel.

"What?"

"They've arrested the husband."

Edwina sniffed.

"Isn't that usually the solution?" she commented acerbically.

"Not when you're Malcolm Gordon. With his billions, he wouldn't have to resort to murder to get rid of his wife."

"Maybe he didn't want to share his billions."

"He didn't have to. Remember the pre-nup."

Edwina looked up.

"That doesn't mean a thing. Do you think a pre-nup would stop me from taking you to the cleaners if you did anything to annoy me?"

Edwina turned back to her book. Beary knew better than to attempt a rejoinder, but he paid for a paper as well as the coffees and came to join his wife at the table. "No, seriously, listen," he insisted. "This doesn't make sense."

Edwina sighed, abandoned P.D. James and picked up her latte.

"Go on, then," she said.

Beary stabbed his finger at the article in the paper.

"The autopsy results indicate that Petrenko died from a toxin that stopped her heart. Her maid discovered her in the late afternoon."

"Where was her husband?"

"Out of town. He'd flown to Washington the previous day."

Edwina set her coffee mug down and frowned.

"If he was out of town, how could he have killed her?"

"He collected rare spiders. Every room in the penthouse contained glass tanks filled with insects and reptiles that he'd brought back from various parts of the world. One of these, an Australian funnel-web spider, is missing from its tank. It's one of the most dangerous spiders in existence and it was found, also dead, in Petrenko's bed."

"Perhaps it escaped from the tank," theorized Edwina. "Her death could have been an accident. Why are the police insisting on foul play?"

"Because the buzzer in the bedroom had been disconnected. If Petrenko had tried to call for help, no one would have come. But why are the police targeting Malcolm Gordon? Anyone could have put a spider in the bed."

"That's true, but would anyone have necessarily known which spider bite would be fatal?"

"Anyone who had murder in mind. You can find anything these days on the Internet. You can bet your boots the reporter who wrote this story wouldn't have heard of funnel-web spiders before one became headline news for dispatching a diva, but the story he wrote is loaded with biological detail."

The bell on the door jangled, but Beary and Edwina were too intent on the article to notice Philippa entering the coffee house.

"It's a nasty way to die," Beary concluded sadly, staring at the photograph of the spider that adorned the second page of the newspaper. "If untreated, the bite is fatal, but death is not instantaneous."

"Is there no antidote?" Edwina asked.

"Yes, there is, and it says Gordon kept a supply of the serum in case of emergencies. This article claims that a vial of the antidote went missing along with the spider—but it wasn't in Petrenko's room, so it must have been taken by the murderer."

"Grisly, isn't it?" interjected Philippa, sliding into a chair beside her father. "If only she'd known what had happened, she could have saved herself."

"Hello, dear," said her mother. "Are you joining us for the day?"

"I thought I would. Robin's in rehearsal and I figured I'd find you here. What's on today's agenda?"

"Wall Street," said Beary. "I want to find the bull."

"That shouldn't be difficult," said Edwina. "I imagine it's knee-deep everywhere around the stock exchange."

"Very funny. I'll have you know there actually *is* a bull, and a very photogenic one at that. All the tourists have their pictures taken with it. I'll take one of you grabbing it by the horns."

Edwina ignored her husband and turned to Philippa.

"Is your nice policeman friend working?"

"Yes, unfortunately—he's great company. It was very clever of you to find him for me."

"Am I missing something?" asked Beary. "What nice policeman friend?"

"The one you photographed me with," retorted Edwina. "Don't you pay attention to anything? Philippa met him again at the Empire State Building and he invited her out. She had lunch with him yesterday, and his sister has offered to have us all to dinner at her house when we return to Vancouver."

"I can't keep up," said Beary. "I thought young Adam was the one and only."

"Adam might eventually prove to be the one and only," said Edwina, "but he happens to be in Europe, and Philippa is far too sensible to wait around for someone who may or may not come back. This young policeman is extremely personable—bright and ambitious too. I had a very interesting conversation with him while you were fiddling around trying to find your camera."

"Well, he's obviously smart enough to comprehend that if he wants to make time with the daughter, he has to spend the pre-requisite half-hour chatting up the mother," Beary grunted.

"Don't be ridiculous," snapped Edwina.

"Bill's taking me to a matinée and dinner on Friday," Philippa cut in. She was adept at heading off confrontations between her parents. "He's off the night before we leave too, so he's suggested we all go out to dinner."

"And who would 'all' be?" asked Beary. "And more importantly, who will be paying for 'all'?"

"Me and Robin, Bill and Karen—"

"Karen?"

"His sister—and you and Mum," Philippa concluded, answering the first half of her father's question. "And of course, Bill wouldn't expect it, but I kind of hoped …" She paused and raised her eyebrows beseechingly.

"Of course your father will pay," said Edwina firmly. "Bill and his sister are being extremely hospitable, and Robin has put you up for the holiday. She also got us opera tickets. It's time to reciprocate."

"And this is a nice way to do it," agreed Philippa. "Anyway, we need to make a fuss of Robin. She's down in the dumps because her accompanist is about to take up again with his old girlfriend. She needs a night out to cheer her up."

"Never mind the social calendars and soap operas," said Beary, tapping the newspaper impatiently. "If you've acquired a cop friend, you must have some inside dope on this soprano's murder. What's his take on the situation? Does he have any ideas?"

"Quite a few, actually," said Philippa. "Bill may be a rookie, but his goal is to join the detective branch, so he's very interested in the case. It's a pretty unusual homicide."

"Why are they picking on the husband?" demanded Beary. "That's what I want to know."

"Bill thinks politics might be playing a part. The detective in charge of the investigation is one of those tough, chip-on-the-shoulder individuals who figures anyone with that much money has to be guilty of something—and of course, there's a big fat motive that hasn't appeared in the newspaper yet. Robin told me all about it. The gossip at the opera has been about nothing else. Evidently, Mariana Lendl is Gordon's mistress and it turns out she's pregnant. It sounds as if Gordon was planning on divorcing Petrenko in order to marry Lendl, but—and this is why you saw her sobbing her eyes out at the Frick Gallery—Petrenko delivered a bombshell of her own the day her husband left. It turns out she was pregnant too. That must have been what Gordon told Lendl when she phoned him. The rotten part is that he was wavering about the divorce, and yet given Petrenko's history, who knows if it was her husband's child or not. She really was a venomous creature."

"And met a venomous end," said Beary. "Bizarre."

"What Bill finds puzzling," Philippa continued, "is that the maid says she made up Petrenko's bed late that afternoon, and there was no sign of the spider. By then, Malcolm Gordon had already left for the airport."

"Perhaps it was tucked down at the foot of the bed."

"But Petrenko had a nap after lunch. That's why the maid re-made the bed later on. If the spider had been in the bed, it would have bitten Petrenko before she left for the theatre and she would have started to show symptoms halfway through the opera. I know she had that little flub at the end and she didn't look well during the bows, but there's no way she could have sung Gilda if she'd been bitten by that spider seven hours before the performance. The toxin wouldn't take that long to take effect. The bite had to have occurred late in the evening."

"Then someone must have come to the penthouse and put the spider in the bed while the opera was on," said Edwina.

"No," said Philippa. "The maid remained at the penthouse until Petrenko returned from the theatre and she said no one entered the apartment. She offered to make tea for Petrenko, but she was dismissed. She said the prima donna seemed very tired and insisted that she simply wanted to turn in. She said not to disturb her and to let her sleep in. She said she'd ring for the maid in the morning when she wanted her."

"Was anyone in the penthouse earlier that day?" Beary asked curiously.

"Several people. Mariana Lendl was there first thing because she was accompanying Petrenko's husband to the airport, and after they'd left, Marco Rubini and Mary-Anne James came by for a brief musical consultation. The dresser was there for a fitting just before lunch, and Narumoff came storming in around noon and threw a big tantrum until Petrenko chucked him out. But according to the maid, none of them went anywhere near the bedroom, because she was in there all morning cleaning the room and en suite and seeing to Petrenko's wardrobe."

"It's a conundrum." Beary shook his head and got to his feet. "Well, let's head out. Maybe the Wall Street bull will have some answers for us."

The air was cold as they walked to Liberty Harbour, so Philippa was thankful to get onto the ferry and out of the chill wind. As the boat carried them across to Pier 11, Philippa could see the Statue of Liberty, green and stately, watching from the distance. On the far side of the river, the trio disembarked and followed the commuters along the jetty. This side of the Hudson was much busier, with water taxis darting in all directions and choppers buzzing overhead. The ferries leaving and entering the docks crisscrossed at high speed, replicating the expert manoeuvres of the yellow cabs on the street.

The Bearys made their way up Wall Street. They passed the New York Stock Exchange and walked round to the bronze bull, which appeared to be participating in a colourful ceremonial ritual, draped with tourists in assorted poses and surrounded by individuals pointing cameras. As Philippa waited with her parents for an athletic Swede to clamber to the nape of the bull's neck so his girl friend, who carried an ancient-looking Minolta, could immortalize him on film, her cell phone rang. It was Robin.

"I'm on a break. Where are you?"

"Wall Street. The bull."

Robin laughed. "We should have one at the rehearsal hall. You should hear all the gossip flying around here. The schemes and plots in *Rigoletto* pale by comparison."

Robin chattered on. As she listened, Philippa watched the Swede astride the bull's neck. His girlfriend, apparently not part of the digital age, was signalling that she had run out of film. The young man swung his backpack round in front of him and delved inside. Suddenly, he gave a yowl of pain, scowled, and pulled out a corkscrew.

Philippa's eyes were riveted to the scene in front of her, but she was vaguely aware that Robin was still talking about the cast of the opera.

"Narumoff is pretty depressed," said Robin, "but he's much calmer. Given a bit of time, he's got to realize he's better off without Natalia. He may have been crazy about her, but there wasn't much love in the equation—it was really all about sex. His last session with Natalia must have been pretty wild, because he's got a love bite on his neck the size of a walnut. Oh, and there's something else that I just found out—"

Philippa barely took in what Robin was saying, for as she watched the Swede holding his thumb, a sudden thought occurred to her, and she cut in and interrupted the flow.

"Robin, the night of the opera, you said something about the props mistress being annoyed because things had been moved and the sack for the last act was missing. Did it ever show up?"

"Yes, it had been pre-set on the revolve. I guess one of the stagehands had placed it there earlier. Why? Is that significant?"

"I'm not sure. There's something else niggling at me too. The Lendls told my parents that on the night she died, Natalia was going on about a sharp projection on the set. Do you know anything about that?"

"I did hear something, now you mention it. One of the stagehands said Natalia cried out as she was dragged onto the stage in the sack. The inn has a lot of open beams and cracked walls, and the steps are designed to look jagged—after all, the building is supposed to look tumbledown and ancient—and Natalia claimed that she'd been pulled against something sharp as she made her entrance. I gather she got pretty nasty, but let's face it, once she'd discovered about the affair between her husband and Mariana, she'd have used any excuse to raise hell. Look, I've got to go—we're being called again. I'll see you later."

Robin rang off, and Philippa put away her phone and pulled out her camera. The Swede had climbed down from the top of the bull and her parents were now posed on either side of its massive head. As she raised her camera, she looked at the blank, yet strangely expressive eyes in the bronze head. The creature seemed to be smiling at her in amusement, as if to acknowledge the truth of her mother's joke. She took the photograph; then she tucked the camera back in the case. She barely noticed her father returning to her side for she was preoccupied with the idea that Robin had planted in her mind.

"You look serious," said Beary, observing his daughter's expression. "That must have been an important call."

"It was Robin. She's given me an idea. Dad, what did it say in that article about the antidote to the spider venom? Would there be any visible symptoms if someone were bitten, but had taken the antidote?"

"Probably a red swelling that would reduce over a couple of days and then disappear. That's all."

"Then I'm pretty sure who killed Natalia," said Philippa solemnly. "I wonder if a blood test would show the presence of the antidote."

"I don't know. It might. What prompted this train of thought?"

"Robin said that Narumoff had a dark mark on his neck. What if that were the remains of a spider bite?"

"You're suggesting that he stole the spider and was bitten in the process?"

"Yes," nodded Philippa.

"But how could he put the spider in Petrenko's bed?" Beary countered. "As I recall, he didn't go into her bedroom that day."

"I don't think the spider was in her bed—not until later. I think it was stolen in the morning and put into the sack at the theatre. Robin says Natalia complained about being stabbed by something sharp as she was dragged on stage. Robin also told me that the props mistress was angry because someone had pre-set the sack on the revolve. I think Narumoff placed it there, knowing that when Petrenko curled up in the sack, the spider would bite her. In the process of being dragged onto the stage, the insect would most likely be crushed, so all he had to do was retrieve it and place it in the bed the following day. I'll ask Bill—I bet we'll find Narumoff rushed over to the penthouse when the news broke of Natalia's death."

Philippa pulled out her cell phone again and called Bill Gunsen. She reached his voicemail, so she left him an enigmatic message: "Bill, call me right away. It's important. *Gilda died for love*." Then she turned back to her father.

"What do you think? Does it make sense?"

"It's possible, I suppose."

"It's more than possible. It's extremely likely. Don't you see? Natalia gave an almost flawless performance, but something went wrong towards the end. I couldn't understand why she missed those notes, but if she'd been bitten by the spider, she would have been physically affected almost immediately."

"Yes," agreed Beary, "but she was a large woman, so the envenoming might not have produced more than minor symptoms in the first hour."

"Exactly. Robin says Natalia left the theatre very quickly, and her penthouse is only two blocks from the theatre, so she would have been home when the toxin started to have a major effect. She'd dismissed her maid, and the buzzer had been de-activated, so once she became really ill, she was alone and no one came to help her. That has to be the solution."

"If you're right," said Beary, "Gilda really *did* die for love—but there's one thing seriously wrong with this theory."

"What?"

"It's not in character. It's furtive, and cold-blooded. There's a deliberateness about it that doesn't fit Narumoff at all. I could see him strangling her in a fit of jealous passion, but I don't believe he'd commit premeditated murder. You're getting hung up on the concept of opportunity and motive, and ignoring the character of the man. I just don't see it."

Philippa paused. Then she conceded the point.

"Yes, you're right, and yet the scenario fits so well in every other way. I wonder what I'm missing."

"I have no idea," said Beary. He gave an aggravating grin and tousled his daughter's hair. "Just remember," he added, gesturing towards the sphinx-like figure at the centre of the square, "you have to look beyond the bull."

"I've hardly noticed the bull," complained Philippa. "I have this mental picture in front of my eyes and it's obliterating everything else. I keep seeing Rigoletto dragging the sack that contains the body of his daughter—but there's a shadowy figure in the wings that won't come into focus."

"Then stop thinking about it," said Beary firmly. "Forget about Natalia Petrenko for a while. Come on. We should make a pilgrimage to Ground Zero and pay our respects to *those* tragic murder victims. You know," he added as they gathered up their bags and prepared to move on, "I can't help feeling there are similarities between the two crimes, even though one was a horrendous mass murder where the victims were random targets, and the other was a carefully planned attack on a deliberately selected individual. I have this instinct that a bizarre fusion of raw hatred and fanatic love are at the root of both." Beary straightened up and struggled into his backpack. "Now, let's get moving." He looked around the square. "Where's your mother?"

"Over there. Under the flag."

Philippa pointed to the far side of the street where Edwina was chattering volubly amid a cluster of fellow tourists. Beary marched across the square, extracted his wife from her new acquaintances and propelled her down the sidewalk. Philippa set off after her parents, watching with affectionate amusement as they embarked on a heated debate over her mother's city map.

The argument lasted the length of the walk, but once they reached their destination, Beary and Edwina fell silent. The site commanded silence. People spoke in hushed tones as they clustered along the chain-link fence that surrounded the bleak, sad space where the World Trade Centre had stood. Philippa moved past a peddler who was ignoring the signs that prohibited souvenir sales and looked down at the rubble and the rusty girders, which were all that remained of the twin towers. The scene seemed to resonate with the cries of the unfortunate souls who had lost their lives during the historic attack. After a while, her thoughts drifted back to Natalia Petrenko, and she found herself reflecting on her father's comments. It seemed odd to draw comparisons between the murder of the soprano and the 9/11 catastrophe, yet Beary did have a point. Passion and intensity did seem to be at the root of both crimes, however cold-bloodedly they had been planned.

She frowned thoughtfully, but as she furrowed her brow in concentration, her cell phone rang, and when she answered the call, Bill Gunsen's voice came through so loud and clear that Beary and Edwina could hear him from where they were standing.

"Bill," Philippa began, "this is important. Did Andrei Narumoff go to Natalia Petrenko's penthouse on the day that she died? I'll explain the details later, but I think the spider was already dead when it was put in her bed. I believe the fatal bite occurred at the theatre, and the spider was returned to the apartment the next day in order to take suspicion away from the opera house and throw it on Malcolm Gordon."

"Sorry, girl," said Bill. "You can't pin this on Narumoff. He didn't go near the place. When he got the news of her death, he fell apart and had to be sedated. However," he added, "you've come up with a great theory and I'm going to pass it along, because there was one person from the theatre who *was* there the next day. That's why the body was discovered when it was. The maid didn't want to disobey Petrenko and disturb her before she rang, but a member of the company came by and insisted the maid go in and wake up her mistress. The excuse was that the soprano had to try on a costume."

"A costume?"

"Yes," said Bill. "It was the dresser. Gotta go. I'll pick you up at noon tomorrow."

He hung up before Philippa could reply. She blinked and looked at her father.

"We heard that," said Beary.

"What's the significance of the dresser?" asked Edwina. "Surely she didn't murder Petrenko because she reprimanded her over a faulty costume?"

"Robin might know," said Philippa. "In fact, she was trying to tell me something when I rang off. I shouldn't have been so impatient. Hold on a sec."

She gestured to her parents to wait; then she dialled Robin's number, praying that her friend was still on a break. After a couple of rings, Robin answered the call.

"Robin," said Philippa, "what was it you were about to tell me when I interrupted you just now?"

"I don't honestly remember," said Robin. "Look, I'm glad you called. I'm going to have to bow out on dinner tomorrow night. Tim called me from Seattle. He wants me to join him and his friend for dinner," she said plaintively, "and he sounded so happy about it, I couldn't refuse."

"Don't be an idiot," said Philippa. "Why torture yourself?"

"I'm going to be working with him for a long time," Robin sighed, "and he is a good friend. I might as well make friends with the fiancée too and get used to her. The sooner I bite the bullet and do it, the sooner I'll recover. Don't be cross."

"Of course I'm not cross—I understand. But look, try to remember what you were going to tell me. It really is important."

"Remind me, what were we talking about?"

"You were giving me all the backstage gossip and you were talking about Andrei Narumoff—"

"Oh, of course," Robin chimed in. "I know what it was. Remember how I told you that he was raised by a mother who worked her fingers to the bone to get him where he is today—well, I just found out that Narumoff's mother is Natalia's dresser."

◆   ◆   ◆

The following evening, while Philippa and her mother pored over the Sardi's menu and Karen Jacobsen made recommendations for entrées, Bill Gunsen gave Beary an account of the end of the investigation.

"Your daughter was right," he concluded. "Gilda really did die for love."

Beary nodded.

"But it wasn't passion. It was a mother's love for her son."

"Exactly. Anna Narumoff envisioned Petrenko systematically destroying her son's brilliant future—the future she'd devoted her entire life to—so she decided to get rid of her. This was no spur-of-the-moment crime—she planned the murder. A library book on poisonous spiders was found in her apartment—it had been taken out three weeks ago—and Malcolm Gordon says Anna Narumoff showed a lot of interest in his collection any time she came to the penthouse."

Edwina emerged from her menu.

"But she could have killed her own son," she protested. "He had to handle the sack. What if the spider had run out and bitten him?"

"She was prepared because she had stolen the antidote," said Bill. "As it happened, the only person bitten was Petrenko. The mark Robin noticed really was a love bite, but it did serve a purpose, because it helped put Philippa on the right track."

"It's all so cold-blooded," said Edwina.

"Completely premeditated," Bill agreed, "and Anna Narumoff shows no sign of remorse. To her way of thinking, Petrenko deserved to die and she would do the same thing again if she had to. She's quite a scary woman."

"Formidable," Beary acknowledged. "I don't envy the lawyer who has to defend her."

Edwina shivered.

"Remember what the Lendls said about the tantrum Natalia Petrenko threw backstage—the dresser stood and smiled politely. Just think—she knew that the prima donna would be dead in a few hours. How horrid!"

The crimson-jacketed waiter materialized at the table with a tray of drinks. He delivered the round of cocktails, suavely fielded an inquisition from Edwina regarding the entrées, collected the menus and retreated to the kitchen with the various orders. Philippa settled back contentedly and stared at the portraits that lined the restaurant walls.

"Isn't this lovely!" she said. "What a thrill to be sitting here in Sardi's."

"I don't recognize many of the faces," Edwina complained, frowning at the pillar opposite their table.

"The pictures are mostly Broadway stars," Karen explained. "Theatre actors rather than film people."

"There's one I know," said Beary, sipping the manhattan that had, out of deference to the location, replaced his usual Scotch. He waved his glass in the direction of a caricature of Lucille Ball. "And," he added, "there's someone else I recognize."

"Where?" asked Philippa.

"Over there," Beary indicated, "and she's not on the wall. Isn't that your friend?"

Philippa stared where her father was pointing. Sure enough, Robin and Timothy were being led to a table on the far side of the room. With them was an elegantly dressed woman, but as the maitre d' hovered attentively at her side, all Philippa could discern was a slim figure in black velvet and the rear view of a blonde and expensive hairstyle.

"For someone who's depressed, Robin is putting on an admirable show of good cheer," Edwina remarked. "She looks positively radiant."

"No wonder," said Karen. "That nice-looking man looks like he adores her."

Philippa watched with a growing sense of wonder as Timothy slid into the booth beside Robin and put his arm around her. He noticed Philippa watching from across the room and he smiled and waved to her. Robin swivelled round to see where her companion was pointing and her face lit up with delight. As she stood up, clearly intending to come to see her friend, the other woman turned to look across to the Beary table. She was stunningly attractive and, Philippa noted with relief, probably the same age as her parents.

One step ahead of the waiter, who was bearing plates and heading for their table, Robin soared across the room and waved her left hand under Philippa's nose. The diamond in the ring on her third finger was as brilliant as her smile. Philippa leapt up and took Robin's hand.

"She's his mother!" Robin whispered. "We're going to be married next spring."

She hugged Philippa warmly, waved to Bill and Karen, wiggled her finger at Edwina, and kissed Beary on top of his head. Then, with the radiant smile still glowing, she floated back to her own table.

Philippa beamed as she sat back down.

"What a perfect ending to our stay in New York," she said.

Beary had acquired a pink glow and looked particularly mellow. He stared after Robin's retreating back and took a large draught of his manhattan.

"Yes," he agreed complacently. "It certainly is."

He set down his glass and turned with gleeful anticipation to his steak tartare.

"That," he said happily, "is one soprano who won't be dying for love."

Sisters in Crime

Penelope Tudge tucked into her crème brûlée with gusto and wondered how she was to broach the subject of the problem that had been bothering her for the last two weeks. Bertram Beary, who was fonder of liquid desserts than the sweet variety, sipped his Scotch, looked fondly at his goddaughter, and wondered why she had invited him to lunch. Having known her since she was a babe in arms, he could tell when she had something on her mind. Since he already knew that she and her husband, Jonathon, were in the process of renovating their home so that Penelope's mother, who sadly had dementia, could live with them permanently, he took an educated guess and opened the conversation.

"How is your mother settling in?" he asked.

Penelope swallowed the last mouthful of her dessert and wiped her mouth daintily on her napkin.

"She's doing all right," she said.

"More to the point," said Beary, "how are *you* doing?"

"Borderline," Penelope admitted honestly. "It'll be better once the suite is built. It's stressful having a house full of workmen, especially as Boris has to be incarcerated upstairs all the time in case he chews their limbs off."

"That's what you get for having a dog with the same obnoxious temperament as your husband. Where on earth are you keeping your mother amid all this chaos?"

"We've given her our room. The children are in Paris on a school trip, so Jon and I are using Katie's room—which is fine from my point of view, but you know what Jon's like—all he can do is complain about being evicted by a geriatric terrible-two and having to lie in bed at night with Orlando Blume staring at him from the ceiling."

Beary nodded.

"Yes, Jonathon is not renowned for his patience. Is your sister doing anything to help?"

Penelope's older sister was a corporate lawyer, married to a successful, if henpecked bank manager, and well known for her ability to tell other people how to organize their lives.

"Marjorie? She's paying her share for the addition and caregivers, but that's as far as it goes. However," Penelope added, "she's sending Jane to help with her grandmother during the holidays, so that's useful if Jon and I want to go out and the hired help is off duty."

"Poor Jane," said Beary. "Seventeen years old and her mother regiments her life as if she's a ten-year-old at boarding school."

Penelope smiled mischievously.

"Jane doesn't mind," she said. "Our contractor, George, has a young assistant named Mark. He's a very handsome lad, so Jane comes over like a rocket whenever we need her."

"What does your sister think of that?"

"She took one look at Mark and christened him 'Galahad of the Gutters'. She's forbidden me to let Jane have anything to do with him."

"And are you complying?"

"Of course not—he's a very nice young man. He comes from a good family and his summer job is to help him save for medical school. But Marjorie has made her mind up that he's 'just a labourer' and there's no point in even trying to argue. You know what she's like."

Beary nodded and shifted to a different topic.

"Is your contractor satisfactory?" he asked.

"George? He's a sweetie—though, of course, Jonathon is always finding fault. He's quite smitten with Stephanie—that's the domestic we hired to help with Mother."

Beary blinked.

"Jonathon is smitten with your domestic?"

"No, not Jonathon—George, the contractor. Not that his interest is reciprocated. Stephanie can't stand him. She gives him the cold shoulder. Actually," Penelope continued, "Stephanie Keane gives everyone the cold shoulder. She's incredibly efficient and I couldn't manage without her, but she's a bit overwhelming. Jonathon finds her incredibly irritating. He calls her 'Matron'."

"Well," said Beary firmly, "if you can't manage without her, then Jonathon will just have to put up with her. Thank goodness your father left you and Marjorie with enough money to take care of your mother. Good job someone's going to benefit from his being such a miserable old tightwad."

Penelope looked uncomfortable. She stirred the froth on top of her cappuccino and then set the spoon down decisively. *Aha*, thought her godfather. *Now we're going to come to it.*

"Uncle Bertram," Penelope began—even though she was a married woman with teenaged children, Penelope could not break the habit of giving Beary the title of uncle—"Marjorie and I have a problem. It's to do with our inheritance."

"Don't tell me the old idiot made bad investments at the tail end of his life. He made a pile all those years he worked in San Francisco. Surely he didn't blow it."

"No, the portfolios are fine. There's lots of money, but we have a terrible moral dilemma on our hands."

"Tell me about it."

"Well … you know how Dad always liked the ladies."

"That's an understatement, my dear. Even when he was on his last legs in hospital, I remember him smooching with that chain-smoking accountant who used to hover around his ward like an asthmatic bumblebee."

"Oh, the Puff Adder. Yes, wasn't she awful? We were sure she was after his money."

"Your mother should have whacked her with the bedpan, preferably when it was full."

Penelope giggled. "That I would love to have seen."

"Still," Beary continued, "one thing I'll say for your father—he may have enjoyed the attention from his lady friends, but he was much too canny to be wheedled out of a penny of his assets. At least he made sure his money went to his family, even if he didn't spend it on them when he was alive."

"Well, that's the problem," said Penelope. "He didn't endow *us* with more than the necessities, but it turns out he did spend rather a lot on someone else. Do you remember Mum and Dad's next door neighbour, Magdalene?"

"The one who wore her bikini to prune her hydrangeas? How could I forget?"

"Yes, well according to Magdalene, all those years Dad worked in the States, he had a lady friend who had the gall to use our family name. She called herself Mrs. White, and Dad used to squire her around to parties and conventions. Even after my mother put her foot down and insisted he return to work in Canada, this woman continued to telephone him. Marjorie and I never knew about it, but it must have been awful for Mum."

"What else did Magdalene tell you?"

"That Dad used to pay for this woman to live quite lavishly—he even sent her on overseas trips." Penelope scowled. "It made me so mad I could spit."

"Understandable," said Beary, "but this is all water under the bridge. How does it create a moral dilemma?"

Penelope looked grim.

"A couple of weeks ago, Jane brought over a box of old papers from Mum's house—the property is up for sale, so we're gradually emptying the personal stuff—and in this box, we found a letter to Dad from a lady called Angela Blackwell. It was obvious from the letter that she was the long-term mistress that Magdalene had told us about, and," Penelope gulped, "it was also apparent that the affair had gone on for years and that there were two children!"

"Good God!" said Beary.

"Yes," Penelope growled, "and the letter also made it clear that Dad had been very generous with them. The two daughters got to go on the overseas trips too. Marjorie and I were never sent anywhere other than summer camp," she fumed.

"Your mother was a long-suffering woman," pronounced Beary, "and much too easy on your father. His first wife wouldn't have put up with that sort of nonsense."

Penelope looked speculative.

"Did Dad talk to you about his first marriage?" she asked. "He never told us anything, except to say that his wife was killed during the Second World War. He said she died during the evacuation of Singapore."

"That's all he told me, too. He said the ship she sailed on went down, but he made some remark about her being one tough bunny who could have withstood anything except the bloody German torpedoes."

"That's so sad." Penelope sighed. "Still, the first wife isn't our problem. It's the Blackwell woman that concerns us—well, not actually her. I gather she died of cancer years ago. It's her daughters I'm worried about. Marjorie and I had a fit when we realized there were two little illegits running around. I mean, what if they come up and try to claim a portion of our inheritance? I'm just getting used to being a rich bitch after all these years of making-do, but if they are entitled to a portion, then I suppose I have to come to terms with the fact. What do you think I should do?"

Beary pondered for a moment.

"What exactly was the wording of your father's will?" he asked finally.

Penelope thought carefully. Then she recited, "*I, Eustace White, bequeath one half of my estate to my dear wife, and the other half to be divided equally between our two daughters, and in the event of my dear wife predeceasing me, the entire estate is to be divided between our two precious daughters.* Well, it didn't actually say 'precious'," Penelope admitted. "I threw that bit in."

"Well, there you are then," said Beary with satisfaction. "The little illegits wouldn't stand a chance."

"Yes, but one almost feels morally obliged to do something."

"Don't talk rot. The only reason the old man had so much money is because he made you and Marjorie and your mother scrimp and scrape all your lives, and it sounds, from what you've told me, that while you and your sister were putting up with mere necessities, the little illegits and their mother were being sent on trips to England and whooping it up living in the most expensive part of San Francisco. No," Beary concluded firmly. "You keep your money and don't give it another thought."

The shadow lifted from Penelope's face and she beamed at her godfather.

"Thank you," she sighed happily. "You're such a darling. You always sort things out so nicely."

"You are most welcome, my dear," said Beary. "Now," he added, looking at his empty glass, "what about another crème brûlée? I could certainly manage another Scotch."

◆   ◆   ◆

Penelope arrived home to find a large cement truck in the driveway, so she parked on the street and went round through the back garden. George greeted her as she approached the French doors.

"The interior work in the basement is almost done," he informed her, "so today we're going to start on the foundation for the addition. Is it okay if we pile the lumber on the deck? I want to start framing in the morning."

"Yes, George, thank you," said Penelope. "Is Stephanie still here?" she added.

"She's with your mother," said George, picking up a pile of two-by-fours and shifting them onto the deck. "Fine figure of a woman, that," he added heartily. "So efficient and energetic too. Must be that U.S. blood. She's from California."

"Is she?" said Penelope. "I didn't know."

"Actually," confided George, "we had a chat while I helped her move boxes the other morning. She told me all about her early years. Evidently her mother died when she was seven and she and her sister were raised by their godmother."

"Why did she come to British Columbia?" asked Penelope curiously.

"She married a Canadian, but it didn't work out. However, she liked Vancouver, so she stayed on. She seems to think she'll have no problem getting a work permit."

The window beside the French doors opened and Jonathon's face bobbed through.

"George," he said peremptorily, "why is this window frame ripped off? I thought we were keeping the heritage house woodwork."

"We are," George assured him, "but that window doesn't work properly. The sash weights were broken off the cord. I just have to reattach them. Then I'll put the frame back."

"Interesting," said Jonathon, wedging the window open with his shoulder and testing the weights. "That's how those old windows work. God, that's heavy."

"Yes," agreed George. "Whack someone with that and they'd never get up again."

"Good heavens," murmured Penelope, moving to the window and staring at the open frame. "What a great gimmick for a detective story!"

"Isn't it?" said George. "The killer could put the weight back and reframe the window, and no one would ever find the murder weapon."

"That's right," said Jonathon, "so keep that in mind when you're presenting your bill."

He disappeared back inside and the window slammed shut.

Penelope went through the French doors and set her purse on the coffee table. She noticed that a cardboard box, obviously one of the cartons that had come from her mother's house, had been placed prominently on the sofa table, so curiously she opened the top and started to unpack. The boxes generally proved to be a treasure trove of wonderful childhood memories, *apart from the occasional snake in the Garden of Eden*, she thought, remembering the offending love letter. This box promised to be less disquieting as it appeared to contain nothing more harmful than Old Country Roses dinner dishes. She shifted a layer of tissue paper and pulled out a china teacup.

"Oh, I loved this set!" she exclaimed.

Her husband came out of the study.

"Shouldn't Matron be doing that?" he asked.

"No," said Penelope. "This is stuff from Mother's house. I want to look through it. And," she added severely, "you really shouldn't call Stephanie 'Matron'."

"Nonsense, it's the perfect name for her. She makes me feel like I live in an institution. Have you heard her with your mother? 'Come along, Granny, time for tea, teeth and a Tum on the terrace.'"

"I know she's a bit overpowering, but she's fitted in awfully well. Anyway, I need her. *You* don't do much to help."

Jonathon wagged a reproving finger. "Remember," he reminded her, "this renovation project was your idea—yours and Bossy-bun's. I merely agreed on condition that I should not be inconvenienced in any way."

"My sister's name is Marjorie."

"Bossy-buns and Matron," groaned Jonathon. "What a pair! Though at least we only have to put up with your sister occasionally. Matron's in our face all the time."

Penelope coughed.

Jonathon looked startled. "Ahem, what?" he demanded.

Penelope rolled her eyes towards the hall. Stephanie was standing at the bottom of the stairs. Her expression was impassive.

"Excuse me, Mrs. Tudge," she said, "I just wanted to let you know that I've taken down the Constable in the dining room. I imagine it's very valuable, and it would be terrible if it got damaged."

Penelope looked surprised. Then she smiled.

"Actually," she said, "it isn't at all valuable, but thank you for the compliment."

"Compliment?"

"I painted it. It's a copy."

Stephanie raised her eyebrows. "Really," she said. "It's quite outstanding."

"I know. I was an art teacher. Jonathon always said I should quit education and go in for forgery."

The eyebrows elevated another inch.

"That would be most unethical."

Jonathon opened his mouth to utter a retort, which Penelope knew would be sarcastic, so she nudged him in the ribs.

"Yes, I know, Stephanie," said Penelope. "I think he was joking."

"I see."

With a superior look that generated the impression that her employer was gaining significantly on his mother-in-law in the dementia stakes, Stephanie glided out of the room.

Jonathon scowled.

"She walks as if she has hypodermic needles in her underpants," he grunted.

Penelope tousled his hair.

"Come on, Jonathon," she urged him, "look on the bright side. Stephanie is wonderful with Mother and she's a terrific help with the household chores. I'd be a basket case without her." Penelope paused and looked thoughtful. "Actually, she reminds me of someone, though I can't think who."

"Bossy-buns."

"No, it's not Marjorie, but there's a vague familiarity."

"There's a lot more than vague familiarity with Matron. There's a complete overstepping of the mark. You should stand up to her. Remember, you're the mistress here. She's an employee."

"Oh, I'll try." Penelope went back to her box and pulled out a brown envelope that had been wedged between plates. "I'm just not used to being the lady of the manor yet—I still tend to feel like the parlour maid. I'll get the hang of it in time."

"Yes, well just keep saying to yourself, 'Daddy died and left me a bundle.' That should do the trick. Any chance of a cup of coffee?" Jonathon added hopefully.

"Get it yourself," retorted Penelope, opening the envelope and extracting the document that had been inside. "Or ask Stephanie. Remember, I'm not the parlour maid any more."

Jonathon looked pained.

"I can't ask Stephanie. All I'll get from her is a cup of tea and a Tum."

"Oh, my God!" shrieked Penelope. "I don't believe it!"

Jonathon blinked.

"OK. You don't have to take that tone. I'll make my own coffee."

"No! Look!" Penelope thrust the document towards her husband. Jonathon looked it over.

"What's the big deal?" he said. "It's your father's first marriage certificate. We knew he was married before. The lady died."

"No! We just thought she did. Look at the name."

Jonathon studied the document more closely.

"Angela Blackwell?" he said finally. "It sounds familiar."

"Of course it sounds familiar," growled Penelope, glowering at her husband. "Don't you remember the letter we found last week?"

Jonathon gasped. "Your father's girlfriend!"

"Exactly. Dad's girlfriend with two daughters!"

"Oh, my God!" said Jonathon. The import of his wife's words finally registered. "She's not his girlfriend with two daughters—"

"No!" wailed Penelope. "She's Dad's *wife* with two daughters!"

"She must not have gone down with the ship after all," groaned Jonathon. "It's incredible. What a disaster!"

"I know. My God. Don't you realize what this means? It's me and Marjorie who are the little illegits! What on earth are we going to do?"

The sound of footsteps in the hallway put a stop to the conversation, and Stephanie materialized in the doorway. Her expression was that of the cat who was about to swallow an entire bucketful of cream.

"Did I hear you talking about someone called Blackwell?" she cooed. "I wonder if it's a relative of mine."

Penelope jumped as if she had been stung. She glared at Stephanie suspiciously.

"You said your name was Keane," she hissed.

Stephanie appeared nonplussed.

"That's my married name," she said serenely. "My maiden name was White, and my mother's maiden name was Blackwell. Angela Blackwell. She died of cancer when I was very young, but I still remember what a lovely lady she was."

Penelope began to hyperventilate.

"I need air," she gasped. She reeled across the room, opened the window by the French doors and leaned out over the sill. Jonathon watched anxiously as his wife gripped the sides of the window and gulped in deep breaths. Gradually, Penelope's body stopped heaving and she pulled herself upright, but instead of turning back into the room, she froze and remained where she was. There was something about her stillness and the set of her shoulders that disturbed Jonathon. With a growing sense of unease, he noticed that his wife's eyes had acquired a steely expression, and her glance appeared fixed on the open frame of the heritage window.

◆   ◆   ◆

Three weeks later, Bertram Beary found himself invited to a second lunch, this time with his goddaughter's husband. Jonathon seemed unusually tense. He ate very little, though kept up with Beary in the consumption of Scotch.

"I'm worried about Penelope," Jonathon stated flatly. He drained his third drink, set down his glass and glowered at his mashed potatoes.

Beary was surprised.

"Why?" he asked. "I think Penelope is looking wonderful. Your new lifestyle obviously agrees with her."

"That's the problem," said Jonathon gloomily. "She's so different."

"In what way?"

Jonathon elaborated.

"I've been married to Penelope all these years, and we've struggled along and raised two children, and she never seemed to mind coping with the muddle and confusion and shortage of money, and she's spent her time accommodating everyone and doing the laundry and cleaning the toilets—I mean, she was just your average, good-natured, run-of-the-mill—"

"Doormat," supplied Beary.

"Housewife," corrected Jonathon.

"Doormat," Beary insisted. "Living with you, definitely a doormat."

"Yes, well, look at her now. Daddy leaves her a bundle, and suddenly it's like living with Imelda Marcos. You should see our closet."

"I hardly think a few pairs of shoes qualify a sweetie like Penelope to be compared to Imelda Marcos."

"Well, that's just it. Penelope has always been so sweet and good-natured, but there seems to be this steel core ... I don't know how to describe it, but it's disconcerting. I never knew it was there. And there's a ruthlessness in the way she talks about our new lifestyle—she's been behaving very oddly."

"I don't understand," said Beary. "I know you've all had a difficult time with this fiasco over the San Francisco family, but from what Penelope tells me, everything has been sorted out most satisfactorily. She sounded exhilarated when I called her yesterday. She'd hired a new caregiver and been on a shopping spree for an evening gown for some golf-club dance that David and Marjorie have invited you to."

"That's tonight," Jonathon grumbled. "I have to wear my tux."

"There you are then. Go out and celebrate the fact that Stephanie Keane decided to leave and didn't press her case."

Jonathon stared at Beary. His expression was desperate.

"But that's just it. *Why* didn't Stephanie press her case? She was positively gloating when she realized she had a legal claim on Penelope and Marjorie's money."

"Did she get a lawyer?"

"No, I think she was canny enough to realize a court battle would eat up the estate, and she made a big thing about not wanting to hurt her half-sisters, so she suggested an even split between the two families. And there it hung in limbo—until suddenly, she disappeared."

Beary looked startled. He put down his glass and frowned.

"Disappeared?"

"Yes. She simply vanished."

"Hmm," said Beary. "Penelope didn't tell me that. You'd better explain."

Jonathon took another swig of Scotch. Then he set down his glass and recounted the events of Stephanie's last day on the job.

"There was a big row that day," he began.

"With Stephanie?"

"No, no. She'd already left. Pen and I were in the study with George—we were going over some bills—and Jane was digging under the furniture pile trying to find the box with the dog's toys. I gather Mark came in to talk with her—the two of them have been thick as thieves throughout the whole business. I suspect Jane's been spilling all the family dirt to Mark and asking his advice."

"Does Jane know the family dirt?"

"She does, actually. Marjorie took all the boxes home so she could ferret around and see what else she could find out about the San Francisco family, and true to form, she's been making Jane sort and file all the letters and documents. Anyway, to go back to the day of the big brouhaha, Mark offered to help Jane find the dog's toys, so he ended up under the dustsheets too. Well, you know what young people are. They started horsing around with the various stuffed animals, and unfortunately, at that moment, Marjorie came by. When she heard Mark's voice coming from under the sheet, along with her daughter's giggles and a cacophony of grunts, snorts and squeaks, she went ballistic."

"I can imagine," said Beary with a complacent smile. He took great pleasure in picturing the scene. In Beary's eyes, Marjorie was as irritating as her sister was lovable, and deserved to be discomfited on a regular basis.

"Anyway," Jonathon continued, "she handed Jane her keys and told her to go wait in the car, and Jane exploded into tears, yelled all sorts of nasty things at her mother, and stormed off—but instead of waiting for her mother in the car, she put the keys in the ignition, screeched out of the driveway, tires squealing, and left her mother stranded."

Beary's grin grew wider.

"Oh, dear. What happened then?"

"Well, Pen and I calmed Marjorie down. She was actually quite hysterical—unusual for her—but the reality is she was as stressed as we were about the mess with Stephanie, and the row with Jane was the last straw. Marjorie admitted as much. For once in her life, she had no idea what to do. And then," Jonathon's face clouded, "Pen stepped in and took charge."

"In what way?"

"She assured her sister that everything was going to work out all right, and she insisted that I drive Marjorie home and stay there for the evening to mediate between Jane and her parents."

"You, mediate? That's like suggesting Boris could oversee negotiations between the neighbours' cats."

"Exactly," agreed Jonathon. "I thought it was pretty lame too. But Pen insisted. She said she wanted to have time to think—but as she acknowledged later, as soon as we'd left, she called Stephanie and asked her over for a chat." Jonathon paused and directed a meaningful stare across the red-and-white checked tablecloth. "And nobody saw Stephanie again after that night."

"She'd left when you got home?"

"Yes. As I was coming home, I passed Stephanie's car going the other way, but I couldn't see who was driving. I just saw the glare of the headlights and a glimpse of the car."

"Well, there you are then. Stephanie left of her own accord."

"Not necessarily."

"What are you getting at? Who else would be driving Stephanie's car?"

Jonathon looked despondent. "Penelope wasn't there when I got home," he said. "Her mother was in bed asleep, but Pen was nowhere about. She came back on foot about fifteen minutes later."

"Where had she been?"

"She said she'd been out for a walk. But it's not like her to leave if no one was there with her mother."

"If her mother was in bed asleep, she wasn't going to come to any harm if Pen popped out for some fresh air," Beary reasoned.

Jonathon looked agonized.

"But what if it were Penelope driving the car? What if Stephanie's body was in the back? There's a wooded ravine just down the road. It's an ideal place to dispose of a corpse and a car. Ever since that night Penelope has been acting evasively. I know she's hiding something. What am I to do?"

Beary looked aghast.

"You can't be serious," he said finally. "Are you really suggesting that a dainty little thing like Penelope popped off a strapping female like Stephanie? What on earth would give you an idea like that?"

"A window weight."

"I'm going to need another drink if you're going to spout cryptic clues," Beary complained. "Sherlock Holmes may have had three-pipe problems, but this is gearing up to be a five-Scotch problem."

"That's a good description." Jonathon flagged down the waitress. He ordered another round of drinks and proceeded to elucidate.

"Our contractor showed us a perfect murder scenario," he explained. "The frame was off the window by the French doors and the counterweight was loose. George told us he was going to re-attach the weight and close the frame—and after Stephanie dropped her bomb into our midst, Penelope couldn't take her eyes off that window. I can always tell when she's plotting something, and there's no doubt in my mind it was that particular moment that gave her the idea of how to solve our problem and get rid of Stephanie."

Beary whistled.

"You're not imagining this? You honestly believe that Penelope whacked Stephanie with a window weight?"

"I'm horribly afraid she did. What am I going to do?"

"Well," said Beary resolutely, his anarchistic tendencies coming to the fore, "do you have to do anything? We all love Penelope. If she did lose it and do something desperate, you surely wouldn't want her to be caught."

"But I've got to know," Jonathon insisted. "Besides, how can I go on living with her thinking she might have homicidal tendencies? What if *I* did something to thwart her?"

"That's true. The way you behave, you'd be living in constant terror. If Penelope decided to whop you with a window weight, it would be justifiable homicide. Well," Beary concluded, ignoring Jonathon's hurt expression, "there's only one thing to be done. If you're determined to find out the truth, you'll have to find some reason why the window has to be opened up again."

The waitress arrived with the drinks, and Jonathon took his glass of Scotch and downed it in one gulp.

"That's a great idea," he said. "I'll do it tonight."

Beary nodded reflectively.

"Yes, that should resolve matters one way or the other. When you see how Penelope reacts, you'll have your answer."

◆   ◆   ◆

Jane and Mark were having an argument, but since their discussion was punctuated by kisses, the debate was hardly acrimonious. Penelope had asked them to Granny-sit while she and Jonathon attended the golf-club dance, and having dutifully administered the appropriate quantities of tea and Tums, they were cuddled together on the couch, with a somnolent Boris contentedly snoring at their feet. Jonathon had been correct in his assessment that the two teenagers were as thick as thieves, for Jane, like her mother, had been extremely put out at the prospect of the newly acquired family wealth disappearing as quickly as it had materialized, so she had unburdened herself to Mark and told him all the details of the San Francisco crisis. Mark, living up to the nickname that Marjorie had bestowed on him, had gallantly set out to help his girlfriend and her beleaguered family. Through some careful research, plus a stroke of luck due to the fact that his father worked at the hospital where Jane's grandfather had died, Mark had discovered some startling facts about Stephanie Keane, and he was bursting to provide the other family members with the results of his endeavours. Jane, on the other hand, wanted to let sleeping dogs lie. Her mother and aunt seemed to have returned to normal, and she saw no reason to stir the pot again, especially since Penelope had stated that her intention in inviting Mark there that evening was to overcome Marjorie's prejudice against the young man.

A further round of debate ended with a most satisfactory embrace, but it was cut short when a flash of light outside the window signalled the return of the adults. Boris awoke and padded expectantly to the front door, and Jane jumped up and looked anxiously towards the hall, waiting for the telltale sound of a key in the lock. When the door opened, Penelope appeared, resplendent in a white sequined gown and floating in a cloud of alcohol and Chanel No. 5. She beamed at the two young people as she pulled off her long gloves and deposited them on the telephone table in the hall.

"Hello, darlings," she said. "Oh, Jane, do relax. You have a couple of minutes before your parents get here. Your father isn't a maniac on the road like your uncle."

"Where is Uncle Jon?" asked Jane.

"Putting the car away. What's this?" Penelope pointed to a pile of envelopes on the table.

"It's your mail," Mark explained. "The next-door neighbour brought it over. It was delivered to her by mistake."

"I think the mailman does that on purpose," sighed Penelope, putting the letters back. "It's his revenge for Boris. I'll look through them later."

"It's really nice of you to have me here, Mrs. Tudge," said Mark.

"Not at all," said Penelope, coming into the room and giving both teenagers a hug. "It's time my sister realized that 'Galahad of the Gutters' is Prince Charming in disguise. However," she continued, firmly steering the youngsters towards the French doors, "we'll break her in gradually. You two go and stroll in the garden. It's a lovely evening. I'll feed Marjorie a large brandy and get her mellow; then I'll bring you in later."

Penelope ushered Mark and Jane onto the patio and pushed Boris after them, since she had no desire to listen to Marjorie's complaints about dog fur on her evening gown. Then she shut the French doors and closed the pleated shades. She did not want her sister to discover Mark's presence until she had educated her as to the young man's sterling qualities.

The door in the hall slammed and Jonathon entered the room. He looked suspiciously at his wife, who had moved to the sideboard and was humming something vaguely melodic and completely unrecognizable as she poured herself a large glass of sherry from the decanter.

"You seem to be in a good mood," he observed.

Penelope twirled into the centre of the room and flopped onto the couch.

"Oh, I am," she purred. "Life is such fun these days, isn't it? I do love being rich. Now that I know how fabulous it is to have money, I don't think I could bear to be without it. I'd do anything rather than be poor again."

Jonathon glanced at the heritage window.

"Anything?"

"Well, wouldn't you? Oh, it's such a relief that everything has sorted itself out."

"Yes, very convenient Stephanie taking off like that. I can't think what made her give up so easily." Jonathon walked over to the window and peered moodily into the night. Penelope had the grace to look uncomfortable.

"I told you. She and I had a little talk."

"A talk?"

Penelope fidgeted, and her eyes refused to meet her husband's.

"Yes," she said evasively. "I explained that the onus of proof would be on her, and as she didn't have access to any of the documents, she would have a great deal of trouble getting anyone to believe her story, and that Mother's rights would be supported in court since she was the one Daddy actually lived with … and that was that."

Penelope's speech tapered off rather lamely, but to her relief, the sound of a car in the driveway prevented Jonathon from questioning her further. She helped herself to another glass of sherry, since the prospect of an evening negotiating her sister's acceptance of Jane's relationship with Mark required fortification, and went to greet the others as they entered.

Marjorie sailed in regally. With her red hair sparkling with sequins, and a billowing dusty-blue taffeta gown emphasizing her slender diet-and-spa-induced waistline, she looked as magnificent as the Virgin Queen—*and equally as daunting*, thought Penelope, taking a large gulp of her sherry. David, grey-haired and debonair, followed his usual three steps behind his wife.

"Isn't this lovely!" Marjorie declaimed, looking around the room. She had not visited the house since the renovations had been completed. She handed David her stole and settled herself gracefully in the wing chair.

"George really came up trumps, didn't he?" smiled Penelope.

Jonathon scowled.

"He certainly did. He'll be able to retire on what he made out of us."

"True," agreed Penelope. "The first thing he did after the job finished was head for the Bahamas."

Jonathon's scowl intensified. He gestured to David to follow him, and the two men headed to the kitchen where the hard liquor was kept. Penelope poured Marjorie a glass of brandy, then sat down opposite her and pondered how to broach the controversial subject of Mark and Jane. Before she could think of an approach, Marjorie spoke.

"Things have worked out well, haven't they?" she said.

Penelope was surprised. Hearing Marjorie open a conversation with a positive remark was unusual, and therefore disconcerting. She looked more closely at her sister. Yes, there was no doubt about it. Marjorie looked different. For want of something better to say, Penelope finally came up with, "Yes, thank the Lord."

With uncharacteristic fervour, Marjorie responded, "Oh, I do hope the Lord is the one we have to thank."

"What on earth do you mean?" Penelope asked.

"Well, it was so strange," said Marjorie. "I mean, Stephanie just disappeared."

Oh, Lord, thought Penelope. *Not another one.* She decided to try a blatant lie.

"Actually," she announced, "Stephanie went back to the States."

"Are you sure?"

"Absolutely," insisted Penelope, and downed the rest of her sherry.

Marjorie let out a breath and suddenly looked much more cheerful.

"Oh, good," she said.

"Why so relieved?"

Marjorie looked sheepish.

"Well, that night ... you know, the evening we had that awful row over that wretched young workman ..."

"Mark isn't wretched," Penelope protested, seeing the opening she had wanted, but Marjorie waved her silent and continued.

"Let me finish," she said. "This is really rather embarrassing, but I need to talk about it—and after all, you're my sister. Anyway, after I got home that night, I taped Stephanie's name on one of Jane's old Barbie dolls and ..." Marjorie's voice tapered off and she bit her lip. Penelope felt a surge of glee.

"Go on," she urged. "You can't stop now. What did you do?"

Marjorie hung her head and stared fixedly into her brandy glass.

"I stuck pins in it," she muttered.

Penelope gurgled with delight.

"Marjorie, you didn't!"

"I did," insisted Marjorie, "and she disappeared the next day. I've been suffering agonies of guilt ever since."

"And so you should have," Penelope said remorselessly. "Voodoo indeed."

"Who's doing voodoo?" asked Jonathon, re-entering with the Scotch bottle and two glasses.

"Ma …" began Penelope. Marjorie glowered daggers at her sister. "… other," Penelope finished. "It's a product of her dementia."

"God, is she really?" Jonathon chuckled. "She must be demented if she's sticking needles in her enemies."

Penelope's eyes acquired a wicked glint. "Yes, mustn't she be?" she agreed. "Absolutely potty."

"Off her rocker."

Penelope dissolved into giggles.

"Nonsense," she spluttered. "Granny never gets off her rocker."

Marjorie went red.

"That's quite enough!" she snapped. "Don't make fun of Mother. Come, Penelope. We should go in and say goodnight."

Marjorie stood up, swept the room with a gorgon-like glare and marched into the hall. Penelope pressed her lips together firmly, regained her self-control, and meekly followed her sister out of the room.

As the sisters left, David returned from the kitchen with the ice bucket. Jonathon leaped into action. He poured two drinks, passed one to his brother-in-law, and gestured to him to be quiet.

"David!" Jonathon glanced towards the window. "You have to help."

David looked bewildered.

"Help? With what?"

"I have to find out what happened to Stephanie."

"We know what happened to Stephanie," said David. He sat down in the wing chair and nursed his Scotch. "Penelope dealt with her."

"Exactly. And I don't believe her cock-and-bull story about their little chat. I think she did something desperate."

"She wasn't the only one," chuckled David. "You should have seen Marjorie. She doesn't know I know, but I actually found a doll at home with pins in it and Stephanie's name stuck on it. Can you imagine it? Marjorie doing voodoo."

Jonathon chortled. "Well, what do you know? Granny isn't off her rocker after all."

David blinked. "What?"

"Nothing. Go on."

"Well, that's the point," said David. "We were all desperate. I even tried a little stratagem myself."

"Really?" said Jonathon curiously. "What did you do?"

David looked embarrassed. "I told Stephanie that George was an eccentric multi-millionaire who only did contracting jobs because he liked the work and that he didn't want people to know how rich he was. I thought that might divert her."

Jonathon snorted.

"That was feeble."

"I know. All I'm trying to point out is that we were all behaving idiotically, and if Penny bent the truth a bit—well, she's no different from the rest of us."

Jonathon fixed his brother-in-law with a prolonged stare. "David—I wouldn't care about white lies and witchcraft, but I think Penelope went further than that." Jonathon was about to elaborate when he heard the ladies coming back. "Oh, hell! Look, never mind the details. Just back me up. Follow my lead."

David watched in astonishment as Jonathon walked to the window, poured his drink onto the sill, and glowered at David to keep silent. As the ladies returned, Jonathon beckoned to his wife.

"You're not going to like this, Pen," he began, tapping his hand on the windowsill, "but David and I have noticed a problem with the renovations. We have a leak. Don't we, David?" He glared meaningfully at his brother-in-law. David nodded obediently.

Penelope came over to the window and peered at the damp patch. She looked puzzled.

"But it hasn't been raining," she said. "How on earth would you know?"

Jonathon paused, nonplussed. David came to his rescue.

"The sprinkler was on," he improvised, "and it's all seeped through."

Penelope looked more closely at the frame. Jonathon whipped out his handkerchief and mopped up the damp patch before she could investigate further.

"Damn. Can you caulk it or something?"

"No," said Jonathon firmly. "It'll take more than that. The whole window casing will have to come off."

Penelope paled and stared, panic-stricken at her husband. Then she threw her back against the window and held out her arms.

"No!" she shrieked. "You can't. I won't let you."

Jonathon's heart plummeted into his boots.

"Oh, my God," he groaned. "You did it! You killed Matron. Now what are we going to do?"

◆   ◆   ◆

The following morning, the phone rang in the Beary household. Edwina answered the call.

"It's your goddaughter," she informed Beary as she handed him the phone. "She wants to take you to lunch at the Cannery." Edwina sniffed disapprovingly and scowled at the bulge in her husband's waistcoat. "You'd better tell her," she admonished, "that she should learn to solve her own family problems because all these restaurant meals are detrimental to your health."

Beary arranged to meet Penelope at twelve-thirty. That morning, as he walked MacPuff, he speculated curiously on the outcome of the Tudge family crisis. Penelope had refused to yield to Beary's persistent questions, merely insisting that all would be revealed when he met her for lunch.

He set off for the Cannery at noon, having ignored Edwina's warnings about the effect of rich foods on his digestive tract, and arrived in time to order a large Scotch and a plate of oysters before his goddaughter arrived. Penelope breezed in ten minutes later. *We are definitely getting used to being a rich bitch*, thought Beary, noting the drop-dead-elegant white linen suit and the fashionably tousled hairstyle that had probably provided the hairdresser with the cash equivalent of half-a-dozen bottles of his favourite Glenlivet.

Penelope sat down and aggravatingly took her time perusing the menu. Then, having ordered, and with a large margarita in front of her, she smiled impishly at her godfather and filled him in.

"Jonathon actually thought I'd murdered Stephanie," she said, "just because I went berserk when he said we had to open up the window frame. I was furious at the time, of course, and you wouldn't have believed the ding-dong row at the house that night. The stinker tried to tell me that the sprinkler had soaked the window and the water had leaked through, but when I smelled the Scotch on his handkerchief I knew he was up to something, so I threw open the French doors to look, and there on the terrace was Jane and Mark snogging like there was no tomorrow. Of course, Marjorie went berserk. You should have been there."

"I'm very glad I wasn't," said Beary sincerely.

"Well, of course, once they all calmed down and let Mark speak, it turned out the dear boy had actually been doing detective work on our behalf, and guess what he'd discovered."

Beary disposed of another oyster and waited for the next set of revelations.

"Stephanie," Penelope announced dramatically, "wasn't our relative at all. She was a fraud."

"Good heavens. So who was she?"

"The Puff Adder's daughter."

"The Puff Adder! You're kidding."

"I'm not. Clever young Mark figured it out. You see, he thought he'd seen Stephanie Keane before—she looked familiar, but he didn't really think much about it—but then, when Jane kept on about her, he remembered. He'd seen her at the hospital last year."

"The hospital?"

"Yes. Mark's father is a doctor. Mark had been walking across the parking lot with his father and they'd stopped to chat with one of the specialists from the cancer clinic. Anyway, two ladies who were getting out of their car greeted the oncologist and he introduced them. They were a mother and daughter who regularly visited an elderly gentleman in the palliative care unit. Mark hadn't remembered any of the names, but he said the older one had been chain-smoking like mad—and the younger one was Stephanie Keane."

"And, of course," finished Beary, "the elderly gentleman was your father."

"Exactly. Daddy had told the Puff Adder about his shenanigans in the States, so she thought up a scheme to get money out of the family. She knew which home-care agency we were registered with, so her daughter signed up and took on the job that we posted."

"Stephanie was taking an awful chance, wasn't she? What would have happened if the real Blackwell girls had turned up?"

"She knew they wouldn't."

"How could she possibly know that?" demanded Beary.

Penelope enlightened him.

"Because," she said, "it turns out that the Blackwell girls were not Dad's daughters."

"But you found the marriage certificate. Angela Blackwell was your father's wife."

"Let me explain. Dad married Angela Blackwell in 1939. She and her brother, William, were stationed with their parents in Singapore. William left to join the armed forces and made it through the war but his sister died during the evacuation of Singapore. Dad stayed in touch with William over the years, but lost contact with him after he immigrated to the United States in 1950."

"Just a minute," Beary interjected. "If Angela Blackwell was killed at sea, how did she become your father's girlfriend years later in San Francisco?"

"It wasn't the same woman. William Blackwell married an American girl in 1954 and her name was Angela Birch."

"Oh, I get it," said Beary. "Her name became Angela Blackwell. William married a girl who had the same Christian name as his sister."

"Yes, and they had two daughters, one in 1957 and one in 1959, which was the year Dad first went to work in the States. I guess he looked up his brother-in-law and became a friend of the family."

"I thought the letter you found was loaded with purple passion."

"Oh, it was." Penelope made a face. "William was killed in a car crash in 1960, and Father continued working in the States until 1965."

"Ah," said Beary, with a knowing wink. "Your father started out as moral support for the grieving widow, and graduated to immoral support."

"Precisely—and the Puff Adder knew about the coincidence of the names and the fact that we'd been kept in the dark. She also knew there would be documents that would support the claim, and with Stephanie in the house as caregiver, she had all the time in the world to sort through the boxes and pick out relevant items that could be used to extort money from us."

"Well, what do you know? A tempest in a teapot after all! I hope your sister was suitably appreciative of Mark's efforts. It sounds as if he's a winner, that young man."

"That was the best part," giggled Penelope. "Marjorie thanked Mark politely, of course, but she was still only snottily gracious. Then I tossed my little grenade into the conversation and informed her that Mark's father is head of neurosurgery at Vancouver General and that 'Galahad of the Gutters' is not only following in Daddy's footsteps, but was only working for us because he believes in paying his own way through school. I also pointed out that he doesn't need much extra cash because he had a four-point-zero average in Grade Twelve and he's got a huge scholarship. He'll be at Harvard in September."

Beary beamed with delight.

"Did Marjorie eat crow?"

"Not at all. She merely flashed her teeth, switched in mid-phrase to the manner she uses on her wealthiest clients and criticized David for not having invited Mark's parents to dinner."

Beary rolled his eyes.

"Trust Marjorie," he said. "But you know," he frowned, "there is one thing still puzzling me. Three weeks ago, you didn't realize Stephanie was a fake, so what did you do to make her leave? Why did she give up so easily?"

The waitress materialized at their table, served Penelope a gourmet prawn salad, and set the dinner-sized lobster thermidor in front of Beary. Penelope picked up her fork, daintily speared a prawn and popped it into her mouth. Beary looked at her sternly across the table.

"I think," he intoned, "that there's something you've left out of the story?"

Penelope paused with another prawn on her fork and stared back innocently.

"No, I don't think so," she said. She resumed eating her entrée.

Beary shook his head sadly.

"Come on, Penelope. Why did you get upset when Jonathon said the heritage window needed to be opened up?"

Penelope wriggled uncomfortably.

"Oh, that. Well, it was nothing really."

"Penelope, I have known you since you were a newborn, and I can always tell when you are lying. What did you hide inside that window frame?"

Penelope sighed.

"Oh, damn," she said finally. "I suppose I'll have to tell you." She set down her fork and explained. "There was an old *decree nisi* in one of Mum's boxes—it was for Uncle Robert's divorce back in 1943—and I kept looking at it and thinking if only Dad and this Blackwell woman had got a divorce ... if only I had some document that would prove that her mother had not been legally married to Dad ... Well, you can't blame me for wishful thinking."

"Not for thinking—no." Beary continued to look stern. "Go on," he commanded.

Penelope gulped and stared ruefully at the two remaining prawns nestled in her plate of greens.

"Well, you know how good I am at art," she said finally.

"Yes."

"And you know how Jonathon always said I could go in for forgery ..."

Beary got a dangerous glint in his eye. He nodded and fixed his goddaughter with a sombre stare.

"Well," said Penelope, "I did some judicious work with white-out and paint and a script pen, and Uncle Robert's decree became the divorce papers for Daddy and Angela Blackwell."

"You forged a divorce document!"

"Yes," said Penelope, still scrutinizing her lettuce. "Then I called Stephanie round and showed it to her. It seemed to do the trick. She left without another word."

Penelope's declaration was met with silence. She looked up at her godfather and saw that he was staring at her in amazement. Finally he spoke.

"Fraud, larceny and imposture, and you retaliated with forgery. What on earth did your sister say?"

"Oh, she was much worse than me," Penelope told him gleefully. "She tried witchcraft. Get her to tell you about her voodoo pins."

"My God," said Beary. "Talk about sisters in crime."

"Oh, come on, Uncle Bertram. Admit it was clever."

"Clever, maybe, and it explains why Stephanie backed off. But," continued Beary severely, "it still doesn't explain why she disappeared off the face of the earth."

Penelope flashed her godfather a dazzling smile.

"Oh, that's easy. She didn't disappear off the face of the earth. She went to the Bahamas."

Beary blinked. "The Bahamas?"

"Yes. There was a postcard from George in the pile of mail on the hall table. It explained everything. Evidently, when he arrived to start his holiday, he found Stephanie staying at the same hotel."

"George?"

"My contractor."

"The one your caregiver couldn't stand? He and Stephanie are holidaying together?"

Penelope speared her last prawn and grinned wickedly at Beary.

"Exactly," she said merrily. "They're on their honeymoon."

A Grim Ferry Tale

Tragic Death in Horseshoe Bay

The body of Lucy Boyle was discovered yesterday morning by her cleaning lady, Mrs. Tilda Jones of North Vancouver. Mrs. Boyle had been beaten with a brass candlestick and had suffered massive head injuries. She was found lying on the carpet in the living room of her home in Horseshoe Bay. The back door was open, and the window in the door had been broken, so it is suspected that Mrs. Boyle interrupted an intruder who was breaking in with the intent to rob the house. None of the neighbours heard any disturbance in the night, and police are asking anyone who lives in Horseshoe Bay to report strangers in the area on the evening of July 20th. Lucy Boyle was the owner of Margison Steel. Twice-widowed, she inherited a fortune from her first husband, Grant Margison, and after he died, she became noted for her charity work on the North Shore. She was president of the North Vancouver branch of the SPCA, and also served on the Lions Gate Hospital board. She re-married in 2004, but her second husband, Ronald Boyle, owner of Burron Software, died tragically in February of 2006 when he fell from the car deck of the Queen of Surrey during a crossing to Langdale. The accident was particularly poignant as the Boyle's dog was left in the pet-enclosure, and ferry staff had thought the animal abandoned until it became apparent that the owner had fallen overboard. The large malamute was in the garden at the time of Mrs. Boyle's murder so, for a second time, the animal has suffered the trauma of the death of its owner.

"Well, I'll be damned," said Bertram Beary, putting down the newspaper and picking up the cup of tea that his daughter, Juliette, had placed on the table beside his deckchair. "First Ronald Boyle, and now his wife—a family as ill-fated as the characters in a Greek tragedy. I was on that ferry crossing," he added, shaking his head sorrowfully. "I remember the dog, too. He and MacPuff had a bit of a 'fisticuff' at the Horseshoe Bay terminal."

"Really," said Juliette, putting her coffee mug on the table and settling into the chaise longue beside her father. She picked up the paper and looked at the article.

Her father nodded. "It was an evening crossing during the week, and there were very few people waiting to board, just a handful of cars and one walk-on, which was Boyle with his dog. After we disengaged our dogs, we chatted briefly. He lived in Horseshoe Bay but had waterfront property on Frances Peninsula, so he kept a pickup truck at Langdale and walked on the ferry when he wanted to come across."

"Oh, how awful," said Juliette, her head still in the newspaper.

"Not really," said Beary. "Quite sensible, if you can afford to maintain an extra vehicle. You avoid those ghastly waits, and you can hop on the ferry at the last minute and never have to worry about whether you're going to get on or not."

"Not the car," said Juliette. "The poor dog." She stroked Quasar who had padded to her side when he heard her exclamation. "There's nothing worse for a dog than losing its owner," she said sadly, looking into the German shepherd's soulful brown eyes, "and to go through it twice would be inconceivably traumatic."

"How is Quasar settling in?" her father asked, remembering Juliette's sorrow at Margaret Witherspoon's arrest and her enforced separation from her pet. "Does he get along all right with Purdy?" He looked towards the garden where, under the eagle eye of his wife, Juliette's own dog was frolicking exuberantly with MacPuff and Beary's grandchildren.

"Yes," said Juliette. "Quasar's patient with the children too, just not particularly playful. I take him to visit Margaret once a month," she added. "She's in the women's correctional centre at the Fraser Foreshore. I'd go more often if it weren't such a distance and I didn't have to deal with the ferry crossing."

"Ah, yes," agreed Beary. "That grim ferry crossing. In the summer it becomes unbearable, doesn't it? Thank goodness I'm retired and don't have to travel on the weekend, which," he added, "is how I met Ronald Boyle. He wasn't retired, but when you own your own company, you have the freedom to travel whenever you like."

"What was Boyle like?"

"Bit of a Young Turk, fortyish, designer jeans, expensive jacket, but he seemed very pleasant. He was most apologetic when his dog lunged at MacPuff. Evidently his dog—its name was Karloff, by the way—had been adopted from the pound when it was four months old. The poor fellow had been abused in his first home—his puppy collar had been left on until it was cutting into his neck, and he'd probably been beaten because it took months before he could be patted without flinching—so Boyle and his wife had to be very careful because they never knew what would trigger a bad memory and cause the dog to bite."

"Poor thing," said Juliette sympathetically. Juliette was the softest-hearted member of the Beary family.

"Actually," Beary continued, "Boyle's wife was the one who adopted Karloff. Basically, when Boyle married, he acquired a pet as well as a wife, but the dog obviously liked him, which, as he said, just went to show that Karloff wasn't a mean animal, just mistrustful, and once people had taken the time to make friends, he was perfectly harmless. I gather Karloff had a circle of people that he loved and accepted—in other words, he was trained not to eat relatives or the home-help—but beyond that inner circle, beware."

"It's difficult having a dog like that," acknowledged Juliette, "but they're often wonderfully loyal to the people they love."

"Karloff was fine with me," said Beary, "because I had the sense not to stick my hand out or move into his space, but I'm quite sure he'd have taken a chunk out of me if I'd tried to get close. Boyle told me that Karloff was one hell of a guard dog."

"He sounds like a nice man. How on earth did he manage to fall overboard?"

"The finding at the inquest suggested that he was leaning against the bulwark and took his cell phone out to make a call. He must have accidentally dropped it over the side. The deck juts out and forms a wide ledge three feet below the railing, but unlike the rest of the car deck where there are openings at the bottom of the bulwarks—scuppers, they're called—the side of the dog-enclosure is solid because otherwise animals could slip through the gap at the bottom. The crew found the cell phone on the ledge, and there was a fragment from Boyle's coat on a sharp piece of metal just below the rail, so the theory is that Boyle bent over the bulwark to retrieve the phone and lost his balance. I only found all this out later, of course. There was a news item in the *Coast Reporter* and a more detailed report later in the *Vancouver Sun*. And when I was driving back to Langdale the following week, there was an item on the radio news. It was quite eerie," said Beary. "I was coming down the big hill just before the ferry landing and I remember looking across at the mountains—they had that two-dimensional appearance that you get sometimes in winter—flat layers of pale blue, rather like cardboard cutouts—and the sheer vastness of it made me think of poor old Boyle trying to survive in the icy water—and it was as if I'd sent out telepathic waves, because just as I pictured the image in my mind, the news announcer's voice came over the air informing me that his jacket had washed ashore on Keats Island. Of course, that put the accident firmly back into my head, so on my return trip to the Lower

Mainland, I chatted with the ferry crew and got a bit of first-hand information from them."

"Did none of them hear the poor man cry for help?" Juliette asked.

"Evidently not. One of the crew members who was patrolling the car deck said he heard the dog bark and he thought he heard a short cry, but then there was silence and he just assumed that the voice he heard would have been the owner telling the dog to be quiet. The reality is," said Beary, "that once the poor sod hit the water, the noise of the engines would have drowned out any calls for help. Of course, nobody would have seen anything, because the dog area is separated from the car deck by a white wall with portholes—all very nicely done-up for our four-footed friends—and you can't see inside unless you go right up to the window. And it was a February evening, so it was already dark."

"Who else was on the ferry?"

"There were only half-a-dozen cars and one oversized vehicle—a flatbed truck with an Ontario licence plate. I was driving our motor-home—it's more comfortable for MacPuff, and besides, your mother wanted the car while I was away—so I was on the lower deck along with the flatbed truck, but the deckhands also loaded the cars there as there were so few of them. I didn't pay a great deal of attention to the other passengers—not at the time, anyway—but I remember being intrigued by the licence plates on two of the cars in the lane beside me."

"Why?"

"They were complementary," said Beary. "There was a red Ford with the plate, SIN 142, and right beside it was a jeep with a Quebec licence plate with the letters and numbers, FUN 241. The woman driving the Ford was utterly humourless. I made the comment, 'my sentiments exactly', and she gave me a look that could have frozen a volcano. The fellow in the jeep smiled, though. Actually," said Beary reflectively, "I think he may have tried to pick her up, which would explain why she was so frosty. I saw him speak to her as she got out of her car, but it was a very brief exchange so she must have given him the cold shoulder too. Mind you," he added, "when you consider that he was wearing an orange baseball cap and an execrable check jacket—not to mention the fact that even though he'd turned off his engine, his car radio was blaring rap music—one can't blame her for not being interested. Not that her own sartorial tastes were anything to write home about—pink spiky hair, panda eyes, earrings the size of footballs and jeans so tight I'm amazed she could walk, let alone sit."

"You don't remember anyone else?"

"Well, I have some recollection of the evening, because after I read in the paper about Boyle going overboard, I had a good hard think about the details of the crossing and jotted down some notes—well, you know what a suspicious mind I have, and I thought I might be asked about it afterwards. I do remember that the driver of the flatbed was a surly-looking individual, and as far as I know, he remained in the cab of his truck for the entire crossing. I was thirsty, so I left MacPuff in the camper and went up top to get a cup of coffee. There was a middle-aged couple in front of me at the coffee machine, and I had a brief interchange with them, then I found a seat in the forward lounge and did my crossword puzzle. Pink-hair was sitting by the window on the opposite side of the lounge, but she only stayed long enough to finish her pop and then she wandered off. I didn't see her again, so she must have already been back in her car by the time I returned to the bottom deck. I didn't see the sartorially challenged Ford driver until I returned to my vehicle—his car was next to the motor-home—so he either stayed on the car deck or was sitting at the other end of the vessel. I also remember seeing a smartly dressed woman who materialized halfway through the crossing, so she was obviously one of the other drivers. She was thirtyish and elegantly dressed—unusual on that route—and she sat in a chair in the centre section and pulled out a romance novel. I honestly can't remember any of the other people on board. It was a very quiet crossing."

Edwina returned from the front lawn in time to hear the tail end of her husband's narrative.

"Quiet crossing! You must be joking!" she said indignantly. "The ferry was overrun with screaming babies, Asian tourists, loudmouthed teenagers in totally inadequate scraps of clothing, and unsupervised children running up and down the corridors. It was a nightmare." She sank into the second chaise longue and fanned herself with her sunhat. "Is there any more tea?" she asked.

"I'll get some." Juliette sprang to her feet. Her mother had thoroughly ingrained the habit of obedience into the various members of her family, and irrespective of age, they were all aware that Edwina's requests were to be considered commands. While Juliette went to the kitchen, Beary enlightened his wife about the subject of the discussion.

"Good heavens," said Edwina, "I remember you talking about that crossing—and now you say the man's wife has been murdered?" Beary handed her the newspaper and pointed to the headline. Edwina proceeded to read the article from beginning to end. She was still engrossed in the newspaper when Juliette returned and deposited a cup of tea at her side.

Beary took advantage of the silence to pause and reflect. The garden was a riot of colour, with pansies and California poppies lining the flowerbeds. The camellia tree at the centre of the lawn still retained a scattering of pink blossoms, and the pale violet blooms of the lavatera cascaded over the railing of the deck. Beyond the cedar fence, the lagoon sparkled in the afternoon sunlight and a sprawling mass of wild roses and snapdragons blanketed the edge of the water. But Beary barely took in the glorious scene, for his mind was preoccupied visualizing a dark car deck on a cold February night.

"It's rather coincidental," he said suddenly, "and therefore suspicious, that both husband and wife have died in tragic circumstances within the space of eighteen months—especially," he added, "when one considers the massive wealth in the family. And yet," he continued thoughtfully, "there's no way that Boyle's death could be anything but an accident because nobody could have got near him without Karloff going into attack mode."

"But didn't you say the dog was tied up?" asked Juliette.

"Yes," Beary replied, "but that wouldn't have deterred him. I wonder if Boyle came out of the enclosure for any reason."

Juliette's mind was still focussed on the problem of the abandoned dog.

"How did the crew get Karloff out afterwards?" she asked.

"With difficulty," said Beary. "The deckhand I spoke to took great delight in describing the incident. The captain was beside himself having never had to deal with a deserted killer canine before, but fortunately there was a lady from the cafeteria who has a way with animals, so the crew had to wait patiently for half an hour while she sat with Karloff, dispensed cookies, and generally won him over before she attempted to untie him. Good job it was the last run of the night. Just imagine if it had happened on a holiday weekend in the summer. Actually," Beary continued, "that's why the boarding staff felt sure that the dog hadn't been simply abandoned. Because it was the last crossing of the evening, they were doing a head- and car-count, and the number of people that left in the cars was exactly the same as the number that came on board, but no one walked off the ferry. That's what set the alarm bells ringing, metaphorically speaking. I remember wondering where Boyle was when it was time to unload. Usually, by the time those huge doors yawn open, the walk-on passengers are in position at the rope across the bow because they're the first ones to get off. And I noticed that the deckhands were looking a bit concerned—with only one foot passenger they could hardly fail to notice he wasn't there—and one of the boarding crew—those are the ones with the orange vests—went scurrying off, so presumably he was sent to look for him. We all sat there, waiting in our vehicles. It was dark and cold, and quiet as the grave on that deck. After a moment, a voice came over the PA, though I couldn't make out the exact words as I had the windows closed—I always do that because of the fumes when the cars start their engines—so I imagine they were making an announcement asking the owner of the dog to report to the car deck. But then they started unloading the cars, and that was that. Poor old Karloff was left behind."

Juliette's husband, Steven, armed with juice packs and cookies, strolled out through the French doors and semaphored to the children to come and get their snacks.

"What about Carl Orff?" he enquired. Steven was a music teacher.

"Not the composer," Beary explained. "Karloff, as in Boris. He's a dog."

"Silly name for a dog," said Steven.

"Not this dog. His story is a real chiller."

"My goodness, yes," agreed Edwina, finally putting down the newspaper. "What a terrible thing. If only the dog had been in the house with Mrs. Boyle," she said sadly. "He could have protected her."

"Yes," nodded Beary. "But that raises a rather interesting question."

Jennifer and Laura raced onto the deck, followed by Purdy and an overheated MacPuff, who padded over to Beary's chair and flopped, panting heavily, at his feet. Steven and Juliette busied themselves dispensing drinks and cookies, but Edwina was still intent on the subject of the murder in Horseshoe Bay.

"What interesting question?" she asked her husband.

His reply was annoying and unsatisfactory.

"The same one that Sherlock Holmes asked," he said.

◆   ◆   ◆

The next day, Beary suggested to Edwina that they take a boat ride to the other side of the harbour. Having been reassured that the trip did not involve setting prawn traps or stopping to throw a line in the water in the hope of catching a lingcod, Edwina agreed to go along, and sensibly armed with sun-block, bug repellent, hat and comfortable shoes, she followed Beary down to the dock. Beary gallantly pulled out a canvas deckchair from the cabin—the *Optimist* was not renowned for luxurious accommodations—and set it out at the stern. Then he raised the large, blue-and-white striped umbrella that he kept on board, and with the *Optimist* looking vaguely reminiscent of the *African Queen*, they set off across the bay.

It took less than five minutes to reach Madeira Park, and Beary sidled the boat into a space at the end of the government dock, then tied up and helped Edwina ashore.

"They've made some improvements," Edwina commented when they reached the top of the gangway and she saw the small, but well-appointed park, complete with flowerbeds, benches and a picturesque gazebo overlooking the water. There was also a small coffee shop nestled amid the shrubs. Knowing his wife's penchant for the fashionable and complicated coffee concoctions that were currently popular with the masses, Beary bought her a large latte, along with a plain black coffee for himself, and they settled on a bench and spent a harmonious half-hour enjoying the combined sensations of sunshine, ocean view and caffeine. They watched the aluminum pontoon Slo-Cat discharge its passengers and take on board another cluster of tourists before setting off for the other side of the harbour, and they observed the captain of a gill-netter selling prawns from the dock. Another smaller group of holidaymakers was negotiating a fare with the operator of the blue and yellow water taxi, which nestled in its mooring, its bulging bowlights and yellow hull stripe making it resemble a predatory shark. The view, Beary thought, was his idea of the perfect action movie—a constantly changing panorama of fishing boats, zodiacs, and every kind of recreational watercraft propelled by oar, motor or sail.

"Now," announced Beary, when they had finished their drinks, "let's walk round to Blue Bay Marina. I want to talk with the Vernons."

"That's on the other side of Whisky Slough," Edwina protested. "What do you want to go to the marina for? We're not having problems with the boat—and we never go to Blue Bay anyway. Billy Brown does our repairs."

"I know," said Beary, "but the Boyles had waterfront property on Frances Peninsula, and according to Billy, the Vernons did all the work on their boat. Angie Vernon knows everything about everyone on this side of the harbour, so if anyone has some background on the Boyles, she will."

"Oh, I see," said Edwina. "A little detective work. All right."

The road to Whisky Slough had very little shade, and they were relieved to find a slight sea breeze blowing onshore when they reached the marina. Angie Vernon was in the shop, but she was busy with a customer, so Beary and Edwina waited patiently beside the giant squid constructed from polished arbutus and driftwood that had pride of place on the window ledge. Not surprisingly, it sported a blue ribbon indicating it had won first prize in the spring craft fair.

When Angie finished her transaction and her customer had left, she greeted Beary and Edwina like old friends. Angie, as Beary often described her, was as friendly as a Labrador puppy, as good-hearted as Mother Teresa, as big-eared as an elephant, and as capable of retaining information as a sieve was of containing water. He had no difficulty in leading the conversation around to the tragedy of Lucy and Ronald Boyle.

"Wasn't it awful!" Angie's eyes were as big as saucers. "Such a dear couple. The only consolation is that they're together again." Beary believed she actually meant it. "They had so little time together," Angie said sadly.

"How did they meet?" Edwina asked, genuinely curious.

Angie's eyes lit up. "It was such a wonderful romance," she said. "Lucy was so down after the death of her first husband, and all she had left was dear old Karloff—people say that dog is mean," she added, "but I never had any problem with him." Beary believed that too. "Anyway," continued Angie, "Lucy used to walk Karloff in Lighthouse Park—she had a lovely house in Caulfield, you know—and one day, there was Ronald, looking out to sea at Juniper Point. He'd recently lost his own dog so, of course, he admired Karloff, and they ended up walking together. After that, there was no turning back. He'd just moved to West Van, which is why Lucy had never met him in the park before, and he'd bought a beautiful home in Horseshoe Bay. After they married, they moved there—so convenient for the ferry. Lucy used to drop in for coffee sometimes when they were here. She didn't come as often as Ronald—he was the real fishing enthusiast—but she still enjoyed the occasional vacation on the Peninsula."

"Where was Lucy when Boyle had his accident?" asked Beary, interrupting the flow.

"She was on holiday in France with her sister."

"Ah," said Beary. "She has a sister. Is that the only surviving relative?"

Angie made a face. "Yes," she said, with an obvious lack of enthusiasm, "and she's going to inherit a bundle."

"You don't approve?"

Angie sighed. "Oh, I suppose Julia's all right. She just isn't the lovely warm person Lucy was. Lucy loved dogs and gardening and looking after her home, and even though she could play the fine lady for her committee work in town, she was a very down-to-earth individual. For all her wealth, she wasn't a snob. She and Ronald would come for a drink at the Peninsula Pub—Ronald went there when he was here on his own too—and they both got along great with the locals. Julia isn't like that. She's very glamorous and charming, but it's all on the surface. She works in the film industry, special effects, make-up, that sort of thing—in fact, she was in Italy on a shoot when Lucy was killed." Angie leaned forward conspiratorially. "Julia," she said meaningfully, "tried to hook Grant Margison herself, but he was much too smart to be taken in by her. He didn't trust her an inch, so much so that he insisted that he and Lucy have identical wills leaving everything to each other, but if they both died, they were to leave their assets to the SPCA, with the condition that the society would always take care of Karloff. Grant was an animal fanatic too."

"Wasn't that a bit extreme?" said Edwina. "What if they'd had children?"

"Grant didn't want children. Actually—" Angie paused and leaned even closer, lowering her voice as if somehow Grant Margison were eavesdropping on their conversation from some astral plane beyond the grave—"I think Grant realized he didn't have long to live, and I suspect he was sterile because of his illness so children were never an issue." Beary stifled a chuckle but Angie was oblivious to the pun. "Anyway, the huge fortune was all his money so I don't see why he should have felt an obligation to leave it to Lucy's sister. Julia had a good job and was perfectly capable of making it on her own so I think it was rather nice that they wanted to leave billions to the animals."

"But you seem to think Julia will inherit now," said Beary, "so I take it Lucy made a new will after she remarried."

"Well, yes, of course. She would, wouldn't she?"

"No clause for the SPCA?"

"No. Lucy told me all about it after Ronald died. I went to visit to give her my condolences, and we had a cup of tea together and a real heart-to-heart chat. The poor love really needed to talk. I was there all afternoon."

"So," Beary persevered, steering Angie back to the question in hand, "why did the animal kingdom get left out of the new will?"

"Ronald wanted children so it was a totally different picture," said Angie. "As far as I know, they made wills with each other as the beneficiaries, so unless Lucy changed anything after he died, it'll all go to Julia as next of kin. To be fair to Julia," she acknowledged, "she really rallied around after Grant died. She'd been in Quebec on a shoot, but she returned right away and came to stay with her sister for a couple of months. Julia was very kind and supportive, and she was happy for her sister when she married Ronald so everything was harmonious. Julia was matron of honour at their wedding. I think," Angie added, "that she was actually relieved when Lucy remarried because she was able to travel again with her work and not worry about her sister going into a depression."

"And then she had to go through it all over again after Boyle died," Beary observed. "What a shock."

"Yes. Julia moved in with Lucy. Well, she pretty well had to. Lucy had a complete breakdown. She lost interest in doing anything around the home, so Julia took charge. She supervised the gardener and hired a new cleaning lady to replace the agency cleaners—they're never as good as one hard-working regular, are they? She got in a full-time cook too, so Lucy was well looked after."

"How on earth did Karloff manage with all these new people in the place?" Beary asked suddenly.

"Oh, he was fine. He hated the gardener so they had to keep him in when the grounds were being done, but he worshipped the cook—all she had to do was bribe him with tidbits—and he got along great with the cleaner. She loved him to bits."

"A nice motherly charlady, no doubt."

Angie laughed.

"You're out of date, old fellow. Lucy's cleaner is a real sharp young woman. She was there the day I went for afternoon tea. She looks like she stepped out of one of those rock videos, but she's a great worker."

"It sounds as if Lucy's sister managed very well for her," Edwina noted approvingly. "She's obviously very efficient."

"Oh, yes, she's that," said Angie. "The support system worked well. Lucy started to come out of the doldrums in the early part of this year. She went back to her committee work, and she even started dating again. She came up here in April and I saw her down at the pub. She was having a drink with a very attractive gentleman, and she introduced him and said he was on the hospital board with her. They looked really happy. Isn't it rotten?" Angie sighed. "Just as life was starting to look up again …" She finished the phrase with a roll of her eyes. "Poor Lucy. What a crappy deal she got."

"She did indeed," agreed Beary. "Do you think," he added, "that Lucy was serious about the new man in her life?"

Angie thought for a moment.

"Probably," she said. "Lucy was one of those women who always needs a man in her life, and she tended to be influenced by her husbands too. I know the feminists would have my hide for saying it, but for all Lucy's capabilities, she was born to be a wife."

When Beary and Edwina left the marina, they walked silently around to the government docks. Both were thinking over the wealth of information that Angie Vernon had given them, some of which was difficult to process, given their lack of personal knowledge of the couple. However, as they climbed aboard the *Optimist* and untied the lines in preparation for the return crossing, Beary finally spoke the thoughts that had been tumbling around in his mind.

"The new suitor would have had a long wait if he intended to marry Lucy," he reflected. "Boyle went overboard in the middle of the channel. It was a high evening tide—a winter tide, those are even higher—so it's more than likely Boyle's body has been carried out to sea and won't be recovered."

Edwina shivered. "Poor man," she said.

Beary continued. "The point I'm making is that in those circumstances, it takes seven years before a person is declared legally dead. That isn't a problem with family property, but it is an issue with matters like insurance or remarriage. Lucy's new gentleman would have had to be prepared to be very patient."

Edwina sniffed.

"Well," she said dryly, "given what we've been told about Lucy's charms and her astronomical wealth, I imagine any man would be willing to be patient."

"Yes," agreed Beary. "If you think in terms of the billions of dollars at stake, a person could easily afford an investment of several years if that kind of money was going to be available at the end of the waiting period. I wonder," he added.

"You wonder what?"

"I wonder what car the new boyfriend drove—and whether he liked dogs and rap music."

"Good heavens," said Edwina, "you don't suppose ..."

"I'm not sure what I suppose," replied Beary, "but it seems to me something smells like a bucketful of rotting herring, and whether or not the sister managed to be out of town at the significant times, I'm ready to bet that she's flapping her fins somewhere at the bottom of the pail. I'm going to call Richard and pass on what we know, and more specifically, I'm going to give him the licence-plate numbers of the cars I saw on the ferry."

"It isn't Richard's case," Edwina reminded him. "West Van has its own police force."

"I know, but the different forces touch base with each other. Richard will know someone over there, and the officers on the case will take the information from him more seriously than if it comes from an aggravating old bugger from the city council."

"Well," said Edwina, swatting a wasp away with her sunhat, "you said it, not me."

"And what's more," Beary concluded huffily, "I'm going to tell Richard to instruct the investigating officers to read their Conan Doyle."

He set his eyes firmly on the far shore and steered the *Optimist* on a steady course for home.

◆   ◆   ◆

Although Richard lost no time in communicating the salient details to his colleagues on the West Vancouver force, the investigation took time and Beary and Edwina did not hear the end of the story until the fall. In late October, Richard came to Sunday dinner and revealed what the combined forces of the North Shore and the RCMP had discovered. The grim ferry tale he told his parents was as potent on the dead-herring scale as Beary had anticipated.

"You were right to be suspicious of the man in the red Ford, Dad," said Richard. "We traced the licence plate. The car on the ferry belonged to a man called Jack Cowland. He was Julia Martin's lover and they were in it together. He owned a moderately successful computer business in Montreal—it was called JC Electronics—and he met Julia when she was there working on a film. They became lovers—they were obviously well suited, both greedy and unscrupulous—and they concocted an elaborate scheme so that Julia could inherit her sister's wealth without having a trace of suspicion attached to her. Cowland came to Vancouver under the guise of starting a secondary office there and he continued to run his company from the new base. These days, with cell phones and computers, you can keep an operation going from the other side of the world. But Julia kept her distance. They had to make sure that there was no way anyone could connect her with Jack Cowland." Richard took another slice of roast beef from the platter at the centre of the table. "This is delicious, Mum," he added to Edwina.

"You should come to dinner more often," said Edwina, passing the potatoes down the table. "So should Philippa. We haven't seen her for ages. The law and the stage demand far too much from you both."

"How is Philippa these days?"

"Down in the dumps," said Beary. "She has a big New Year's event coming up, and now it turns out Adam isn't going to make it home for Christmas."

"She should try to persuade her buddy from New York to come out. Doesn't he have a sister in Vancouver?"

"She's working on him, but he's just been promoted to the detective branch of the force so he may not be able to get away."

"Stop gossiping about Philippa," ordered Edwina. "I want to hear the rest of the story. What was the scheme? To push poor Mrs. Margison's husband off the ferry, then come back six months later and bash her head in when the sister was safely ensconced in Europe? That doesn't sound very elaborate to me."

"Let the boy finish," said Beary, helping himself to more gravy and ignoring Edwina's gimlet eye glaring reproof at his ample waistline.

"Julia and Cowland planned the murder some time ago," explained Richard. "Julia had been resentful towards her sister for a long time because Lucy had landed the billionaire husband that Julia had wanted for herself. Grant Margison had Julia sized up pretty well. He didn't trust her and he wanted to make sure that his assets wouldn't ever end up in her hands, so he insisted that he and Lucy have identical wills naming each other as heirs, with the SPCA as legatee after the last survivor. There was only a small bequest for Julia, so she had nothing to gain if anything happened to either one of them."

"But the situation changed after Grant Margison died of cancer," put in Beary.

"Exactly. Julia came to stay with her sister and did her best to be supportive in the hope that her sister would change the offending will, but Lucy was one of those women who are completely influenced by the men in her life and there was no way she would insult the memory of her husband by going against his wishes."

"That's so archaic," Edwina said severely. "Haven't these young women got any idea of what the sixties were all about?"

"Obviously not," observed Beary. "Lucy was probably a very charming woman," he added sincerely.

Edwina ignored the implied insult and turned back to Richard.

"I think it's appalling," she proclaimed, "that Lucy Boyle only changed her will when the new husband came on the scene."

"It's too bad she changed it at all," commented Beary. "By doing so, she signed her death warrant. Once Ronald Boyle was eliminated, Julia didn't have to be named in the will. She was simply in line to inherit."

"How wicked," said Edwina, "and how calculating. The whole thing was an appalling case of premeditation on a grand scale. Imagine plotting a murder a year in advance."

"Oh, it was much longer than that," Richard informed them. "Julia and Cowland met three years ago. The plan to murder Lucy started shortly after Grant Margison died."

"I don't understand," said Edwina.

"I do," said Beary, taking a slice of beef and passing it to MacPuff who was sitting under the table with his head in his master's lap. "They might have waited even longer," he added, "but once Lucy started getting interested in another man, they had to act quickly. So Julia went to Europe, and Cowland staged the burglary and killed Lucy. And if it hadn't been for Karloff and MacPuff having a scrap at the ferry terminal, they'd never have been caught. What a good job Karloff has a difficult temperament."

"What does the dog's temperament have to do with it?" Edwina asked impatiently.

"Everything," said Beary.

Edwina's eyes grew wide and her expression became thoughtful.

"Oh, yes," she mused. "It's very odd that it didn't bark when Cowland came that night."

"Exactly," said Beary. "Well done, my dear. Sherlock Holmes all over again."

"What on earth are you talking about?"

"Dad means you asked the right question," said Richard. "*Why didn't the dog bark in the night?*"

"Well, why didn't the silly thing bark?" snapped Edwina.

"Because," said Beary, "Jack Cowland was Ronald Boyle."

◆　　　◆　　　◆

Over dessert, Richard explained.

"Julia Martin arranged her sister's second marriage," he began. "She and Cowland hatched the plan between them. Identity theft is so easy these days. Cowland surfed the Internet—tombstoning, they call it—so he could acquire the necessary ID to create his new identity; then he drove to Vancouver, rented a townhouse under his own name, and kept his car there. He maintained a one-room office from where he could officially run his company, so from the point of view of his two employees in Montreal, Cowland was doing business as usual. However, having established dual identities, he altered his appearance by shaving off his moustache and dying his hair, and under the name of Ronald Boyle, he set up a new company called Burron Software. Thus, he was able to run both companies."

Edwina looked appalled. "You mean he deliberately set out to woo and win Lucy Margison with the intention of murdering her?"

"It happens," said Richard. "There are many documented cases of men who seek out women with assets, marry them, and bump them off. Some murder wives on a regular basis and it takes years before they're caught."

"The women don't even have to be loaded like Lucy Margison," added Beary. "Some are dispatched for far less—just a house and a few dollars in the bank is often enough—so let that be a warning," he added gleefully. "You'd better take good care of me, because you'd have enough assets to be a target if I weren't around."

"I'd like to see anyone try," sniffed Edwina.

So would I, thought Beary.

Richard smiled.

"Dad's right," he said. "These predators are skilled con-men and they put on a show of being as rich, or even richer, than their victims. Cowland had to appear well heeled, so Julia coughed up some of her own assets, and Cowland took out a huge loan against his company so he could buy a new car and acquire a house in Horseshoe Bay. He also made up a story about recently losing a dog because Julia had told him about Lucy's daily walks in Lighthouse Park, and that provided the easiest way for him to meet Lucy, strike up a friendship, and ultimately marry her."

"But how did they stage the so-called death of Ronald Boyle?" Edwina asked.

"Cowland isn't saying anything, but the police found a piece of information that may be the link they need. Cowland, or Boyle as he was known, spent a fair bit of time at the Peninsula Pub and he'd made the acquaintance of a man called Harry Morgan, a bit of a loner who was a temporary worker on the construction site at Sakinaw Lake. The building project had wrapped up and everyone assumed Morgan had returned to town or moved on somewhere else, but the police haven't been able to track him down and I'm betting that Cowland found some pretext, either a job or a fishing excursion, for having Morgan come back up the coast. All he had to do was arrange for Morgan to pick up his car and drive it on the ferry, with the understanding that Cowland would walk on and meet him in the dog-enclosure. When Morgan arrived, Cowland knocked him out and dumped him overboard, first removing Morgan's hat and coat and retrieving his own car keys. Cowland probably weighted the body too—all you'd need would be a couple of ten-pound weights, the sort of thing exercise-fanatics use, and the body would stay on the bottom. Then he just had to reach over the rail, plant his cell phone on the ledge, and snag his coat on the sharp metal edge. After that it was easy. He took off his own coat and threw it overboard. Then he put on Morgan's hat and coat. He left Karloff tied in the dog-enclosure, got in his car, and drove off the ferry. After that, he simply resumed his proper identity. He dyed his hair to its normal colour, grew back the moustache, and continued operating JC Electronics, flying back and forth between the Montreal and Vancouver offices, until Julia let him know they were ready to move to the next stage of the plan. Then he returned to the house in Horseshoe Bay, cold-bloodedly murdered Lucy, closed down the Vancouver office of JC Electronics and returned to Montreal. When the RCMP caught up with him, he was in the process of selling off his business, so I suspect the plan was for him to move to a totally different location where he could wait for Julia to claim her inheritance, sell up in Vancouver and join him."

"Dreadful," said Edwina. "To think they might have got away with it!"

"Yes," agreed Beary. "Any villain who is prepared to abandon a dog, however cantankerous, deserves the worst the courts can throw at him. What will happen to poor old Karloff now?"

"I asked about that," said Richard. "The SPCA has taken care of him."

"Poor animal. They'll have a hard time finding him a new owner, given his temperament, but it's doable if they work at it. I hope they try."

Richard smiled. "They already have," he said. "Lucy's cleaning lady is taking him, and the SPCA is going to make sure she has lots of dollars to provide him with everything a dog could desire. They can hardly do otherwise. He's proved a very valuable dog for them."

Beary's eyes glinted.

"Wait a moment … don't tell me … Yes!" he crowed. "The will!"

Edwina looked mystified.

"But it was the first will that left the estate to the SPCA," she argued. "Even if Julia can't inherit now because of her complicity in her sister's death, there's no clause for charity in the second will."

"No, but think for a moment. The second will designated Ronald Boyle beneficiary, but Ronald Boyle didn't really exist. The name was false."

Edwina's face lit up in a wide smile.

"Oh, I see!" she exclaimed. "The second will was invalid."

"Exactly," said Beary. "So the dogs will inherit the lot."

He bent down, ruffled MacPuff's ears and handed him the remains of his dish of ice cream.

"Karloff will be in clover for the rest of his life."

The Mystery of The Black Widow Twanky

"Oh God! Look what the hellcat dragged in," exclaimed Milton Lovell. "It's the Black Widow Twanky. I'd like to murder the bitch!"

Philippa Beary looked towards the restaurant lobby. She saw a debonair gentleman of middle years, with the build of a linebacker and the sophisticated attire of a matinée idol from the 1930s. Hanging avidly on his arm was an elegant lady wearing a turquoise suit that screamed Armani. Philippa recognized her as Ingrid Lindstrom, the director of the local Christmas pantomime.

Philippa's dinner companion made a vicious stab at his moussaka.

"I've been the Dame in our panto since the club was formed. It's tradition!" he said indignantly. He popped a morsel of food into his mouth and banged the end of his fork on the table. "It's all because Andrew was ill and couldn't direct this year. I can't believe that cow they brought in from Surrey has demoted me to a genie! Imagine," he snorted, "hiring a Swede to direct an English pantomime! The board has gone mad."

"Ingrid is third-generation Canadian," Philippa pointed out. "She has an English mother and she's been directing pantos for twenty years. Anyway," she added, "it's hardly a demotion. The Genie of the Lamp is one of the plum parts in *Aladdin*."

"Nonsense," Milton contradicted her. "The Magician and the Dame are the show-stealers. The Genie is usually played by some skinny teenager who's top of the choreographer's ballet class."

"So you'll turn it into a comedy part. The director is probably thinking of Robin Williams."

"All Ingrid Lindstrom is thinking of is how many times Norman Green can bonk her during the run of the show."

Philippa adored Milton. He was one of her most entertaining friends, but she was well aware of his tendency for creative hyperbole.

"Now you don't really know that, surely," she challenged him.

Milton's face was turned towards his plate, but he stared reprovingly at Philippa over his glasses.

"Darling, would I say that if it weren't true? Two days after we started blocking, Sandeep went into her costume room and caught them hard at it."

"How excruciatingly embarrassing, especially for a nice girl like Sandeep. What on earth did they say?"

"Oh, they didn't see her. Fortunately she saw them before she flicked the light on. Of course the poor love backed out in a hurry, but not before she'd seen Ingrid's panting physiognomy bobbing up and down over Norman's shoulder. They were doing it against the *wall*," Milton added gleefully.

"How could she be sure it was Norman if the lights were out?"

"My dear, it was mid-afternoon and there is a little window, albeit high up. It wasn't that dark. And she recognized his jacket." Milton sniffed. "Fancy not even taking off his coat. They must have been in a tearing hurry. But then of course, at Ingrid's age, she's probably all too aware of time running out. And since that windbag she's married to is such a boozer, she'd have to activate his fading libido before sunup if she wanted action at home."

Philippa giggled. "Milton, you're awful!"

"I know. And don't you love it?"

Philippa peered round a potted plant and looked across the restaurant. She and Milton were eating in an atrium that had been created by enclosing an outdoor deck, but they could see into the main room as the glass from the windows had been removed and the apertures were framed with fake-plaster ledges and ivy-draped columns. Philippa had a clear view of Ingrid Lindstrom and Norman Green. They were seated under a mural depicting ancient Greek ladies bathing in an impossibly brilliant aquamarine river, and the intimacy with which the couple locked glances appeared to verify Milton's item of gossip.

"How did Ingrid find Norman Green?" she enquired. "Someone told me he was an equity performer from Toronto—both stage and film."

"He is, but Jimmy Green—that's his cousin—is the house tech at the Colosseum, and as Norman was in Vancouver on a film job, Jimmy suggested he stay over and try out for the panto. Ingrid took one look at Norman's middle-aged manly charms and cast him on the spot." Milton looked peevish. "I don't object to her post-menopausal lust," he said, "but to make him the *Dame*! I mean ... it's perverse."

"Is he good on stage?"

Milton nodded grudgingly. "He can act—I'll give him that—but only within a very limited repertoire. He was born in England after the war—which makes him much too *old* to play the Dame—imagine running around in drag when you're pushing sixty? His hair's dyed, you know—and he trained in rep over there, so he knows the panto tradition and he's a master of the 'Who's for tennis?' drawing-room comedies that seem to get regurgitated regularly no matter how out of date they are."

"What about his film jobs?"

"Just as limited. He gets TV and film work whenever they need a stiff-upper-lipped officer to defend the Empire—the highlight of his career was getting blown apart by one of 007's arch-foes back in the Connery days, and that was *yonks* ago—but these days, if he gets anything, he's just a back-room boy tapping a pointer on a map."

"It sounds as if he's competent," Philippa reasoned, "so you can't really complain."

Milton sent a reproving glare across the top of his wire-framed lenses.

"Oh yes I can," he said. "He's treating the current gig like a holiday. His behaviour is absolutely criminal—we ought to be calling that gorgeous brother of yours in to arrest him. How is the handsome detective, by the way?" he added, diverting to another tangent. Milton's conversations were as complex as an operatic sextet.

"Richard is fine." Philippa steered Milton back to the main theme. "What sort of behaviour? Do be specific, Milton."

"He plays jokes on the other performers, particularly Princess Sheherezade and the Magician. There's a dramatic scene where the Magician whisks the Princess away to Africa, so Norman got Jimmy to rig a water bomb with a timer so the thing came down just as the Princess complained that the desert was dry." Milton sniffed. "He's very immature," he concluded with a flourish of his napkin.

"Isn't that a case of the pot calling the kettle black? Remember when we performed in *Land of Smiles* together. You taped a *Playboy* centerfold to the middle of my scroll."

"Yes, dear. But that was just a little bit of innocent fun. Anyway, if you remember, it backfired on me because you unrolled the scroll upside-down and the only people who saw the picture were the musicians in the orchestra pit. I had a very hard time keeping a straight face seeing the entire string section rolling around in hysterics." Milton assumed a sanctimonious tone. "Norman's stuff is different. He's got a mean streak. He throws people off. He's not a *generous* performer," he concluded, uttering the ultimate damnation of a fellow thespian.

Milton finished his last mouthful of moussaka and arranged his cutlery neatly on his plate.

"This place is deliciously kitschy," he declared, staring at a statue that rose naked from a column at the end of the atrium. "Don't you adore the friezes around the walls and those wrought-iron lanterns hanging from the ceiling? The gold bulbs in the greenery are a bit much, but the overall effect comes together rather nicely—other than the fact that these square-backed wooden seats are exceptionally hard on the bum. Of course, the service is the pits—the waitresses are as humourless as the village crones in *Zorba the Greek*—but the food is fabulous, so that makes up for staff that look like they'd just as soon stone you with the black olives as stick them in your salad. I shall retreat here regularly during the course of the run and console myself with souvlaki, baklava and ouzo."

"You'll be a well-lit Genie of the Lamp," laughed Philippa.

"How's your dinner?" Milton asked. He was always an impeccable host, considering it his duty to ensure that his guests were comfortable as well as entertained.

"Excellent," Philippa assured him. "And you're right, it is a pretty setting. Look at that string of lights reflected in the glass." She pointed to the far side of the window where the evening sky was bisected by a line of golden orbs that stretched the width of the atrium. Below, the Fraser River, slate-grey and rippled at the center where the current flowed faster, was gradually changing colour as the sun shifted across the sky.

"It gets better," said Milton. "You watch. The river will turn to indigo, then gold as the sun sinks to the horizon, and ultimately the water will be black, but you'll still see the waves in the light of the halogen lamps on the docks. Look at the bridges."

Philippa swivelled round and looked in the other direction. The Skytrain, its red and blue zigzags just visible in the fading light, was arcing across the sky between monolithic concrete towers. A red light blinked atop each gigantic column but the support cables that extended across the river were already fading from view. Behind the train loomed the Patullo Bridge, transformed from its Nelson's-hat curve to a shimmering red tiara as the taillights from rush-hour commuters streamed across the girders.

"Another fifteen minutes," predicted Milton, "and all you'll see will be dock lights, bridge lights, and the navigation lights on tugboats and barges, not to mention a swath of sparkling diamonds from the houses and high-rises on the far shore. Once it's dark, Guildford Shopping Centre looks like a castle tower, and the casino on the paddle-steamer glitters like a maharajah's elephant."

Philippa gazed affectionately at her friend. For all Milton's cynicism, he was very much a connoisseur of beauty.

"Speaking of the casino," Milton added, reverting to his earlier tone, "that's a favourite hang-out for Twanky-Wanky. He and his cousin love to gamble. They always seem to win too," he said petulantly.

"In my experience," Philippa said disapprovingly, "gamblers only tell you when they win. They never admit to losing."

"Not these two. How do you think Norman can afford expensive suits and restaurant meals? He couldn't do it on an actor's pay. The minute he's through at the theatre, he pops over the road and gambles the night away. Jimmy's just as bad."

"They sound quite a pair."

Philippa changed the subject before Milton could begin another diatribe on the subject of Norman Green.

"Who else is working the show?" she asked.

"The only performer you'd know is Dieter Volkow. Wasn't he your leading man in *Vagabond King*?"

Philippa scowled.

"Awful, isn't he?" said Milton. "Not as a performer, of course. He's a good actor, but such wandering hands."

"That's the understatement of the year."

"He's in his element on this show. Dieter likes them young—*really* young, if you know what I mean—and except for Norman and me, all the cast are practically infants. There was a lot of talk when he played Captain Von Trapp last year. Little Liesel didn't make it to the age of consent until halfway through the run, and according to my sources ..."

Milton's facial expression spoke volumes.

"I can imagine," Philippa muttered. "I had to endure his advances on *and* off-stage. I had to say, 'Kiss me, Villon,' and die in his arms. He certainly made the most of it."

Milton grinned.

"I bet you expired faster every night."

"I did. By closing night he was kissing a corpse. But enough about Dieter." Philippa steered Milton back to her original question. "Who's on the production team?"

"Joy Carter is choreographing—she doesn't like the casting any better than I do. With me playing the Genie, she has one less opportunity to showcase her studio stars—and she *does love* her little girl protégés—rather too much, if you know what I mean."

Milton's eyebrows shot two inches above the rims of his glasses as he gave Philippa a knowing look that would have read well in a fifty-thousand-seat stadium. "And Bill Brent is musical director," he continued, when his eyebrows returned to Earth. "Not a bad sort, but a bit of a plodder—he never gets my tempos right. Joe Lennox is stage-managing. The poor fellow would love a chance to tread the boards, but he's such a good stage manager that he's never cast because directors want him running the show."

"That's hardly surprising. Joe is extremely reliable."

"A veritable rock," agreed Milton, "and one needs a bit of granite to deal with the cast Ingrid's assembled—hysterical infants who see this as their *big* chance and pros who don't take panto seriously. And on that subject," Milton chattered on, "I think the gambling fever's catching. I saw Dieter handing Jimmy a bundle of notes the other day, and it's my guess he was getting him to place a bet for him."

Milton paused for breath and looked towards the kitchen.

"Now, before we indulge in more gossip," he said, "let's order dessert. The dress call is six-thirty so we just have time—especially since *you-know-who* is still stuffing down his main course, and he's in the opening number. At least I don't have to pop out of my lamp until Scene Three. Let's see if we can flag down a waitress."

"I'm really looking forward to the rehearsal, Milton," said Philippa. "I'm glad you invited me. And I do appreciate being treated to dinner. What a lovely evening."

"Ah, but remember, I expect payback. You promised to help me gift shop."

"That's no big deal. I love Christmas shopping—I love everything about Christmas."

"Well, if you love everything about Christmas, you should have auditioned for the pantomime. You'd make a much better Aladdin than our current principal boy."

"I couldn't audition, you know that. I was already committed to the Bach Choir, plus I'm in rehearsal for *Fledermaus*."

"How can you prefer Handel's *Messiah* to British panto? Soooo solemn—and speaking of solemn, where is the politically correct, po-faced harpy that served our meal?" He craned his neck to see over the ivy-covered plaster. "Did you hear how she called you *Mizzzzzz?*" he added, relishing the syllable with the gusto of a hyperactive mosquito.

"She'll appear in a minute," said Philippa. "I need a rest to digest my steak."

Milton shook his head.

"Steak in a Greek restaurant—Handel instead of panto! You're going down-hill fast, my girl."

"I'm practical. Spicy food gives me indigestion and the Messiah gives me a better pay-cheque." Privately Philippa much preferred the majesty of Handel's oratorio to the screaming children, silly puns and cross-dressing of English panto-mime. Although her parents had been born in England, she was too far removed from the tradition to feel a sentimental attachment for the medium. However, she kept those thoughts to herself as she did not want to hurt Milton's feelings.

As Milton resumed his vigil for the elusive waitress, Philippa turned and looked at the view. The sky was now black, though a hint of white cloud remained, gleaming faintly above the lights of the far shore. The lower halves of the diamond-shaped transit buttresses had disappeared and only the tops were visible, golden and freestanding against the night sky. The Skytrain had trans-muted into a glowworm, arcing across the black void, and below it, the green starboard light of a speedboat snaked along the river. Philippa glanced up and saw the lights of a plane gliding over the glass roof of the atrium. She was woken from her reverie by Milton's penetrating tenor.

"There she is!"

The sober-faced woman who had served their meal had emerged from the kitchen. Milton wildly semaphored in her direction, but to no avail, for she bla-tantly ignored him. Milton took a deep breath and projected his voice in the tones he used to reach the back of the Queen Elizabeth Theatre. "Excuse me! Waitress!"

Unable to ignore what the entire restaurant had heard, the woman came over and took their dessert order. As she tucked her pad in her belt, she looked Milton straight in the eye and said, "Where have you been the last few years?"

Milton looked blank.

"I'm your server, not your waitress," the woman snapped. She turned abruptly and marched towards the kitchen.

Milton was unabashed.

"Shouldn't that be serviette?" he called after her.

Philippa slunk down on her chair. Sometimes Milton was too much even for her.

◆   ◆   ◆

The Colosseum was one of the oldest theatres in the Lower Mainland. It had started life as a vaudeville house; then moved through various stages of dilapidation to exist as a concert hall, movie theatre and a bingo establishment; but a burgeoning enthusiasm for heritage restoration in the nineties had saved it from demolition, and loving care and a monumental fundraising campaign had restored it to its original glory. Philippa leaned back in her velvet-upholstered seat and admired the exquisite murals that graced the ceiling, framed the proscenium and decorated both balconies. Where the lower balcony curved around the walls of the theatre, two ornately embellished boxes overlooked each side of the stage. A massive chandelier, worthy of *The Phantom of the Opera*, hung at the centre of the auditorium, and the stage curtain, which was still down, was trimmed with gold tassels and made from a pleated orange brocade that matched the piping on the luxuriously padded seats.

The musical director was already in the pit, talking earnestly with the small ensemble he had assembled for the show, and thumps from the far side of the curtain suggested that the choreographer was taking the dance troupe through some last-minute paces. A lonely spot travelling the width of the stage indicated the presence of someone in the lighting booth, but otherwise, nobody was in sight. Philippa looked at her watch. The rehearsal was late starting and she suspected it was going to be a long evening.

The auditorium doors banged open, and Sandeep Sihota shot through and hurried down the aisle. Her arm was draped with a gauzy costume in turquoise and gold, and she flashed a smile at Philippa as she passed. The doors opened a second time to admit an Arabian princess wearing an indecorous bodice that would have resulted in a prison sentence or worse in the current Saudi kingdom. She was accompanied by a white-faced demon garbed in flowing black and silver—presumably the evil Magician from Africa. As the pair reached the aisle, Philippa recognized the devilish face under the elaborate mask. It was Dieter Volkow. Dieter was listening to his companion and did not notice Philippa in the back row of the auditorium.

The Princess spoke petulantly. Her voice sounded young, and although her tone was angry, Philippa sensed she was on the brink of tears.

"Norman's cousin is as bad as he is." The young performer radiated fury and indignation. "When I complained about the whoopee cushion on my throne, Jimmy told me I had no sense of humour. I can't stand either of them."

Dieter stared sympathetically down the Princess's cleavage and attempted to comfort her. His voice was a deep rumble, but his well-trained baritone projected to the back row.

"You must not let them get to you. Focus on your part."

"How can you be so calm? Look at what Norman did to you. He pulled a cap gun in your big scene."

"Well, it was funny," Dieter admitted philosophically. "Ingrid told us to keep it in."

"But aren't you furious?"

"Not really. The Greens are like silly English schoolboys. They've never grown out of their passion for comics, commando movies and war toys. I don't take them seriously."

A sharp voice rang out overhead, and Philippa looked up to see Ingrid Lindstrom at the rail of the stage-right box. Margaret Chang, the assistant director, stood behind her, armed with notepad and pen.

Ingrid looked toward the booth.

"I'd like to get started," she called. "We have a long evening ahead." She sat in the armchair at the front of the box and gestured for Margaret to join her. The musical director took his seat at the synthesizer and the other members of the ensemble picked up their instruments. The thumping backstage ceased, indicating that the technician had cued the stage manager, and the lights in the auditorium dimmed. *Aladdin* was about to begin.

The curtain went up on a colourful market tableau, the chorus singing with gusto while a trio of gaudily clad merchants, who Philippa suspected were the senior pupils at Joy Carter's ballet academy, performed a vigorous, vaguely oriental dance. As the chorus ended, Widow Twanky lumbered to the front of the stage and declaimed the opening lines. The Dame's delivery was good, and Philippa found herself laughing at the atrocious puns as the actor cavorted through the first scene. In spite of her loyalty to Milton, she had to admit Ingrid had made a good casting choice. Norman Green was hilarious in the part. The garish make-up and outlandish costume looked hysterically funny on his massive frame, and he did nothing to disguise his deep, masculine voice. He loped through the role as if he were organizing a team on the football field. He had an easy manner with asides and a nice touch with the songs. *Audiences will love him*, Philippa decided.

As Milton had indicated, the majority of the cast was young, but the performers had boundless energy and lots of enthusiasm. Aladdin had a pleasing musical comedy style, Princess Sheherezade had a bright, well-trained soprano, and Dieter, predictably, was particularly fine as the Magician. Philippa had to acknowledge his skill as a performer even if she abhorred his off-stage behaviour.

She sat up straighter when the cave scene began. An eerie blue light hovered centre stage as Aladdin summoned the Genie of the Ring, a young dancer with exquisite lines, who led a jewel ballet, clearly designed as a Carter Academy show-case. Then Milton appeared, heralded by a puff of purple smoke, and Philippa saw right away that Ingrid had made a wise decision. However annoyed Milton was to be deprived of the Dame, he was brilliant in his assigned role. His twin-kling eyes and merry smile were utterly captivating, and Philippa was certain that the Genie of the Lamp would be the favourite of every autograph-seeking child who mounted the stage at the end of each performance.

The rehearsal proceeded smoothly until the close of Act One. Aladdin's hut had been transformed into a palace and he had duly wooed Sheherezade; and now he made his exit, issuing strict, but predictably vain warnings that she should guard the lamp and not let it out of her hands. The lights dimmed to a soft rose, and the Princess, alone on stage, began a lyrical rendition of a currently popular love song which bore little relation to the plot. As she sang, she picked up the lamp and moved slowly downstage. Her voice was lyrical and bright, and surpris-ingly mature for her age. Philippa was impressed. The girl really was extremely talented. As the song rose to a penultimate phrase that was obviously leading to a spectacular high note, the Princess opened the lamp, as if trying to understand the mystery of its power. The music swelled as she glanced down, and Philippa waited with anticipated pleasure for the end of the soaring phrase. Then sud-denly, the girl's face twisted in horror and the glorious note erupted into a shriek. She threw the lamp across the stage, stared angrily towards the box where Ingrid sat, then ran off in a flood of tears.

Ingrid stood up and bellowed towards the booth. The auditorium lights blazed on. After a moment, Joe Lennox came out of the wings. He was carrying a shoebox, and before coming forward to face Ingrid, he looked round the stage floor, then bent, scooped something from the boards and tucked it into the box.

"What is going on?" Ingrid demanded.

"A joke gone wrong," Joe stated flatly. "There was a frog in the lamp."

"What! For heaven's sake, this is a dress rehearsal."

"I'll find the culprit and straighten him out," said Joe shortly. He had a good idea who it was, but was too fair-minded to make assumptions without proof. Joe was unflappable. Nothing fazed him.

"All right," snapped Ingrid. "Since we've stopped, we'll take the break now. However, I should warn you all that I will be giving notes after we finish tonight, and if you want to get home before breakfast tomorrow, I'd suggest that no one else decides to indulge in juvenile antics." She turned, peremptorily nodded to her assistant, and disappeared through the velvet curtains at the back of the box.

Philippa got up and stretched. She was desperate for a cup of coffee but the theatre bar was closed and she was too professional a performer to march back-stage uninvited. However, to her relief, Milton, resplendent in purple and silver, appeared at the foot of the auditorium and came up the aisle to meet her.

"There's food and drinks in the green room," he announced. "Come on, fol-low me."

"So who did it?" Philippa asked as she accompanied him down the aisle.

Milton gave her a bug-eyed look.

"You really have to ask? The Black Widow Twanky strikes again."

"How can you know for sure it was Norman?"

"He admitted it. Little Tina is livid. I'm surprised you couldn't hear her screaming at him. Very un-princess-like language—I was afraid she'd damage her precious vocal chords."

"Did he apologize?"

"Are you kidding?" Milton led Philippa through the double doors and down a flight of stairs. "He had the nerve to tell her she was over-reacting and that a true professional would have taken it in her stride, shut the lid of the lamp, and fin-ished the aria."

"He sounds like an idiot." Philippa sympathized with the young singer. She wasn't sure that she would have managed to keep control in the circumstances.

"He is," Milton agreed. "I told you. He's good at three things: gambling; act-ing anything that requires an English accent; and the other thing that Ingrid likes so much. Otherwise, he's a case of arrested development. Would you believe he still has a collection of fifties toys? Down here," he added, indicating a second, shorter set of steps. "Yes, Norman is totally self-centered and his cousin isn't much better. A good technician, but no sensitivity to what the performers might be feeling—oh, whoops—speaking of ..." He paused as a tall man in jeans and T-shirt came into view at the base of the stairs. Philippa looked curiously at the man. He had the same stocky build as his cousin and his features were not dis-similar, but his cropped hair had been allowed to stay its natural grey, and he lacked the arrogant expression and dynamic presence of the Black Widow. He was stuffing an envelope into his pocket and barely glanced their way.

"Hello, Jimmy," said Milton impassively as they crossed on the stairs.

Jimmy Green nodded brusquely, took the last few stairs two at a time and dis-appeared round the corner.

"He looks like his cousin," noted Philippa, "but without the dash or style—and he certainly doesn't make much effort to be charming."

"He doesn't have to. Good technicians are much harder to find than actors. He hangs and sets lights, and he trains a team of underlings to run the booth. Mind you, everything is computerized, so once he's entered all the cues and set the show, it practically runs itself. Hello, Joy," he added. Joy Carter had materialized at the bottom of the stairs. She seemed preoccupied and looked startled when Milton spoke to her. She smiled thinly and hurried past.

"And goodbye, Joy," muttered Milton. "So nice to chat. One of her little twinkle-toes must have given her the cold shoulder," he speculated, as he ushered Philippa down the hall.

They went through a door into a small vestibule. Here, there were three more doors, two of which sported signs for the ladies' and gentlemen's washrooms, and a third that led into the green room, which was a long, narrow rectangle with chairs, chesterfields, and a small kitchenette at the far end. Beyond the fridge, Philippa could see another door, presumably a second entrance. The green room was a mass of colour that belied its name, and a motley crew of peasants, sultans and jewels greeted Philippa and Milton as they entered. Princess Sheherezade was sitting in a corner nursing a bottle of water. Dieter hovered nearby.

"Where's the bad boy?" asked Milton.

"I think he's hiding," Dieter replied, tearing his eyes from Tina's décolletage. "There was a shady-looking character asking after him earlier this evening. He said he was from the casino so Norman probably owes him money."

"I doubt that," said Milton.

"Well, whatever the reason, he's skulking in his dressing room."

"That's another bone of contention," hissed Milton to Philippa. "There are four double dressing rooms and two large chorus rooms. Norman insisted on taking one of the doubles, while all the other principals are sharing. He says he needs the space because of the padding and wigs and hoop-la that the Dame has to wear. Utter nonsense—I never indulged in such prima donna tactics. He's an absolute hog, darling. You have no idea."

The door opened and Joe Lennox peered in.

"Five minutes, please. And dancers, don't change after the bows—Ingrid will want you on stage immediately for the notes." He ignored the chorus of groans and continued. "Principals, you'll get a half-hour break. Ingrid's doing the ensemble first."

"What!" exclaimed Dieter. "But that's most unreasonable."

"No, it isn't," said Joe firmly. "Most of the dancers are still in school." He left before Dieter could protest further.

"Sorry, darling," said Milton to Philippa. "You're going to be waiting for your ride until the bitter end."

A crackling voice over the intercom called, "Places," and the green room gradually emptied. As Philippa followed Milton to the landing, a sallow youth in jeans, combat jacket and ball cap hurried along the corridor and brushed past them before loping up the stairs.

"Rude," remarked Philippa. "Who was that?"

"That's Mario—the ASM. He's actually quite nice-looking if you see him with hair. I abhor the ubiquitous baseball hats," Milton complained, "especially since the young never wear them the right way round." Milton was well known for his sartorial elegance. "And the combat jackets seem to be all the rage too," he grumbled. "Mind you, Mario's entitled to wear one. He's supposed to be a crack shot. When he's not running shows, he likes murdering ducks. He belongs to the Westburn Fish and Game Club—your father's a member there, isn't he?"

"Yes, but Dad doesn't hunt. He just likes fishing."

"Well, after all, he is a politician. I know the infamous Councillor Beary is renowned for his feisty independence, but even he probably has to make some concessions to public opinion. Off you go, dearie," Milton added, opening the door that led to the front of house. "This is where we come to a parting of the ways."

Philippa returned to her seat and waited for the show to proceed. To her relief, the second act went without a hitch. Ingrid's warning had been effective and no pranks interrupted the proceedings, other than the Widow's attempt to shoot the Magician with a cap gun; but since Philippa had overheard Tina and Dieter talking earlier in the evening, she knew the director had instructed the performers to keep the business in.

The show concluded with the customary grand finale, followed by a series of frenetically choreographed bows, although Philippa was surprised to see that Norman Green appeared to be flagging. Perhaps Milton was right, she mused—the demands of playing a pantomime dame might be too much for a man of sixty. However, the final tableau was spectacular, for when the curtain descended, the ensemble continued playing and a huge grid covered in lights that spelled *Aladdin* came down at the front of the proscenium. The chorus could be heard singing backstage, and it was apparent that audiences were going to be treated to a lavish lighting display with rousing orchestral accompaniment as they exited the theatre—an impressive end to an enjoyable production.

The exit music continued for five minutes, ending with a noisy drum roll as the grid disappeared back into the fly gallery. In the eerie silence that followed, the curtain was raised to reveal dancers and chorus straggling into position for their notes. The performers perched their weary bodies on the palace steps and along the edge of the apron. Their dazzling smiles had been replaced by bored expressions and the energy that had vitalized the show was completely dissipated. Ingrid waved towards the booth, disappeared through the curtain at the back of the box, and emerged a moment later at the front of the lower orchestra. Margaret Chang, carrying sheaves of paper, was close behind. Philippa looked at her watch. It was ten-thirty. She wished she had brought a book to read.

As she contemplated moving closer to the stage—at least that way she could listen to the director's comments—Milton bobbed his head through the door at the side of the pit. He ducked low and tiptoed up the aisle so as not to disturb Ingrid.

"Come on," he urged. "We're not called for forty-five minutes. You might as well come and socialize in the green room."

Philippa followed him downstairs. The green room was empty except for Sandeep and Joe Lennox who were both helping themselves to coffee. Joe greeted Philippa and left with his drink. Sandeep sank onto the couch and rolled her eyes.

"What a night!" she groaned. "Pantomime is the worst challenge for a costume mistress."

"A lot of bodies to fit," agreed Philippa.

"It's not just that. The majority of performers are so young, and they don't look after their things. I feel like putting up a sign: 'I am not your mother!'"

"You should put one by the sink." Philippa grimaced at the pile of dirty dishes as she poured herself a coffee. She turned to Milton. "Don't worry about entertaining me," she added. "If you want to take off your make-up, I'll be fine here."

"I can't. The cow has ordered the principals to stay in full costume for the notes. We have to stand around indefinitely while Ingrid tells Sandeep where to stick our turbans."

Sandeep nodded. "That's why I said, 'What a night!' Ingrid's got a long list of last-minute adjustments." She downed the rest of her coffee and stood up. "Well, I'd better get up there." She sighed and left the room.

"Where are the other principals?" asked Philippa, looking around the empty room.

"Either in their dressing rooms or up in the auditorium. I saw Dieter with a coat over his robes. He said he was going to grab a burger from the café across the street. Hope he doesn't give the girl at the counter a heart attack."

"You know, that's a great idea." Philippa suddenly realized how hungry she was. It was more than four hours since their dinner. "I'm going to pop over and get dessert. Can I pick up something for you?"

"I wouldn't mind a doughnut. Hold on, I'll get some change."

"No, you won't. You treated me to dinner. I'll get it."

Philippa hurried out before Milton could argue. The short flight of steps from the green room led to a corridor that ran underneath the stage, and she correctly deduced that this would take her to the street side of the building. The passage had doors on both sides, presumably the dressing rooms, and at the far end, as Philippa had anticipated, there was another flight of stairs that led to the stage door.

Once out of the theatre, she saw Dieter Volkow leaving the café on the far side of the street, so she walked to the end of the block and crossed at the light. Dieter cut across the road and was already back inside the theatre by the time Philippa reached the door of the café. It took less than five minutes for her order to be filled, and when she came out, she cut straight across to the theatre. She looked at her watch. It was five past eleven. As she came back down the stairs, she heard a sharp bang. *Norman and his cap gun*, she thought. *He's obviously getting bored waiting around.* When she reached the green room, she found Dieter ensconced between Princess Sheherezade and the Genie of the Ring. Milton was nowhere in sight. Philippa acknowledged Dieter's greeting—fortunately his mouth was full so he could only manage a wave—and poured herself another coffee to go with her doughnut. As she settled on the couch, the door opened and Milton entered.

"I'll have to scoff mine down, darling," he said, taking his doughnut. "Ingrid's finished with the masses so we'll be called any minute."

"You're being called now," announced Joe, sticking his head around the door. "Where's Norman?"

"In his dressing room. Didn't you hear him firing his cap gun?"

"He's not there," said Joe. "I knocked and there was no answer."

"Maybe he's asleep," suggested Tina. "We're all exhausted. Didn't you look inside?"

"The door was locked," said Joe, "but he doesn't seem to be anywhere else. I guess I'll get the master key from the house-manager's office."

Joe left, and the others got to their feet, disposed of their garbage and straggled out the door. Philippa took a second cup of coffee and joined the exodus. She followed the group up the first flight of stairs, and as she crossed the landing, she saw Joe coming along the passage from the far end. She had been about to follow Milton onto the second staircase, but now she paused and turned back. Curiously, she watched as Joe stopped at the dressing room and unlocked the door. He disappeared into the room; then almost immediately, he uttered a strangled cry and backed out into the corridor. His normally phlegmatic expression was replaced by one of horror.

Philippa ran to join him and looked into the room.

The Widow Twanky, resplendent in full costume, was seated in front of the mirror. The pink-and-purple striped hoop skirt ballooned across the floor, framing the green-velveted torso that was slumped against the counter. The Dame's red wig appeared hideously garish and strangely lop-sided in the blazing lights from the bulbs surrounding the mirror. Widow Twanky showed no sign of life.

Philippa's eye was drawn to the mirror where the reflection showed the Widow's deathly white face. The wig had slipped sideways and revealed a small, black-red hole in the left temple. Suddenly, above the Dame's still form, Joe's face materialized in the mirror beside her own.

"Can you stay here?" he asked. "I'm going to call the police."

"Here," said Philippa, opening her purse. "Use my cell."

Joe took the phone and dialled, and Philippa turned back to look at the body.

"God knows what Ingrid's going to do now," said Joe, while he waited for a reply at the other end. He had recovered from his initial shock and had reverted to the practical mode that made him invaluable as a stage manager. "Even if the cops don't shut us down, we don't have an understudy for Norman."

"I don't think that's going to be an issue," said Philippa.

She pointed at the grey hair that had been revealed where the wig had shifted away from the hairline.

"This may be a dead Widow Twanky," she said, "but it isn't Norman Green. It's his cousin, Jimmy."

◆   ◆   ◆

Richard Beary watched as the members of the forensic unit conducted their work. The body had been removed and the dressing room looked bare without the trappings of the Dame's costume. The only furnishings were two chairs by the counter, a set of square-boxed shelves, which were empty except for a bundle of clothing and a pair of men's running shoes, and a mobile costume rack laden with coat-hangers. An array of make-up was strewn along one end of the counter and an open book entitled *How Weapons Work* sat incongruously in the middle of the pile. Now that the mirror bulbs had been turned off, the only illumination was from a fluorescent light in the ceiling, which did little to improve the flesh-tone of the walls or the utilitarian brown carpet. The wall to the left of the mirror contained a small, solitary window.

A metal wastebasket stood in the middle of the room, not far from the chair where the body had sat. It was full of what appeared to be old bills, but a patch of red velvet and what looked like the arm on a pair of glasses jutted through the paper. Richard watched as the bills were extracted and the remaining contents were spread onto a plastic sheet. It appeared that Norman had been throwing out his joke shop. Richard found himself staring at a whoopee cushion, a package of balloons, a ball of purple silly-putty, a small metal ball on a string, and a pair of glasses complete with bulbous nose and bushy moustache. A paper screwed into a tight ball was caught in the cavity created by the plastic nose. As it was extracted and flattened out, he was interested to see it was a threatening letter regarding Norman and Jimmy Greens' gambling debts.

The door opened and Constable Jean Howe entered the dressing room.

"We've tracked down Norman Green, sir," she said. "He was at the casino."

"Good. I'll come up shortly. How is Martin managing with the hordes of hysterical actors? If anyone can cope with these British comedy types, he should be able to."

"Fine. They love his accent. The director offered him a walk-on part."

"She doesn't realize how tough he is under that Constable Plod exterior." Richard looked at his watch. It was three o'clock. "How much longer will it take you to finish with the people in the auditorium?"

"Not too much longer. We've got the names and numbers for the cast and crew, and with your permission, we'll send the majority home. Most of them remained in the auditorium or on stage after the bows, so they're all accounted for. The only individuals who were backstage at the relevant time were your sister, the stage manager, the ASM and four of the principals, plus the choreographer very briefly. I gather she came down to get a coffee when the musical director was giving the chorus notes. The director was also away from the auditorium for a brief period during the dance notes, though she says she didn't come backstage but went onto the street for a cigarette. By the way, your sister heard what sounded like a shot shortly after eleven, and that time has been confirmed by two of the actors who heard it too. They assumed the noise was made by the cap gun that's used in the show, but since the cap gun is still on the props table, it's likely that they heard the shot that killed Jimmy Green. The time frame is right. He went downstairs immediately after the rehearsal ended at ten-thirty, and his body was discovered at eleven twenty-five."

"Which four principals were backstage at the time?"

"Tina Trent, Milton Lovell, Dieter Volkow and Amy Chow. The Chow girl is only thirteen. She's a student at the choreographer's dance school—the star student, one gathers. Her mother is here and hopping up and down in fury, so it might be diplomatic, given the girl's age, to send her home too. We can question her later."

Richard nodded.

"Dismiss the people who were in the auditorium," he said, "and get Martin to take statements regarding the exact whereabouts of the individuals who left the area, even briefly, and to ascertain when they'll be available for further questioning. Then he can send them home. Thank God we don't have to bring an entire busload of performers and musicians downtown for interviews. Ask my sister to wait, if she's not too tired. I'll give her a ride home. I'd like to get her perspective on the situation."

Jean Howe left the room and Richard moved to the window. Upon closer examination, he saw that the latch was undone, so he raised the lower section of the window and peered out. He found himself looking out at ground level onto a loading bay which abutted the lane that ran from the main road to the river promenade. The bay was empty except for a dumpster, but a similar window, presumably belonging to another dressing room, was set in the wall on the far side of the recess. Richard made a mental note to find out who occupied the room. He ducked back inside and released the window. It slid back and closed of its own accord. He nodded to the remaining members of the forensic unit, left the room and made his way to the theatre lobby.

Bill Martin had commandeered the house-manager's office as an interview room. Norman Green sat in the corner, anxiety causing his complexion to match his name. The dyed black hair emphasized the pallor of his skin and he looked every minute of his age. Martin paused as Richard entered. Richard introduced himself, sat on the edge of the desk and, without preamble, asked Norman about the items from the wastebasket.

Norman looked surprised. It was not the question he expected.

"My joke collection? I chucked it out." Receiving no response from Richard, Norman expanded. "Little Tina threw a fit after the incident with the frog and Joe Lennox started playing the heavy over my contract—I'm one of the few getting paid—so I thought I'd better do something to demonstrate compliance."

"You need the money?"

"Jimmy and I were both a bit short—temporarily, of course. We'd had a run of bad luck at the tables. The sods at the casino had threatened us but I never believed they'd actually do anything. They knew we were going to pay up."

"How much money did you owe?"

"Ten thousand dollars."

"What about your cousin?"

"Close to one hundred thousand."

Richard flinched.

"Did he often incur those sorts of debts?"

"Occasionally. It had happened before."

"And he'd managed to extricate himself?"

"Yes. Jimmy is pretty resourceful. He usually managed to land on his feet."

Richard looked Norman straight in the eye.

"You implied that this murder is connected with your gambling debts, and given the fact that your cousin was unrecognizable in your costume, we have to investigate his death as if you were the intended target."

Norman shrivelled in his chair and his complexion paled to chalk-white.

"Yes, I know," he muttered.

"So why would you be the target when you owe so much less than your cousin?"

"I think they were going to write me off literally and figuratively as a bad debt. If they killed me, it would be a warning to Jimmy that they were serious. He'd have been terrorized into paying up."

"And where would he get that kind of money?"

"My mother is quite wealthy. She was always willing to help if I ran short. I'm an only child and she tends to spoil me—but she'd have helped Jimmy too. She's done it before. Jimmy's parents died when he was twelve, so he's been part of our household for years. Actually," he added, his eyes suddenly widening, "if I'd been killed, Jimmy would have been rich. He'd have been next in line to inherit from my mother."

Richard frowned.

"If your mother is so well-to-do and willing to give you money, why didn't you ask her to pay off your debt?"

"My mother is old and not very well. She has cancer and I doubt if she's going to last more than a few months. I didn't want to worry her, and as it happened, I didn't really have to as I had prospects of my own. That's why I wanted to get out on time tonight."

"And what prospects would these have been?"

Norman looked smug.

"There's a charming, twice-widowed lady who frequents the casino. She's loaded, and she seems to have me marked down as husband-number-three. It

won't be the end of the world if it doesn't work out because my future inheritance is going to take care of me nicely, but if it does come off, it could be rather
fun."

"You're not married?"

"No, I have always successfully avoided that state, but I suppose we all have to
succumb at some point. Anyway, my lady friend had asked me to meet her
tonight and I had no intention of letting her down, so I asked Jimmy to fill in for
me."

"Are you telling me that your cousin was dressed in your costume so you
could keep a date at the casino?"

"Well, yes. I didn't want to annoy our lady director so that seemed to be the
perfect solution. The Widow Twanky has a huge part in Act One, but the second
half is all Aladdin and the Magician once the first scene is over. The Widow isn't
on for the last thirty minutes, so once I shoot the Magician with my cap gun, I'm
free to twiddle my thumbs until the grand finale. Jimmy met me in my dressing
room. I helped him into the costume; then I took off to meet my friend—who,
by the way, didn't get there until eleven—and all Jimmy had to do was go on
stage and lope through the finale—there weren't any lines at that point—and
then return to the dressing room until the principals were called for their notes.
After that, he just had to go on stage, sit silently and nod whenever Ingrid gave a
note for the Dame, then bolt for the dressing room and head home before anyone
had a chance to speak to him. Simple." He shook his head regretfully. "Nobody
ever needed to have found out," he said sorrowfully. "It would have worked perfectly."

Bill Martin looked sceptical.

"Are you sure? Isn't it possible that someone in the production recognized
your cousin?"

"I doubt it. They're all young and totally preoccupied with their own over-
developed egos. I suppose Joy might have noticed if the dancing was a bit off, but
she'd have just put it down to fatigue. The only one that might have twigged
would be Dieter Volkow. He's a savvy old pro, and he and I do a bit of a routine
in the finale. But he wouldn't have said anything—he gets up to enough on his
own. He could be arrested for the way he fondles that teenaged tart who plays the
Genie of the Ring. He had her in his dressing room a few days ago—it's the next
one along the corridor—the window is directly opposite mine so one can see in if
the lights are on. Anyway, Jimmy had run down to my room to return a book
he'd borrowed, and he looked across to the other window and saw the two of
them together. Dieter had his hand ... well, never mind that—you're here to

investigate a murder—but the whole point is, Dieter's not likely to blow the whistle on anyone else."

"Is Volkow the only occupant of that dressing room?"

"No, he shares with Milton Lovell. That's the actor playing the Genie of the Lamp. Bit of a silly ass—he can't stand me because I got the part he wanted—but he's good on stage."

Richard steered the conversation in a different direction.

"You say you've never married, and you have a rich mother who is dying of cancer. Are you her only heir?"

"Yes," said Norman.

"Has she not included your cousin in her will?"

"No. He got money from his own parents. Besides, my mother has done a lot to help him over the years so she has made it quite clear that her assets all come to me."

"How much money are we talking about?"

"Her condo is worth around two hundred and fifty thousand, and she has about that much again in the bank and investments."

"So you're looking at a half-million-dollar inheritance?"

"Yes. Not megabucks by today's standards, but a comfortable sum to keep me in my old age."

"What happened to your cousin's inheritance? The money he got from his parents?"

"He's blown most of it."

"Gambling?"

"Pretty much. I enjoy a flutter at the tables, but if I get a bad patch, I settle up and back off for a while. Jimmy's addicted. He can't stop. Do you think," he added, leaning forward with intense concentration, "that the thugs at the casino figured they'd kill me, knowing that he'd not only be terrified into co-operating, but that he'd inherit enough money to pay off his debts and have cash left over to burn at the tables? Is that possible?"

"Anything is possible," said Richard, "but if that was their intention, it certainly backfired on them. Your cousin won't be paying off any debts now."

◆　　　◆　　　◆

After Norman had left, Richard brought Philippa into the interview room. It was nearly four o'clock, and the theatre was empty except for members of the force and a night watchman who had come on duty at midnight and found a vastly different atmosphere than that of his usual tranquil shift. Richard frowned. He was tired, and it was getting increasingly hard to concentrate.

"We won't know for sure until we get the autopsy report, but the most likely time of death is just after eleven when you heard the shot," he told Philippa. "The dressing-room door was locked from the inside but the latch on the window was open, so either the killer came from outside and shot Green through the window or he was in the room with him, shot him, and then left via the window."

"If it was a hit from the casino, it's most likely the former," said Martin.

"Exactly," Richard continued, "and if it was someone from the theatre who wanted to make it appear that the killing was not connected with the show, the murderer could have easily locked the door and left via the ground-floor window, then re-entered through the opposite window—which was the dressing room of Dieter Volkow and Milton Lovell—or even come back into the theatre through the lobby or the stage door. All the doors were open."

"Have you found the gun?" Philippa asked.

"No," said Richard. "We've had two constables scouring the area, but so far, the only gun in evidence is the cap gun that was used in the show, and that never left the props table after it was used on stage."

"We're right by the river," Philippa reminded him. "The murder weapon could be at the bottom of the Fraser. Of course, if the killer's a hit man, the gun will have gone with him."

Martin nodded. "Let's leave the hit-man scenario for a moment and focus on the suspects from the production. How did the actors get on with Norman Green?"

"Not well. Norman was disliked by most people in the cast. He played tricks on other performers."

"Yes, we know," said Richard. He described the contents of the wastebasket in the Dame's dressing room.

"Of course, the one notable exception was Ingrid Bjornsen," said Philippa. "Surprising, when you consider the havoc Norman caused."

"Yes, amazing what sex will do," said Martin. "I gather she was hot to trot any time he gave her the nod. Mind you, he's in for it now she's discovered he was two-timing her with a lady at the casino."

Philippa raised her eyebrows.

"Really? I didn't know that. Are you sure?"

"He told us himself, and we've had a constable over to check," said Richard. "The lady in question is a Mrs. Beresford. She's buxom, blond, and extremely well heeled. She didn't arrive until eleven, but Norman Green was there to meet her, and there are several witnesses who chatted with him prior to eleven o'clock, not to mention a cashier who sold him some chips at ten-fifteen. He seems to have been a popular character there—especially with the ladies."

"What a louse," said Philippa. "And what a slap in the face for Ingrid."

Richard nodded. "Yes, she seemed pretty distraught. Anyone would have thought it had actually been her lover that was killed."

"Ingrid wouldn't go to pieces over a dead lover," said Philippa. "She's much too practical. If she was in a state, it was more likely a combination of rage at finding out Norman had betrayed her and anxiety in case the police were going to close her show."

"There's another possibility for her distress," suggested Martin. "What if she thought she'd killed Norman Green and then found out she'd got the wrong man?"

"Could Ingrid have committed the crime?" Philippa asked. "Physically, I mean? Wasn't she on stage?"

"Not during the choreographer's notes," said Richard. "She went outside for a cigarette just before eleven. She says she stayed on the road, but she could have slipped down the lane. The time is right. She didn't come back inside until quarter past, so it's feasible. I think the choreographer is out, though. She was giving notes on stage at the time. She did go downstairs, but not until eleven-fifteen, which is ten minutes after the shot was heard."

"Who did you see backstage?" Martin asked Philippa.

"Tina and Amy were with Dieter in the green room, and Joe Lennox was wandering the corridors—and of course Milton was there, but there's no way he'd pull a gun and shoot someone. I know him well. He talks an acerbic line but he's really a sweetheart."

Richard smiled. "We've heard that before. Some of the worst psychopaths have been described as 'sweethearts'."

Philippa scowled.

"All right, I know you have to take that attitude, but believe me, I'm right. So who else is in the frame?"

Martin checked his notes. "Just Mario, the military thug who's assisting the stage manager. I gather he has guns, so we'll check his weapons."

"Several suspects, but not much in the way of motives," concluded Richard, "so ultimately, we have to come back to the gambling debts and the possibility of a hit man from the casino."

Philippa raised her eyebrows.

"Gambling debts?"

Richard proceeded to fill Philippa in. Her eyes widened as she listened, and when Richard finished, she nodded wisely.

"That's what I said to Milton. Gamblers never tell people when they lose. Isn't it strange?" she added. "Norman is the one with the assets—well, potential assets, anyway—and if Norman had died, Jimmy would have been the obvious suspect because he would have become the heir; but in fact it was Jimmy who was killed in Norman's place. Everything seems a bit upside-down."

"Yes, it's confusing, but that's why we want you to keep your ears and eyes open. The theatre is dark tomorrow and our forensic unit will be able to finish their work, so that means the show can open on Friday as scheduled. I'd appreciate you being there. You know these people, and you might pick up on something significant that a member of the force wouldn't notice."

"Yes, I can do that. My concerts don't start until next week." Philippa gave a huge yawn, and guiltily, Richard noticed how pale his sister looked.

"Come on, you're exhausted," he said. "I'd better get you home."

Philippa nodded.

"Yes, you'd better. I have an important engagement tomorrow."

"Not an audition, I hope," said Martin. "You won't be in very good shape to sing."

"No," agreed Philippa. "Actually, it's something much more fun." She flashed Bill Martin a smile. "I have to go Christmas shopping."

◆   ◆   ◆

Robson Street was a turbulent mass of frenetic people bundled in heavy coats and laden with bags and parcels. Inside the small space of the Bijou Gallery there was an uncomfortable sense of confinement as last-minute shoppers vied for space at the counters. The piped-in sound of Bing Crosby bidding the customers to have themselves a merry little Christmas was punctuated by intermittent strains from cell phones and the jingle of bells from the sidewalk Santa outside the door. As Milton went from shelf to shelf in search of a present for his aunt, Philippa watched the crowds streaming past the window. The street looked dark, even though it was mid-afternoon, and the sky was ominously grey and overcast. The passers-by on the sidewalk created clouds of mist as they exhaled.

"The temperature is dropping," said Philippa. "I think it's going to snow."

"Never mind chit-chat about the weather," grumbled Milton. He glared at the price tag on a crystal butterfly and set it back on the display. "You still haven't filled me in about last night. What on earth was Jimmy Green doing in the Dame's costume?"

Philippa turned back from the window.

"He was stepping in so Norman could meet a lady at the casino."

Milton's owl eyes grew larger.

"Two-timing Ingrid, was he? Madam Director wouldn't have liked that. Maybe she potted him in a frenzy of hormonal rage."

"It's possible, I suppose, but I can't really see Ingrid as the type to commit a crime of passion." Philippa steered Milton to a cabinet stocked with china dogs. "How about these?"

"Perfect. Auntie prefers canines to humans. Yes, you're probably right—Ingrid may like sex, but I suspect she's pretty calculating about her affairs, and she'd never do anything to rock the boat with her husband because *he's* loaded and *she* likes money." Milton picked up a porcelain poodle and scrutinized it. "Have you noticed her clothes?" he added. "All her outfits come from designer stores in Holt Renfrew."

"Well," said Philippa, "if it wasn't love, let's try hate. Who disliked Norman enough to kill him?"

"Only me," said Milton. "I'm still ticked that he got my part."

"I wouldn't joke about it if I were you. You're one of the eight people who went backstage during the critical hour. You're on the police list of suspects."

"Ouch! That hurt. Who are the others?"

"Ingrid is one. She went outside for a cigarette, but she could have come in by the stage door. Joy and Mario are possibilities too—both came backstage for coffee—and Dieter, Amy and Tina have to be considered because they were hanging out in the green room, but each one of them left at some point. Then there's Joe. He was wandering about letting people know when they were needed."

Milton exchanged the poodle for a golden retriever. "Well, we've ruled out Ingrid and a crime of passion, and I can't see Amy and Tina as first and second murderers—nor Joe—he's much too placid. Now Joy and Dieter might have it in them. There are some hidden depths there. And Mario has the ability to kill, though as far as I know, he sticks to wildfowl." Milton pursed his lips and looked anxious. "This is getting scary. Do you really think I'm under suspicion?"

"Not seriously, but you haven't been ruled out. Still, I don't think you have to worry. I'm pretty sure this murder was motivated by money. Given that Norman and Jimmy had run up huge debts, a gangland killing is the most likely solution."

Milton gasped. "You've just reminded me of something," he said, gesticulating wildly with the golden retriever and causing the lady behind the counter to tense like an outfielder watching the progress of a home run. "Dieter said there was a shady-looking character from the casino looking for Norman earlier that evening. That must have been the killer."

"It's distinctly possible," said Philippa, taking the ornament from him and gently returning it to the shelf. "Did anyone else see the man Dieter mentioned?"

"I don't think so. No one said anything."

Philippa frowned.

"So we only have Dieter's word for it? He could have made it up."

"Yes, but why would he lie? You don't think he killed Norman—unless, of course, he hadn't got over the nonsense with the water bomb, but that would be rather an extreme comeback. Besides, for all that Dieter was annoyed, I think his Germanic love of mechanics rather appreciated the device that was used for the trick."

Milton turned back to the display, lunged forward and reached to the very back. He emerged with a china collie and nodded approval. "This'll do," he said triumphantly. "Auntie has a mailman-eating mutt that looks like Lassie. We all hate it, but she thinks the sun rises and sets around its fuzzy rear end." Milton scooped up his parcels and headed for the line at the cash desk. "Nearly done," he said happily. "I just need a present for my niece, and that's easy. We'll stop at the mall and get a Cinderella doll at the Disney store—if, of course, we ever get through this line." He gestured towards the desk where a determined-looking dowager was trying to negotiate an exchange.

He hoisted his shopping bags into battering-ram position and earned a glare from the woman shopper in front of him.

"Patience, Milton," Philippa counselled. "It's five days to Christmas. What did you expect?"

"I expected all the cashiers to be open—*and*," Milton added, his penetrating tenor accelerating to stage-delivery decibels, "I assumed people wouldn't be bringing returns that require a half-hour debate at a time when legitimate customers are trying to make purchases."

Philippa steered the conversation back to the subject of the murder.

"Richard seemed to think the Greens were pretty sharp operators. Did Norman have financial dealings with anyone on the production?"

"Possibly, though Jimmy was more of a hustler than Twanky-Wanky—but then, *he* wasn't the target."

"Yes, we have to assume that. The only person who knew that the 'Widow' was Jimmy was Norman himself, and he left for the casino before the finale."

Milton frowned.

"I think Dieter guessed," he said.

The stately woman at the cash desk concluded her transaction and the line shifted forward. Philippa moved to stay alongside Milton.

"Why do you think Dieter guessed?" she asked.

"Because I commented that Norman hadn't been up to snuff during the finale, and our venerable Magician got a smug little smile on his face and said he wasn't surprised. He said, 'Norman isn't himself.' It was as if he was laughing at a private joke. But I'm sure no one else knew."

Philippa stiffened.

"Didn't you say you once saw Dieter giving Jimmy money?"

"Yes. I figured he was getting him to lay a bet for him."

The shopper in front of Milton finished her purchase and cleared the cash desk. Milton set down his parcels, deposited the collie on the counter and dug out his charge card.

"What if it were something more sinister?" Philipa suggested. "Dieter is an ideal target for blackmail and Jimmy was desperate for money."

"Well, if it turns out to be Dieter, could you not tip your brother off until the middle of next month? We open tomorrow night and the Magician doesn't have an understudy. Yes, of course I want it gift-wrapped," Milton added imperiously to the girl behind the counter, "and preferably with more speed than it took to reach your till."

"Actually," said Philippa, "Dieter couldn't be the killer. At the time I heard the shot, he was in the green room with Tina and Amy—a fact that would eliminate them as well, and Joy too, because she was back on stage at that point."

"Now that's too bad," said Milton heartlessly, "because she's a potential target for blackmail if anyone is, and we don't need her once the show opens."

"Well, she's out, so that just leaves you, Joe, Mario and Ingrid—or the sinister hit man from the casino."

"True." Milton signed the charge slip and put down the pen. "Well, I opt for the gangland solution," he stated firmly. "It won't interfere with the run of the show."

Philippa raised her eyebrows heavenwards and went to wait by the door. She looked through the glass pane at the street scene beyond. The sky had darkened to slate grey, but the store windows gleamed with light, and the twinkling bulbs decorating the sidewalk trees sparkled and glimmered as if in motion. Suddenly, Philippa realized that the effect was the result of snowflakes floating past the bare branches.

She turned back to see Milton tucking his wallet in his pocket and giving the girl at the counter a theatrical smile that was worthy of Lady Bracknell.

"Thank you, dear," he said graciously, taking his parcel. "Do try for better timing in future—the pace was appalling." He nodded regally and sailed towards the exit. He opened the door for Philippa and stood back to allow her through. Then he followed her onto the sidewalk and beamed as he noticed the white flakes drifting by the store windows.

"Snow!" he carolled. "Christmas is here."

Not hearing a response from Philippa, he turned to look at her. She appeared to be in a trance.

"You don't look very 'ho-ho-ho'," said Milton. "What did you do? Swallow a holly leaf?"

Philippa ignored the witticism. She continued to look perplexed.

"It was what you just said."

Milton blinked.

"What did I just say? Something about Christmas?"

"No," she replied. "You were talking about timing."

Philippa faced Milton and fixed him with an intense stare.

"Tell me how the water bomb worked," she said.

◆   ◆   ◆

Philippa met Richard at the theatre at five o'clock. They went backstage and proceeded to Norman Green's dressing room where a uniformed constable was still on duty by the door.

"You were right," said Richard, as he ushered Philippa into the room. "The metal ball was a cap bomb. Those were popular toys in England during the post-war era and they work on the same principle as a cap gun. The two halves of the ball close around a cap, and when the bomb drops, it detonates. Landing in a metal wastebasket, it would have made a bang loud enough to be heard right down the corridor."

"The basket was full, though," said Philippa. "Wouldn't the other stuff muffle the sound?"

"No, we tried it. If the solid items were stacked along one edge with the light pieces of paper on top, the bomb had a clear path to the metal base. The jolt as the bomb hit made the paper cave in and bury the bomb."

"Clever."

"Very—in theory—but now we have to see if it was feasible to rig a timer in this room."

"Where was the wastebasket?" asked Philippa.

"Right here. Under the fluorescent light."

They looked up at the long light fixture. It appeared perfectly normal. Richard pulled a chair over and climbed up so he could see above the fitting.

"Well," urged Philippa. "Can you see anything?"

Richard nodded.

"There's a timer with a rotating dial wedged on top of the fixture." He pulled the device out, stepped down and showed it to Philippa. "Look," he said, "there's cotton thread attached to the dial. If the other end had been tied to the cap bomb, the mechanism would have gradually shortened the thread until it reached the metal edge of the light, and at that point, the pressure would have broken the thread and released the bomb."

"So Jimmy didn't die after eleven. It could have been as early as ten-thirty."

"Exactly."

"And that brings Dieter back into the picture."

"Yes, in which case Jimmy was probably the target."

"How will you proceed from here?"

"We'll start by checking Volkow's bank records for unexplained withdrawals that could tie in with a blackmail scenario."

"But how will you get proof?"

"The forensic team has finished in here." Richard climbed back onto the chair and set the timer into its former position. "I'm going to open up this dressing room for tonight's performance, and you're going to leak your theory to your pal, Milton, who will be sure to spread it to the entire cast and crew." Richard got back down and ushered Philippa out of the room. "We'll give Norman Green a police guard," he continued, "just in case we're wrong about Jimmy being the target, but when Norman's on stage, the guard will be in the wings, which means our friend will have the opportunity to retrieve the timer. What he won't realize is that another constable is going to be on duty right outside the window."

Richard smiled.

"I think that should do the trick."

◆   ◆   ◆

Philippa stood in the wings and watched as the Widow Twanky drew the cap gun and fired at the Magician. The roar of laughter from the opening-night audience was loud, even from where she was standing. *Aladdin* was clearly a big success. The scene drew to a close and the Widow loped into the wings.

"That's it!" Norman beckoned to Jean Howe who had been assigned as his bodyguard. "I'm done until the finale. Come on, coffee time—and then I'll need a bathroom break, and you've no idea what a challenge that is in *this* costume! You'll be able to drink the entire contents of the carafe by the time I come out."

Jean's expression remained impassive. She followed Norman to the stairwell and they disappeared from view. Philippa turned back to watch Dieter, who was still on stage. Suddenly Milton materialized at her elbow.

"I've done as you requested." Milton looked smug. "The entire world knows there was a trick to delude everyone into thinking the murder occurred later than it did. I must say it's all very exciting. I've never been a police spy before."

"Glad you're enjoying it," Philippa whispered back at him.

"I won't enjoy it if we lose our Magician and the show closes," said Milton. He watched Dieter menace the Princess. "Anyway, I have a better theory."

"You do?"

"Yes, and I hope you realize what it cost me. I was awake all night thinking about it. My Genie is probably going to be vilified by the press as the most somnolent player ever to crawl the boards." Milton vigorously poked at his hairline. "I must say these long fingernails are great for scratching under my turban," he added.

"So what is this fabulous theory?"

Milton stopped scratching and fixed Philippa with his black-lined oriental eye.

"Remember how we said Ingrid likes money. Well, I suddenly had a brainwave. What if Sandeep could have been mistaken when she saw Ingrid going at it with her lover? The two cousins were very alike. What if Ingrid's lovey-dovey public antics with Norman were a front to cover the fact that Jimmy was her boyfriend? Maybe Ingrid wanted to leave her husband and knew that if Norman died, Jimmy would inherit and the two of them could team up. I mean, when you're a director, there's nothing more useful than being married to a techie—and it's the perfect solution because the director is always officially off the show after opening night, so Ingrid is quite dispensable."

Philippa stopped him in mid-flow.

"Milton, you can't pin a murder on someone just because they're not needed for the run of the show. And if Ingrid is so keen on money, she wouldn't have wanted to team up with someone with a gambling problem."

"She might not have realized how much Jimmy was in debt," Milton argued, raising his voice and eliciting a reprimand from Joe. "Anyway," he continued in a whisper, "from what you've told me, Norman's mummy would have coughed up, so Jimmy didn't really have money problems at all." Milton paused. "Why are you staring at me like that?" he said. "It's not that far-fetched."

"No," said Philippa. "Milton, you're brilliant."

"You think I'm right?"

"I didn't say that. I said you were brilliant. Now, let me get by. I'm going to find Richard."

"Just like that! You'll miss my big scene."

"I've seen your big scene. It's wonderful. See you in a ..."

Milton nudged Philippa and pointed at the stage.

"What?"

"Dieter's exited. It looks like he's going down the stairs in the other wing. You'd better go and see what he's up to."

"It doesn't ma ... Oh, never mind. I'll see you later," said Philippa.

She swept past Milton and sped down the stairs to the lower corridor. As she reached the bottom, she was just in time to catch a glimpse of the swirl of the Magician's cloak as Dieter disappeared into a room halfway down the passage. She hurried to the far end of the corridor, climbed the steps to the stage door, and exited onto the street; then she raced down the lane at the side of the theatre and joined Richard and Bill Martin who were huddled behind the dumpster. They gestured for her to be quiet, and she crept down beside them.

There was a light in the room that was shared by Dieter and Milton, but Norman's dressing room was dark.

"Listen," Philippa hissed at her brother. "Milton said something that gave me an idea. I think you'll find there was a different reason for Dieter giving Jimmy money. I don't think Jimmy was a blackmailer."

"Ssssh," Richard warned, and pointed to the lighted window. Dieter had appeared. Philippa ducked lower behind the dumpster. The window slid open and Dieter leaned out over the sill. He stared back and forth; then he looked across at the window on the far side of the alcove. Silently, he pulled his robes around him and slid over the windowsill. Then, with another quick look about the lane, he glided across to the window of the Dame's dressing room. As he passed, Philippa caught her breath. She could see something in his hand but the object was concealed by his cape.

Dieter paused by the window. He pressed his face against the glass and peered through, but suddenly there was a glimmer of light as the door to the dressing room opened and the light from the passage spilled through. Someone was entering the room.

The light was flicked on. Dieter slid back and the watchers in the lane had a clear view into the room. The Widow Twanky had returned.

"Damn," whispered Richard. "Norman's come back to his dressing room. We've lost our chance. Dieter won't do anything now. He'll go back."

"Dieter isn't moving," said Philippa. "What on earth is he up to?"

"I don't know," muttered Richard. "And where the hell is Jean?"

"Oh, my God! Look!" cried Philippa. "What's he doing?"

Dieter had moved back in front of the window. Suddenly, he raised his hands. His cape fell back from his shoulders and his arms became visible. The object he had been clutching was now pressed against the glass.

"Christ!" said Richard, and lunged forward. As he tackled Dieter, there was a flash of white. Then the two of them went sprawling onto the blacktop. Richard grabbed Dieter's arm and pinned him to the ground. Then, as he pulled back, he saw the object that Dieter had been holding. It was a camera. Stunned, Richard looked up to see Philippa and Martin staring into the dressing room. Bill Martin's expression was one of utter amazement. Richard released Dieter and stood up so he could see what had caused his partner's reaction.

The Widow Twanky, alias Norman Green, was standing on a chair in the middle of the room. He seemed frozen in time, like a gargantuan Technicolor statue. He turned towards the window and stared, open-mouthed, at the trio on the other side of the glass. In his hand, he held the timer.

◆   ◆   ◆

Milton wanted to hear the end of the story, and as Philippa had to go downtown for last-minute shopping on Christmas Eve, they met for lunch at his favourite hotel. Milton greeted Philippa exuberantly and led her into the lobby, where a huge Christmas tree, sparkling with white lights and silver bows, reached almost to the ceiling of the three-storey entrance hall. As they entered the restaurant, the lyrical strains of Leontyne Price singing "Oh, Holy Night" floated from overhead speakers and mingled with the chatter of diners.

"This is such a delightful establishment," beamed Milton, taking in the seasonal decorations. "They know how to do Christmas properly—Santa, Frosty, nativity scenes, classic recordings of my favourite carols—I love this time of year."

"Me too," said Philippa. She opened her menu and studied the lunch entrées.

"Now, while we wait for our chestnut soup, fill me in," Milton demanded. "I want to know why Norman killed his cousin, and how he managed to do it."

"I already told you how—he used the timer to create an alibi. He walked over to the casino as soon as he'd changed, and he bought some chips, thus establishing that he'd arrived by ten-fifteen. Then he whizzed back to the theatre and waited for Jimmy in the dressing room."

"But what if he'd been seen?"

"He knew he wouldn't be. Everyone was on stage for the finale. It would only have taken a moment to set the timer. He knew Jimmy was going to come to the dressing room the moment the finale was over, and when he came in, Norman was hiding behind the door. As Jimmy sat down, Norman shot him."

"Where did Norman get a gun?"

"He'd kept an old service revolver from one of his war movies," Philippa explained. "In those days, they actually used guns with blanks—they didn't remove the firing mechanisms like they do today. He'd hid it above the fluorescent light when he arrived at the theatre, and taken it down when he set the timer."

"Why didn't we hear the shot?"

"The exit music—full chorus and orchestra—remember."

"Ah, of course," nodded Milton.

"Once Jimmy was dead, Norman left via the window, ran back to the casino, and threw the gun in the river as he went on board. He was only away for ten minutes, so with the crowd in the casino, nobody would have missed him and everyone assumed he'd been there the whole time."

"Tricky—just like his commando movies. We'll have to rename him the Widow Hanky-Panky." Milton looked bewildered. "But what was his motive? Why did he want to kill Jimmy?"

"Money. I said so right from the beginning. This murder was all about money."

"But Jimmy was broke. Norman was the one with the money—well, prospective money anyway."

"Exactly."

"So he had nothing to gain."

"No, but he had everything to lose. Norman's mother was ill, but she still retained control of her finances. Although she was leaving her assets to her son, she never minded helping her nephew—and Jimmy had been taking full advantage of her generosity. Three years ago, he'd accumulated a whopping great debt and she'd paid it off for him. Eighteen months later, he'd had another run of bad luck, and once again she helped him out. With her failing health, she didn't seem to realize how fast she was depleting her fortune."

Milton gasped. "I get it! Her assets and Norman's inheritance."

"Yes. Now there was another huge sum due and the poor old woman would have given Jimmy another blank check. Three years ago, Norman's inheritance was close to three quarters of a million dollars, but at the rate Jimmy was going, Norman would be lucky to get the condo. His cousin was bleeding his mother dry."

"Jimmy was a scuzz, wasn't he? One can almost feel sorry for Twanky-Wanky. Was Jimmy blackmailing Dieter and Joy too? I wouldn't put it past him."

"Actually, no. Jimmy was in charge of collecting the society membership dues. That's what Dieter was paying him. And Joy looked so annoyed that day because she'd been forced to pay the fees for her student, Amy, who'd spent the money her parents had given her going to a rock concert with Mario."

"Ooh, yes. That would annoy Joy—not just because she had to cough up money to keep her little star in the show, but because her budding ballerina liked boys."

The waitress appeared with two bowls of steaming chestnut soup and placed them on the table.

"Try it," ordered Milton. "It's to die for." He took a sip and raised his eyes blissfully to heaven. "There's one other thing," he continued. "What was all the to-do with Dieter in the lane? Someone told me he was taking pictures."

Philippa nodded.

"You were right when you said Dieter had guessed about the substitution in the finale. He had to stay to sing the exit chorus, but afterwards he went down to Norman's dressing room to find out what was going on. However, the door was locked and nobody answered. Later, he heard Norman was at the casino, so thought no more of it, but when he heard you spreading the story about a timing device, he became suspicious, and given his feelings about the Widow's antics on stage, he was only too happy to have a chance to catch Norman out. The police are going to find his photograph very useful."

"Dieter's such a slime-ball. I'd hate to think of him getting a commendation."

"Don't worry. I saw Jean Howe having a lengthy conversation with young Amy, and I suspect that Dieter may be facing his own come-uppance before too much longer."

"Horrors. Not before we close!"

"Milton, you're utterly unscrupulous. There is a world outside theatre, you know."

"No there isn't—you know what they say: 'The play's the thing.' And, by the way, on that subject, don't you want to know how the show is going?"

"Well, since every cloud has a silver lining, I suppose you're going to tell me that Norman's arrest resulted in you getting your part back. Who did they get to fill in for the Genie?"

Milton looked haughty.

"No one. I'm not giving up my role as Genie of the Lamp. You should have seen the line of children asking for autographs on opening night. They all headed straight for me. None of them even noticed that the Dame hadn't been in the finale."

Philippa sputtered into her soup. When she recovered, she set down her spoon and stared at Milton.

"You're not serious?"

"I am. One little child asked where the funny lady was, but when I said she'd had to leave, he said he didn't care because everyone liked me best."

"Well," said Philippa. "So forfeiting the Dame's part wasn't Milton's *Paradise Lost* after all."

"No. Definitely not."

"So perhaps you'll listen to your Auntie Philippa in future."

"I will never doubt your word again." Milton took another mouthful of soup and peered roguishly at Philippa over his glasses. "Well," he said, "you've answered my questions. But aren't you failing to ask one yourself? Don't you want to know who's playing the Dame?"

"Yes, of course I do," said Philippa. "Why didn't I think of that? Who on earth did they get to come in?"

"They didn't have to bring anyone in. Poor old Joe always plods through the parts when actors miss rehearsals—that's part of the stage-manager's job, after all—so of course, he knows the show pretty well."

Philippa beamed. "That's so nice. He's finally getting the chance to be on stage. He's such a good sort, I guess no one minds if he's a bit pedestrian. At least the show can go on."

Milton reached over and patted Philippa's hand.

"Tut-tut," he admonished. "Don't you know that the first rule for a detective is never to make assumptions?" He smiled mischievously. "You should see him," he continued. "Everyone was amazed. Joe donned the costume and roared out of the wings like the Sugarland Express. He's fabulous in the part."

Milton finished his soup and leaned back with satisfaction.

"In fact," he concluded, "it would be safe to say that the mystery of the Black Widow Twanky is why ever didn't Ingrid cast Joe in the first place?"

A Black Tie Affair

"You should have heard her," cooed Octavia Bruni. "She tossed off high notes as if they were middle-C's. And she wasn't just a great singer, she was a consummate musician. She did that gorgeous Lehar number from *Paganini*, and she sailed out of the wings with a violin, sang 'Liebe du Himmel auf Erden' better than I've ever heard it, *and* played a section of the melody along with the orchestra. Incredible!"

Octavia snatched a quick breath and embarked on another lengthy phrase. She was a highly proficient mezzo-soprano, so it was impossible to get a word in edgeways when she was on a roll.

"She was stunning to look at—one of those glamorous East European blondes—and you should have heard her sing *your* number. She threw in a high F! That certainly isn't going to be in *your* rendition of the 'Audition Song', is it? Hardly the same spectacular start to the New Year."

Philippa gritted her teeth while her co-star raved about the soprano that had performed at the "Salute to Vienna" concert the previous year. Philippa had been thrilled to get the role of Adele in Westburn Opera Company's production of *Die Fledermaus*, particularly as the opening performance was to be a celebrity New Year's Eve gala with the mayors of the two participating cities in cameo roles and a champagne ball to follow. However, sharing a dressing room with Count Orlovsky was proving to be a trial.

"Speaking of New Year's Eve," Octavia continued mercilessly, "I gather you couldn't get a date for tonight. Surely if Adam Craig really cared about you, he would have flown back to cheer you on—but then, he's probably surrounded by adoring Fräuleins, and you know what those German girls are like. Couldn't you have got that nice-looking brother of yours to round up someone from the cop shop? Beggars can't be choosers and all that."

A knock on the door stopped the flow, and rescue came in the form of Peter Hampton, a quietly but expensively dressed, grey-haired man who happened to be president of the young opera company. Hampton owned the largest accounting firm in the Lower Mainland and had contributed generously to the production. His arms were laden with three large bouquets of carnations and roses, and he deposited two of the offerings on the counter.

"Flowers for my lovely leading ladies," he announced.

Philippa was touched. She thanked him politely, but Octavia leapt to her feet with outstretched arms and delivered an extravagant hug and kiss. Peter went slightly pink.

"I'll have to give flowers more often," he said lightly.

Octavia's neon smile switched off the minute the door closed behind the middle-aged widower.

"You know where the third bouquet is going," she snapped. "How can he be so taken with Darleen? She's over fifty, for heaven's sake."

"So is he," said Philippa shortly. "Probably over sixty. And Darleen does happen to be rather special. She's a local heroine. Everyone loves her."

"Just because she lucked out and won the Met auditions in 1981. Everyone is making such a thing about the fact that she had the big international career, then chose to come back to live in Vancouver—but the reality is if her husband hadn't been murdered last year, she'd have still been in New York. She's getting past it anyway, but because she's famous and everyone feels sorry for her, she's nabbing roles that should be coming to younger singers. This company is all about giving chances to up-and-coming professionals so she hardly belongs here, does she?"

"She isn't getting past it," Philippa retorted indignantly. "Darleen is superb—and she's singing Rosalinda because Peter asked her to. He knows that her presence will give such a high profile to the company that he'll be able to capitalize on it with future sponsors. In the long term it's going to benefit local singers. Darleen is doing us a big favour."

"You mean she's doing her weaselly nephew a big favour. Imagine giving that ugly little runt the part of Frosch. Talk about nepotism."

Philippa felt exasperated. Octavia's negativity was putting her on edge. She tried to inject a positive note.

"Roy Winner may not be physically attractive," she said, "but he moves well and he's funny in the part. I think he's going to do well with his acting career. Most TV sitcoms are so goofy these days that his manic brand of comedy will fit right in."

"His manic brandy of comedy, as you put it, isn't a product of stage training and technique; it's the result of the stuff he ingests. Haven't you noticed his perpetually runny nose? He has no sense of ensemble playing either. You watch out—he'll upstage you all through your big number in Act Three."

"He will not," said Philippa firmly. "I didn't suffer through opera workshop for nothing. I can hold my own. Anyway, I feel sorry for Roy. He can't help his appearance and he's had a rough time. It was bad enough losing his father to cancer ten years back, but he must have been utterly traumatized when his mother and uncle were shot. He was the one who found the bodies."

Octavia looked slyly speculative.

"Doesn't it strike you as odd that Darleen's husband and sister were together in her New York apartment when they were shot? Maybe there was something going on between them. Just think—Darleen might have killed them herself."

"Darleen was at a rehearsal when it happened," said Philippa flatly. "The police figured that her husband had taken Roy's mother gift shopping and the two of them were unfortunate enough to return and catch a couple of thugs in the act of breaking into the apartment. If Roy hadn't been out sightseeing, he might have been killed too."

Octavia stared at Philippa.

"How can you possibly know that?" she demanded.

"I have my sources," Philippa said smugly. "Anyway, that explains why Darleen feels responsible for Roy. She's all the family he has left."

"Not so," Octavia contradicted. "Darleen's mother is still alive, and she's loaded. She's old and unwell, by the way, so there could be lots of lovely money coming Roy's way from a rich, doting granny."

"Roy's seventeen—too young to manage big money and too wild for an ailing grandma to handle. He needs Darleen. She's the mother figure in his life now."

Octavia snorted rudely.

"He already has one of those. Haven't you noticed how cozy he is with our ASM? He's been practically living at her apartment."

"Sophie Blau—you're joking. She's in her late-twenties. What on earth would she see in him?"

"Money, obviously. Sophie would screw Quasimodo if she saw a prospect of getting rich quick."

"Well, if Roy's into drugs and being hit on by older women, then he definitely needs Darleen around. She's one of the most sensible, down-to-earth prima donnas I've ever met."

"You're such a Pollyanna, Philippa," Octavia said dismissively. "There are hidden depths to Darleen and I intend to find out what they are." Octavia adjusted her powdered wig and stood up. "I'm not going to let her get her talons into Peter Hampton," she spat, her voice dripping with venom. "She's got pots of money of her own, she'll get a bundle more when her mother dies, and she's got an adoring, well-to-do business manager who, according to what I've been told, wants to marry her. That should be enough for anyone."

"It's interesting that she has two accountants wooing her," Philippa mused. "It rather supports the much-touted theory that math and music go together. Still, I know who I'd pick if I had to choose between John Granger and Peter Hampton. Granger is so serious—all money and no passion—whereas Peter Hampton is loaded with charm."

"It's so unfair." Octavia pouted. "Things were really starting to happen between me and Peter. He was incredibly attentive when we were on the San Francisco Opera tour. I know he was getting interested, and given a couple more weeks, I'd have got him to be my escort tonight. As it is, I've had to fall back on Eisenstein—he's been making cow's eyes at me all through rehearsal ... or should that be bull's eyes? They'll certainly be striped by the time he drinks the bottle of vodka he's stashed in his dressing room for tonight's party. It's going to be the crappiest New Year's Eve I've ever had."

"Oh, come on, it's not that bad."

"Yes, it is. I'm going to be spitting nails watching Darleen with Peter. How can I enjoy myself? Now that she's back, it's as if I've ceased to exist."

"Octavia, this is ridiculous. You shouldn't read grand passion into one lunch date. Anyway, Peter's not the sort to want a young trophy wife. He's interested in you as a singer, that's all. I'd say he and Darleen are ideally suited."

Octavia glared daggers at her roommate.

"I fail to see why you're standing up for Darleen," she said spitefully. "Her dramatic spinto completely drowns your birdlike coloratura in the 'Calamity, Catastrophe' trio." Octavia stood up and delivered a parting shot. "The lyrics are so apt, aren't they? You could be describing your own performance."

After a last petulant, but admiring glance at her white satin form in the mirror, Octavia flounced out of the dressing room. However, much to Philippa's surprise, the door did not slam shut behind her, and after a moment, a familiar face peered in through the opening.

"Hello, dear," said Bertram Beary.

"Dad! You look magnificent. I can't believe Mum actually got you into your tux."

"She didn't," said Beary. "This is at the behest of your wardrobe mistress."

"I don't understand."

"Darling Gwendolyn has backed out, so now that the management has lost one of the celebrity mayors, I've been delegated to fill in—since, of course, I was going to be here anyway to see your Adele."

"Mayor Pye can't do her cameo role?"

"No. Family crisis, or so she said. I don't believe it for a minute. She probably figured she was going to swan around the stage in a gorgeous gown, but someone will have tipped her off that the mayors' cameos are merely maid and waiter, and you know Gwennie. She'll have decided she wasn't going to demean herself by carrying a tray all through Act Two."

Philippa grinned.

"So you're going to be on stage with me. What a hoot! You'd better behave yourself," she warned.

"I always behave," said Beary with dignity. "What do I have to do, anyway?"

"It's easy—you just carry trays and hand out champagne glasses."

Beary perked up.

"Full ones?"

"Full of watered-down iced tea, actually, but don't despair. The auxiliary ladies are serving a sandwich buffet in the green room prior to the last act, and after that you'll get to hand out real champagne—it'll be during the bows. At that point, everyone will be joining in a chorus of 'Auld Lang Syne'."

"Ah," said Beary. "So avoid the pre-prandial cocktails but be sure to indulge in the post-prandials. And is this a general free-for-all, or do I get some kind of direction?"

"There'll be three of you, obviously all waiters now, and no maid—"

"Three? I thought it was just Gwennie and Pinko Rogers. That would have been easy to direct, wouldn't it? Extreme stage right and extreme stage left. What will they do with a feisty independent like me?"

"Heaven knows," said Philippa. "But to answer your original question, the third waiter is John Granger. He's Darleen's business manager, and he's been here during rehearsal so he knows what the director wants. Simply stay with him, or go where he tells you and you'll be just fine."

"Just as long as I don't have to go anywhere near the glamorous transvestite that stormed past me as I came in. She looks a proper vixen. What was wrong with her anyway?"

"She's been devoured by the green-eyed monster. Furthermore, she projects her own poisonous personality onto other people and assumes their motives are as selfish as her own. Put more specifically, Octavia Bruni has her heart set on marrying Peter Hampton, and now that Darleen is back in town, she sees her dream slipping away from her."

"Oh," said Beary. "That's why she looked like murder."

Before Philippa could respond, there was a knock at the door. It opened, and her mother's blonde and elegantly coiffed head popped into view. Edwina came into the room and gave her daughter a hug.

"You'll be wonderful, darling," Edwina predicted. "Isn't it thrilling! Your first Adele, and you'll be on stage with Darleen Winner. Oh my," she added, eyeing the glittering turquoise creation hanging in the open closet. "Is that what you wear in Act Two? I can't wait to see you in it. Thank goodness I brought my camera. Don't you dare change until I've had a chance to come back and get a picture."

"Hello, Bertram," grunted Beary. "Break a leg, why don't you? Thank you, Edwina. So kind of you to come back to wish me good luck."

Edwina ignored the rumble from the corner and continued to address Philippa.

"And whatever you do," she added, "please make sure your father doesn't make a fool of himself."

Having issued this queenly directive, she removed her arm from her daughter's shoulder, straightened the jacket of her full-length green brocade suit and sailed from the room.

◆   ◆   ◆

"*Fabuloso!*" boomed the maestro, as he joined the artists backstage after the first-act curtain. "Well done, everyone."

"Could you hear me in the trio?" Philippa asked anxiously.

Her conductor looked puzzled.

"Of course I could hear you," he assured her. "You project well, and Darleen knows to keep it light. The balance was perfect. I can't think why you would ask."

Philippa breathed a sigh of relief and mentally cursed herself for letting Octavia rattle her. She turned to leave the stage and smiled as she noticed her father and a thin, anxious-looking man being coached in the wings. She had not met the second celebrity mayor, but judging by the way he was hanging on John Granger's every word, he was taking his assignment seriously, unlike her father, who appeared to be scrutinizing the paintwork on the baroque door frames and ignoring the orientation provided by Darleen's business manager.

"Come on, Dad, pay attention," she said, joining the group. "You don't want to end up wandering the stage like a lost puppy."

"What's so difficult about handing out glasses of champagne?" demanded her father. "This gentleman is acting as if the bows have to be performed like army drill."

"Bows do have to be drilled," Philippa said firmly, seeing that Granger was becoming red in the face. "What is it you want, John?" she asked, turning to the other man. "I'll make sure he does it."

"It's very simple," said John. "Your father and Mayor Rogers are to be positioned on stage right and left respectively—"

"That's appropriate, anyway," muttered Beary.

"And," continued Granger, ignoring the interruption, "after the final chorus, they are to come out from the wings, each carrying a tray with one glass. Mr. Beary is to take his glass to Rosalinda, and Mr. Rogers delivers champagne to Eisenstein. The two leads will toast each other, and while they enact the business, our celebrity waiters will have returned to their wings to get the other trays, which will be loaded with enough glasses for the rest of the ensemble. Then the three of us will come back and circulate, passing out the champagne. The orchestra will continue playing until everyone has a glass; then there will be a drum roll, and Rosalinda will gesture to the audience to join in as we sing 'Auld Lang Syne'."

"OK, Dad, got that?" Philippa demanded.

"Yes, of course I've got it. I had it half an hour ago. Now can I go for coffee?"

John Granger nodded wearily, and Philippa led her father through the door at the rear of the stage and guided him down to the green room.

"Very uptight, that man," Beary commented as they progressed down the hall.

"He doesn't want anything to go wrong with Darleen's performance. It's understandable."

"I can't believe anyone would be that strung-out over a stage show," grunted Beary. "The man's a nervous wreck."

"He's probably unhappy," observed Philippa. "He has a rival in love who appears to be making very good time with the lady he wants to marry."

"I assume you mean Miss Winner?"

"Yes. He's been her business manager right from the start of her New York career, so he's known her for years and probably has a long-standing affection for her, but if the malevolent Octavia is to be believed, Darleen is gravitating towards Peter Hampton."

"Hampton, eh? If she marries him, it'll be a case of money marrying money."

"I think Granger is pretty well heeled too."

"Yes, but Hampton is one of the wealthiest businessmen in the Lower Mainland."

"Is he? No wonder Octavia is spitting nails."

"Are you coming in for coffee?" Beary asked as they reached the green room.

"No, I have to don my ball gown. I can't go to the party in my maid's dress. That would be most inappropriate."

"Speaking of inappropriate," remarked Beary, staring over Philippa's shoulder, "who's the shrimp-sized thug practicing mouth-to-mouth resuscitation on the redhead in designer leather? They look like a couple of goldfishes."

Philippa turned to see Roy Winner and Sophie Blau locked in an embrace in the stairwell.

"That's Darleen's nephew—and the girl he's kissing is Sophie Blau—she's the assistant stage manager."

"Bit old for him, isn't she?"

"Yes, but he obviously doesn't care."

"Not the most prepossessing of individuals, is he? Doesn't have Auntie's gorgeous looks."

"No, Roy's the poor relation, in more ways than one."

"No money?"

"I gather not. Darleen has tended to keep the family afloat. Roy's mother was pretty hard up."

"Was?"

"She was murdered, along with Darleen's husband—a robbery gone wrong, so they think. It happened in New York. Bill Gunsen is on the case, which is how I know about it. He emailed me a couple of weeks back as he wanted to see if I had any inside knowledge on the people involved."

"Nice young fellow, that," said Beary, eyeing his daughter speculatively. "Any chance of his coming out to visit you?"

"Actually, when I knew Adam wasn't getting home for Christmas, I asked Bill if he could be here for the New Year's gala, but he said it was impossible because of the homicide investigation."

"Too bad." Beary turned back to watch the couple in the stairwell. His eyes narrowed. "What the hell is that?" he muttered, seeing a small envelope in the young man's hand. Before Philippa could comment, Roy noticed that he had been observed. With indolent grace, he pushed Sophie away, gave her the envelope and smiled innocently at Beary.

"Anacin," he said. "She has a headache."

"That doesn't surprise me," said Beary equably, as he opened the door to the green room. "She's probably suffering from oxygen deprivation. And," he added as an aside to Philippa, "she'll be as blue as her surname if she gets hooked on the stuff he's giving her."

Philippa continued down the hall to her dressing room. To her relief, Octavia was not there so she was able to prepare for the second act in peace. However, when she returned, her serene state of mind was disrupted, for she heard raised voices as she neared the green room. She rounded the corner and saw Darleen and Roy Winner involved in an altercation. Darleen appeared angry and frustrated. She gripped her nephew's arm with one hand and gesticulated wildly with the other, but Roy seemed indifferent to his aunt's distress. He looked mulish and rebellious, and after a moment, he broke away and flounced off, leaving Darleen looking anxious and biting her lip.

Philippa held back. She did not want to be intrusive for she was still very much in awe of the prima donna, but as she hesitated, John Granger came down the hall. Darleen seemed relieved to see her business manager, and she took his arm and pulled him into the stairwell. Granger listened attentively, then gestured to Darleen to wait. He went to the door of the green room and called inside, and after a moment, Peter Hampton appeared. The two men joined Darleen in the stairwell, and once the trio was deep in conversation, Philippa slipped by. As she passed, she overheard enough of the discourse to realize that Octavia's prattle about drug abuse was not idle gossip.

By the time Philippa took her position in the left wing, Sophie Blau was already ensconced in the ASM's corner. She was talking quietly and efficiently into the mouthpiece of her headset, and the hand that rested on the stand in front of her sported a silver bracelet with a distinctive design which Philippa recognized immediately. The last time she had seen one like it was on the third floor of Tiffany's in New York. Sophie was totally focussed on her score and paid no attention to the performers beginning to cluster at the side of the stage. Philippa joined her father, who was chatting with a stagehand nearby.

Beary looked up as his daughter approached.

"Love the fan," he said, eyeing the huge feathered concoction that dangled from Philippa's wrist.

"Love the décolletage," said the stagehand cheekily.

"Watch it, young fellow," Beary cautioned him. "This is my daughter." He turned back to Philippa. "All ready for your big number?" he asked.

Philippa nodded tersely. She had sung the "Laughing Song" so often she could do it in her sleep, but this was a big night and she was feeling fluttery inside.

"Where's your co-star?" she asked, conscious of her mother's edict. "Have you got your moves down pat?"

"Pinko? He's practicing his walk—he has trouble staying on the beat. He's a musical illiterate, that man. I had to explain to him that the English title of *Die Fledermaus,* literally translated, would be *The Bat.* He thought the words meant a whipped mousse."

Conscious of the voice still murmuring in the ASM's corner, Philippa drew her father further upstage until she was sure they were out of earshot.

"Dad," she said, "that envelope you noticed—do you think it's possible that Sophie had given it to Roy, and when he saw you watching, he gave it back to her?"

"Yes. It's possible. Why do you ask?"

"Because nothing about Sophie Blau suggests that she uses drugs, but Roy shows all the signs—and he's so much younger than her. Sophie seems to have a lot of money for someone working as a techie. What if she's getting the drugs for him? What a great way to hook a plain and impressionable young man who's going to be mega-rich one day! He'd become utterly dependent on her."

"True, with a face like his, he's not likely to get his sex and rock and roll the normal way, but where would he get the money for drugs? I thought he was the poor relation."

"He is, but I just overheard Darleen talking with Peter Hampton and John Granger. The subject of their conversation was Roy's use of cocaine, plus the fact that there's money missing from Darleen's accounts."

"Well, if there's something like that going on, you should probably email back to your friendly New York cop and let him check it out—or better still, tip Richard off. Then the information can go through proper channels."

Beary's head swivelled as a rustling sound heralded the approach of Darleen Winner. It was Beary's first sight of Rosalinda dressed for the ball, and Philippa could tell that her father was impressed. Darleen looked ravishing. Her blonde hair cascaded in ringlets over her white shoulders, and her black and crimson ball gown was a sea of ruches and sequins, draped and gathered so that it swirled as if it had a life of its own.

"My goodness," exclaimed Beary, "speaking of whipped mousse! That gown is the most sumptuous confection I've ever seen."

"Wait until you hear her sing the Czardas. You'll be even more impressed. That's the aria she sang for the Met auditions twenty-six years ago. The audience will go wild."

"I can believe it," nodded Beary. "Sentiment as well as artistry—what a combination."

Octavia materialized at the back of the wing. She smoothed her white jacket over her lean trousered thighs and sauntered past Darleen.

"Gorgeous dress, Darleen," she said sweetly. "Flattering too," she hissed snidely, as she reached Philippa. "Those fashions hide a lot of bulges. Good luck with your aria, by the way," she added. "Make sure you get them laughing with you and not at you."

Octavia smirked at her own witticism, then, noticing Peter Hampton on the far side of the stage, immediately forgot Philippa, waved seductively and strode across to the other wing.

"The transvestite had better watch out," observed Beary. "One could hide a lot more than the odd love-handle in the frills and ruffles of nineteenth-century evening gowns. You and Darleen could tuck vials of poison in your bodices to slip into her champagne."

"Tempting thought," muttered Philippa. "Octavia is very trying."

"Trying hard by the looks of it," Beary agreed, nodding towards the far wing. "And it appears our prima donna has noticed her efforts," he added.

Darleen's hitherto motionless form had sprung to life. Her skirt swirled as she swept downstage and her expression was resolute. She stopped as she reached Philippa and squeezed her hand.

"Courage, darling," she said. "You're going to be marvellous."

Then as quickly as she had come, she crossed to the other wing, extracted Peter Hampton from Octavia's grasp, and drew him upstage. As they disappeared from view, a ripple of applause indicated the presence of the conductor in the pit. Act Two was about to begin.

◆   ◆   ◆

To Philippa's relief, her father acquitted himself well. In spite of his aggravating lack of concentration before the show, Beary had absorbed Granger's instructions, and the three waiters pranced out of the wings, a perfectly synchronized unit, tripping neatly in time to the music, faces turned toward the footlights, and Beary sporting the seraphic grin that had been known to induce apoplexy in his council opponents. The celebrity waiters' entrance was greeted with cheers from the audience, and once into the scene, Beary moved about the stage, delivering his champagne glasses with rhythmic grace and a great deal of élan. However, like a true professional, he dutifully froze during the solo arias, and when Philippa witnessed the glowing pride on his face as she concluded the "Laughing Song", she felt tears come to her eyes. Her father's delight was even more moving than the silently mouthed "bravo" from Darleen Winner or the thunder of applause from the partisan crowd in the house.

By the third and final act, spirits were running high. As Philippa waited for her cue, she had to concentrate hard to keep her focus. Adele's third-act aria was even more demanding than the "Laughing Song", and steady support for the voice required inner calm, even if her exterior façade had to be vivacious. She positioned herself for her entrance and watched Roy's antics on stage. He was drawing guffaws from the audience, well deserved, Philippa admitted, but she hoped the howls of laughter would diminish during her aria. Otherwise it would be a terrible waste of her hard-earned high notes.

"Funny guy, isn't he?" commented Beary, coming up behind Philippa. "Come on, Pinko," he urged Mayor Rogers, who had followed him into the wings. "Stand over here."

"What are you two doing up so early?" Philippa demanded. "You're not on until the bows."

"Your father said I had to watch your number," said Rogers.

"Oh, that's sweet. Thank you. I hope you enjoy it."

"It's not right at the end, is it?" the mayor enquired nervously, noticing that the trays of champagne glasses had already been set out on the props table in readiness for the finale. "I have to be in the other wing for the bows."

"No. You'll have lots of time to get across. Oh, excuse me." Philippa heard another burst of applause from the house. "Here's my cue."

She drew herself as tall as her diminutive five-foot frame would allow and sailed out onto the stage. Frosch immediately detracted from her entrance by pretending to be overcome by her beauty and doing a pratfall. Philippa gritted her teeth as another howl from the audience drowned her opening line. With eyes gleaming purposefully, she slipped her cloak from her shoulders, dragged it behind her across the stage and dumped it over the recumbent form of the jailer. The volume of the laughter doubled. *And that should fix you*, she thought with satisfaction.

◆   ◆   ◆

"What did you think of that?" said Beary proudly as the last ringing note of the "Audition Song" came to an end.

Mayor Rogers beamed approval.

"Utterly charming," he said. "She has a bit of the old man in her too, doesn't she?" he added perceptively. "She kept that jailer character firmly in his place. They were both hilarious, but it was definitely her number. She must have watched your tactics in the council chamber."

"I've never held a fan in front of a colleague's face," said Beary. "She learned that one all on her own."

Roger's eyes sparkled.

"This opera business is great fun, isn't it? And the music is really quite catchy. One could almost hum along."

"God forbid," muttered Beary.

He leaned sideways to get a better view of the action on stage, but suddenly he sensed another presence in the wing. Before he could move, a mellow voice spoke in his ear.

"You're Philippa's father, aren't you?"

Beary turned to see who had crept up behind him. To his delight, it was Darleen Winner.

"You must be so proud," she said. "She's an enchanting girl—lovely to work with."

Beary glowed.

"Thank you, dear lady," he crooned in his smoothest politician's manner, for once not assumed, "and may I say how thrilled we are being on stage with you—truly a memorable experience."

Before Darleen could respond, John Granger appeared and interrupted the conversation. He held a champagne bottle in each hand, and he gestured with the right bottle towards a small table, tucked in the corner below a wide ledge that was laden with bouquets.

"That's the tray with the glass for Darleen," he told Beary, indicating an already-filled flute standing in isolation on a silver platter. "I've set it aside so you can't get mixed up. The other trays have fourteen glasses each and they're on the long props table at the rear of the stage."

"What about us?" Beary demanded. "Where are our drinks?"

"Same table. Take whichever one you want. There'll still be enough for the cast and chorus. I'm going to fill them now."

Granger took his bottles upstage, and Beary was surprised to see Darleen's normally serene countenance furrow anxiously as she watched the manager go. *Hampton must be in the lead*, he reflected. As if his thought had summoned the man in the flesh, Peter Hampton materialized out of the gloom and glided to Darleen's side. He was already holding a champagne glass, and as he held it up to toast the prima donna, the couple locked glances with a fervour that would have made Octavia Bruni's heart plummet.

"I think I should be getting over to the other wing," Mayor Rogers ventured, breaking into Beary's contemplations. "It must be getting close to the end."

"Lots of time," said Beary heartily. "Why don't you get yourself a drink? I'm going to."

"I don't normally drink." Mayor Rogers pursed his lips. "Tonight's champagne will be an exception, but I'll just stick to the one glass on stage. You'd better not have too much either, Beary. We do have an image to maintain, you know."

"*You* might have an image to maintain," retorted Beary. "Nobody expects me to be teetotal."

He marched upstage, helped himself to a drink from the props table and drained it. Then, having done a quick count of the champagne flutes on the trays and a mental head-count of the cast and chorus, he took a second glass and returned downstage. As he came back, he passed Roy Winner who had exited and was leaving the wings.

Darleen was now on stage, singing robustly in Eisenstein's ear, and other than the stage manager who was huddled over his score in the corner, the only remaining occupants of the wing were Peter Hampton, whose eyes were fixed on the prima donna, and a disgruntled Octavia, who had taken her position in readiness for the bows.

Darleen's sparkling potable remained in solitary splendour on the small table and Beary took his position beside it. He sipped his champagne and watched the finale. Noticing that his cufflink had become loose, he set down his glass and set out to reattach it, but it slipped from his fingers and rolled beneath the table. He bent down to retrieve it, but his hand touched another object that had fluttered against the wall. It was a small white envelope, very much like the one he had seen passed to Sophie Blau earlier in the evening. Curiously, he pulled it out and stood up.

"Hey, Pinko, did you see anyone drop this?" he asked Rogers, who was standing behind Hampton, smiling blissfully, and bouncing on his heels in time to the music.

"What?" Rogers turned and looked at the envelope. "No. Funny though—I heard someone talking about an envelope earlier."

"Do you remember who it was?"

"It was that girl." He pointed across to the far wing. "The one with the headset."

Rogers looked disapproving. "She's not at all nice, you know," he digressed. "Neither is that young fellow playing the jailer."

"Never mind the sermonizing," Beary said impatiently. "What about the envelope?"

"That girl asked the jailer what he'd done with it, and he said it had been confiscated."

"Is that all? Think man. Didn't he say who took it?"

Rogers looked blank.

"No ... well ... let me think." He furrowed his brow in concentration. "It must have been a woman, because then he said something about wanting to kill her—that's why I said they weren't nice, because the girl then said as cool as cucumber, 'That can be arranged.' And she added something about there being lots more where that came from, but then they saw me and started talking in German. I couldn't pick out much after that. The only words I recognized were 'the alto'."

"The alto? They were talking about Octavia Bruni?"

"I suppose so. They pronounced it strangely though."

"Repeat the phrase as they said it. What were the exact words?"

Rogers frowned and thought for a moment.

"*Der Alte*," he managed finally.

Beary raised his eyebrows heavenward.

"*Alte* means old," he informed Rogers. "They were talking about 'the old man'. I wonder which one they were referring to."

"I've no idea," apologized Rogers. "Sorry. Has any of this helped?"

"I don't know," said Beary thoughtfully. "For once I'm at a loss."

A burst of applause signalled the end of the act. Rogers' eyes bulged in panic.

"That's it? Already!"

"Yes. Better hoof it, man."

As Rogers sprinted upstage, Beary turned and stared at the drink sitting in isolation on the tray beside him. It seemed to have taken on a sinister hue. *It's just your cynical, suspicious mind*, Beary told himself, but the thought that had taken hold would not release its grip. There was very little time before his cue, but impulsively he took the glass and tucked it at the back of the ledge behind the row of bouquets. Then he picked up his salver, darted upstage, and took another glass from the props table. He was just in time. The champagne chorus began, and without further ado, he straightened his bow tie, marched to centre stage, and presented Darleen with her drink. To his delight, she rewarded him with a kiss. Then she passed him to his daughter as the orchestra broke into the familiar strains of the *Die Fledermaus* waltz.

◆   ◆   ◆

Edwina was dewy-eyed.

"Such a thrill—to see you dancing on stage with your father like that—I'll never forget it," she trilled. "Where is your father, by the way?"

Philippa frowned.

"He dashed off the moment the curtain went down. He said something about having to find Richard. Ah, here he is," she added, as the dressing-room door opened and Beary popped through.

Edwina turned to her husband and reduced the rhapsodic tones to more utilitarian decibels. "Well," she acknowledged, "you did quite well. I didn't have to flinch once."

"Good," said Beary, firmly taking his wife's arm. "Come on, Cinderella—off to the ball. I need some decent Scotch to wash down all that bubbly."

"Where's Richard?"

"He had to go to work," Beary said abruptly. "He sent his apologies," he added, turning to Philippa, "and said to tell you that you were wonderful. He'll try to join us later. Now," he continued, edging Edwina towards the door, "let's get moving."

"Shouldn't we wait for Philippa?"

"Nonsense! She doesn't want to make her entrance with a couple of old fogies like us."

A knock on the door halted the argument and a devastatingly handsome young man bounded into the room. He was resplendent in a gleaming tuxedo and he engulfed Philippa in a huge bear hug.

"Pippy! You were fabulous!"

Philippa pulled back and gaped at the newcomer.

"Conrad! What are you doing here? I haven't seen you in over a year."

"Don't you read your sponsor list? My computer company gave money. We got six comps—for the show and the ball. You're coming of course."

"Of course. It's going to be wonderful."

Conrad acquired the sheepish, little-boy-lost look that deceived women into thinking he was helpless.

"Is there any chance you're on your own tonight?" He paused and looked hopeful.

Philippa hesitated, weighing the pros and cons of an evening with Conrad, who for all his charm, good looks and wealth had a vocabulary problem with the word, "no". Her first and only date with him had been sufficiently tiresome that she had vowed it would be her last—but then she thought of Octavia.

"Actually, I don't have a date," she said. "Why? Didn't you invite someone to come with you?"

Conrad flashed his toothpaste-commercial smile.

"No. I gave five comps to my office staff and came on my own. I was rather hoping we could team up."

"Then we shall." Philippa stood up and pushed Conrad towards her parents. "Go wait in the lobby with Mum and Dad. I'll be there as soon as I've changed."

She ushered Conrad and Edwina through the door of the dressing room, but Beary hung back and glowered at his daughter.

"I thought you said that man was only interested in sex and Ferraris," he muttered. "I seem to remember you said being out with him was like dating an octopus that had swallowed a tape recording of an automotive manual."

"It doesn't matter. He's rich and good-looking, and when I swan in on his arm, Octavia will choke. Come to that, if he gets overly amorous, I'll simply pass him over to her as the evening wears on." Philippa paused and looked sternly at her father. "And what was all that about Richard going to work? What's happened?"

"Possibly nothing," said her father, "but just to take precautions, I did a little switching of champagne glasses at the final curtain and the drink that was intended for Darleen Winner is now on its way to the police lab for analysis."

Philippa gasped.

"You're kidding! You think someone tried to kill Darleen?"

"I don't know, but I had a hunch and I acted on it."

"Did you tell Darleen?"

"I did. I also informed her nephew, her business manager, the sexy ASM, Peter Hampton and the malevolent transvestite."

Beary paused and gave his daughter a meaningful stare.

"And I suspect," he concluded, "if my hunch was right, one of them will fail to turn up for the champagne ball tonight."

◆   ◆   ◆

By eleven o'clock both the ball and Beary were in full swing.

"They should write a sequel," Beary intoned, noticing his wife glowering from their table as she watched him purchase his fourth Scotch from the no-host bar. "*Die Alte Fledermaus*. Edwina could star in it."

He took his drink and made his way back through the host of dancers swirling about the ballroom floor. Darleen Winner had not yet made an appearance, neither had her nephew, and although Beary looked carefully around the hall, he could not see Peter Hampton or John Granger anywhere in sight. Sophie Blau had also failed to appear, but as Beary continued across the room, Octavia Bruni floated into his line of vision. She was surrounded by a throng of admiring males. Beary made a detour in her direction and joined the circle.

"My, my," he said, "you're much better as a girl. Is that red satin glued or painted on?"

"Why don't you ask me to dance?" suggested Octavia. "You can find out—and you can tell me all about that handsome stud who's sitting with your daughter."

"Fancy him, do you?" purred Beary, leading the mezzo onto the dance floor. "You know, I bet he's just your type."

"Your father's in good form," remarked Conrad, admiringly watching from the table. "That's quite the woman he's steering round the floor. Are you sure you wouldn't like to dance again, Pippy?" he wheedled. "I'm pretty good at the Viennese waltz."

"Not just yet, Conrad. We'll wait for something more up-tempo."

"But slow dancing is my forte."

Exactly, thought Philippa. *That's why I'm holding out for rock and roll.*

As the waltz came to an end, Beary rolled back to the table and lowered himself into his chair.

"You know, the transvestite isn't so bad after all," he announced. "She actually has a sense of humour. I asked her if her voice was one, two or three Octavias, and she gave a ribald laugh and told me it depended on the size of the instrument. What's the matter with you?" he added, seeing Conrad gaping in horror.

"That woman's a transvestite!"

"Fancies you too," said Beary wickedly. "I told her you wanted to dance with her. She's coming over in a moment."

Conrad turned pale. Philippa giggled, but before she could reassure him, Conrad was on his feet. He declared his intention of rounding up more champagne and shot off in the direction of the bar. As she watched him scurry across the hall, Philippa noticed her brother enter through the glass doors at the far end of the ballroom. Richard pinpointed the Beary table and strode across to join his family.

When he got to the table, he gave his sister a hug, slapped his father on the shoulder and then sank into a chair beside his mother.

"Well done, Dad," he congratulated Beary. "There was enough cocaine in that glass to kill a horse. You saved Darleen Winner's life."

"Well I'm damned," said Beary. "So I was right. Thank God I didn't hesitate. Have you got someone keeping an eye on the suspects I told you about? None of them are here yet, other than Octavia Bruni."

"We've done better than that," Richard informed him. "We've made two arrests. We've nailed Sophie Blau for possession of drugs—she, by the way, had nothing to do with the attempted murder—and we've got our killer." He turned to his sister. "Philippa, did you know your NYPD buddy was out here?"

"Bill Gunsen! You're joking, surely. He's still in New York working on the Winner case."

"He was, but based on the background info you sent him a few weeks ago, he made the necessary breakthrough. The so-called robbery was staged. The murder of Darleen's husband was deliberate and premeditated, and her sister's death was a tragic result of being in the wrong place at the wrong time. Yesterday NYPD figured they had enough evidence to pull in the killer. They sent Bill out here to co-ordinate with us in making the arrest."

"Why didn't he let me know?"

"He was told not to. You were working with the people he was investigating. But he said to tell you he'll do his best to get through at the station as quickly as possible and with any luck, he should be here by midnight."

"Oh," said Philippa. She bit her lip.

Edwina furrowed her brow.

"Goodness, that's a little awkward," she murmured.

Beary chortled.

"Would you like me to run back to the theatre and retrieve your mask?" he asked his daughter.

"Very funny." Philippa thought for a moment. "It's OK," she decided, looking speculatively towards the bar. "Octavia has had her eye on Conrad ever since we arrived. Once I tell him she's all woman, I won't see him for dust."

She turned to her brother.

"Now, go on, Richard," she insisted. "Don't keep us in suspense. Give us the rest of the story."

Richard helped himself to a glass of champagne from the bottle at the centre of the table.

"The motive was money, pure and simple."

"Yes, but who—"

A sudden drum roll cut Philippa off in mid-sentence, and the orchestra burst into the *Die Fledermaus* waltz. Darlene Winner swept into the room on the arm of Peter Hampton, and behind her followed Roy Winner, who was escorting the pretty teenager who had played Ida. John Granger was nowhere in sight.

Beary raised his eyebrows and gave his son a quizzical look.

"Well, well, well. So it was the business manager after all—a pretty vicious reaction for a rejected suitor."

Richard nodded.

"Was he really in love with Darleen," Beary asked, "or did he just want to marry her for her money?"

Richard took another sip of champagne; then he embarked on an explanation.

"Granger already had a lot of Darleen Winner's money," he said. "He'd been embezzling the Winners' funds for years, and I suspect Darleen's husband had become suspicious. Granger killed him and staged a robbery, figuring that he could marry the widow and continue managing her investments, and no one would ever know what had been going on."

"But then she fell in love with Peter Hampton, who was also an accountant," said Philippa. "Granger must have been frantic. It wasn't just a case of missing out on marrying Darleen, he must have realized that Hampton would look at the books and immediately figure out what he'd been up to."

Edwina looked shocked.

"But why try to kill Darleen? What would that have accomplished? Surely he'd have been found out anyway?"

Philippa shook her head.

"No," she said. "Don't you see? Darleen's estate would have gone either to her ailing mother or to her drug-addict nephew, neither of whom would have had a clue about the fraud. Granger would have offered his services on the basis that he'd been managing the family accounts for years, and they'd have simply kept him on."

"What a wicked man," said Edwina severely. "And thank goodness they brought you in to replace Gwendolyn Pye," she added to Beary. "She never sees anything beyond the end of her nose. Darleen Winner was very lucky to have you there."

"Did I hear a compliment?" said Beary. "That calls for another drink."

"No, it doesn't," Edwina retorted. "This may be an opera ball, but I'm not having you turn into The Flying-high-as-a-kite Dutchman. Well," she continued, ignoring her husband's mutinous expression and looking across the room to where Darleen Winner and Peter Hampton were locked in an intimate embrace as they danced a slow foxtrot at the centre of the ballroom floor, "this is most satisfactory. A murder was averted, and by the looks of things, we'll be celebrating a wedding before too long."

"I think you're right," agreed Philippa, "and between Hampton and Darleen, they'll get Roy straightened out before he has to manage anything more than an equity pay-cheque. A happy ending all round."

"Not quite," Beary interjected. "You still have to get your story straightened out before NYPD arrives."

"Bill will understand," said Philippa firmly. "It's not as if I knew he was coming."

Before her father could answer, a waitress materialized beside the table.

"Excuse me, Miss." The woman handed Philippa a note. "There was a phone message for you, but rather than call you, I was asked to give you this."

"Maybe it's from Bill," Edwina speculated. "Perhaps he won't be able to get here after all."

Philippa opened the note and read it. She blanched.

"Oh, my God!"

"What dear?" Her mother looked concerned.

"It's from Adam. He's here!"

Richard chortled.

"How did that come about?" he asked.

"He says he was going to surprise me and fly in for the show, but his plane was delayed. He's just landed at the airport and will grab a cab and come straight here. He says he'll be here in time to see in the New Year."

Richard emptied the last of the champagne bottle into his sister's glass.

"Here. Drink enough of this and you'll just think you're seeing double."

Philippa leaned on the table and put her head in her hands.

"Now what am I supposed to do?"

Beary drained the last of his Glenlivet.

"Well," he said, unsympathetically enjoying his daughter's discomfiture, "I thought *Die Fledermaus* was entertaining, but ..."

Beary paused and patted his daughter on the shoulder.

"This black tie affair," he concluded, "promises to be even funnier."

978-0-595-42850-2
0-595-42850-9

Printed in the United States
123736LV00003B/145-171/P